Praise for #1 *New York Times* bestselling author

LISA JACKSON

"Bestselling Jackson cranks up the suspense to almost unbearable heights in her latest tautly written thriller."
—*Booklist* on *Malice*

"When it comes to providing gritty and sexy stories, Ms. Jackson certainly knows how to deliver."
—*RT Book Reviews* on *Unspoken*

"Provocative prose, an irresistible plot and finely crafted characters make up Jackson's latest contemporary sizzler."
—*Publishers Weekly* on *Wishes*

"Lisa Jackson takes my breath away."
—*New York Times* bestselling author Linda Lael Miller

LISA JACKSON

STRANGERS

Recycling programs
for this product may
not exist in your area.

ISBN-13: 978-0-373-77578-1

STRANGERS

Copyright © 2011 by Harlequin Books S.A.

The publisher acknowledges the copyright holder
of the individual works as follows:

MYSTERY MAN
Copyright © 1991 by Lisa Jackson

OBSESSION
Copyright © 1991 by Lisa Jackson

This edition published by arrangement with Harlequin Books S.A.

For questions and comments about the quality of this book
please contact us at Customer_eCare@Harlequin.ca.

® and TM are trademarks of the publisher. Trademarks indicated with
® are registered in the United States Patent and Trademark Office, the
Canadian Trade Marks Office and in other countries.

www.Harlequin.com

Printed in U.S.A.

CONTENTS

MYSTERY MAN

CHAPTER ONE

"I THINK I'VE found your man."

Chelsea Reed froze. She glanced up sharply from the jewelry counter where she'd been taking inventory. "Devlin?" she asked, focusing on the short man with unremarkable features and small eyes. Adrenaline surged through her. "He's alive?"

Ned Jenkins tapped the countertop with his blunt fingers and a smug smile played on his lips. He was one of the best private investigators in the bay area, and Chelsea had hired him three months before to find Devlin McVey. Now, surrounded by silk dresses, brilliant scarves and designer handbags in the boutique, Jenkins looked like the proverbial fish out of water.

"I'd bet money on it," he said, seeming satisfied with himself.

"Where is he?"

Jenkins snorted. "The Caribbean. Looks like he wanted to disappear, but good."

"The Caribbean..." Chelsea swallowed against a suddenly dry throat. Her fingers gripped the counter. So Devlin, damn him, had run away, leaving her alone to deal with her grief.

Memories—some wonderful, some filled with pain—swam before her eyes. Her heart began to knock in her chest. She glanced quickly around the three connecting rooms of the old converted row house. A few customers browsed lazily through the racks and Melissa, a sales-girl for the boutique, was standing in the front window display case, pinning a bright pink belt around the slim waist of a mannequin.

"Melissa—can you hold down the fort a few minutes?" Chelsea asked unsteadily. She could barely concentrate on anything other than the fact that Devlin McVey was alive. Now he had a lot to answer for.

"Will do," Melissa said around a mouthful of pins.

"Sally will be back shortly and Carrie will be in at four. If you need me, I'll be in the kitchen." Her knees threatened to buckle though she'd waited for this day for over a year.

"Got it," Melissa replied, making an "okay" sign with her fingers and thumb.

Chelsea turned back to the small investigator. "Let's go into the back room where we'll have a little more pri-vacy."

He shrugged. "Wherever you want."

He followed her through a door behind the counter and down a short hall to the kitchen of the old house. To keep her hands occupied Chelsea poured them each a cup of lukewarm coffee, then motioned for Jenkins to sit at a chipped Formica-topped table.

"Okay," she said, finding her voice. "Let's start over. Where exactly is he?"

"On an obscure island called Paradis. Believe me, this place is off the beaten path."

Her fingers clamped around her cup. "And you've seen him—you're sure it's Devlin?"

For an answer he snapped open a battered old brief-case, pulled out a manila envelope and dumped the con-tents of the packet onto the table. There were several snapshots and a large, glossy eight-by-ten color photo which he slid across the table. "Unless I miss my guess, this man is McVey."

Chelsea picked up the photograph, heart racing at the sight of a handsome, roguish-looking man with tanned skin, bladed cheekbones and unruly black hair that brushed across the collar of his faded denim jacket. His eyes were hidden by mirrored aviator sunglasses, his jaw disguised by a dark beard. He was grimacing and he looked tough and hard. "I don't know," she said quietly, remembering Devlin as he had been—dark and sensual, with a hard edge that hinted of danger. This man could be him, but then again...

"Well, he's changed his looks, of course. People usually do when they want to get lost," Jenkins said, leaning forward and tossing another picture, a photograph of Devlin taken six months before the accident, onto the table. "But check out his cheekbones—hmm? And the way his hair parts a little off center? And his nose—" he pointed to the larger photograph, then to the small snapshot "—compare them. Identical. Looks as if that nose was broken somewhere along the line—maybe more than once."

"Several times," she thought aloud. There was a similarity in the two pictures; she, too, could see it. Her pulse started to pick up speed but she willed herself to remain calm. Even if this man did prove to be Devlin, there were still so many unanswered questions. She studied the photograph as the minutes ticked by. Yes, the man could be Devlin, but she wasn't sure.... "I'd feel better about this if I could see his eyes."

"I know." Jenkins gave a snort of disgust, as if he wasn't used to being outfoxed by his quarry. "The only time he took off those damned glasses was in the café and it was too dark to get a shot."

"What color?"

"Pardon?" Jenkins's reddish brows inched upward.

"His eyes. What color?"

"Oh. Blue—intense—piercing," the investigator replied with a frown of dislike. "Kind of creepy, the way he stares at you. His eyes are the first thing you notice about him."

"Yes," she agreed, remembering the force of Devlin's gaze. "Did you speak with him?"

Jenkins shook his head. "Nope. Didn't want to tip my hand." His mouth drew into a defensive frown. "You did say you wanted him located but not confronted."

"Yes, that's right," she assured him. "But I want to know everything there is to know about this man."

"Mitch Russell. That's the name he goes by." Jenkins sipped from his cup and scowled. "I did a little poking around and found out that he claims to be from Chicago, just one more disillusioned American looking for the good life in a tropical paradise. It's crazy, if you ask me. Why would anyone want to leave the U.S. of A?"

Good question, Chelsea thought, but kept her face noncommittal. Why, indeed? Unless he was hiding something. Her heart wrenched a little. "Tell me about—what did you call the island? Paradise?"

"Paradis. It's French for paradise, located about thirty miles southwest of St. Jean in the Caribbean. The only way to get to it is by boat or hydroplane." He waved impatiently. "There was a landing strip once, but it's overgrown and no one uses it anymore."

Narrowing her eyes, she examined the photograph again and the more she studied it, the more she was certain Jenkins was right. The man in the picture was Devlin! She'd found him, at last! She couldn't help but smile as she envisioned confronting him. What would he say? What *could* he?

"Did you find out anything else?" she asked, and Ned Jenkins grinned, a wide, toothy smile that made her uncomfortable.

"Here's the report." He reached into his shabby briefcase again and tossed a buff-colored file onto the table. "Not a whole lot in it. I didn't ask too many questions because I didn't want Russell to know I was on to him." He gave her a wink. "You said to keep this low-key and I always aim to please."

"Good." She skimmed the report and frowned. The typed pages didn't give her much more information than Jenkins had already told her. Seeing the bill tacked onto the last page, she reached into her purse, withdrew her wallet and wrote Ned Jenkins a check for services rendered. "Just tell me one more thing," she said, handing him payment.

"Shoot." Jenkins eyed the figures she'd written, nodded to himself and tucked the check into the inside pocket of his jacket.

"How did you find Devlin?"

Jenkins's blue eyes sparked. "I hate to admit it, but I got lucky. That happens sometimes. No one around here knew from nothing and even my friends down at the San Francisco Police Department weren't any help. Everyone acted like he really did bite it in the boat accident. But I checked back with the airlines and flashed his picture around. Eventually a stewardess on a cross-country flight recognized him—or thought she did. Even then he looked a little different from the pictures I had—he was starting to grow a beard—but she was sure it was our guy. There seems to be something about Mr. McVey that the ladies remember."

Chelsea didn't comment—she didn't want to think about the raw sexuality that was as much a part of Devlin McVey as the badge he wore, or had worn, for the SFPD. Nor did she want to think of the string of beautiful women who had fallen in love with him in the past few years. After all, she wasn't interested in his love life, or his sexual charms, she told herself. She only wanted to find out why he had disappeared and what had happened in the accident—the accident from which Devlin had disappeared and that had taken her fiancé's life. Her heart wrenched a little at the thought of John. If only she knew why Devlin had been so insistent that John meet with him that day. What was so all-fired important that they had to talk privately on Devlin's boat in the middle of a storm?

Jenkins scraped back his chair. "Is there anything else I can do for you?"

"Yes," she said impulsively. "I'm going to have to go to Paradis. While I'm gone, I want you to keep poking around. See if anything surfaces around here."

"It hasn't for over a year," he speculated.

"I know, but it's always possible."

"Okay, I'll nose around. Maybe I can find someone at SFPD who's willing to talk. And if you change your mind, and want your friend back on American soil, just let me know. McVey wouldn't be the first man I tracked down and brought back home."

"No, thanks. I think I'll handle this my way."

Jenkins paused, his brow furrowing. "There's something I don't understand about this. You were planning to marry McVey's best friend, the guy who drowned in the accident, right?"

Chelsea swallowed hard. Grief stole into her heart. John Stern's death was still hard to accept. "Yes."

"So why all the interest in McVey?"

Chelsea had a ready answer for a question she'd asked herself a million times. "Because Devlin was John's best friend and he was supposedly killed, as well. I never believed it. And this—" she tapped on the large photo of Devlin "—proves I'm right. I think he might know something about John's death—something that hasn't come out in the police reports."

"Stern's death was ruled an accident."

"I know, but I'm not convinced."

Jenkins eyed her and rubbed the back of his neck thoughtfully. "Listen, I'm going to give you some free advice."

As if she hadn't heard enough from everyone on the planet, she thought.

Jenkins rambled on. "Drop this thing. If your fiancé died in an accident, it's over. If there was something else involved, let the police handle it."

"I just want to know why Devlin disappeared," Chelsea replied. And why John died.

"He might have his reasons. Some people who vanish like it that way."

Too bad, Chelsea thought, catching a glimpse of the bearded man in the picture. If this man were truly Devlin—and she had begun to believe he was—he had a lot to answer for.

Jenkins reached for the door handle just as Chelsea's partner, Sally Bedford, flew into the room, nearly running him over.

"Sorry," she said automatically, then spied Chelsea in the chair. "Oh, God, Chels, I didn't mean to interrupt." Sally was immediately contrite. Her kinky blond hair glistened with raindrops and the shoulders of her raincoat were damp. "It's a downpour out there! I'm soaked to the skin." She shook some of the rain from her hair. "Can you believe it—it's nearly June and we're having a rainstorm that won't quit!"

"It's okay, we're through here."

"Good, because I just dashed through the shop and the floor's crawling—and I mean crawling—with customers." Her boots squished as she walked to a small closet and hung up her coat.

"I'll take care of the customers," Chelsea replied with a quick grin. "You dry off."

"Hey—what's this?" Sally looked at the photographs scattered across the table and her perky face fell. "Oh, no, Chelsea, you're not still trying to find Devlin, are you? Can't you face the fact that he's gone? He and John both?"

Chelsea didn't bother to respond. She gathered up the photographs and stuffed them into Jenkins's manila envelope. "We'll talk about this later," she said over her shoulder as she tucked the envelope into her oversize bag, then shepherded Ned Jenkins back through the store.

Sally was right on one count. The floor was a madhouse. Melissa was busy with two women vying for the latest creation by Marcel De Vasia. Three teenage girls fingered the hand-painted jewelry. A harried young woman was trying on hats and another woman in her twenties was eyeing a fuchsia jumpsuit.

Chelsea helped three customers choose accessories to go with the dresses they'd picked out while Carrie manned the shoe department. Melissa sold two De Vasia originals and managed to keep both women happy.

Two more customers strolled in and Sally, revived, emerged from the back room with a ready smile. She sold the jumpsuit and two raincoats within fifteen minutes.

As the afternoon wore on the crowd thinned.

It was well after seven when the last customer, laden with a package containing a silver belt, peach scarf and two pairs of slacks, finally walked out the front door of the store. Sally turned the bolt, lowered a Closed sign, and, sagging against the door, whispered, "Another day at the zoo!"

"Amen." Chelsea straightened the racks while Sally headed for the till to balance out for the day.

Carrie and Melissa had already taken off and the shop, aside from the soft notes of jazz drifting from hidden speakers, was quiet. Chelsea slid out of her pumps.

As Sally added the checks and cash, she grinned, showing off deep dimples. "Well, at least it was a profitable day at the zoo."

"That's good."

"No, that's great," Sally said, slamming the till shut.

Sally and Chelsea had been friends since college and had opened this shop four years before. Located near Ghirardelli Square, the boutique had grown and flourished, become chic and popular enough to expand until it now filled the entire first floor of the old remodeled house. Sally was talking of opening another store, either in Union Square or out of the city entirely in Sonoma, but Chelsea hadn't been able to work up the necessary enthusiasm.

In fact, she could hardly think past the accident that had taken her fiancé's life.

"I don't suppose this is a good time to tell you that I'm going to need a few weeks off," Chelsea said as she snapped out the lights.

Sally sighed. "Come on—let's talk." Stuffing the receipts for the day into the bank bag she would drop into the night depository on the way home, she added, "I'll buy you a cup of coffee."

"You're on."

The kitchen had grown dark with the evening. Chelsea flipped on the overhead fixture and Sally grabbed the handle of the glass coffeepot.

Wrinkling her little nose, she swished the dregs of brown liquid down the drain. As she started a fresh pot, she glanced over her shoulder at Chelsea. "Okay," she said, "so now it's later. Out with it. You think you've found Devlin, is that it?"

"I'm not sure," Chelsea admitted, dropping into a chair and retrieving the envelope with Jenkins's photographs from her purse. "But I have to find out."

"Why?"

"Because there are so many questions that don't have any answers," she replied quickly.

Shaking her head, Sally scrounged in a cupboard for sugar substitute, then waited as coffee began to drizzle into the pot. "Devlin and John are dead," she said quietly. "We both know that."

Chelsea whispered, "Devlin's body never washed up."

"That's not unusual. San Francisco Bay is a major piece of water, you know. And there was a storm that day. They were crazy to be out there. Anyway, Devlin's body could have been washed out to sea."

"I don't believe it. I won't." Chelsea looked at her friend as Sally poured them each a cup of fresh coffee. "Devlin was a cop—he always landed on his feet. I just can't believe he's dead."

"Can't believe it—or won't believe it?" Her lips drawing into a thoughtful frown, Sally dropped into the chair across from Chelsea. "It does happen, you know."

Chelsea didn't answer, just swallowed a mouthful of hot coffee.

But Sally didn't give up. She propped her chin on one

hand, and studied the pictures spread across the table. "This guy—he's supposed to be Devlin?" she asked, pointing to the image of the man with the heavy beard.

"Yes."

"How can you tell?"

"I just feel it."

Sally's lips pursed. "He could be anyone with that beard." Her blond brows pulled into a tight knot as she glanced up at Chelsea. "Look, I know how you feel—"

"Do you?" Chelsea flung out, her frustration of the past year surfacing. "I don't think so. I don't know if anyone does."

"Maybe not, but you've been through a terrible loss."

Chelsea's throat closed. The boating accident and storm had been unexpected. John and Devlin had left her at the docks. She could still remember John, squeezing her, whispering that he loved her. She'd clung to him, her dark hair blowing across her face, her gaze, as she looked past John's shoulder, landing squarely in Devlin's mocking blue eyes. The air was heavy and gusty and filled with the tangy salt-sea scent. She'd felt a premonition then—a tiny trickle of fear that had dripped into her heart.

"It's not easy to lose someone you love," Sally was saying, adding sweetener to her cup and stirring slowly.

Chelsea thrust up her chin. "I know you and the rest of the world don't approve. I also know you think I'm on some wild-goose chase. But believe me, finding Devlin is something I have to do. I have to find out what happened to John."

"Or what happened to Devlin?"

"Both!"

"What if this man isn't Devlin?" Sally asked, holding up the eight-by-ten and staring at the print. "Will you give up? Or will you go on searching—clinging to a dream that Devlin's alive somewhere and, once you find him, will give you all the answers you're looking for?"

"I don't know."

"John's gone, Chelsea. So is Devlin. Accept it."

"I can't. Not until I'm sure."

Sally shook her head and threw up her hands in exasperation. "Well, do what you have to do, heaven knows you're going to anyway. And don't worry about anything here, I can handle the store."

"I don't know how long I'll be gone. It may be longer than a couple of weeks."

Sally stared at her friend. "I said I can handle it. Do what you have to—be gone as long as you need. Just take care of yourself, okay?"

"I will," Chelsea promised, but she wondered what would happen when she ran into Devlin again.

"I WISH THERE WAS SOME way to talk you out of this," Chelsea's older sister, Felicia, said the next afternoon. Felicia had stopped by her apartment when she'd learned from their mother that Chelsea was planning to leave for Paradis. And, as usual, Felicia was fit to be tied.

Pacing in front of the couch, her long plum-colored skirt swirling around her calves, Felicia sighed theatrically and rolled her eyes in typical exasperated big-sister fashion. "Why don't you just give it a rest, Chels? Get on with your life. Sally said you were thinking of expanding the shop and I think it's a good idea—so much healthier than this—" she pursed her lips and motioned to the photographs neatly stacked across the coffee table "—this morbid obsession you have with Devlin McVey!"

Chelsea bristled. "I'm not obsessed."

"Sure."

"You know I have to check it out."

"Oh, so now you have a mission—a quest, right?" Felicia said sarcastically. She rubbed her temples, as if she felt a headache coming on. "God, Chelsea, why don't you grow up?"

"I just want to know the truth."

"Oh, do you?" Felicia lifted a skeptical dark brow. "Well, the truth is that you keep hanging on to a dream, Chels, and somehow that ridiculous dream is wrapped up in Devlin McVey. For the past year—no, thirteen months—you've thought of nothing else."

Chelsea didn't argue, just let her older sister rant on. When Felicia was on a roll, there was no stopping her. Chelsea glanced at Felicia over her shoulder, as if she were listening, but she kept tossing clothes from the small closet of her studio loft onto the couch. Blouses, dresses, tank tops and shorts were draped over the back of the sofa-sleeper and her two beat-up pieces of luggage stood ready near the kitchen alcove.

When Felicia paused to take a breath, Chelsea cut in, "I don't need another lecture, you know."

Felicia tossed her straight red-brown hair over her shoulder and her eyes narrowed. "You know your problem, don't you?" Felicia demanded, crossing her arms over her chest. "You're too much like Dad."

Chelsea froze, a beige blouse dropping from her fingers. "I'm not—"

"You two are cut from the same cloth—always searching for something more, something dangerous, something…a little wild. And you don't fool me. I know that you've tried to look like you've been playing it straight, but it's an act, Chelsea. Mom has probably forgotten, but I remember you as a kid. You were always the one getting into trouble in school."

"And you were always ready to run and tell Mom and Dad."

Felicia colored a little but added, "It was a good thing we were never in one place long enough for your reputation to catch up with you!"

"My reputation?" Chelsea repeated, stung.

"Of taking dares, you know, that sort of thing. I was always bailing you out! Remember when you talked three kids into skipping school with you and sneaking into the country-club pool in the middle of December—"

"Enough already," Chelsea cut in quickly. "What does how I behaved in grade school have to do with this?"

"It's all the same thing. You were never satisfied, just like Dad."

"Dad has nothing to do with this!"

Felicia lifted a shoulder. "You even had Mom convinced that you'd finally settled down—not that I ever believed it, mind you. But I live with Mom, I saw the change in her when you started dating John. And then, when you and Sally started your business, Mom was proud, I mean really proud."

Chelsea felt her shoulders droop a little.

"And then there was John." She sighed. "He was too good for you, you know. Too straight and narrow. An architect, for God's sake! But he wasn't enough, was he? Oh, no, not for you," Felicia added with an envious glint in her eye. "You had to get involved with Devlin!"

"I wasn't—"

"Sure you were." Felicia slid her younger sister a knowing glance. "It was obvious. I'm surprised John didn't catch on. You were different around Devlin. I could tell. I could almost feel the energy between you two. All this charged sexual attraction just simmering under the surface. It was downright disgusting!"

"That's nonsense!" Chelsea argued, but felt a tell-tale blush creep steadily up the back of her neck. Guilt prickled at her mind.

"And I know what appealed to you. Devlin was sexy—damned sexy—in an earthy kind of way." Felicia colored and added quickly, "But he was all wrong for you—in so many ways. He was a cop, for crying out loud! Like Dad! Can't you remember the hell we all went through with Dad's jobs? And think about how hard it was on Mom. Why you'd want to involve yourself with a man—"

"I don't want to get involved with Devlin, Felicia," Chelsea said through tight lips. Why did she and Felicia always fight? "I just want to locate him and find out what happened to John!"

"Devlin's dead," Felicia said flatly.

"I don't think so." Chelsea snatched the snapshot of Mitch Russell from the tabletop and stormed across the room. "This man looks too much like him for me to give up now," she said, shoving the photograph under Felicia's disapproving nose. "There's a reason John died, Felicia, and a reason Devlin's hiding down in some God-forsaken island in the Caribbean—and, no matter what, I'm going to find out what it is!"

"So now it's an adventure!" The lines around the corners of Felicia's mouth turned bitter. "Dad thought it was an adventure, too—remember? But he was never satisfied, was he? Hauling us from town to town all across the country didn't do it, becoming a cop didn't do it, divorcing Mom didn't do it, and taking up with that…well, that girl half his age didn't do it, either! Think about it. John didn't make you happy and Devlin, even if he were alive, wouldn't, either!"

"I don't remember asking for your advice," Chelsea said tartly. She stripped a pair of white slacks from a hanger and tossed them into her suitcase. "You're saying I'll never be content."

"I'm saying you're wasting your time and chasing a dream that doesn't exist." She eyed her sister speculatively. "You know, I think you *like* following in Dad's footsteps."

"That's crazy! I'm just trying to get to the bottom of John's death."

"Yeah, sure." Felicia rolled her eyes, then studied her nails.

"I am."

"And this has nothing to do with any hidden feelings you might have had for Devlin?" Felicia taunted.

Chelsea's shoulders tightened at Felicia's tone. She whirled on her sister. "The only feelings I have for Devlin McVey are friendship. Period."

"Uh-huh. Right. And that's why you can't believe he's dead."

Chelsea held up her palms. "There's no reason to argue, Felicia," she said through clenched teeth. "This is just something I have to do, okay?"

Felicia's mouth drew into an unforgiving line. "I'll tell Mom why you're going."

"I already did. Now, all I want from you is your assurance that you'll come in here once a week and water the plants. If that's not too much to ask! And if it is, I'm sure Mrs. Murphy across the hall—"

"I'm just trying to spare you some heartache, that's all," Felicia insisted, her brows lifting in feigned innocence. "Someone's got to look after you."

"I can take care of myself."

"Can you?" Felicia mused. "I wonder." With a long-suffering sigh, she tucked her tiny purse under her arm. "Well, if you want to throw away your money and waste your time and set yourself up for a major—and I'm talking major, here—fall, that's certainly your prerogative."

"Thanks." Chelsea wanted to say more, to snap back an equally hot retort, but she held her tongue. Felicia had, after all, remained at home, staying with their mother after their parents' divorce, trying to help her pick up the shattered pieces of her life. Though now she could move out and find a place of her own, Felicia preferred to stay with Mom and play the part of the martyred older sister, and Chelsea tried her best to keep her temper in check.

"Just think about one thing," Felicia suggested cattily as she grabbed her umbrella, snagged her raincoat from the hall tree near the door, and glancing back over her shoulder, lifted a lofty brow.

Chelsea hated to ask, but couldn't help saying, "What's that?"

Felicia skewered her younger sister with a knowing glare. "If and when you run into Devlin McVey again, take a good long look in the mirror and ask yourself why you've been so hell-bent to find a man who's trying his damnedest to remain dead!"

CHAPTER TWO

THE PLANE, A SMALL PROP, touched down with a jarring thud that pushed Chelsea's already queasy stomach right up her throat.

She gripped the arms of the seat and sighed in relief as the pilot taxied to the tiny airport—if that's what you'd call it. Little more than a few landing strips, several hangars and a low, flat building that served as terminal, the tiny airport of St. Jean left a lot to be desired.

As she climbed off the plane, the tropical heat of the island hit her full force. Beams of sunlight reflected off the whitewashed buildings. A whisper of a breeze brushed Chelsea's cheeks. The gentle gust caused the fronds of palm trees to sway high overhead. Shifting shadows danced gracefully on the tarmac.

Chelsea picked up her luggage in the terminal and checked through customs. Once she was outside again, she approached a cabdriver who was leaning on the front fender of his Chevrolet while perusing a magazine written in French.

"I need a ride to the docks to catch a boat to Paradis," she said. "Can you get me there?"

"No problem," the driver, a heavyset Creole man with graying hair and a thick accent, promised. He tossed the magazine into the open window of his beat-up old Chevy and stuffed her bags into the trunk. He held the door for Chelsea, then slid behind the wheel. Flashing her a blinding smile in the rearview mirror, he said, "Twenty minutes to the docks."

The cab bounced along rutted, winding roads, past grand hotels with red tile roofs and wide verandas guarded by lush vegetation. They traveled to the heart of the lazy, sun-washed city of Lagune where only a few high-rises competed for the view of a pristine bay.

The docks were a madhouse. Fishing boats, cabin cruisers, sailboats and yachts filled the crescent-shaped harbor.

Sunlight shimmered on the aquamarine water and sailboats skimmed across the sea. Chelsea's throat grew tight as she watched a sloop slice across the bay. The small boat wasn't unlike Devlin's. Once again, she remembered the last time she'd seen John and Devlin, just before their fateful outing, and shoved the unhappy thought aside.

Shivering a little, she found her sunglasses, slid them onto the bridge of her nose and stepped onto a small cruiser named the *Anna Marie*. It would, the round-bellied captain assured her, take her on the final leg of her journey, from St. Jean to Paradis.

Other people crowded aboard, their different voices and dialects rising over the soft lapping of the water and the thrum of the boat's idling engines. Chelsea surveyed the group heading for Paradis, but she kept to herself, her thoughts racing ahead of the small craft as it chugged into the open sea.

Why would Devlin, who had grown up in California, hide here on a remote tropical island, letting everyone he'd known think him dead? What had happened during the storm that had taken John's life?

John.

A hot pain knifed through her heart and, as she stood against the rail, she glanced down at her left hand where once she'd worn his engagement ring. Swallowing hard, she remembered John's athletic good looks, wavy blond hair and easy smile. He'd been her friend for years and falling in love with him had seemed natural and right, the easiest path for her life. And safe. John had been safe. As far removed from her father as any man she'd known.

Felicia had been right in one respect, she admitted grimly to herself. Their father, Paul Reed, had been a man who had sought danger, a man whose professional as well as personal life had been lived on the edge. A man, in the end, who had disappointed and hurt his family.

She'd vowed never to fall for a man like her father, and John Stern had been Paul Reed's antithesis. Her chest grew tight as she thought of the man she'd chosen to marry, a kind, gentle, fun-loving man who was as rock-solid as he was handsome.

Only one person had challenged her love for John, and she frowned as she remembered the night John had told Devlin they were getting married.

"Can you believe it?" John had cried, grabbing Chelsea around the waist and swinging her, laughing, from her feet as they stood near the Christmas tree that glittered by the balcony of John's bay-front condominium. "She's finally said 'yes.'"

"Imagine that," Devlin drawled, the lines around his mouth showing white against his tanned skin.

"I've been asking her for months!"

"Well—" Devlin's inky gaze had moved slowly from John to Chelsea's flushed face and lingered a second too long before he'd held up his bottle of beer. "Congratulations. I hope you're both happy."

His gaze left her as he drank slowly from the long neck of his bottle and Chelsea remembered studying his Adam's apple as he swallowed and noticing the way his black hair brushed the back of his neck. She'd wondered what she felt for him then. Anger? Disgust? Or unwilling attraction...

"Stop it," she told herself now, refusing to continue a memory that had burned in her mind for over a year, a memory that had made her question everything she'd ever believed in, a memory that had eclipsed all her memories of John.

She squeezed her eyes shut for just a second, willing away the sardonic look in Devlin's features, the mockery in his gaze. He'd always set her on edge, and yet she had to find him, had to know the truth about the accident.

Shoving her hair from her face, she stared at the blue-green water, feeling its spray as she leaned over the rail. Far ahead in the distance, a small island rose from the sea—a tiny emerald-green cone poking out of the ocean.

Soon they would be docking. Her heart began to race. What if the man wasn't Devlin? What would she say to him? How would she deal with the disappointment? Or, conversely, what if Mitch Russell *was* Devlin McVey? There must be a reason he was hiding down here, and he might not take kindly to her bulldozing her way back into his life.

Too bad.

She'd come this far—she wasn't about to turn back now. Besides, he deserved it. If he had left his friends and relatives to think him dead, then he deserved to have his life thrown out of kilter, and she had the right to some answers about what had happened on that windy day in April in San Francisco Bay.

As the captain guided the *Anna Marie* into harbor, Chelsea strained to see the port, a tiny town named Emeraude sprawled around several weathered docks that jutted into the shimmering water. Fishing boats, canoes and sailboats, rocking gently with the tide, were lashed to the moorings. A plank boardwalk curved over a sandy stretch of beach and led to the town, which was little more than a few sunbaked buildings lining the waterfront.

This village seemed so remote, so unlikely a spot for a big-city cop to end up. Unless he were running from something. But that was ridiculous. To Chelsea's knowledge, Devlin McVey had never run from anything in his life. Until now.

"There's a first time for everything," she told herself.

The captain tossed ropes that looped over moorings on the docks as the *Anna Marie* settled into port.

It's now or never, Chelsea thought, grabbing her bags and climbing onto the bleached wooden pier. Her stomach was in knots, her jaw set. Within hours, she could come face-to-face with Devlin again.

She shared a taxi, a decrepit gray station wagon, with an older couple, the Vaughns, from Miami. The apricot-haired woman, Emily, chatted nonstop while her husband, Jeff, suffered in silence, only interjecting a grunt or two when Emily would pause and ask, "Isn't that right, dear?"

Chelsea couldn't wait to get out of the cab. Her nerves were already strung tight and Emily's senseless chatter only set her more on edge as the old wagon snaked up the winding, rutted road to the one resort on the island. Lush green vegetation encroached on the dusty road and provided a leafy canopy high overhead, but the inside of the cab was hot and stifling.

"...so we decided to try something more secluded, a little less touristy, if you know what I mean," Emily went blithely on, "and Paradis seemed perfect. We heard all about the Villa from a friend. It was originally built in the twenties by some rich oil baron who wanted a private spot where he could get away from it all, probably to keep a mistress or two. Isn't that right, dear?"

"Right," Jeff said on cue as the driver pulled into the circular drive of what, years ago, must have been a glorious resort. A two-storied Mediterranean-style mansion with once-white stucco walls, wide verandas and a sloping tile roof stood shabbily behind an overgrown courtyard. The roof of the hotel had been patched over the years and the dingy walls were in sad need of paint.

Grass poked through the cracks in the pavement and the gardens rambled untrimmed. A fountain, rusted and no longer operational, stood in the middle of an empty wading pool and unkempt vines crawled across the ornate grillwork on the balcony surrounding the second story.

"Welcome to the Villa," the cabdriver said as he collected their fares.

"Isn't it spectacular," Emily gushed, eagerly climbing out of the cab.

Spectacular wasn't the word Chelsea had in mind. Run-down maybe, or once-grand, but definitely not spectacular. The sun was beginning to set and shadows stole over the main courtyard as if trying to hide the tired building's most obvious flaws.

A porter carried her bags into the main lobby and Chelsea felt a stab of regret for the old resort. Inside, the floors were tile, the staircase hand-rubbed walnut and the carpet running to the second story wine-red and worn. Circular fans moved lazily overhead and fading sunlight drifted through tall paned windows.

But the condition of the hotel didn't matter, she reminded herself. She was here with a purpose: to find Devlin.

To that end, she checked into her room on the second

floor, and spying her reflection in the mirror over the
vanity, cringed. She'd been traveling since dawn and she
looked rumpled and tired. Her slacks and blouse were
wrinkled, and her unruly red-brown hair was springing
out from her ponytail in wild clumps.

She quickly showered and changed into white slacks
and a red tank top, then brushed her wayward hair and
wound it into a knot at the base of her skull. A dab of
makeup and a shot of eyedrops, and she was as ready as
she'd ever be to meet Devlin.

She headed for the door, but stopped dead in her
tracks. What if he'd left? Jenkins had been gone four
days. What if, in that time, Devlin had taken off? Or
what if he's really not Devlin McVey and you've traveled all this way for nothing? Her heart nosedived.

"Think positive," she told herself, squaring her shoulders as she marched through the door and turned the key.

According to Jenkins, Mitch Russell, as he called himself, spent some of his evenings in the bar at the Villa.
Otherwise, he frequented several other watering holes
in town.

Chelsea decided to start downstairs.

The bar was at the back of the hotel and in no better shape than the rest of the Villa. A single bartender
served drinks and waited the few tables scattered around
the dark room. Candles flickered and the windows had
been cracked open, allowing the sound of insects to in-
filtrate the whispered conversations, clinking glasses and
occasional burst of laughter. Paddle fans fought a losing
battle with smoke and the hint of a breeze brought with
it the scent of the sea.

Chelsea sat in a corner of the room, ignoring the curious glances local patrons cast in her direction. She sipped

from a glass of wine and nibbled on the salted nuts, but her eyes were trained on the door from the lobby.

Within a few minutes a lanky man in his early thirties settled onto a stool at her table. His wheat-blond hair was long, tickling his ears, and he had a lean face with a narrow nose, teeth that overlapped just a little and eyes that stared straight into hers. "Mind if I join you?" he asked.

"I'm waiting for someone."

He scanned the bar and apparently seeing no one who was any competition, he shrugged. "It wouldn't hurt if I bought you a drink."

Chelsea didn't want anything to do with this man or any other man—aside from Devlin. Her stomach was already in knots and she didn't need to try and make small talk with this stranger. "I don't think so," she said, offering him a cool smile.

"Well, I'll just wait until your friend shows up."

Chelsea bristled a little. "I'd rather wait alone."

He arched a skeptical blond brow. "You're sure?"

"Positive."

"Okay." Lifting a shoulder, he added, "I can take a hint, especially when it's hurled at me." He offered her a confident smile. "The name's Chris Landeen if you change your mind or if your friend doesn't show up."

"Thanks," she said, feeling suddenly foolish. What if Devlin didn't show up? Well, she hadn't come all this way only to stop now. She sipped her wine again and settled in for a long wait, her gaze once again on the door.

She didn't have to wait long. She felt a prickle of apprehension as a gust of wind caused the candle on her table to flicker and dance.

At that moment, a tall, broad-shouldered man in snug-fitting jeans entered the room.

Her heart kicked into double-time as she stared at him.

Dressed in faded jeans, a black T-shirt, and a well-worn denim jacket, he crossed the room in an easy, fluid gait. A full, black beard covered his chin and his gaze, a deep, calculating blue, swung lazily around the room, landing full force on Chelsea.

She swallowed hard and rose, smiling, thanking God that he was safe—for when she gazed into his electric blue eyes, she knew for certain she'd found Devlin McVey. Now, at last, she could put together the missing pieces of the puzzle of John's death and get on with her life.

"I can't believe it," she whispered, crossing the room, her heart pumping furiously.

One dark brow lifted curiously. "Believe what?"

"That you're here—I mean, oh, God, Devlin, why?"

"Excuse me?" he drawled, his expression blank.

"What're you doing down here? What happened on the boat?"

He glanced from her to the eyes of several men at the bar, then his gaze came crashing back to hers. "Did I miss something?" he asked slowly. "Do you think you know me?"

"Of course I do. Devlin—"

"The name's Russell. Mitch Russell." A trace of irritation edged his words.

"But—" She was about to touch him, but stopped and let her hand drop to her side. "You're telling me that you're not Devlin McVey?"

"Lady, I think you've made yourself a big mistake."

"But…your voice, your walk…" The world spun crazily for a second. This couldn't be happening. He *was* Devlin. He had to be! "Devlin—"

He stared at her as if she'd gone mad. "Look, I don't know who this Devlin character is, but you've got the wrong guy!" Turning toward the bar, he motioned to the barkeep. "The usual."

Chelsea stood in the middle of the room, caught between the present and the past. Was her mind playing tricks on her, or was Devlin playing a cruel game?

Mitch glanced over his shoulder. "You want a drink? You look like you could use one."

"No...I don't think so." She licked suddenly dry lips and tried not to feel like a fool. She'd come all this way, spent all this money, wasted all her time for what? To confront a total stranger and act like an idiot?

She noticed the way people let their glances slide away, the manner in which their lips curved in amusement. Well, the show was over. Drawing on her courage, she walked to the bar and slid onto the empty stool next to Mitch's. "I, uh, didn't mean to—"

"Don't worry about it." He shook his head and she stared at his profile—identical to Devlin's. Her breath caught in her throat.

"But, it's just that you look so much like a...a friend of mine who's missing."

"Look," he said, turning toward her, "I told you to forget it." He lifted his shoulders easily. "It was an honest mistake."

"But—" she paused, confused. "You really do look like—"

"It happens."

"No, you don't understand," she said in a rush, wanting to shake him, to make him listen. "Devlin was supposed to have drowned but his body was never found and—"

"Are you coming on to me?" he asked suddenly.

"W-what?"

"I asked you if you were coming on to me. Either

you're trying to get me interested or you're a nutcase. Now, which is it?"

Chelsea's jaw dropped open in shock. "It's just that you bear this incredible resemblance—"

"Yeah, sure." He took a swallow of his drink, then looked her slowly up and down, his gaze nearly burning through her clothes as it rested on the stretch of fabric across her breasts.

Chelsea's heart thumped crazily.

"So what's it going to be?" he demanded, his eyes centering on her lips. "You and me? Upstairs?" He glanced through the open lobby door to the curved staircase and Chelsea's temper skyrocketed. "Your room?"

"Not on your life!"

His expression turned cynical and cold. "Then leave me alone. Okay? I'm not your friend Devin."

"Devlin—Devlin McVey."

"Whatever." He turned his attention back to his drink.

Mortified and furious, Chelsea slid off her bar stool. How could she have made such a disastrous mistake? She glanced back at the man at the bar, his profile hard-edged and rough, his features carved and angular, his black, unkempt hair curving over the frayed collar of his jacket. He had to be Devlin. He just had to be!

She walked quickly out of the bar, ran upstairs and once in her room, sluiced water over her burning cheeks. As she stared at her reflection in the mirror, she gritted her teeth. She hadn't come this far to give up so easily. No matter how insufferable he planned to be!

She intended to confront Mr. Mitchell Russell again, but the next time, she'd meet him in a more secluded spot—away from the interested eyes of the other guests at the Villa.

She had pictures of Devlin with her, and pictures of

John. She'd wave those photos under his nose and watch
for his reaction. He couldn't be that immune.

Or could he?

It had been over a year since she'd seen him, a year
since he'd disappeared from San Francisco.

She closed her eyes. Why had Devlin disappeared?
Why? She couldn't stop the questions from pounding
against the back of her mind.

There had to be a reason Devlin was pretending to be
Mitch Russell, but what was it?

Opening the window of her room, she stared out at the
moonlit night and let the sea-laden breeze cool her face.
The scent of jasmine and lemon filtered in, ruffling her
hair and cooling her burning cheeks.

Her fists clenched in renewed determination as she
watched the moon slowly rise over the ocean. If Mitch
Russell wanted a fight, he'd get it, but she wasn't giving
up until she was convinced that he wasn't Devlin.

And what then?

Chelsea cringed at the thought. The man in the bar,
the cruel man with the hot blue eyes, was Devlin. She
could feel it. All she had to do was prove it.

CHAPTER THREE

WHAT IF HE skips out?

The thought struck Chelsea like a thunderbolt as she dropped to the corner of her hotel room bed.

Now that she'd come face-to-face with Devlin, how could she be sure that he wouldn't leave? He'd already avoided the police and any friends or family he had back in San Francisco. Since she'd tipped her hand in the bar, he would now realize that he was found out in Paradis. What was to prevent him from sailing to St. Jean and taking the next plane to God-only-knew-where?

"You've bungled this, Reed," she growled at herself as she yanked off her clothes and tossed them onto the bed. She couldn't let him slip through her fingers! Not after she'd spent so much time and effort and come so far to locate him. No, she thought, changing into a pair of black slacks and a black pullover, she had to make sure that he would stay put and find out where he lived.

And you're going to do that by spying on him? the rational side of her mind questioned.

"You bet I am!" She pulled her hair from the neck of the pullover, donned running shoes, then headed quickly downstairs. Feeling a little foolish in her cat burglar outfit, she dashed through the side door not far from the bar, then lingered in the shadows by the empty wading pool, her eyes trained on the entrance.

Nerves strung tight as bowstrings, she spent the next

forty minutes checking her watch, drumming her fingers impatiently on the wall and telling herself that she was acting like a certifiable lunatic.

And what if Devlin waltzed out of the bar and climbed into his vehicle? There were several trucks and cars parked in a side lot, and if Devlin climbed into one of them she'd be stuck with nothing more than a license-plate number.

She considered calling a taxi, and asking the driver to wait until she needed him, but discarded the idea. On the deserted island roads, Devlin would spot a tail instantly. After all, he had been a cop, an undercover detective no less, and her amateur sleuthing skills were no match against him.

Despite her arguments with herself, she stuck it out and eventually he emerged, alone, hands plunged deep in his pockets, walking with the same quick, athletic stride she remembered. She held her breath and crossed her fingers, smiling to herself when, instead of heading toward the parking lot, he walked around the corner of the hotel.

Chelsea didn't waste any time. She took off after him. The glow from the windows of the Villa and the moonlight filtering through the dense foliage gave her some illumination, but she had to hurry to keep pace with Devlin's swift steps.

She rounded the corner of the hotel and followed a flagstone path that skirted the swimming pool, then flanked the edge of the forest. Her quarry, a mere hundred feet ahead of her, never once glanced over his shoulder.

That worried her. If this man were indeed Devlin, he would surely remember her and he'd know that she wouldn't give up easily. He'd *expect* her to follow him.

So, what if Mitch Russell wasn't Devlin?

The thought struck her cold and she shoved it angrily from her mind as she half ran to keep up with him, staying in the shadows, careful that her shoes didn't scrape against the stones. Mitch Russell was Devlin—he had to be! No one person could look and sound that much like another! No, her every instinct told her that this man was not only Devlin, but that he had something to hide.

He disappeared at the edge of the hotel grounds and vanished into the trees edging the east side of the resort. Great, Chelsea thought as she followed. The flagstones gave way to a sandy path. Chelsea slogged on, hearing the sound of the sea, the rush of water and feeling the air grow cooler as she squinted against the darkness to stay on the trail.

She hadn't thought to bring a flashlight, but wouldn't have used one if she had. A single beam would only alert Devlin to the fact that he was being followed. So she walked on, clenching her teeth and biting her tongue when her toes stubbed the root of a tree and she almost yelped. Hang in there, Chels, she mentally encouraged, squinting against the darkness and wishing she could quiet the hammering of her heart.

Where was he going?

Eventually the path widened and the trees gave way to a stretch of beach that glimmered silver in the pale light from the moon. She took one step onto the beach and glanced north and south, sweeping the waterline in both directions. Her heart plummeted. The sand was deserted. Devlin was nowhere in sight.

How had she lost him? She was sure she'd followed him. There had been no fork in the path, no trail angling in another direction—at least none that she'd seen.

She swung her gaze left and right again, but the beach

was empty. Deserted. Desperately, she narrowed her gaze on the sea, but the shimmering water stretching from the sand to the night-black horizon was unbroken. No solitary swimmer appeared and no shadow lurked near the water's edge.

"Damn! Damn! And double damn!" she swore. How had he eluded her?

Tossing her hands into the air, she stepped farther out onto the beach and kicked at the sand. Some detective she'd proved herself to be! She couldn't even follow one man less than a mile. Pathetic, that's what this entire scenario was—downright pathetic! Nancy Drew had nothing to worry about in the competition department.

Furious, Chelsea thrust her chin forward in determination. Well, she wasn't about to give up. So he'd lost her tonight. Tomorrow was another day. And tomorrow, things would be different. Unless he decided to take off in the middle of the night! In frustration, she shoved her hands through her hair. He wouldn't be able to pack up and disappear in just a few hours, would he?

Since she'd blown tailing him, her only other option was to find out about him from some of the regulars in the hotel. They would know where he lived, what he did for a living, maybe some detail from his past...

Muttering under her breath she turned and started back along the path.

"Giving up so soon?" a male voice boomed.

Chelsea froze. Her heart slammed in her chest. She whipped around, facing the edge of the forest on the northerly side of the path and saw him.

Devlin, damn him, was leaning insolently against the trunk of a large palm tree. His hands were plunged in his pockets and his shoulders rested against the bark. His face was shadowed but she didn't doubt that he'd been hiding there since she'd emerged from the thicket of trees. He probably watched her scour the beach for him while he silently laughed at her.

"You nearly scared the life out of me!" she flung out, her pulse jackhammering.

"You deserved it." He shoved himself upright and closed the short distance between them. If he'd been smiling, his expression had changed. Now his face was dark and dangerous, his bearded chin rock hard.

"I was just…"

"Out for a midnight stroll?" he mocked. "Sure."

There was no use lying, so she didn't. Instead she stood her ground, inches from him, tilting her chin defiantly upward, her shoulders automatically stiffening.

"I guess I didn't get through to you in the bar," he said evenly, his teeth flashing white against his beard. "I don't like people spying on me."

"I wasn't—"

"You weren't following me?" he asked, towering over her.

She'd already decided she couldn't lie and, truth to tell, she had always been a lousy liar. "Okay, I was following you," she admitted.

"Why?"

"I told you why in the bar."

"Because I look like your boyfriend."

"My friend," she corrected.

The moonlight cast a silver sheen to his eyes. "Okay, lady, what's your game? Who set you up to this?"

"No one. And the game's simple. I'm here looking for—"

"Yeah, I know. Well, you haven't found him so you can just leave me alone!"

She couldn't let him go that easily. "Don't you remember me?"

"I already told you. I've never laid eyes on you before. Now, if this is your idea of a joke—"

"No joke, Devlin."

Quick as a striking snake he grabbed both her upper arms in a hard, viselike grip. His fingers closed over her skin. "The name's Russell. Mitch Russell." His face looked nearly sinister. "I suggest you remember that." Frowning, he loosened his grasp a little. "And just who are you?"

"You don't remember me—?"

"Hell, no!"

"Chelsea," she replied, shaken to her roots. She'd been so sure. He even smelled like Devlin and his earthy scent brought back memories she was better off forgetting.

"Chelsea what?"

"Reed. You know—"

"I *don't* know. Not a damn thing! Except that you're down here, making up some wild stories that just don't make any sense." His lips tightened and he sucked in a short, angry breath. His gaze, rigid and calculating, skated down her front. "Why did this Devlin character leave you?"

"He didn't leave me—not exactly."

"Oh, yeah, he was supposed to have died…right? But somehow he's resurrected down here."

"Devlin disappeared in a boating accident. His friend died. John Stern. My fiancé." Was it her imagination, or did his eyes flicker a little? Or was it just the shadow of a passing cloud scudding across the moon?

"Let me get this straight. You were engaged—to another guy?" he asked incredulously. "But you're down here looking for the one who was just a friend."

"Yes."

"Geez, woman, this just gets better and better!"

"Please, just listen, Dev—er, Mitch." The name stuck in her throat and she had to force it over her tongue. "I just want to talk to you. Show you some pictures."

His mouth lifted at the corner and his eyes darkened seductively, but he didn't let go as he studied the contours of her face. "So this *is* a come on."

"No!"

"Then I'm not interested!" His grip relaxed, his arms dropped to his sides and he let out an exasperated breath. "Just leave me alone, okay? I don't like women who try and mess with my head."

"I need to talk to you—"

"You need to talk to a shrink!"

"But—"

His smile slashed coldly in the darkness. "I'm not interested in anything you're peddling. If you've been set up for this and someone's paying you to play some kind of sick joke on me, tell him the last laugh's on him. Or, if you're just looking for a little fun," he added suggestively, "I'm only interested in one thing. Got it?"

The bastard! Her skin crawled at his suggestion. Who was this guy? "In your dreams," she said.

"No, lady. In yours." With that he shoved his hands into his pockets, turned, and strode quickly up the beach.

Chelsea was left furious, insulted and downright angry. "Of all the insufferable, egotistical, revolting…" She bit her tongue to keep from swearing soundly.

What did you expect? she asked herself as she turned and headed back to the hotel. Anger burned up her cheeks, but she forced it back. She'd have to hang on to her patience in order to deal with Mitch Russell.

Don't give up, she told herself. Remember John. Remember Devlin!

She spotted the lights surrounding the hotel and started running, through the forest and along the flagstones flanking the pool. She walked into the main lobby and climbed the stairs, slowly counting to ten and calming herself. If this was the way Devlin planned on playing the game, fine. Two could play.

In her room, she kicked off her running shoes and headed for the shower. She'd had enough for one day, but tomorrow, watch out—round two! If Mr. Russell thought she would back down so easily, he damn well had another think coming!

THE NEXT MORNING, CHELSEA wrapped herself in a yellow sundress, stepped into white leather thongs and decided to explore Emeraude. Maybe if she poked around she could find out more about the mysterious Mitchell Russell without having to square off with him again.

There had to be more to his character than the fact that he insulted women for a hobby, she thought ruefully. At least she hoped so.

Swinging a straw bag over her shoulder and plopping a matching hat on her head, she marched downstairs. Outside, the sun was hot, the temperature already soaring, the moist earth steamy as the ground began to bake.

Chelsea asked a dark-skinned taxi driver to drop her off near the docks in town, then she stared out the cab's window, seeing flashes of silvery-blue water through the trees as a glimpse of ocean appeared through the dense greenery.

Within twenty minutes, the taxi was grinding to a halt. Chelsea paid her fare and then set about exploring the town where Mitch Russell lived.

Emeraude was little more than a sleepy fishing village—a tourist town that had faded in popularity over the years as the larger, more commercial islands had gained favor with trendy vacationers. But the dusty streets were lined with a few shops—boutiques, bakeries, bookstores, craft shops and an art gallery or two. Two blocks from the waterfront, a shaded, open-air market was laden with fresh fish, produce, island art and jewelry.

Several cafés were strung along the docks, and a block inland, a jumble of brick and concrete buildings housed apartments, the local government, a bank, a real estate firm and a few miscellaneous business offices.

The mood of the town was slow and lazy, and Chelsea didn't mind. In fact, if her head hadn't been filled with Devlin or Mitch or whoever the devil that arrogant man was, she might enjoy the lazy, sun-drenched pace of Paradis.

Her stomach rumbled, reminding her that she hadn't stopped for breakfast. She strolled into a small café overlooking the waterfront and slid into an empty booth upholstered in worn yellow vinyl. The menu was written in French and Chelsea's high-school fluency stopped on the second item.

A slim, dark-skinned girl, with an easy smile and sleek black hair braided past her waist, sauntered over to her table and helped Chelsea choose a breakfast of shrimp creole, eggs and island bread, whatever that was.

"You'll love it," the waitress assured her in a French accent. "Everyone does."

Chelsea wasn't convinced, but within minutes the pretty girl returned with a large, steaming platter.

The shrimp was so spicy it nearly brought tears to Chelsea's eyes, but it tasted divine and the chewy island bread, spread with honey and butter, melted in her mouth.

"Hot, *non?*" the waitress asked, refilling Chelsea's iced tea glass as Chelsea took a bite of shrimp.

"Hot, yes!" Chelsea replied with a smile. She sipped the cool tea and thought about Devlin as the waitress, whose name tag read Simone, poured coffee at nearby tables.

Why was Devlin eluding her, lying to her, and worse yet, mortifying her? Devlin had always earned a reputation with women, but Chelsea had suspected that his exploits were vastly overestimated by John. She, herself, had never seen any indication that Devlin was into fast women and one-night stands. In fact, in the few double dates she and John had shared with him, the women, never the same one twice, had seemed far more interested in Devlin than he had been in them.

And then there had been Devlin's wife, Holly, who had died long before Chelsea had met him. He'd never spoken of her, but John had mentioned that Devlin had been destroyed by her death. Chelsea had never learned how Devlin's wife had died. "It's something he never discusses," John had warned her.

As for the other women—those ladies who found Devlin's cool aloofness so attractive—Chelsea had never become friends with any of them. Some women went for the distant, disinterested type—a male who presented a challenge. Chelsea didn't.

She stared out the window and sighed. Mitch Russell was far from cool and aloof. He was frank about his intentions; in fact, he was rude to the point that no sane woman would want him. But maybe that was the point. Maybe his challenge of offering to take her to bed was just a bluff. There was the possibility that he was just trying to scare her off.

But why?

The question rattled around in her mind for the next fifteen minutes while she finished her tea. She still didn't have an answer as she walked to the front desk and dug into her purse for some cash to pay her bill.

As Chelsea opened her wallet, a petite woman with short red hair and a burst of freckles across her nose bustled through the door and hurried up to the counter.

"The usual, Simone," she said as the waitress tallied Chelsea's bill. "Two coffees, a tea and whatever pastry you've got—preferably something with marmalade." She fanned herself with her hand, "Can you believe this heat?" she asked no one in general, as she looked in Chelsea's direction.

"Aren't you used to it?" Chelsea asked.

"Me?" The redhead laughed. "Heavens no! I doubt I'll ever be used to the temperature. And the *humidity!*"

"But you came in here ordering 'the usual.'"

The petite woman laughed, crinkling her freckled, upturned nose. "Well, it's the usual down at the shop where I work, but I've only been here a couple of years." Her brown eyes twinkled. "I know that sounds like a long time, but I'm far from a native. I'm from Idaho, about fifty miles from Boise, and sometimes I miss winter—I mean real winter with snow and ice and frostbite!"

Chelsea was intrigued. "Do you?"

"Oh, don't get me wrong, I came here for the sun and sand, but once in a while the heat gets to me, really makes me swelter, and I'd just about kill for subzero temperatures. Oh, by the way, I'm Terri. Terri Peyton. I'm the manager of the Boutique Exotique just down the street." She extended her hand.

"Chelsea Reed," Chelsea replied.

Terri's handshake was as enthusiastic as she was. "Here for a visit?"

"Mmm." Chelsea nodded, finding the right amount of cash and leaving it next to an ancient cash register.

"How long are you staying?" Terri asked.

"I'm not sure yet—probably a couple of weeks."

Simone returned with Terri's order.

"Paradis is a great place," Terri enthused, obviously forgetting the charms of winter in Boise. "So romantic, you know."

So far, Chelsea hadn't noticed.

Terri handed Simone some bills. "Keep the change," she said, then turned back to Chelsea. "If you're interested in shopping for something out of the ordinary—jewelry, scarves, clothes, gifts or island art, we've got it at the B. E.—that's what we call the boutique." She fluttered a wave with her fingers, and carrying two white sacks, opened the door with her backside and left.

"Terri, she knows everyone on the island," Simone commented as she picked up Chelsea's tab and cash.

"I thought she said she's only been on Paradis a couple of years."

Nodding, Simone grinned widely. "This is true, but Terri, she makes it her business to know everyone. Come back again."

"I will," Chelsea promised. She shoved open the door, adjusted her hat and thought about the pert little redhead. Terri was friendly and warm. Obviously she met people easily. No doubt she'd come across Mr. Russell. The wheels turned in Chelsea's mind. Perhaps Terri would like to help Chelsea fit together some of the pieces of the intriguing puzzle that was Mitch Russell.

CHELSEA SPENT THE AFTERNOON exploring the town. She picked out a hand-knit sweater for her mother and even found some straw place mats dyed a raspberry shade for

Felicia. After all, Felicia wasn't so bad, Chelsea thought with more than a little twinge of guilt for the fight they'd had at her apartment. Felicia, in her own perverse way, was only looking out for her younger sister's best interests—or so she thought.

At four-thirty Chelsea's feet were killing her. Aching from walking in thongs along the hot cobblestones, she rested on the corner and spied the hand-painted wooden sign for Terri's shop.

With a weary smile, she yanked open the screen door of the Boutique Exotique. And exotic it was. A blue-and-green parrot whistled loudly from a huge aviary near the window and a cockatoo plumped his feathers in a large wire cage in the opposite corner of the room. Artwork and crafts decorated the walls and tables. Bright clothing hung from spiraled racks. Straw, canvas and leather bags swung from pegs planted in the ceiling near the walls.

"Chelsea!" Terri called, glancing over her shoulder. She stood at a counter, draping shell necklaces over a rack.

"I thought I'd come in and look around," Chelsea explained. "My partner and I own a boutique in San Francisco."

"Do you!" Terri cried. "Well, come on, let me show you everything." And she did. While another salesclerk dealt with the few other customers who drifted in, Terri gave Chelsea the grand tour.

Chelsea bought two pairs of wild earrings, a pair of hand-painted sunglasses, another hat and a white sun dress with a pink-and-green belt.

"You didn't have to buy out the store," Terri said, grinning as she rang up the sale.

Chelsea laughed. "I think I left a few things for your other customers."

The parrot cawed and Terri rolled her eyes.

Chelsea said, "My partner calls our shop a zoo. If she only knew…"

"This bird, too, can be yours," Terri teased, motioning to the parrot. "For a nominal fee—"

The parrot ruffled his wings loudly and repeated, "Nominal fee."

Handing Chelsea her bag, Terri leaned across the counter and stage-whispered, "Don't let him know, but he's a real pain sometimes."

"But the customers adore him, I bet."

"They don't have to clean his cage," Terri said with a sour look, then added, "If you wait a few minutes, I'll close up and we can go somewhere for a drink."

"I'll wait." Chelsea dug in her bag, shoved her new pair of sunglasses onto her nose and strolled outside.

Twenty minutes later, the two women were seated at an outdoor café overlooking the docks. A striped umbrella shaded their table as they sipped iced tea and lime. Terri was explaining her life story—how she ended up in Paradis after a painful divorce. "I just wanted to get away—escape, I guess you'd call it—from Rob. So I found a spot as far away as I could from Boise and the rest is history!"

"That's when you started working at the shop?"

"Mmm, actually, I'm part owner." She swirled her drink. "Believe it or not, I'm actually a kindergarten teacher, but when I left Idaho, I wanted to start all over. You know, new location, new career, new man—only trouble is, I haven't found the new man yet."

"You will," Chelsea predicted.

"I hope so."

Chelsea eyed her new friend. "Is that how a lot of people end up here? Because they're leaving something or someone behind?"

Terri lifted a tanned shoulder. "You mean the Americans?" At Chelsea's nod, she added, "I suppose."

It was now or never. Chelsea plunged on. "Simone said you know most of the people on the island."

"Not most, but some."

"Have you ever met Mitch Russell?"

Nodding, Terri smiled dreamily. "Of course. He showed up in Emeraude about eight or nine months ago, I think. And he was definitely the most interesting man to walk off the boat in a long time."

An arguable point, in Chelsea's estimation. "What do you know about him?"

"Not much," Terri admitted. A small crease formed between her brows. "He's a mystery man of sorts. You know the type—doesn't get too close to anyone, hangs out at the bars some nights."

"No wife?" Chelsea asked.

Terri shook her head. "Well, no wife down here. Who knows what he left behind."

What, indeed?

"So—you already met him?" Terri asked.

"Mmm. Last night in the bar at the hotel," Chelsea said, then gambled. Reaching into her purse, she yanked out her wallet and flipped it open to a page with a picture of John, Devlin and herself on Devlin's sailboat. She slipped the photo from the wallet and handed it to Terri. "That's a picture of my fiancé, John, his best friend, Devlin McVey, and me. It was taken over a year ago."

Terri set down her drink and pushed her sunglasses into her hair. "You're engaged?" she asked.

"Was. My fiancé was killed in a boating accident and I'm looking for his friend."

"This guy—right?" she pointed to the picture of Devlin.

"Yes. He disappeared after the accident."

Terri didn't react, just studied the photograph. "What do you mean 'disappeared'?"

"He left San Francisco, didn't tell anyone where he was," she explained, not mentioning Devlin's deception of letting everyone think he was dead. "I think Mitch Russell might be Devlin."

"You're kidding!" Terri's reddish eyebrows skyrocketed. She stared at the photograph with new interest.

"I'm dead serious. Take a long look—" she encouraged, mentally crossing her fingers that Terri would agree with her. She needed reinforcement.

"I don't know…"

"Picture Devlin with a beard like Mitch's."

Terri's face pulled into a knot of concentration. "It's possible, I suppose, but why would he change his name?"

"I wish I knew. Obviously, he doesn't want to be recognized."

"And you saw him last night? Talked with him?" Terri asked, her eyes rounding. "What happened?"

"He claimed he didn't know me, but…"

"But, what? You think he's lying?"

"I wish I knew," Chelsea admitted, blowing her bangs out of her eyes and staring at the ice cubes melting in her drink. "Somehow, I have to find out."

"Is there a reason he'd want to hide?"

"That's the million-dollar question," Chelsea said. She decided to keep the fact that Devlin had been involved in the boating accident a secret. At least until she confronted Devlin or Mitch or whoever he was.

"Well, I don't know much about Mitch Russell." Terri dropped her sunglasses back onto the bridge of her nose. "No one does. As I said, he showed up here several months ago and he keeps pretty much to himself—lives in a cabin about two miles up the beach from the Villa, just around the northern point. Oh, he hangs out with a few locals occasionally—usually at the bar in the Villa or at the Dauphin Bleu, or someplace like that, but he doesn't have a lot of friends."

"What about women?" Chelsea asked impulsively, despising the question. Mitch Russell's interest in the female population wasn't really any of her concern. Chelsea was only in Paradis to find out the truth.

Terri's lips pulled down at the corners. "I've never seen him with a woman—not like on a date or anything. And his name hasn't been linked with anyone in particular. Sometimes he hangs out with a couple of guys who live somewhere else and there's usually a girl—well, woman really, she must be twenty-one or two—with them."

For an unfathomable reason Chelsea's heart dropped.

"And, of course, he's around women, but as for anything serious—" she lifted her palms toward the sky "—I haven't heard about it—not that I would, necessarily." Terri slid her sunglasses back onto her nose. "Believe me, he's gotten his share of attention from the women tourists."

"I'll bet," Chelsea said dryly. Just like Devlin.

"He comes from somewhere in the midwest—Chicago, I think."

"What does he do for a living?"

"Nothing that I can tell," Terri said thoughtfully. "Though I heard he was working on some book."

"A book?" Chelsea repeated with a twist of her lips. Oh, sure. Devlin—writing a book? Restless, ever-moving Devlin sitting down at a computer or typewriter for hours on end? No way!

"That's the rumor."

"Do you know anything else about him?"

"Not much. Once in a while he goes over to St. Jean, but I don't know why."

"Regularly?" Chelsea asked, interested.

"Fairly—maybe once every week or two. But that's not so unusual. Paradis is pretty small, especially if you're used to a big city." Terri finished her drink and studied the picture again. "This man—" she tapped a peach-colored nail on the photograph "—if he had a beard, I suppose, could be Mitch, but it's pretty hard to tell."

"I know," Chelsea agreed in frustration. "I guess the only way I'll find out is by talking to him again."

"That shouldn't be such a hardship," Terri teased.

If you only knew, Chelsea thought.

THAT NIGHT, SHE WAITED in the bar again. Self-consciously, she sipped her wine and ignored the curious looks sent over the shoulders of several men—men she recognized from the night before. She heard a few of the whispers and laughs, caught more than one smirk or interested eyebrow lifted in her direction, and she knew the knowing smiles were at her expense.

Still, she sat alone at a tall table, absently twirling the stem of her wineglass, nibbling on pretzels and pretending not to notice the speculative glances cast her way. Three different men tried to occupy the other chair at her table and one asked her to dance, but she made it clear she was waiting for someone and acted as if she didn't see the mockery in each man's eyes.

Staring through the haze of cigarette smoke, she lingered for nearly three hours.

Mitch didn't show up.

She'd probably scared him off, she realized fatalistically. Great. So what was the next step? She'd already wasted a day on the island—well, perhaps not wasted.

Terri had been helpful and she'd enjoyed the petite red-head's company. However, as for Devlin, she didn't know much more than she did when she arrived in Emeraude yesterday.

She left her second glass of wine half-full, tossed some change on the bar and walked through French doors to a patio outside, away from the noise and the smoke.

Fresh, salty air blew in from the sea, snatching at her hair and cooling her face. The moon, three-quarters and shining brightly, hung low in the sky. Thousands of stars winked overhead.

Shoving her hands into the pockets of her new sun-dress, Chelsea shoved on a rusted wrought-iron gate that squeaked in protest as it opened. She followed an over-grown sandy path that skirted the old Villa and forked into the same flagstone trail she'd followed the night be-fore. Without thinking twice, she hurried past the swimming pool and started down the path that led through the woods to the beach.

Terri had said that Mitch lived past the north point on the beach, and Chelsea intended to check it out and wait for him if need be.

The path widened and unconsciously, Chelsea glanced at the trunk of the tree where Mitch had waited for her the night before. But tonight, she was alone. The strip of white sand was deserted and the sea lapped lazily at the shore. A ribbon of moonlight rippled on the shadowy water.

On a lark, Chelsea kicked off her sandals and waded in the warm sea, wondering at the rashness of her plan to wait for Devlin at his house.

If he hadn't already left Paradis.

She plucked her sandals from the ground and gathering her courage, started north along the beach, cool sand squishing between her toes. She'd wasted enough time trying to learn something about him. It was time for a showdown.

Trying to convince herself that she wasn't about to make the biggest mistake of her life, she followed the deserted stretch of sand around a curve and past a few cabins with lights burning brightly in their windows.

The beach narrowed to a path that twisted around a rocky jetty. Chelsea followed the overgrown trail along the edge of the ocean until it widened again for a short distance.

Only one house occupied this tiny northerly beach, a small cabin with a tile roof and a broad front porch that faced the sea. A beat-up vehicle—a truck or rig of some sort—was parked in a rutted lane and a couple of chairs occupied the porch. A hammock stretched between two trees. Farther away, at the ocean's edge, a long, sun-bleached dock stretched into the dark ocean. Against the pier, a sailboat was lashed to the moorings and rocked gently with the tide.

Chelsea's teeth bit into her lip. Obviously Devlin's love of sailing hadn't been destroyed in the accident. Her heart hammered loudly as she approached the house.

What if this were the wrong place?

Just because Terri had given her general directions didn't mean that this little cabin belonged to Mitch Russell. The windows were open, no shades drawn, and lamplight glowed in the darkness.

Closer to the cabin, her hands beginning to sweat, Chelsea craned her neck to peer cautiously into the living room.

The inside of the cabin was sparse, furnished with a worn couch, coffee table and chair. The walls were stucco, the floor, weathered boards covered by an old rag rug.

"It's now or never," she whispered to herself as she walked stiffly up the two rickety steps to the front door and knocked loudly.

Her stomach twisted.

The seconds ticked by.

Sweat gathered between her shoulders.

No one answered.

What now? she wondered, but even as she did, she reached forward, her fingers wrapped around the doorknob. She pushed and the door creaked open on rusty hinges.

Her heart thundered. She shouldn't be doing this. She was trespassing, for God's sake! And she didn't know anything about Mitch Russell. He could be on the run. Maybe he owned a gun. She glanced around, but couldn't see anything.

Swallowing against a suddenly dry throat, Chelsea took a step forward, but couldn't cross the threshold. Even though the door hadn't been locked, this seemed a little like breaking and entering—well, entering at least—and she didn't want to have to try to talk her way out of a complaint lodged by Mitch.

But then, she'd come this far, hadn't she?

"Mitch?" she called, and her voice sounded little more than a whisper. This place was giving her the creeps! "Mitch?"

Behind her, the breeze picked up, tickling her neck. She felt someone's gaze upon her back and froze. The deep male voice, hard-edged and sounding so much like Devlin, stopped her cold. "Take one step inside and I'll call the authorities."

His voice was like an electric shock. Chelsea nearly

jumped out of her skin. Heart thudding, she whirled around.

"What the hell are you doing here?" he demanded, glaring angrily at her. Standing near the curved trunk of a palm tree, his silhouette was just visible against a backdrop of moon-dappled water. He wiped a hand over his face and shoved wet hair from his eyes. He wore cut-off jeans and nothing else. His hair shimmered in the moonlight and his wet shorts clung to him, hanging low on his hips. His chest was bare and dark hair stretched across the broad expanse only to narrow into a thin trail that disappeared beneath his exposed navel and nearly indecent low-slung cutoffs.

Chelsea's mouth turned to cotton at the sight of him half-naked. His abdomen was flat and hard and his chest rose and fell, as he breathed raggedly from his swim.

"I called for you but no one answered," she said lamely.

His expression murderous, Mitch ground out, "You sure don't know how to take a hint, do you?"

"I just wanted to talk to you."

"Yeah, right," he said with a disbelieving snort.

"I did. Really."

"So talk."

"I have pictures—pictures of Devlin. I'd like to show them to you."

"I'm not interested."

The man was absolutely maddening! "What would it hurt?"

He didn't answer for a long moment. His eyes regarded her with sultry appraisal.

Chelsea could barely breathe. She felt his hot gaze, so much like Devlin's, and it caused her blood to quicken through her veins.

Scowling, he crossed the sand that separated them, then climbed the two steps of the porch, stopping only inches from her. She had to tilt her head up to look into his eyes and it was all she could do to meet his gaze—hooded and darkly sensual. He smelled of salt, sea and musk, and droplets of water still clung to his beard.

He was too close and she wanted to back up a step, to put some distance between her body and his, but she held her ground, rather than retreat into his house.

"Will you leave me alone if I trip down memory lane with you?" he asked, his breath hot as it whispered across her hair.

"I—I don't know."

"What will it take to convince you that I'm not your boyfriend?"

"I told you, he wasn't my..." She swallowed hard as he crooked one lofty brow. "Just look at the pictures—hear me out."

"And then you'll be on your way?"

"Yes."

"And you won't bother me again?"

She hesitated. She'd always been an awful liar, but she knew if she told him the truth, he'd shut her out and that would be the end of it. "I—I'll try not to."

His jaw slid to the side. Leaning one shoulder against the rough walls of the house, he reached forward and touched the tip of her chin with one long finger. "Maybe we can work a deal," he said silkily.

Chelsea shuddered. "A deal?"

"Yeah. I listen to you and you—" he cocked his head toward the interior of the house "—you spend the night with me."

She hesitated just a heartbeat. "No way."

"No?" His fingers slid easily along her chin and down her throat. Chelsea quivered inside but didn't move. Staunchly, she held her ground.

"I'm not here to bargain sexual favors," she said tightly.

His gaze slid downward to the swell of her breasts. "I wonder."

To her horror, her traitorous pulse leaped. "Well, you can wonder and rot in hell while you do it!" she snapped, though the constriction in her lungs was nearly painful.

He clucked his tongue and his eyes glinted mischievously. "Strong words for a woman who wants something so badly."

"All I want is information—nothing else."

Mitch's lips twisted beneath his beard and his finger moved lower, to the circle of bones at her throat. "This guy—Devlin—he must've meant a lot to you."

That was a tough one. "He did."

"You were friends?"

"Yes," she whispered, trying to concentrate on the conversation while Mitch's fingers slid lower still, closer to her breast.

"Lovers?"

"No!"

"No?" he asked, disbelieving and she stepped back and flung his hand away.

"No!" she repeated, her voice sounding torn even to her own ears. "I—I was in love with his best friend."

Mitch's blue eyes darkened to midnight.

"If you'll just listen to me, I'll explain everything."

Eyeing her thoughtfully, he shoved his hands into the back pockets of his cutoffs. "Okay, lady, I'll listen. But on one condition."

"And what's that?"

His eyes glinted like blue fire. "After you spin your little tale and I look at your scrapbook, you either leave me alone for good or spend the rest of the night in my bed."

CHAPTER FOUR

CHELSEA TOSSED HER HAIR over her shoulders and angled her chin upward rebelliously. "Get this straight, Russell. I'm *not* interested in sleeping with you—"

"Even if I turned out to be this Devlin guy?"

Her heart pummeled against her ribs. "Even then."

He crooked a dark, disbelieving brow.

"And as for leaving you alone, I can't do that. At least not yet!"

"Then I guess we don't have anything to talk about." He leaned down, as if the consequences of their conversation meant nothing to him, and brushed the sand from his still-wet legs.

She couldn't believe he was turning her away. After practically undressing her with his eyes, he didn't have the decency to hear her out! Narrowing her eyes, she asked, "Don't you even want to see the pictures?"

"I couldn't care less."

"But—"

"Look, lady, I already told you I don't know you and I don't give a damn about your boyfriend."

"I thought I told you, Devlin *wasn't* my boyfriend."

"You've told me all right, but you seem pretty interested in him. How far have you traveled, hmm? How much money have you wasted to get here? From where I stand, you seem to have more than a passing interest in your lover's friend."

That did it. Her temper went through the roof. It was all she could do to keep from slapping him. "If you'd just hear me out," she said through clenched teeth. "You'd understand—"

"Why don't you just leave me the hell alone?"

"Because I can't!"

"Give it up, lady!" He flicked an angry glance at her, eyeing her dress with disdain. "Paradis isn't a place for a wealthy woman, or haven't you figured that out yet? Why don't you go chase your petty fantasies in Martinique or Bermuda or the Bahamas? I'm sure you can find someone willing to go along with your fairy tale—"

"Because you're here," she interrupted.

He didn't move a muscle. His blue eyes turned as dark as the night sky as he silently appraised her.

Chelsea's breath caught in her throat. Her pulse leaped crazily and she had to battle the emotions that tore at her soul.

"Not me, Chelsea," he said quietly. "You're looking for someone else."

"I don't think so," she whispered, her gaze locking into the inky depths of his.

"You think I'm lying?"

"Yes."

"Why?" he demanded, his face a knot of consternation.

"Because you know something that you'd rather keep secret."

He shook his head slowly. "You really expect me to believe this?" he said, nearly laughing. "Lady, if you could only hear yourself. If you ask me, you've watched one too many TV movies."

Refusing to be ridiculed into submission, she crossed her arms over her chest. "Why won't you just admit that you're Devlin?"

"Because I'm not, dammit." He plowed stiff fingers through his wet hair and the brackets surrounding his mouth turned white. "What does it take to get through to you?"

"Just listen to me. Let me show you the pictures…"

He tensed suddenly, every muscle turning rigid.

When she opened her mouth to continue, he whispered a soft, "Shh." He placed a staying finger against her lips and gave a curt shake of his head.

She got the message. Chelsea's words died on her lips. And his apprehension infected her. She strained to listen but only heard the sounds of the night.

Mitch squinted, eyes narrowed against the shadows. His gaze darted quickly across the isolated terrain, searching the darkness of the tropical woods and sweeping across the ocean. Lips tight, he muttered, "Get inside." When she didn't immediately obey, his jaw hardened and without another word he wrapped a strong arm around her waist.

"Hey!"

Hauling her quickly over the threshold, he kicked the door shut behind them.

Chelsea struggled against his tight hold. "What do you think you're doing?"

"Shh!" he hissed. He dropped her unceremoniously onto the couch, then locked and bolted the door, closed the windows and snapped the shades shut.

Frightened by his bizarre behavior, she quickly scrambled to her feet and started for the front door. But he grabbed her hand roughly and spun her around. "Who followed you?" he demanded.

"W-what?" Her stomach slammed against her diaphragm.

"Did you bring someone with you?" He wasn't playing games. His face was hard and set. His fingers tightened over her arm, biting into her flesh.

Chelsea's blood ran cold. "No—I don't know anyone on the island. No one but you."

"Look, lady, for the last time, you *don't* know me!" He gave her arm a shake.

"No one followed me!"

"Are you sure?"

"Yes—I think." Sighing, she threw up her hands, casting his fingers off her. "I didn't really pay attention, but the beach was deserted."

"Not good enough." His back teeth ground together as he snapped off the lights. The cabin was suddenly black as pitch.

"Hey—what're you doing?"

"Just making sure you were alone."

"Why?" she demanded, squinting, trying to get her bearings in case he was playing some trick on her.

"Just shut up for a second, will you?" he asked, peering through the blinds.

The house grew silent except for the island breeze that soughed against the roof and the dull, distant roar of the ocean. Chelsea's nerves stretched tight. Here she was, alone with a man who was either a virtual stranger or a man who couldn't—or wouldn't—remember her—a man who had played havoc with her emotions in the past. Either way, she was in an impossible situation.

A cold sweat ran down Chelsea's back. Had she inadvertently lured someone to Mitch—someone dangerous? Or was this just another of his ploys to get rid of her? Maybe he was trying to scare her off. She wouldn't put it past him.

Slowly, her eyes adjusted to the darkness and she told herself she should be afraid—locked in this unknown house with a stranger. Even if this man proved to be Devlin, he'd changed to the point that she didn't feel at ease with him—not that she'd ever been completely at ease with Devlin. There had been an ominous and rough side to him—a side that had intrigued, yet frightened her. But Devlin had shown a depth of character, a sense of humor, cynical though it might be, and a certain warmth, loyalty and charm that Mitch Russell was sorely lacking.

Yes, there had been times when Devlin had been cold and calculating, when as a detective for the San Francisco Police Department he had been forced to be so. But there had been a human side to him as well—an honorable side. Chelsea wasn't sure that Mitch Russell had any honor. In fact, she decided that he probably had ice water running through his veins.

Her skin prickled as she watched him. He stood at a side window, peering through the slits between the blinds, the corded muscles of his chest stiff and tense.

The minutes dragged out. Chelsea fidgeted apprehensively on the couch. Was he trying to scare her? Well, dammit, he was. She was frightened, but she really didn't understand why. What could be so threatening that he would drag her in here and lock the door? Nothing, she decided. He was just into melodrama, hoping to frighten her away. Well, she'd surprise him.

The silence became deafening. Finally, when she thought she couldn't stand the tension straining in the room a moment longer, he flipped on a small table lamp. But he didn't open the blinds.

"Satisfied?" she asked.

"No." He glared at her as if she were some kind of Jezebel. His gaze raked down the scoop neck of her dress, the full white skirt. "You couldn't have worn anything that would have stood out any more than that, could you?"

"What are you afraid of?"

"Not afraid. Just cautious."

"Or paranoid?" she baited.

To her surprise he actually grinned—a cynical smile that didn't quite touch his eyes. "Probably."

"You really thought someone followed me? Why?"

He lifted a shoulder.

"And why all this secrecy—this cloak-and-dagger stuff? What are you, some kind of spy?"

He snorted. "Hardly."

"No?" She lifted a mocking brow. "Then what? Running away from the law? Or maybe the I.R.S.? Or are you hiding here with a new identity, Devlin?"

In a split second his smile faded and he clenched a fist, raising it as if to crash it against a wall, then, abruptly straightened his fingers. "For the last time," he muttered, his voice strained by his rapidly escaping patience, "I'm not your precious Devlin."

"He wasn't *my* anything."

"Yeah, right. You do a lot of denying but not much convincing."

She ignored that jab. "So who do you think followed me?"

"I don't know." Motioning impatiently with his hand, he said abruptly, "You said you had some pictures. Why don't you show them to me and be on your merry way?"

"Nothing I'd like better," she replied curtly. Quickly, she opened her purse and retrieved the envelope of photographs. She dumped the contents onto a scarred coffee table and watched Mitch's reaction. He crossed the room, but barely glanced at the pictures.

Chelsea's heart constricted. How could Devlin act so callously disinterested when he and John had been so close? Desperately, she handed him a picture of John and a part of her died when not the least bit of emotion crossed his face. Oh, Lord, had she been so terribly wrong about him?

"I don't look like this guy," he finally said, his eyes returning to hers. "Not at all. I don't get this—"

"That's not Devlin," she cut in hastily. "It's John, my fiancé," she said, her throat suddenly hot and dry when she thought of John and all their plans. Why did it seem so long ago—so far away?

Mitch glanced at the photograph, then let it drop back to the table. "If this guy's the one you were supposed to marry, why all the interest in his friend? Or did you have a thing going with him, too?"

Chelsea had to grit her teeth to keep from flinging back a hot retort. "No, I just need to talk to him—to you. I—I need to know what happened."

Mitch's jaw hardened. He kicked the table out of his way, grabbed her by the forearms and hauled her to her feet.

"Hey—stop—"

"I'm only going to say this one more time, lady," he ground out, his breath hot against her face, the tips of her breasts brushing his chest. "I'm not, never was, never will be Devlin McVey! And I pity the poor bastard who is, because you're obviously going to chase him to the ends of the earth—or some poor slob who looks like him." His gaze raked over her face. "Why do you care?"

"Because I need answers," she said, her eyes beseeching his. "I want to know why Devlin insisted John go out on the boat that day—what they had to discuss. And I want to know why he faked his death, what happened on that boat, and why he ran away."

Something deadly flickered in Mitch's eyes and he released his viselike grip on her arm. The hard line of his mouth gentled. "Has it ever occurred to you that McVey might be dead?"

She closed her eyes against that horrid truth. "I can't believe Devlin's gone."

Mitch's head snapped up and his eyes narrowed on hers. "Why not? Just because his body didn't wash up?"

"It's—it's just a feeling I've got. That's all."

"Where did this happen?"

"San Francisco Bay."

"Lord, woman, that's one helluva stretch of water. Couldn't McVey's body have washed out to sea?"

No! "It's possible."

"What do the police have to say about it?"

"They seem to think that Devlin and John got caught in a storm, they had engine trouble of some kind, maybe a leak in the gas line, which caused an explosion, and a swell capsized the boat, smashing it into some rocks and both men drowned." Chelsea gazed steadily into his blue, blue eyes. "But I find it hard to believe that could have happened. Both Devlin and John were expert sailors."

"They wouldn't be the first ones to lose out to the forces of nature," he said cynically. Raking his fingers through his hair, he picked up another snapshot that had fallen to the floor when he'd kicked the table. In the picture Devlin stood on one side of her, John the other. Ironic, she thought, how she'd always felt torn between these two friends.

Frowning, he rifled through the remaining photographs, one after another, eyeing them with maddening calm, not showing the least bit of emotion—as if he really didn't know the men in the pictures—as if he had no memory of Devlin McVey's past.

An overwhelming wave of disappointment flooded through her. She almost believed that this man wasn't

Devlin, but she remembered that Devlin had been an actor, and a convincing one at that. He'd been a man comfortable with lying and assuming roles as an undercover detective for the police force. Perhaps "Mitch Russell" was feigning indifference just to get her out of his life.

"This, I assume, is Devlin," he said finally as he pointed at one small photograph of Devlin. In the picture, Devlin's blue eyes were filled with mischief and a crooked smile slashed across his clean-shaven jaw.

Chelsea's insides clenched. Even in a still photograph, some of Devlin's rakish charm came through. "Yes," she said, aware of the catch in her voice.

"There's some resemblance," he reluctantly conceded, his lower lip protruding thoughtfully, "but I'm not your guy." His eyes met hers again and they were filled with questions. "San Francisco is a long way from here. How'd you find me?"

"A private investigator named Jenkins."

"And he just happened to pick Paradis?" Mitch asked skeptically.

She quickly sketched out how Jenkins had discovered Mitch Russell and returned with the news. As she explained about her hasty trip, she watched Mitch carefully. His expression didn't alter—he still stared at her as if she were a certifiable lunatic. Nonetheless, she continued on with her story, including the events of the past two nights. "…so that's how I ended up here and that's why I know that you're Devlin."

"What do you want me to say? That I'm this guy?" he asked, sounding incredulous. Lifting one hand, he added, "Okay, let's just pretend I'm Devlin McVey— Oh, do I have a middle name?" he mocked.

"Andrew."

"Okay. I'm Devlin Andrew McVey. Now what?"

The muscles between Chelsea's shoulder blades tightened. "Now I ask you what happened on the boat that afternoon."

"I don't know." Not a glimmer of regret crossed his face. In fact, he seemed almost bored with the game.

"It was this day," she gritted out, frustrated beyond belief. She shoved a picture across the table, a picture of John, Devlin and her, arms flung around each other, the sailboat tethered to the side of the dock. The sky was gray and overcast, the sea slate-colored. Wayward strands of her dark brown hair whipped across John's laughing face. "You remember the day—April twenty-sixth of last year! The day the boat went down, the day John lost his life, the day Devlin McVey disappeared!"

"You're crazy!"

"Don't you remember John? Your best friend!" Dear Lord, why was he playing this game with her? Why? Hadn't she suffered enough? Shaking, her throat hot with unshed tears, she took in a long breath. How many times had she relived that fateful gusty day? How many nightmares had caused her to wake up to her own screams, to feel the sheets soaked with sweat as she saw over and over again in her mind's eye, how John had drowned?

Mitch's voice, when he finally spoke, was soft. "I've known a lot of men named John in my life," he admitted, frowning, "but I don't recognize this man." He let out a long, whistling sigh and his hard-edged features gentled. "I'm sorry for all the pain you've gone through, really I am. But I'm not your missing friend. You have to believe me. I know it might be hard to accept, but you'll have to look elsewhere or deal with the fact that McVey obviously drowned along with your fiancé."

"I can't!" she cried, pounding an impotent fist into the worn cushions of the couch.

"Why not?"

She shook her head, wishing she had more than intuition to go on. "If...if Devlin were dead, I think I'd know it. Feel it."

"You cared for him that much?"

The question stopped her cold. Coming from this man, whose gaze was so intense—so damned piercing, she found the words difficult. "No—yes—oh, I don't know." Realizing she sounded as crazy as he obviously thought she was, Chelsea rubbed her arms as if from a sudden chill. "He was—no, *is* my friend and he's not dead. He's not!"

"You certainly are a stubborn thing," he observed.

"When I know I'm right."

He rubbed a hand around the back of his neck and Chelsea tried to ignore the innate sexuality of his muscles moving effortlessly under his skin. "I wish things were different, Chelsea," he finally said, sounding as if he meant it, "but I can't help you."

"I think you're lying to me," she said with difficulty.

"I'm not—"

"Devlin, please!"

"Dammit, woman, give it a rest!" Angry all over again, Mitch shoved the pictures aside. Several slid onto the beaten plank floor. "I hope you didn't already pay this clown of a private detective of yours, 'cause if you did, you just lost yourself a pile of money!"

He'd hit a raw nerve, but Chelsea didn't flinch. "My deal with Jenkins is none of your business."

"Exactly! None of this—" he motioned toward the pictures scattered on the floor and table "—is my business! And I'm none of yours. So why don't you pick up your photographs, stuff them into your purse, waltz out of here and leave me the hell alone?"

"Can you prove to me that you're *not* Devlin?"

His eyes narrowed a fraction. "I shouldn't have to. But if it'll make you feel any better, okay."

He strode stiffly through the kitchen to another doorway, which she assumed led to his bedroom. Within seconds he was back, opening a beat-up wallet. He unfolded the leather and stared at the contents, then dropped an outdated Illinois driver's license onto the table along with three major credit cards issued to Mitchell P. Russell.

"The P is for Palmer—which, by the way, was my mother's maiden name. She was Marian Adair Palmer Russell, my father was Brian Joseph Russell. They're both gone now and I had no brothers or sister or cousins who I was close to. As for pictures, I have a few of my own." He handed her a wallet-sized snapshot of himself and a beautiful blonde woman with laughing blue eyes and a mischievous smile. Tiny dimples graced her cheeks and her arms were thrown around the neck of a black shepherd. "That's Angie," Mitch said quietly. "My wife."

Chelsea's heart dropped. "You're married?" she whispered, hardly believing her ears.

"I was," he replied softly, his lips flattening over his teeth. "We were in an accident." He glanced away. "I was injured—broke my hip and a couple of ribs, got cut up a little, but Angie didn't make it. Neither did the dog."

"Oh." Chelsea felt like a fool. Obviously this man still grieved for the beautiful, smiling woman with the impish blue eyes, easy smile and silken blond hair. "I—I'm sorry."

He shrugged, as if her empathy were of no consequence. "You need any more proof?"

Chelsea swallowed. The suspicious side of her nature required more than one photograph and a few credit cards, yet, there was a ring of truth to his story that she couldn't dispute. "Devlin had a wife, too," she said woodenly. "She died a few years ago."

"Then I feel sorry for him," Mitch said quietly. "It's hell." He rammed the photo back into his wallet. "Satisfied?"

She nodded mutely, wishing she could argue with him. But the pain shadowing his eyes was real and the evidence he'd shown her held up his claim.

"I don't like giving people my life history and I sure as hell don't need to prove myself to you. So, unless you have an ulterior motive for coming here, I think you'd better leave."

Her throat was suddenly desert dry. Nervously, Chelsea licked her lips. She didn't want to leave and yet she knew that staying would be to invite danger. "I don't have an ulterior motive."

One side of his mouth lifted cynically. "No? Well, if you really do think I'm your friend McVey, I sure would like to know what was going on between the two of you. Anytime you want to give me a demonstration, I'll be ready."

All the empathy she'd felt for him disappeared. Fury shot through her, but she quickly counted to ten. She wasn't going to let him goad her. Though her stomach was in knots, Chelsea calmly gathered her pictures from the table and floor. "Would you? I wonder. You know, Mr. Russell, I don't believe you. I think you're just trying to scare me into running off."

He didn't bother to hide the mockery in his eyes. "Try me," he invited lazily.

"No, thanks."

His lips twitched. "No?" He crossed the room, reaching the door and throwing the bolt.

"Not if you were the last man on this island."

He laughed then. "Don't challenge me, Miss Reed," he warned. "You'll lose."

She shook her head and wished she was anywhere else on earth. "You've got an ego that just won't quit."

"You're here, aren't you? And I don't remember issuing an invitation."

Was he laughing at her? What she wouldn't do to wipe that smug smile off his lips! "Don't flatter yourself," she remarked, heading for the door, but as she reached for the knob, he sprang, grabbing her arm and spinning her around sharply. She landed against him with a thud.

She gasped and as she did, his lips captured hers in a kiss that tore the breath from her lungs. Unexpectedly his mouth covered hers and his tongue, wet and sensual, slid between her teeth to touch and explore.

She tried to pull free of his grasp, but his arms tightened around her.

"Stop it!" she cried when he lifted his head, but she was trembling from head to foot.

"It's what you really wanted, wasn't it?" he growled, shoving her against the door, her bare back pressed hard against the painted wood.

"No!"

"Come on, Chelsea, admit it. This cock-and-bull story about dead fiancés and best friends is just for kicks. You're down here—some wealthy woman who's probably tired of her husband or lover—and you're looking for a little adventure. Sure, you found me and I look like the guy in the photos, but that's not what this is all about, is it?" With one long finger, he slowly traced the line of her jaw, causing her skin to tremble expectantly. "That's not why you're so damned persistent when you know I'm not Devlin."

Furious with herself, she shoved his hand aside. "You're despicable!"

"No, just willing," he teased, shifting so that his hips pressed intimately against hers, his thighs hard and demanding, his wet cutoffs creating a damp impression upon her cotton skirt.

"I already told you I don't want to go to bed with you," she said, her voice hoarser than usual.

"And I say you're a liar." He kissed her again and this time his lips were less punishing, his mouth molding gently over hers.

She turned liquid inside and hot spasms pulsed through her blood. Desire, unwanted and long buried, surfaced, yawning and stretching within. As his body trapped hers against the door, he placed both hands on the sides of her face, his tongue rimming her lips, tickling the inside of her mouth and sliding sensitively along her teeth.

"Don't!" she cried, jerking her head to the side, but the sound that issued from her lips sounded like a moan. She reached behind her, found the knob and jerked open the door. "You're the most insufferable man I've ever met!"

"And you just keep coming back for more."

"And you just keep flattering yourself!"

Mitch stepped backward into the house and Chelsea nearly stumbled across the porch. Her breathing was tight and hard. Embarrassment washed up her cheeks and burned in her mind as she glared back at him. Good Lord, the man was actually smiling!

How could she let him touch her so intimately? She'd let him *kiss* her, for God's sake!

"Good night, Miss Reed," he taunted. "Come back when you want to show me more—"

Chelsea straightened and glared across the porch

at him. "I won't give up, you know. If you're Devlin, I swear—"

"Don't waste any more of my time. The next time you come to me, think about your reasons and don't think I'll pretend to be some ghost or fantasy. When you show up here again—and I have a feeling you will—I'll assume it's for me."

"Your ego is incredible!" Her jaw dropped.

"At least I don't delude myself."

"Go to hell!"

His smile fell from his face. "I think I've already been."

Chelsea turned on her heel and, forcing her legs not to run, marched stiffly back to the path. Disgusted with herself and her purely physical reactions to a man she couldn't stand, she trudged along the moon-washed shore and told herself that she wouldn't give up, she couldn't! And if Devlin wanted a fight, damn it, he'd get one!

Get a grip on yourself, Chels, she thought, stumbling along the path through the trees. Angry that she'd let him goad her into so vulnerable a position, she seethed all the way back to the hotel. When he couldn't get her to leave by conventional methods, he'd used his masculinity as a weapon and she'd fallen into the easy trap. All he had to do was pretend to be interested in her and she had turned tail and run.

But what other option did she have? Return his passion—real or construed—with her own? Where would that lead? Right into Mitch Russell's bed—or Devlin's bed. That thought sent unwelcome anticipation through her mind.

"Never!" she spat, but knew she was more susceptible than she was willing to admit. Devlin had proved that once before.

She climbed up the stairs to her room, more determined than ever to find out the truth about one Mr. Mitchell P. Russell. There were ways to check out his story. As she opened the door, she wondered about the beautiful blonde woman—his wife—in his photograph.

How did she know that the blonde wasn't still very much alive? Or that she was his wife?

"You don't," she reprimanded herself as she stepped into her room and locked the door behind her. When it came right down to it, she didn't know much about Mitch Russell.

What if he's really who he says he is? He had the identification and story to prove it. And what did she have to go on? The fact that he looked like Devlin, that he sounded like Devlin, that he smelled like Devlin? What else? What hard evidence?

Dropping her head into her hands, she squeezed her eyes shut and more doubts assailed her. If he were really Mitch, she looked like a fool. It's a wonder he didn't call the police or the mental hospital! And she'd kissed him so passionately.

Because you thought he was Devlin. What if he isn't? She froze inside, mortified beyond words.

She couldn't think about that, not now, not until she was sure. Willing her eyes open, she noticed that the red light on her telephone was flashing, signaling that someone had left her a message.

"Now what?" she wondered, dropping onto the bed and blowing her bangs out of her eyes. She dialed the operator and was told that Felicia Reed had called her.

"Great," she mumbled, hanging up and punching out her mother's number. Just what she needed—big-sister lecture number seven, which repeated just about every other week.

It took several tries before the long-distance, overseas connection finally went through.

Felicia answered on the fifth ring.

"Hi," Chelsea said, pretending she didn't have a care in the world.

"About time you called!" Felicia replied, her voice faint through the poor connection. "Where were you? It must be past midnight there!"

"It is," Chelsea agreed.

"Well, did you find this man—this Mitch Russell?" Felicia asked, worry edging her voice.

"Yes."

"And?"

"He swears he isn't Devlin."

"Good. So you'll be home in a couple of days," Felicia decided for herself. "I'll tell Mom—"

"No!"

"What?"

"Don't tell Mom anything. Just because the man says he's not Devlin, doesn't mean a thing."

"But can't you tell?" Felicia demanded.

"No." And that was the truth. "One minute I believe him, the next, I'm not so sure."

"Oh, great. Now, you're not even sure." Felicia sighed impatiently. "And what does he have to say for himself?"

"He thinks I'm a nutcase."

"I like him better already," Felicia observed dryly.

"Thanks a lot."

"Well, you have to admit it, Chels, this is really reaching. I mean *really* reaching. Even for you."

"I don't think so," Chelsea replied, squirming a little. She did have doubts herself. If Mitch were really Devlin, he was pulling off the acting job of his life!

"Well, I just hope you smarten up and give up in a few

days. This is really taking a toll on Mom. She worries, you know."

"Let me talk to her."

"I can't. She's in the tub. But I'll tell her you called."

"Do that," Chelsea said, just to get Felicia off her back.

"And when can I tell her you'll be home?"

"I don't know yet," Chelsea admitted.

"A week maybe?" Felicia prodded.

"I'm not sure."

There was a tired, long-suffering sigh from Felicia's end of the conversation. "You can't take off indefinitely, you know. You have responsibilities—we all do."

"I'll call Mom later," Chelsea said, adding a quick goodbye and hanging up. She lay back on the bed and flung one arm across her eyes. Some of Felicia's points, she admitted grudgingly, had merit. Maybe this was just a wild-goose chase. And maybe, though she hated to admit it, she had come to Paradis for more than answers about John's death.

Frowning, she rolled over on her stomach and propped her chin on her hands. Thinking of John was difficult. Thinking of Devlin was confusing. Thinking about both of them together was downright scary. She'd been pulled and pushed between them for over a year and a half, caring about them both, but denying any feelings other than friendship for Devlin. Well, most of the time, she thought guiltily, not letting her mind wander too far into that forbidden territory that was reserved for Devlin McVey.

If only it weren't so complicated! If only she could turn back time to the first night she'd met Devlin—the first night she'd come face-to-face with his rakish good looks, confident smile and biting sense of humor.

Life had been simpler before she'd met Devlin, before he'd caused the first of her doubts to surface, before she'd questioned her love for John. She grabbed a pillow and clenched it to her chest, wishing that John were still alive and that they could go back to the easy life they'd shared before Devlin.

Devlin—always Devlin! Why couldn't she just accept that he was gone and forget him?

Because he was unforgettable.

Meeting Devlin had been a turning point in her life and even now, in this lush tropical paradise, she could remember that cold September night when Devlin McVey had caught her so unaware and from that moment on, her life had been turned inside out....

CHAPTER FIVE

WINTER HAD COME EARLY to northern California that year.
Even in the early evening the sky was the color of slate,
the cold waters of the bay reflecting the same somber
shade.

Chelsea didn't mind. She was young and in love and
she smiled to herself as she locked her car and, carrying
her purse and a bottle of wine, walked up the five short
steps to John's condominium. There were still lingering traces of summer in the courtyard, straggling red
and white impatiens and dried yellow-headed marigolds
splashed worn color in the greenery and added to Chelsea's lighthearted mood.

Shaking the rain from her umbrella, Chelsea rang the
doorbell. She and John were going to share an evening
alone and she'd been looking forward to it all week.

The door swung open and John, a chef's apron tied
over his slacks, his oxford shirtsleeves rolled over his
forearms, grinned broadly. "You're in for the treat of
your life," he predicted.

"Uh-oh, you've been experimenting in the kitchen
again," she charged, eyeing his apron.

"Nope, it's better than that."

She walked inside and his brown eyes flashed devilishly. "So what's the surprise?"

"Fantastic news!" He wrapped his arms possessively

around Chelsea's waist. "You're finally going to meet Devlin!"

She'd heard of Devlin McVey, of course. "Ah, so the mysterious friend suddenly appears," Chelsea teased, kissing John lightly on the forehead. Still bundled in her raincoat, she shook the drops of water from her hair. "About time."

"He's been busy." John waited as she handed him the sack with the bottle of chardonnay. He eyed the bottle and wrinkled his nose.

Chelsea untied the belt of her coat. "Too busy to visit a good friend?"

"Come on, Chelsea, you understand about Devlin."

Oh, she understood all right. Devlin McVey, whoever he was, just happened, in John's opinion, to be right up there with the Almighty himself. Tough competition, in Chelsea's estimation. John hung up her coat in the closet near the door and Chelsea rubbed her arms.

John's condominium was warm and cozy. A fire crackled in the tiled hearth and classical music filtered through the rooms from hidden speakers. A huge drafting table occupied a space near the floor-to-ceiling windows and cream-colored leather couches were arranged between teak-and-glass tables. Brass lamps glowed in the corners, and high over the bedroom loft, rain peppered the skylights.

She followed John into his kitchen where the scents of garlic, onions and tomatoes mingled together in John's special primavera sauce. "This must really be a special occasion," she remarked, eyeing the simmering sauce. She hated to cook, but John was as comfortable in the kitchen as he was in his architectural office in Oakland.

"It is. You remember me telling you about Devlin," John said, uncorking a bottle of zinfandel, ignoring the wine she'd spent all of five minutes selecting. She wasn't surprised. According to John, she wasn't a wine connoisseur, nor a gourmet, nor even had an eye for interior decorating, but she didn't let his prejudices bother her. All in all, he was probably right, she thought ruefully.

"Hard not to remember Devlin." John spoke of Devlin often, not that she really cared. In fact, she was intrigued that he was actually going to show up. "Devlin McVey, cop extraordinaire," she said dryly.

"There are worse things in life than being a cop."

"Not in my family," she replied, remembering the horrid nights she'd lain awake worrying about her father. There had been times he hadn't returned home for days and she'd caught her mother crying and praying that he was alive. Paul Reed had survived, though he'd been shot and hospitalized more than once in his career as an undercover detective. No, thank you very much, she didn't need any more reminders of how hard the life as a policeman's wife or daughter could be.

"You'll like Devlin. Trust me," John told her.

"Can I reserve judgment?" she asked, winking at him as he handed her a glass.

John laughed. "Don't I have good taste in friends? I chose you, remember?"

"How could I forget?" She and John had met in college and he'd shamelessly pursued her. They'd studied together, gone to football games and parties and always gotten along well. "The perfect couple," their mutual friends had called them. Practical. Predictable. Fun-loving but levelheaded. Loving John had been safe and comfortable—like wearing a favorite old bathrobe. And everyone, her sister and mother included, had told Chelsea to count her blessings that such an even-tempered, successful man loved her.

"Time you settled down with one good man," her mother had told her during her senior year in college.

"John's perfect," Felicia had cooed. "And an architect! Oh, just think, Chels, when you get married he could build you a house—I mean a real house—something contemporary that hangs out over the ocean or maybe a traditional in the Heights. I'm so glad you found someone to keep you sane!"

Chelsea hadn't been all that comfortable with Felicia's attitude, but as she'd long since given up her wilder tendencies, she didn't let Felicia's comments get under her skin. Because Felicia had been right. Chelsea *had* been wild in high school and her first couple of years in college. But, during her senior year at Berkeley, she'd settled into a comfortable lifestyle with John. He was a great friend and a wonderful companion. Good-looking, athletic, witty, John was every girl's fantasy.

So why had she resisted the natural step of moving in with him? It wasn't that she was holding out for marriage, but, if she delved deep into her heart, she knew there was a small piece missing in their lives—what, she couldn't really say, because, as everyone agreed, John was the greatest.

She picked up a piece of carrot from the counter and munched on it, for which she was rewarded with one of John's mock dark looks. "So why haven't I met Devlin before?"

"My fault," John admitted. "He's a lady-killer." His lips tugged upward at the corners. "I didn't want you to drop me and fall for him."

"You thought I would?" she teased, giggling.

"It's happened before."

"Not with me."

"You haven't met him yet."

"Oh, ye of little faith," she intoned, laughing at John's consternation. She loved him—she did! He was perfect. She'd be crazy not to love him.

"I'm not kidding, Chels. He's got a reputation a mile long. Women drop like flies for him. It must be that birthmark he has," John added slyly. "It's right about here—" he pointed a finger high on his hip, very close to his crotch "—and it looks like a crescent moon—"

"Give me a break," Chelsea said, laughing and punching him on the arm.

"I'm not kidding."

"And *I'm* not interested. Come on, back to your story."

"Okay, okay. Anyway, Devlin and I met a long time ago." John was furiously stirring his sauce. "We were freshmen in college in L.A., before I transferred up to Berkeley."

"Where you met me," she put in.

"Right. Best decision I've ever made." He shot her a knowing glance. "Anyway, back in L.A., Devlin and I ended up in the same dorm and we hung out together, even though we didn't have any of the same classes. We just hit it off."

"So what happened?"

"All hell broke loose. Come spring term, there was some theft going on in the dorm and one of the guys— his name was…Sean…Sean Lavery. Sean insisted that he'd caught Devlin going through his room."

Chelsea was interested. She sipped her wine. "Go on."

"There'd been some thefts on campus. Well, it turned out Devlin *had been* in Sean's room, but not for the reason everyone thought. Devlin was sure the guy was involved in some drug deals on campus and he wanted to prove it."

"He was a policeman—even then?" she asked skeptically.

"Nope. And that's how he got into trouble. There was a
big scandal, the story was written up in the school paper.
Both Devlin and Sean were kicked out of school."

"That's not fair!"

"Devlin *was* trespassing."

"But—"

"I know, but Sean's parents were big school alumni.
Each year, they gave megabucks to the school athletic
program—you know the type—Mr. and Mrs. Joe College. They came unglued and started legal proceedings,
the whole bit, against the school and Devlin."

"How could they?" Chelsea asked.

John lifted a shoulder. "Anyone can sue anyone—all
you need is enough money to pay an attorney's fees."

"So Devlin quit school?"

"He transferred. And, really, it was probably best that
Devlin left, because most of the guys didn't like the fact
that he was playing the part of a narc. Even though Sean
was into pretty heavy stuff. The irony of it was that when
Devlin and Sean left, the thieving stopped."

"Sean was the culprit."

"Yep. Can you beat that? The kid was rich and had
everything money could buy." John frowned as he tasted
his sauce. He reached into the cupboard and scrounged
until he found the spice he wanted, which he added gen-
erously to the copper-bottomed kettle.

"Anyway, I was the only guy on the floor who believed Devlin. I let him bunk with me when no one else
would talk to him. I figured he got a bum deal. After the
year was over, I transferred up to Berkeley." He glanced
at her and smiled. "And then, eventually, I met you and
the fairy tale began." He kissed her lightly on her lips.

"You lucky devil," she said with a laugh. "So what happened to Devlin?"

"He went out of state, finished school and became a cop in Cincinnati. He was married for about a year, but his wife died."

"Died?" she repeated, stunned.

"Yeah, she was killed in a car accident. Devlin always blamed himself for not being able to drive her where she wanted to go that night." He frowned. "Anyway, losing his wife really tore Devlin up and he never talks about it—so don't bring it up," John warned.

"I won't." She felt a pang of pity for John's friend.

"Anyway, since Holly died, Devlin's been in several different cities in the midwest. And he's dated at least a million girls."

"Didn't grieve long," Chelsea remarked.

"People have different ways of dealing with grief and Holly's been gone quite a while." He stuffed a lid back on the saucepan and wiped his hands. "So, about two months ago, he landed a job with the SFPD. He's some sort of detective, I think."

One more strike against him, Chelsea thought, though it didn't really matter. What John's lady-killer friend did with his life wasn't her concern, unless, of course, it involved John.

The doorbell pealed and John asked, "Would you get it?"

"No problem." Chelsea was already on her way. At the entry hall she yanked open the door and stared face-to-face with one of the most darkly sensual men she'd ever seen in her life. He wore a white T-shirt, leather jacket and tight, faded jeans. His hair, a little longer than fashionable, was jet black, his face tanned, his jaw strong and blunt, and his eyes a piercing shade of crystal blue. One side of his mouth lifted into a sardonic smile.

"Don't tell me," he said, his gaze warming, "you must be Chelsea."

She extended her hand and felt his fingers clamp around her palm. "And you're the infamous Detective McVey," she replied, forcing a cool smile as she withdrew her hand. Oh, she could see how this man had earned his reputation, but, fortunately, he wasn't her type—not her type at all. In one glance she could tell he was much too rough around the edges for her—much too stuck on himself. "Come on in," she said, remembering that he'd had his share of pain and trying to sound friendly. "John's doing his best Julia Child impersonation."

"I heard that," John warned, his voice ringing from the kitchen. "Just remember he who criticizes the cook, leaves this place hungry!"

"What's going on?" Devlin asked. "John, are you really *cooking?*"

"Someone has to," John replied and Devlin cocked a dark eyebrow at Chelsea.

"Don't look at me," she replied. "I'm not into domesticity."

At that, his lips twisted into an interested smile and his blue eyes sparked with reserved insolence. "A feminist?"

"At the very least."

"And you're involved with John?" he mocked, causing the hackles on the back of her neck to rise a little.

So what if John was a little on the traditional side? At least he wasn't asking *her* to cook for his irreverent friend.

More agitated than she had any right to be, Chelsea followed Devlin into the kitchen. She noticed his easy, athletic gait and the way his jeans hugged his hips. She forced her eyes upward. The man was obviously aware of his innate sexuality and he didn't even bother concealing it.

John poured Devlin a glass of wine and handed it to his friend. "Salute!" he said, touching his glass to Devlin's.

Devlin smiled—the first real grin Chelsea had witnessed—and took a long swallow of the wine.

"So what do you think of my girl?" John asked, wrapping an arm around Chelsea's waist.

Devlin's gaze returned to Chelsea's face and to her mortification, she felt a blush creeping up her neck. "She'll do," he said.

"She'll more than do," John said boldly. "Whether she knows it or not, she's going to marry me." He squeezed Chelsea then and kissed her cheek and she ignored the uncomfortable urge to wriggle out of his arms. She'd prefer to keep their future out of the conversation for the time being. Besides, what she and John planned was private.

"Is that so?" Devlin asked.

"Well, it's not written in stone, but just you wait, once she gets that business of hers off the ground, she'll run out of excuses for putting me off. And you'll get a chance to be best man."

"I can hardly wait," Devlin drawled sarcastically.

Chelsea wanted to kick John in the shins, but instead, she turned back to Devlin and changed the course of the conversation in a more conventional matter. "So what brought you to San Francisco?"

"The right job at the right time," he replied evasively and fortunately John, seemingly unaware of any friction between Devlin and Chelsea, brought up the Forty-Niners football season.

For the rest of the evening, through the appetizers, wine, salad, main course and dessert, conversation was light. Chelsea relaxed a little. Devlin wasn't all that bad—just a little on the cynical side. And John liked him. That much was obvious as they talked and laughed and eventually moved to the couch in front of a television where they watched a football game already in progress.

Chelsea sat between the two men. John's arm was comfortably slung across her shoulders and now and again he squeezed her, but she couldn't keep her mind on the game or John. Instead, she glanced at Devlin furtively from the corner of her eye. Though she was nestled next to John, it was Devlin's presence she noticed, the way his scuffed Nike was braced against the edge of the coffee table, the bend of his knee, the stretch of denim over his thighs. She wondered what his wife had been like and why he had never remarried.

With effort, she pried her gaze away from him and mentally kicked herself for being one of "those" women who found him attractive.

When the evening wound down, she was relieved. As Devlin walked out the door of John's condominium, she let out a long sigh. The ordeal was over. She'd never have to see him again. Now, she and John could go back to their idyllic existence again.

Of course she'd been wrong. Devlin was back in John's life and in a big way. Friends for life, they began sailing together and Chelsea was always asked to go along. Often she did, ignoring Devlin's masculinity and telling herself that the reason he bothered her was because he was a cop—a detective, no less—in the same line of employment as her father had been. Though, when she thought about it much later, she realized that she'd been deluding herself. Despite her hard lessons growing up, she felt a deep-seated admiration for anyone who was willing to lay down his life for the law and that included a grudging respect for Devlin.

And therefore, in an unconventional way, she admired Devlin.

In late November, John announced they were going to Lake Tahoe for the weekend, with Devlin, of course, and, Chelsea assumed, his latest woman. In the past two months, she'd been introduced to five different women whom Devlin had dated.

"I don't even know how to ski," she argued in the confines of her own apartment, wanting to bag out of yet another uncomfortable situation with Devlin. And a weekend, for crying out loud! How would she survive being caught with him for two days and nights? It would be pure hell! "Besides, I—"

"Don't tell me you have to work. Sally already told me she could handle the shop."

Chelsea clamped her mouth shut. "Fine! Just fine!" She dropped onto the soft pillows of her couch. "Well, what about Devlin? The way I remember it, cops work round the clock. How'd he manage a weekend off? Isn't he low man on the pole?"

"I don't know, but it worked out."

"Great!" Chelsea grumbled, then heard herself and sighed loudly.

"What is it you've got against him?" John asked quietly. He flung one leg over the arm of the couch and, leaning forward, touched the crease between Chelsea's eyes.

"I don't have—"

"He hasn't done anything to you."

"I know, I know, it's just that he rubs me the wrong

way, I guess," Chelsea tried to explain. "Before he came here, you and I, we never fought and now—" she shrugged, finding the words hard to say "—now we argue a lot."

"About Devlin," he said.

"Yes!"

Frowning, John smoothed the wrinkle from her brow. "I think it's your problem, Chels."

"He doesn't like me," she replied, then cringed a little inside. It sounded so petty.

"Maybe that's because you never gave him a chance. You had your mind made up to dislike him the minute you heard he was a detective."

Chelsea couldn't argue with that, though she wanted to. Damn it, she didn't want to like Devlin and she didn't know why. Maybe it was because he seemed dangerous and reckless somehow—reminding her of the wild days of her youth. Whatever the reason, she didn't want anything to do with him.

"Come on, Chels, give the guy a break. The only crime he's committed is being my friend."

John did have a point, she decided ruefully. And it wasn't like her to judge someone so critically or act so childish. "Okay," she finally agreed with a smile. "Lake Tahoe, here I come."

"That's my girl!" John gave her a bear hug and she mentally crossed her fingers that she could get along with Devlin and his girlfriend.

However, things didn't go as planned. John called the afternoon they were to take off and explained that he had to work late, to finish a project for a big client who wanted some last-minute changes on the design of his waterfront home.

"Ride up with Devlin and I'll catch up with you later at the cabin," John said.

"Without you? Are you crazy?" Chelsea's fingers tightened around the receiver.

"Oh, come on, Chels. I thought you were going to try and get along with Devlin."

"I was—I mean, I will, but I'd just be more comfortable with you."

"And so would I," he said, his voice tight. "But I really don't know when I'll be finished."

"I'd be glad to wait."

"Go up with Devlin and Mary, Chels. He won't bite."

She wanted to argue further, but decided against it. John was already in a bad mood and no doubt Devlin was in a worse one. So, for once, she'd try not to make any waves. "Okay, I'll see you later," she said.

"That's a good girl. Love ya," John said and clicked off.

Chelsea tried not to be bothered by his little endearment. It was just John's way. Every once in a while, he had to assert his male authority, and when he did, she usually bristled, but this weekend, come hell or high water, she was going to make the supreme effort to get along with everyone. Including Devlin and his date.

Except that Mary canceled. Her seven-year-old had come down with chicken pox.

Devlin explained all this as he was loading her suitcase and two bags of groceries into the back of his Bronco.

Chelsea could hardly believe her ears. Standing in the pale glow of the streetlight, her breath misting in the air, she realized that for the next few hours she'd be trapped alone with Devlin.

Fog had crept into the city and the night was dark and close. She shivered, but not from the cold. A little frightened at the prospect of being alone with him for hours, she hiked the collar of her ski jacket against the mist and told herself she was being a fool. She wasn't scared of him—well, maybe a little intimidated, but that wasn't so bad, was it? She could handle the situation as well as Devlin McVey. At this point, she had no choice.

Devlin slammed the back door of the Bronco.

"I guess it's just you and me," he quipped, flashing her a crooked smile that touched a forbidden part of her heart.

"For the time being." More than a little on edge, she climbed into the rig. He sat beside her and he shoved the four-wheel drive into gear. The Bronco lurched forward. Without a word, Devlin steered them toward the freeway heading east.

As they drove through the clog of Friday evening traffic, she tried not to notice the length of his leg, so close to hers, or the way his long fingers curled over the gear shift, or the earthy scent of his cologne.

This is all wrong, her mind screamed at her, but she pretended that being alone with him and driving to a remote cabin in the mountains was an everyday occurrence.

Chelsea never had been very good at small talk, and from the long stretches in their conversation, she guessed Devlin was even less adept at talking about nothing than she was.

Licking her lips, she tried to concentrate on the night-shrouded foothills and the forests of the Sierra Nevada mountain range.

Devlin turned on the radio, which eased the need for conversation, but Chelsea felt tense as a springboard.

"Do you have any idea where we're going?" he asked, glancing at her as the road wound through thick stands of pine.

"Mmm, if I can remember," she said, nodding. "John and I were here a couple of years ago. The cabin belongs to a friend of his. But I was here in the daylight."

"Well, I'll have to count on you," he admitted. "All I've got is an address."

"It's near Heavenly Valley Ski Resort."

Devlin laughed and the deep sound echoed through the rig. "That really narrows it down."

"Okay, okay, you just drive and I'll give directions."

He sighed dramatically. "Just like a woman," he muttered, but, for once, she wasn't irritated. In fact, she smiled to herself. Maybe spending some time alone with Devlin wasn't going to end up being a nightmare. There was a chance that they could learn to like each other, at least for John's sake.

Snowflakes began to fall from the dark sky, collecting on the windshield and sprinkling the ground with a fine white powder.

"If you're interested, there's a thermos of coffee and an extra cup in the backseat," Devlin said, shifting down when the Bronco started to climb a particularly steep grade.

"Sounds great. You want some?"

"Absolutely."

Twisting, she rummaged around until she found the thermos, then carefully poured them each a cup. Fragrant steam filtered to her nostrils as she settled back in her seat and started to enjoy the ride. The snow glistened like diamonds in the illumination from the headlights. Chelsea felt an unlikely contentment as she sipped the strong coffee.

If nothing else, she decided, this weekend with Devlin would be an adventure.

It took another hour before they finally located the

small cabin tucked in the snow-dusted pines. Built of
rough cedar, with a pitched roof and paned windows, it
stood alone in a clearing, looking empty and cold.

"Shangri-la?" Devlin asked skeptically.

"Close enough. John would like to buy it someday,"
Chelsea replied. "He thinks Heavenly Valley is appro-
priately named."

"And you?"

Chelsea lifted a shoulder as she climbed out of the
Bronco. "It's beautiful up here," she admitted, "and I
love the snow, but I don't ski."

"And you're engaged to John?" he asked, hauling the
bags from the back of the rig. "That's a situation that will
have to be rectified."

"We're not engaged yet," she said, her boots crunching on the new snow.

"John acts like it's only a matter of time."

Chelsea didn't reply as she fumbled with the key John
had given her. The lock finally clicked and she shoved
open the door, snapping on the lights with her free hand.

The cabin smelled musty and unused. Chelsea threw
open the windows and Devlin went to work on the fire.
Kneeling in front of a river-rock hearth, his head angled
up to check the flue, he lit a match, mumbled something
under his breath, then headed outside for firewood.

Chelsea went to work in the kitchen, which was separated from the living room by a long butcher block
counter. Unpacking the groceries, she furtively watched
Devlin as he returned, crumpled yellowed newspaper
and stacked dry chunks of oak in the grate. She noticed
how snowflakes had melted in his dark hair, causing it
to glimmer. She studied the movements of his hands,
quick and sure, as he prodded the logs with a poker, and
she felt her breath tighten in her lungs as he leaned for-

ward and blew on the flames, fanning them expertly as his breath whistled through his thin lips.

Quickly, she diverted her gaze, pretending interest in making dinner. "I hope beef stew is okay," she said, rattling noisily in the kitchen as she looked through the cupboards for the right size of pan.

"I'll eat anything."

"I'm not the greatest cook," she replied, surprised when she looked up and he was standing next to her. Her stupid heart fluttered a second.

"So you've said," he drawled lazily, eyeing her. "John doesn't seem to mind."

"No, uh, he accepts me the way I am."

Devlin didn't respond, just cocked an interested dark brow.

"You don't believe me."

"I've just thought John was the button-down-collar type."

"Meaning?"

"That he wants the traditional things in life."

"Such as?"

"A house in the city, a mountain cabin for vacations, a station wagon and a Porsche, two point three children, and a wife who can entertain, cook and…" He let the rest of the sentence slide and she knew he'd nearly mentioned something about bedroom prowess.

"Maybe you don't know John as well as you think you do," she said, stung.

"Maybe you don't."

She wanted to argue with him, to tell him that John loved her and nothing else mattered, but she knew she was wading in dangerous waters. Her relationship with John was something private and she meant to keep it that way.

While she worked on the meal—adding the finishing

touches to the stew she'd started the night before, and baking corn bread—Devlin turned on the water and carried her bags upstairs to the loft bedroom. She thought about sleeping under the sloping roof, lying in John's arms while Devlin was bunked downstairs in the other bedroom. The thought made her uncomfortable and she regretted ever agreeing to this trip. She and John had been lovers since college, yet now, with Devlin in the same cabin, she was as flustered as a schoolgirl and for the first time she felt guilty and a little ashamed.

"Ridiculous," she muttered to herself. John wanted to marry her. It was she who was holding out. And for what?

She didn't want to think about all the reasons and excuses she'd come up with for putting off the engagement. She glanced at the phone, hoping John would call.

"It doesn't work," Devlin said.

"Why not?"

"I guess John's friend doesn't want to pay for service when he isn't here."

"But—what if John gets held up? Or his car breaks down? Or—"

"John can take care of himself," Devlin said quickly. "He'll be here when he gets here."

There was no arguing with that deeply intellectual logic, Chelsea thought sarcastically. She scooped steaming, thick stew into two bowls, then cut squares of the corn bread.

Devlin poured her a glass of wine and opened a bottle of beer for himself. "You don't like wine?" she asked as they sat in front of the fire.

"Nope."

"Why not?"

He lifted a shoulder. "Not my style."

"You drank it at John's—the first night I met you."

He slid her a sensual glance. "Well, I didn't want to be rude," he said. "I did have to toast the bride-to-be."

"I'm not—" She dropped the subject. If he wanted to mock her, so be it. She just wouldn't rise to the bait.

They ate in silence and he even took seconds. "You've got hidden skills," he remarked when he'd finally finished.

"Meaning?"

"You *can* cook."

"Don't tell John. It's my secret."

With firelight playing over his features, he leaned back on one elbow, and nudged off one battered Nike with the toe of his other shoe. Then, warming his feet, he eyed her. "So what is it with you and John?" he asked, sipping from his second bottle of beer.

"What do you mean?"

"Seems to me John's a helluva catch."

"So I've been told."

His eyes slitted. "But you don't believe it."

"Of course I do."

"But you don't want to marry him."

"Yes, I do. But not…yet…"

"Most women would lick their chops if a man like John wanted to marry them."

"And you know so much about women?"

He smiled lazily. "I know enough. Women like John. He's good-looking, takes care of himself and makes a pile of money."

"You left out kind, generous and intelligent."

His lower lip protruded in a thoughtful frown. "Because those attributes aren't high on the list for most women."

"Depends on whose list you're reading," she threw back at him. He had some nerve!

"Okay," he said, drinking a long swallow. "Tell me about your list, Ms. Reed. What is it that makes you want—or in this case—not want—John Stern."

"I do want him!"

"Then marry the bastard and put him out of his misery!"

"I don't know what you're talking about."

"Sure you do. He's hung up on you—has been for a few years. And you keep sidestepping him. Why?"

"I don't think it's any of your business."

"He's my friend," Devlin said flatly, as if that explained everything.

"Then you'll understand that he would want our private life kept that way."

He slowly set his bottle aside. Eyeing her, he moved closer. "Privacy is one thing and I'm all for that. But I don't like anyone stringing someone else along."

"And that's what I'm doing?"

"I don't know. Is it?"

"What is this—the third degree? Well, *Detective* McVey, this isn't a police interrogation room and I don't have to answer any of your questions!"

His mouth quirked a bit, lifting into a wicked little smile that she found incredibly sexy.

"I love John," she said simply, hoping that one statement would end the conversation.

His eyes darkened. "How much?"

"What?"

"I asked, 'how much' do you love him? Not enough to marry him."

"The time just hasn't been right."

He slid her a disbelieving glance. "As I pointed out, most women would jump at the chance—"

"I'm *not* most women."

"Amen." He was so close to her that only a hair's breadth separated them, yet they weren't touching.

Chelsea held her ground and pretended that her heart wasn't slamming against her ribs, that her mouth hadn't turned to cotton, that her palms hadn't begun to sweat. She clung to her wineglass in a death grip and realized that her knuckles were showing white.

"What makes you tick, Ms. Reed?" he asked, his breath fanning her cheeks, his eyes searching her face as if she were some intricate puzzle. "You know what I think it is?"

"I couldn't begin to guess and I don't really care—"

"Pride and independence. You can't give up your freedom—at least not to a man like John."

"John's wonderful and—"

"And you don't love him," Devlin said flatly, studying his nails and rubbing his thumb on his forefinger. "At least not enough to marry him."

"I do," she replied quickly. She swallowed hard, unconsciously licking her lips at the lie. Devlin was partially right, of course, but she couldn't admit it, not even to herself. She loved John, but all along she'd known there was something missing in their relationship, something vital, something passionate and wild that she suspected existed between some couples.

She didn't scoot away when Devlin's fingertips touched hers and though she knew she should jump to her feet when he leaned forward, she couldn't move.

"Don't," she whispered, but he only shifted closer and his mouth closed over hers so quickly the breath was trapped in her lungs. His lips were warm and hard and sensual, and it took all her willpower not to respond. Good Lord, she couldn't be kissing John's best friend!

His arms wrapped around her and he lifted his head, his eyes burning with a secret blue flame that caused her blood to race like quicksilver through her veins. "Admit it, Chelsea, what you want is someone more exciting, someone who'll set you on fire."

"This is insane," she whispered, struggling, but his arms held her fast and when he kissed her again, his mouth was demanding, his tongue insistent as it pressed against her teeth. She shoved against him, peeling her lips from his. "Stop—oh, please, stop."

He lifted his head slightly, then glanced at her wet lips and, with a groan of regret, whispered, "I'm sorry."

Then his mouth found hers again.

Passion exploded deep in her soul. Wanton desire flooded her senses and somewhere in the back of her mind she knew she was doing something irrevocably wrong, betraying a precious trust, but she couldn't stop.

Devlin's hand splayed possessively against the small of her back, drawing her close, crushing her breasts against his chest, while his lips moved sensually across hers. Her mouth parted of its own accord and Devlin's tongue anxiously sought and found the wet velvet recess of her mouth.

He groaned against her, shifting his weight, drawing them both down to the hard floor. His legs, taut and muscular beneath his jeans, rubbed against hers.

Chelsea's senses swam dizzily. She couldn't think, could only feel. His hands twined in her hair, forcing her head back, and his lips trailed across her cheeks and throat.

"Chels, sweet Chels—" he growled, and a vibrant answering response tore through her soul. She tingled and returned the fever of his kisses with her own. Though what she was doing was forbidden, she couldn't seem to stop herself.

Devlin rolled atop her and she clung to him, all thoughts of refusing long since shoved from her mind. Moving sensually, he cupped her breast and it swelled in his palm.

He started to lift her sweater and his fingers grazed the skin of her abdomen. Warning bells clanged through Chelsea's mind. "No—" she cried as his fingers found the lace of her bra and her traitorous nipple hardened against his rough skin. "Please, Devlin—" But it sounded like a plea.

He stopped moving and threw his head back, squeezing his eyes closed. With a groan, he rolled off her, and took in one long, steadying breath. Shoving the heels of his hands into his eyes, he swore between clenched teeth. "How could you do that to John?"

"How could *I?*" she flung back, wounded. "How could *you!*"

"I—I was just trying to prove a point." But his hands shook as he shoved his hair from his forehead and his eyes, blue as a sizzling flame, still gleamed with eroticism.

"This was a *test?*" she cried, horrified.

"Yes."

"And what did it prove?"

"That you're not in love with John," he said simply.

"Oh, but I am in love with you?" she mocked, quivering inside when she realized how closely she'd come to making love with him.

He barked out a short, mirthless laugh. "You don't have to love someone to have sex with them."

"I do!"

His brows lifted cynically. "No, you just have to tell yourself you're in love so that your conscience is salved."

"What! No—"

"You want another demonstration?" he asked.

"Is that what it was?" she threw back at him.

His lips clamped shut. "Nothing more!"

"Liar!"

Devlin's eyes shuttered. "You think I feel something special for you?" He let out a sound of disgust. "Why do you women delude yourselves into thinking that sex is more than it is?"

"You bastard! You'd sleep with your best friend's—"

"What? What, exactly, are you to John? His mistress?"

"No—"

"Not his fiancée," he reminded her callously.

"But we're involved!"

"Not so involved that you wouldn't go to bed with me."

"You're the last man on earth I'd—" But his raised eyebrow called her the liar that she was.

The phone rang, jangling her already rattling nerves. She stared at the telephone as if it had miraculously come to life.

"You'd better answer it," Devlin said with maddening calm. "It's probably John."

"You said it was dead!"

He lifted a shoulder. "You're right. I'm a liar."

The phone rang shrilly again and Chelsea, in a fit of anger, stormed across the room. "Hello?"

"Chels!" John said.

Chelsea's throat closed and tears of regret sprang to her eyes. "Where—where are you?" she choked out, wishing he were here, wishing she could erase the taste of Devlin from her lips. Oh, she'd been so foolish!

"Still in the city. This project is taking longer than I thought."

"No—" She stared across the room to Devlin, who sat near the fire, his arms crossed over his chest, his face without emotion.

"Look, hon, I'm sorry, but I can't get out of here until morning."

"Oh, John, please," she whispered desperately, her voice nearly cracking.

"Are you all right?" he asked, and she hated the concern in his voice. Devlin was right, she didn't deserve a man like John.

"I—I'm fine," she said, though she knew her face was ashen. Lord, she'd acted so wantonly, so...

"Well, don't worry. Devlin'll take care of you."

"I don't need anyone to—"

"Sure you do, Chels. That's why I love you."

"I love you, too," she whispered, staring straight at Devlin and defying him with her eyes. She'd never, never betray John again. Not with Devlin. Not with any man.

"I'll see you in the morning. Just hang in there," he said, then hung up.

Chelsea replaced the receiver with icy calm. "He won't be here until morning."

Devlin shrugged. "I guess we'll have to make do."

"Have you lied about anything else?" she asked, motioning toward the phone.

"I don't make it a practice." His jaw hardened. "But what do you care? You're an expert."

"I don't understand."

His eyes blazed. "Every time you kiss John, or tell him that you miss him, or profess to love him, or lie in his bed, you're lying through your beautiful white teeth."

She wanted to throw herself at him and pummel him

with her fists, call him every name in the book, but she stood in the kitchen, gripping the counter and said, "I made a mistake with you, McVey, a horrible one. And I regret it. I'll regret it for the rest of my life. But it won't happen again."

"No?" He smiled crookedly, but she willed herself to ignore any speck of his masculine appeal.

"No!"

"Want me to prove you wrong?" He crooked one eyebrow.

Her stomach began to knot. "No reason. You've shown me that I can be as much of an animal as you are, but there is one difference."

"Oh, and what's that?"

"I won't be looking for an opportunity."

"Neither will I," he said coldly, and for an insane instant she felt a stab of disappointment. "You see, I only wanted to show you that you're not the woman for John."

"That's John's decision."

"John doesn't have all the facts."

"I don't understand—" But she did. In a blinding flash of realization, she knew that he intended to blackmail her. "You wouldn't tell him about this, would you?"

His jaw grew taut. "Only if I thought it would save him a life of misery. But the problem is, when I tell John what happened between you and me, either he won't believe me and I'll lose the best friend I've got, or he will believe me and hate me."

"So we're at an impasse."

"No, lady. I expect you to think about what happened tonight and reexamine your reasons for pretending to be in love with John. Then I think you'll come to the same conclusion I've already drawn—he'd be happier with a more traditional wife."

"How noble of you," she mocked.

For a minute, he let down his guard. His eyes darkened from an inner pain. "It's not all nobility, Chelsea," he said, his jaw sliding to one side. "I've seen a lot of bad marriages in my time—"

"Like yours?" she flung out angrily and watched as he winced. "Is that what this is all about? Did your wife hurt you so badly that you think every woman will betray…"

His jaw was so tight, a muscle jumped near his temple. "Don't bring up my wife."

"Then don't preach to me about John."

For seconds they glared at each other and Chelsea wished she could drop through the floor, but she held his gaze. At last Devlin said quietly, "I'd hate for John to be disappointed or you to be trapped."

"I wouldn't—"

"Just think about it," he suggested, shoving himself upright and crossing the room. Chelsea's heart tripped into double-time, but he didn't touch her. Instead, he found the bar and poured himself a stiff drink.

The rest of the night she could think of little but what had happened between them, and her traitorous body tingled at the memory of his kiss, but he didn't so much as come near her again. In fact, he acted as if they had been friends for life.

Slowly, she began to trust him and fortunately, Devlin had the decency to never bring up the subject of that night alone in the cabin.

Only much later—around Christmas—when John announced that he and Chelsea were to be married, did Devlin react violently.

They were at John's condominium for a holiday celebration. A fourteen-foot tree, resplendent in twinkling lights and glittering silver decorations, stood near the fireplace where a yule log crackled and burned. Soft Christmas carols drifted from hidden speakers, filling the rooms.

John was ecstatic. "Can you believe it?" he asked Devlin. "All these years and she finally said yes."

"No," Devlin said, shifting his knowing gaze to Chelsea. "Congratulations." He lifted his champagne glass and John squeezed Chelsea possessively. "Many years of happiness." Sipping his champagne, he let his gaze move over Chelsea—two blue orbs that cut through her facade and saw right to her soul.

"Th—thank you," she said, disgusted with herself for stumbling over the words.

The phone rang and John rolled his eyes. "I'll get it in the den," he said, hurrying down the short hallway.

Devlin turned and walked quickly onto the deck. Chelsea, hesitating only a second, followed him outside. He stood, staring at the stormy waters of the bay, bracing himself with both hands against the rail. Shoulders bunched, knuckles white, hair ruffled in the stiff breeze, he tensed when he heard her approach. His jaw was so tight, a muscle flexed beneath his temple. "You're sure about this?"

"Absolutely." She stood next to him and her stomach fluttered.

Devlin's lips compressed. His eyes turned a darker shade of blue. He glanced back to the sea again and muttered something under his breath.

Chelsea shivered and rubbed her arms. Why did it matter what he thought?

"What made you change your mind?" Devlin asked.

"I didn't change it. The time's right."

"Since when?"

Since I decided I needed a safe, secure life, a life with no surprises. "Actually, today," she said, feeling the salt-laden breeze tangle in her hair.

"Well, I hope you're happy with your decision and—" he turned, facing her, his expression grave "—you'd better do your damnedest to make John happy, because he deserves it."

"You don't think I will?"

His jaw slid to the side. "You don't want to hear my opinion."

Chelsea could never resist a challenge. She tilted her head upward and said evenly, "Of course I do. You're a friend of John's. Your opinion matters."

His eyes narrowed on her lips and her breath got lost between her lungs and her throat. She was reminded of the night he'd kissed her so passionately, fired her blood as no other man had dared.

"Let's not play any games, Chelsea," he said slowly, his gaze daring her to argue with him. "You and I both know you're marrying the wrong man."

"I don't think so."

"Don't you? Well, I remember a time when I could have proved—"

"You're wrong!"

He stared at her a few seconds and time seemed to stand still. "I hope so, lady," he whispered. "I hope to God I'm wrong about you. Because John deserves better. If you ever cheat on him, I'll make sure he finds out about it."

"But I would never do anything to hurt him!"

"Just don't forget that I have a long memory," he said as John opened the sliding doors and joined them.

"What's going on?" John asked.

"I was just congratulating your bride-to-be," Devlin drawled.

Chelsea felt herself pale, but John didn't notice. "Good," he said. "Then let's celebrate." He whipped out a piece of mistletoe from his pocket, dangled it over Chelsea's head and before she could object, kissed her long and hard. To her dismay, she felt nothing. She tried. Good Lord, she clung to John, tasting of him, willing her blood to race like wildfire, but her heartbeat barely accelerated.

When he lifted his head from hers, she glanced over his shoulder to the railing where Devlin had been standing. But Devlin was gone—only his empty glass a testament that he'd been there at all.

From that night until the stormy day he disappeared in the bleak waters of San Francisco Bay, Devlin never allowed himself to be alone with her again.

CHAPTER SIX

THE NEXT MORNING, Chelsea sat at the vanity and brushed her hair. She'd slept poorly, with thoughts of John and Devlin running through her mind.

Why wouldn't Mitch admit that he was Devlin? What was Devlin trying to hide?

Devlin would never have done anything to jeopardize John's life, she was sure of that. But something had happened on that boat, something that had forced Devlin to drop out of sight and pretend he was dead, only to end up here with an assumed identity.

So what was it? What would cause Devlin to take such drastic measures?

She tied her auburn hair away from her face in a ponytail, and frowned at her reflection. A line furrowed between her dark brows, her eyes were a moody shade of green, and she gnawed anxiously on her lower lip. "Oh, stop it," she muttered, touching up her makeup.

Frustrated, she pulled on a turquoise swimsuit and terry cover up, plopped her straw hat onto her head and grabbed her beach bag. She'd spend the day relaxing on the beach, sorting out exactly what her next step would be. As a private detective, she decided, locking the door of her room, she was a failure.

"Well, I wondered where you've been keeping yourself," a high-pitched voice called to her. "I haven't seen you since the cab ride over here!"

Chelsea glanced up and discovered Emily Vaughn bearing down on her. Decked out in a yellow-and-orange muumuu, sandals, wide-brimmed hat that shaded her apricot-tinted hair and white-rimmed sunglasses, Emily charged down the hall. "Well?" she asked as she caught up to Chelsea, her sandals clicking to her short steps. "What've you been up to?"

"Exploring," Chelsea replied evasively as they walked together down the stairs to the main lobby.

"Fascinating island, isn't it?" Emily quipped.

"And then some."

"And what did you find?"

Not much. "A great little boutique near the waterfront," Chelsea replied.

"Ever locate that man you were looking for?"

Chelsea nearly stumbled on the bottom step. "Man?" she repeated. How could Emily know?

"Mmm." Emily nodded quickly. "Come on, let's have breakfast by the pool. Jeff will find us there."

Chelsea wasn't really hungry, but she decided that she didn't have anything better to do. Until she found a way to observe Mitch Russell, she was at a standstill.

They were served croissants, jam, juice and coffee at a round, glass-topped table positioned near the shimmering water of the swimming pool. Emily, adjusting the umbrella of the table, finally explained. "Jeff saw you in the bar the other night and said you ran up to some man thinking he was someone else."

Chelsea inwardly groaned. "That's essentially correct."

"So—who is this man?"

"The man I ran into is Mitch Russell. I thought he was a friend of mine I hadn't seen in a while," Chelsea evaded.

"But he wasn't?" Satisfied with the angle of the striped umbrella, Emily sat down and began attacking her croissant, spreading thick currant jam over the flaky roll.

"No."

"You didn't come all the way down here just to find him, did you?"

"This is my vacation."

"And a wonderful place for a vacation it is," Emily remarked, temporarily distracted as she munched on her croissant. "Jeff and I have been saving all year just to come down here. Marvelous weather, steeped in history—a lovely spot. Heaven on earth is what I call it." She prattled on and Chelsea only half-listened, her eyes drawn to the path that led to the beach, as if just thinking about Mitch Russell would make him suddenly appear.

"…so I guess I just can't let him out of my sight again," Emily was saying. "First the bar downstairs and then some run-down place on the waterfront. Oh, he saw that man there, too, what did you say his name was—Russ something or other?"

Chelsea's gaze flew back to Emily's face. "Mitch Russell?"

"Right. Jeff saw him last night with a couple of other men."

But last night she and Mitch had been together at his house.

"What time?"

"Oh, it was early. Six or seven, I think. I don't let Jeff out alone too late. I worry too much." She smiled at Chelsea, obviously satisfied that she'd regained the younger woman's attention. "You know, it was the strangest thing. Jeff said your friend and the men he was with were speaking Spanish—well, at least Jeff thought it was Spanish—

but the native language on this island is French. Don't you think that's odd?"

"Jeff's sure?" Chelsea asked.

"Oh, I think so. He took Spanish in college. Of course that was years ago, but—" she lifted a shoulder "—Jeff's not one to get his facts wrong." She washed down a bite of croissant with a swallow of coffee. "So—I take it you haven't talked to your friend in a while—the friend you're looking for. Otherwise you would know where he's staying and would have called to arrange a meeting, isn't that right, dear?"

"I suppose." Chelsea shifted uncomfortably in her chair.

"And he's not in the phone book."

"No."

"So why do you think he's here—on Paradis?"

"I heard he might have ended up here, and since I was planning a vacation anyway, I thought I'd look him up."

"And he looks like this Russell man?"

"Very much," she admitted, deciding Emily talked too much for her to confide her secret. Besides, Chelsea's story sounded so farfetched, who would believe her? "Do you know the name of the bar where Jeff saw Mitch?"

"He'd have to tell you that. But it wouldn't be too hard to figure out. This is a pretty small island."

That much was true.

"Oh, here's the sleepyhead now!" Emily waved wildly and her lined face broke into a radiant grin. Chelsea glanced over her shoulder to spy Jeff walking briskly to the table.

"Look who I found, dear!" Emily said as he sat down. "And see, we saved you some rolls and jelly." She handed him the platter of croissants as a waiter refilled their cups. "Now, you just help yourself. I was telling Chelsea that you ran into that man you saw her with in the bar on the first night we were here! She says his name is Russell Mit—no, Mitch Russell."

Jeff slathered butter on his croissant and grunted an affirmative.

"And they were speaking Spanish, isn't that right, dear? What's the name of that bar?"

Jeff lifted a shoulder and his face pulled into a thoughtful frown. "Can't remember."

Emily glanced at Chelsea. "What did I tell you?" She tossed up her hands. "Oh, it doesn't matter anyway! He'll think of it soon enough. And it's going to be a simply marvelous day! I can just feel it. Maybe we should all go fishing. There are boats you can rent."

"Thanks, but I can't. Not today," Chelsea said.

Emily's face fell. "Why not?"

"I've got plans," she lied, feeling a twang of guilt. Emily and Jeff had been nothing but nice to her and yet she couldn't spend an entire day drifting on the ocean. She was in Paradis for a purpose.

"Oh, can't they wait! We can sunbathe and talk and—"

"Another time," Chelsea promised, standing and reaching for her beach bag.

"Oh, all right, but we'll hold you to it."

"Good." Chelsea smiled and dug through her wallet, but Emily shook her head.

"You put that thing away. We'll just charge this to our room."

"Oh, no, I couldn't—" Chelsea replied quickly, before Jeff could respond.

"I won't hear of it any other way," Emily insisted. "You kept me company and I appreciate it. Now, just go on and see if you can find your friend. If you do, I certainly want to meet him."

Chelsea swallowed a smile. She couldn't picture Devlin and Emily having one thing in common.

"The Dauphin Bleu," Jeff said suddenly as he turned his teacup in his hands.

Emily's brows knit. "What're you talking about?"

"The bar last night. I think the name of it was the Blue Dolphin."

Chelsea grinned. Finally—she was getting somewhere!

"Could you pick out the men again if you saw them—the men who were speaking Spanish to Mitch?" she asked.

"Maybe," Jeff evaded, turning his cup nervously on the table and avoiding Chelsea's eyes.

"Good."

"Stop fiddling with your tea. You're making me crazy," Emily said, shaking her head. "What's wrong with you?"

Jeff scowled. "Well, it wasn't just two men who were with Chelsea's friend. There was also a woman with them."

"So?" Emily asked, but Chelsea's heart had nearly stopped. Jeff was obviously uncomfortable.

"Your friend—Russell—he was with her. She was very attentive to him." Jeff rubbed his hand across his chin.

"I see. And what about him?" Chelsea asked, her fingers gripping the handle of her bag so tightly her hands ached.

"They seemed to be pretty wrapped up in each other." He blew across his tea.

Chelsea's heart dropped. What did she care if Mitch had a woman on the island? Devlin had dated more than she could count. And yet… "Well, thanks for breakfast," she said, forcing a bright smile. "Next time it's on me."

"Oh, go on!" Emily said waving her away, chuckling. "I'll see you later!"

"We'll count on it," Emily replied.

As Chelsea left the table, Emily was rattling on about the weather and Jeff was eating in long-suffering silence.

Chelsea, though she was loathe to admit it, felt more than one pang of jealousy at the thought of this mysterious woman in Mitch Russell's—or Devlin's—life. Who was she? Were they lovers? She certainly hadn't returned to Mitch's place with him. "Don't even think about it," she grumbled to herself later, as she lay on a beach towel and eyed the horizon.

The afternoon sun was hot and intense, beating against her skin until she was covered in sweat and the sunscreen she'd applied was dripping from her skin. She waded in the aquamarine water to cool off, but her mind kept wandering back to Mitch and his woman.

Her heart twisted a little though she didn't understand why. He was young and virile—why wouldn't he have a woman?

Foolishly, she felt betrayed. Licking her lips, she remembered the touch of his mouth on hers, the electricity that licked through her body at the taste of him. So much like Devlin. So damned much like Devlin. His looks, his touch, his voice—everything about him screamed that he was Devlin and yet he denied it. Frustrated, she kicked at a stone in the surf and sent a tiny crab scurrying for cover.

Why does it matter so much? You loved John, not Devlin. Chewing on her lower lip, she wondered if the love she'd felt for John—real though it had been—was more of a sense of loyalty—a duty that she'd felt compelled to fulfill after Devlin had nearly made love to her in the cabin.

Her skin turned hot at the memory. Awash with guilt, she sat in the warm water and propped her chin on her knees. Had she been deceiving John, lying to Devlin and deluding herself? Had she, as Devlin had so coarsely suggested, never really loved John enough to become his wife?

"That's ridiculous!" she chided herself, then sighed. "Oh, Lord, what a mess!" Shoving her hair from her eyes, she thought about Mitch and Devlin and all the conflicting emotions each man wrought from her.

The brilliant day seemed to evaporate, leaving her in a desert of memories. If Mitch had been at the Dauphin Bleu earlier last evening, he'd then come home for a quick swim and subsequently discovered Chelsea on his front porch. At first he'd been angry—and then he'd put on the act of pretending that she'd led someone inadvertently to him. But whom?

And who was the woman he'd been with? Was she young? Beautiful? Was he in love with her? Was he waiting for her when Chelsea had planted herself on his front porch? Was that why he tried so hard to get rid of her?

His big act of shutting the blinds and pulling her into the cabin had all been for show—to scare her off—and to make sure that his girlfriend hadn't spotted her, Chelsea decided angrily, a headache beginning to pound behind her eyes.

Well, he'd find out she didn't scare easily. Struggling to her feet, she walked out of the surf and trudged through the sand to her beach towel. After shaking the sand from the towel, she stepped into her cover-up, then tucked her towel and sunscreen into her beach bag. More determined than ever to find out everything possible about Mitch Russell, she set off down the beach, intending to hike over a mile through the sand to the town of Emeraude.

She'd check out the Dauphin Bleu as well as the other watering holes in town. Surely someone would know something about Mitch, or Devlin, or whoever he really was!

THE DAUPHIN BLEU WASN'T much. Set two blocks away from the waterfront, with yellow stucco walls, a brown patched roof, and a quivering neon window sign—a blue dolphin leaping from a pink wave—the bar had seen better days.

Chelsea shoved hard on the scarred plank door before she noticed the "Closed" sign, which listed the hours of operation.

Sighing, she checked her watch. The bar wouldn't open for two hours. And what will you do then? she asked herself as she headed back toward the waterfront, her sandals scuffing on the cracked concrete sidewalks. Wait for Mitch again? Suffer through the questioning gazes cast in your direction? The thought turned her stomach, but she was determined to do whatever it took to find out what had happened to Devlin as well as to John.

If only John had lived, she thought, pausing at a corner before crossing the street and joining the crowd moving through the shaded, open-air market. Her life would have been simple if John had survived the boating accident. They would be married by now, living in his condominium, planning, perhaps, to buy a house or have a baby.

But all her dreams were behind her now; they'd sunk into the stormy depths of San Francisco Bay when John had been killed. The old pain clutched at her heart as she thought about John—the man she was to marry—the man she'd loved. And she *had* loved him. Despite what Devlin had thought. Perhaps that love hadn't been a raging passion, maybe it hadn't been a billowing lust that had swelled through her each time she'd kissed him, but she'd loved John and had known that they would spend the rest of their lives in friendly companionship, in laughter and love.

But that future was long gone, destroyed when John— an expert seaman and swimmer—had drowned, leaving so many unanswered questions. Questions only Devlin McVey could answer.

The hours dragged by, but finally the bar opened for the evening. She forced herself inside the breathless, dark room and found a bar stool in a back corner that faced the door. After ordering a glass of wine she waited, as she had for two other nights, her gaze wandering around the worn interior. What kind of a man would hang out here night after night? But maybe Mitch wasn't always here or at the Villa. She swirled her untouched wine and wondered how Mitch spent his days as well as his nights.

Men and a very few women began to wander inside. Laughing and talking, they ordered drinks. Chelsea nursed a glass of wine and had started on her second when the same lanky blond man she'd met on her first night at the Villa approached her table. What was his name? Chris something or other. Without waiting for an invitation, he plopped himself down on the bar stool.

"You alone?" he asked, offering her a smile that showed off white teeth that overlapped slightly.

"Yes, but I'm waiting for someone."

"Again," he reminded her.

She smiled and nodded.

"Same guy?"

Unfortunately, yes. "Mmm," she replied noncommittally. What was it about this man and his mocking gaze that put her on edge?

"As I said the other night, there's no reason I can't keep you company 'til your friend arrives."

There was no reason he couldn't stay, she decided. Besides, she was tired of being alone, chasing the ghost of Devlin McVey.

"Oh, come on. Give a guy a chance," he suggested with an easy smile, his eyes twinkling. "What's your name?"

"Chelsea."

"From the States—right? West coast, I'd bet— Seattle?"

"Close. San Francisco."

"Here on a vacation?"

"Of a sort," she evaded.

He ordered a beer for himself and another glass of wine for her. "I'm from Wyoming—not far from Laramie. But that's a long story…" When their drinks had been deposited on the table, he said, "So what's holding up your friend?"

"I don't know," she admitted, wishing Mitch would miraculously appear.

"I'll tell you this much about your friend," Chris said, sipping from his glass. "He's crazy to keep a woman like you waiting. Who is he?"

For the first time, Chelsea decided Chris might be able to help her. Since she wasn't getting anywhere on her own, she decided to try something new. "I'm waiting for Mitch Russell. You know him?"

A flicker of recognition lightened Chris's eyes, but other than that small indication, his cool expression didn't change. "I've met him a couple of times. But he mainly keeps to himself." He eyed her thoughtfully.

"Umm." She nodded, sipping from her glass as a steel

drum tuned up in the corner. "I knew him a long time ago."

Chris studied his beer. "In Chicago?"

"Actually I met him in San Francisco," she said, deciding to keep the details to herself.

"Was he out there on assignment?"

"Assignment?" she repeated.

"Yeah, I thought he worked for some newspaper in Chicago, but he gave it all up when he was in an accident—the one that killed his wife."

So Mitch Russell claimed to be a journalist. "Which paper?" she asked.

"You know, I don't think I ever heard the name of it." Chris thought for a moment, but shook his head. "I know he did some traveling for the paper, but essentially he lived in Chicago or Detroit or Cincinnati or someplace like that.

Chelsea grinned inwardly. Devlin had lived in Cincinnati before he'd moved to San Francisco and an accident had taken his wife's life. Finally, she was getting somewhere.

"And now he's writing a book," she added.

"That's what he says."

"But you haven't seen it?"

"Nope, but I don't really know him that well."

She sipped her wine. "You don't hang out with him often?"

"Me? Nah. He's kind of a loner—but I guess you know that. He's all wrapped up in his book, or so he says, and spends his time with a few of the locals—probably for research or local color or whatever you want to call it."

"His book is set in the islands?"

Chris lifted his shoulders. "Beats me. Like I said, I barely know the guy."

You and me both, she agreed silently, steering the course of the conversation to neutral territory.

The band started playing a familiar tune and Chris asked her to dance, but she declined, claiming to be tired, which she was.

"How about a rain check?" Chris asked as he walked her outside and she found a cab. "Can I see you again?"

Why not? "Sure. I'm staying at the Villa," she replied, more than a little uncomfortable. She hadn't dated since John's death and she wasn't really interested in starting any kind of relationship. But Chris lived on the island. He might be able to help her find out more about Devlin.

"I'll call," Chris promised as she slid into the cab.

Chelsea nodded and waved as she asked the driver to take her back to the Villa.

Tired, she stared through the gritty window of the cab and decided she hadn't learned much about Mitch today, but the little she had gleaned hadn't convinced her that he wasn't Devlin. In fact, little by little, she was piecing together Mitch's past—a past that seemed very much like Devlin McVey's.

Tomorrow, she silently promised herself, barely able to keep her eyes open. She'd find out more tomorrow.

HOWEVER, IN THE NEXT FEW days her luck didn't improve. In fact, she hadn't spotted Mitch once. Now she was contemplating returning to his house. "And do what?" she asked herself as she walked through the streets of Emeraude. What good would another showdown do?

She walked back to the Dauphin Bleu and sighed when she noticed the Closed sign. Could she stand another night lingering in the seedy bar hoping for Mitch to show up, only to end up disappointed again?

Frustrated, she slammed a fist on the door of the establishment and nearly jumped out of her skin when the door swung open and a round-bellied man with dark skin and frizzy gray hair stared at her.

"Can I help you?" he asked in a thick, rumbling accent.

Chelsea didn't even pause to think. "Yes! I'm looking for this man," she said quickly, whipping out her glossy picture of Mitch.

"Aaah. Mr. Russell."

"Yes! Mr. Russell." Maybe she'd finally struck pay dirt!

"Most days he spends at his house or in his boat," the man said thoughtfully. "He lives to the north around the point…" He gave her directions to Mitch's cabin along with a few pieces of information Chelsea had already discovered herself. "He stay mostly to himself."

"Doesn't he have any friends?"

"A few. He be with Mr. Landeen sometimes or Mr. Raoul," he said thoughtfully. "But mainly he be with himself."

This was nothing new, except she was surprised that Chris's name had come up. She thanked the man and with little more information than she had before, she strolled through the open-air market, eyeing the wares. She bought a small bag of oranges, a bottle of wine and two baskets, which she tucked into her beach bag.

The sun was low in the western sky but the heat of the day, still rising in shimmering waves from the pavement, caused sweat to collect between her shoulder blades. Walking lazily along the bleached planks of the docks, she gazed at the sea, where silhouettes of sailboats skimmed the horizon and larger fishing vessels lumbered into port. Sunbathers, catching a few dying rays, were scattered along the beach and swimmers dotted the turquoise water. The pungent odors of fish, seaweed and brine filled her nostrils.

Paradis had a certain charm, she thought, leaning against a rail worn smooth with time. She watched the boats rocking lazily against the docks—outriggers, sloops, ketches—bobbing to the gentle swell of the tide, when she saw him.

Mitch Russell, big as life, was barely a hundred yards from her. His eyes were guarded by sunglasses and he wore tan slacks and a plaid shirt with the sleeves rolled over his forearms. He was talking to two men—both dark-haired and tanned.

Chelsea couldn't believe her good luck. She hoped she blended into the crowd along the piers as she stared at Mitch and the people with him. One man was tall with a thick moustache and greasy black hair. He wore faded denim jeans and a blue jacket. The other man was shorter and thicker, his belly protruding and the beginning of a beard starting to darken his chin. He was dressed in a straw-colored suit and black tie and tugged nervously at his chin as they talked.

However, the two men held little interest for Chelsea. It was their companion, a beautiful woman who stood so close to Mitch that no daylight squeezed between them. With jet-black hair, large eyes and a pointed little nose, she grinned up at Mitch, her generous mouth curved into a smile—as if she and he shared some private joke.

Chelsea's insides twisted as Mitch whispered something to her and she tossed back her head and laughed, her straight black hair shining vibrantly in the fading sunlight.

So he did have a woman.

A painful little ache throbbed in Chelsea's heart. *What did you expect?* her mind taunted. *Mitch Russell means nothing to you—and you mean nothing to him! As for Devlin—well, he never really cared for you, now, did he? If he did survive the accident, he ran from you and the life he'd led in San Francisco and even if he died in the bay with John, you've lost him forever.*

"No," she whispered vehemently as she stared at the man whose features and voice were so like Devlin's, whose smile and laughter reminded her of Devlin's and whose kiss was as powerful and consuming as Devlin's had been.

She reached into her bag and found her camera. Focusing quickly, she snapped off several quick shots of Mitch and the raven-haired woman, of his two acquaintances and of the sleek red sailboat moored nearby as it moved in tempo with the lapping of the tide.

As if he could feel her eyes on him, Mitch glanced her way. In the viewfinder, she saw his lips tighten, though he barely missed a beat before turning his attention back to the group. Slinging one arm around the beautiful woman's waist, he pulled her tight against him and squeezed, his fingers splaying intimately beneath her breast.

Nausea swam in Chelsea's throat. She shoved the lens cap onto her camera. She felt suddenly dirty and sick. How could she care the least bit for that wretched man? Just because he looked like Devlin?

Disgusted, she threaded her way between the other people crowding the docks. The heat seemed abruptly staggering. She swiped her bangs from her eyes and felt sweat against her palm. She just needed a few hours to get a grip on herself, to shower and change and somewhere find the guts to come back to the Dauphin Bleu and observe Mitch again.

And what if you see him take that woman into his arms and kiss her?

"It won't matter," she said aloud, sounding more certain than she felt. Bracing herself, she hazarded one last glance over her shoulder to see Mitch alone on the docks. The other members of his party had boarded a sleek red speedboat, which boasted the name *Lucia,* and Mitch stood, shoulders bunched tightly as he watched the racy boat roar out of the bay.

Though it was ridiculous, Chelsea felt a certain satisfaction that the woman was no longer with Mitch. She was trying to swallow a smile when the boat rounded the far point of the island.

As soon as the speedy craft disappeared from view, Mitch turned and, spying Chelsea, strode swiftly her way. His jaw was set, his eyes blazing as he approached and Chelsea felt more than a tiny prickle of fear.

"Just what the hell do you think you're doing?" he demanded in a harsh whisper. Grabbing hold of her upper arm, he propelled her away from the docks and across a dusty street crowded with tourists. Only a few people even glanced their way.

"I was just sightseeing."

"Ha!" He yanked harder on her arm, forcing her down the street and through the tightly packed shops of Emeraude. "And I suppose you were just taking a few photographs of the view?" he snarled.

"Yes. The bay, the beach, the docks—"

"Me."

"No, I—"

"Sure." He yanked harder on her arm and they passed through the open market, leaving the waterfront behind.

"Where're you taking me?"

"Someplace safe."

"Safe?" she repeated, half running to keep up with him before she understood. "Oh, I get it. Safe because of the other night, when you thought someone followed me to your house and you insinuated that there was some kind of danger?"

His lips pressed so tightly together they turned white against his black beard.

"So what are you afraid of, Mr. *Russell?*" she chided, unable to keep her tongue still. "Were you concerned that your girlfriend would see me?"

He muttered something under his breath, rolled his eyes to the summer-blue sky, then swore softly. Yanking harder on her arm, he said, "Look, I don't need you fouling up my life."

"I'm not."

"Like hell!" He strode, dragging her to keep pace with him, along an old cobblestone street until it gave out and petered into a path that led into an overgrown park. Trees offered shade and fragrant blossoms scented the air. Insects buzzed as they passed, birds pecked at crumbs on the paths and a few people sat on old wrought-iron benches.

"Isn't this far enough?" she demanded, trying to tug her arm away from him.

"Not private enough!" he growled and a feeling of panic swept up Chelsea's spine. Throwing her a dark look, he explained, "I don't want to cause a scene and you, lady, bring out the worst in me."

"You mean you actually have a better side?" she flung out.

That was a mistake. He slid a furious glance in her direction and his fingers dug into the soft flesh of her arm. "Believe it or not, there are times when my sole purpose in life *isn't* centered around wringing your pretty neck!"

"How chivalrous," she mocked.

Growling something unintelligible, he continued to

tug on her arm as the path led through a grass clearing and past an old gazebo in sad need of paint. "We could stop here," she suggested, but Mitch didn't pause for a second.

Beach grass tickled her calves as the sandy trail led upward, switching back and forth through stands of leafy trees and shrubbery. Chelsea's legs began to ache as the path grew steeper. Several times she stubbed her toe, but Mitch continued to climb. "You should have told me to wear my hiking boots," she grumbled.

"I didn't know you had any."

"Well, they're back in San Francisco—"

"A lot of good that does you." He glanced down at her sandals and a frown creased his brow. "Women's fashions," he grunted disgustedly, but the fingers around her arm slackened a little and his pace slowed slightly.

Eventually, just when Chelsea thought her calves and thighs could stand no more, the trees gave way to a clearing.

Chelsea walked onto the grass and her breath caught in her throat at the panoramic view of sky and sea. Far below, past acres of emerald-green treetops, the small shops and docks of Emeraude stretched around the glistening waters of the bay. Boats dotted the horizon and, closer, seabirds swooped to rookeries tucked into the rocks and marshes of the deeper recesses of Paradis.

"Okay," he said at last, finally releasing her. "You and I are going to have it out—once and for all!" Without so much as asking, he reached into her basket, found her camera and opened the back.

"Hey—wait!"

He stripped the film from the camera.

"That's mine—"

Exposing the film to the sun, he tossed the empty camera back to her. "So now you've got it back!"

She caught the camera on the fly. "You have no right—"

"I? *I* have no right? What about you? Sneaking around like some phony private eye, taking pictures, asking questions, generally being a pain in the backside!"

"But you can't just—"

"I can do what I damn well please," he snarled back. "This is my home. You're the foreigner—"

"Foreigner? So you've taken up citizenship? Is that it? Well, even so, you can't—"

"I can!" Advancing on her, Mitch ground out, "Now, you listen to me! You're the one who can't! You can't trespass on my land, you can't take pictures of me or my friends without telling me about it and you certainly can't start asking questions about me of every person you meet on the street!"

"But, I—"

"I know. You think I'm lying to you. You have this insane belief that I'm someone I'm not!"

She just stared at him. Could she have been so wrong? Doubt prickled her mind as she stared at this bearded man who glared at her from the protection of dark glasses. She licked her lips nervously. "Who—who were the people you were talking to?"

"What people?" He shoved his sunglasses onto his head.

"On the docks."

"Look, don't you go bothering them," he warned, his eyes snapping blue fire.

"Who are they? Friends?"

"Acquaintances, and probably not the nicest people

you'd ever want to meet. But I need them, they help me with research for my story."

"Your story?"

"The book I'm writing. Part one is set in South America in a fictional small dictatorship. Those people—the men on the docks—have given me insight to the people, customs and government of their country."

"In exchange for—?"

His lips compressed. "Money."

"Couldn't you just go to the library?"

The look he cast her called her every kind of fool. "Not for the kind of information I need."

Chelsea's stomach knotted. "What about the woman that was with them?"

"Same thing."

She arched a disbelieving brow.

"Haven't you ever heard of the woman's perspective? Well, believe it or not, a woman from an impoverished Third World country has a different outlook on life than most American women who can walk into Nieman Marcus and charge whatever they want."

"What're their names?" she asked and his eyes turned dangerous.

He acted as if he hadn't heard her question. "Since you've been poking around into my personal life, you probably know I'm a reporter."

"I'd heard."

"I protect my sources. And my advice to you is to leave well enough alone. I don't want those people or you hurt."

"I wouldn't—" Then she understood. "What 'customs' do they tell you about? Drugs? Prostitution? Shady government deals with the United States?"

"It's none of your business, Chelsea."

"It is if you're Devlin."

"You are too much!" He threw his hands into the air as if asking supplication. "I'm sorry about your friend— really, I am. It's hard to lose someone—I know. I lost my wife about eighteen months ago. But you just have to go on."

"Like you did," she ventured. "By running down here?"

His jaw clenched and he walked away from her, staring at the sea, his shoulders broad and stretching the cloth of his shirt, the tails flapping in the breeze. He pinched the bridge of his nose and Chelsea's throat tightened. How many times had she seen Devlin, in exasperation, make the very same gesture?

"I had my reasons for leaving," he said slowly, and when he turned back to face her, his eyes were clouded with guilt. His lips pressed firmly together and her gaze was drawn to his mouth. "But I guess you could say that I ran away." His jaw slid to one side. "I wouldn't deny it, but I don't like my life pried open and dissected." He shoved his hair from his eyes. "What is it I have to do to get rid of you?"

"Prove that you're not Devlin," she said, not missing a beat.

"I tried, the other night. Obviously you didn't buy it."

"Would you?"

"Yes! Damn it, woman, why won't you accept what is so patently obvious?" Striding back to her, he shoved his face so close to hers that his beard touched her cheek. "I am *not, never have been* and *never will be* Devlin McVey! Until the other night in the bar at the Villa, I'd never laid eyes on you before and I'd never heard of the man and I wish to Almighty God that I never had. Now, the way I see it, you can keep up with this fantasy of yours or you can accept me for who I am."

"Which is?" she asked, her voice so soft she could barely hear it.

"A man who is disgusted with his way of life in America, a man who lost his wife and it nearly killed him because he was behind the wheel, a man who's trying to rebuild a life that makes some kind of sense and a man who wants and needs his privacy!" His blue gaze delved so deeply into hers, it seemed to scrape her soul and for the first time since meeting him, she felt something akin to pity for this man who called himself Mitch Russell. He must have read her expression because he swore under his breath and plowed his fingers through his hair. "Why won't you believe me?"

"Because I can't!" she cried, aching inside because she hurt so much. Had she come so far for nothing? Good Lord, was this man really who he said he was? She blushed and felt like an utter fool.

When he reached forward with one finger and slowly tilted her chin upward, so that her eyes met the mystery in his, she nearly came undone. Inside, she trembled. Her skin felt cold and hot at once, prickly and tense as his gaze searched the contours of her face.

"You want me to leave you alone?" she whispered.

"Yes…and no. I want you to give up pretending I'm someone I'm not."

She swallowed hard. "And…"

"And…if you won't leave me alone, at least meet me on my own terms, treat me as if I'm not some long-lost dream."

She licked her lips, aware of his one finger so near the pulse beginning to throb in her neck. "If you only knew how like him you are."

"Give it up, Chelsea." His fingers slowly descended, trailing along her neck to rest at the hollow of her throat.

"I'm not your perfect Devlin," he whispered, his throat suddenly raw and hoarse.

"He wasn't perfect and he wasn't mine."

His eyes darkened. "Oh, I think he was. He was probably just fool enough not to know it." His arms circled her waist and he drew her to him. His lips crashed down on hers with a possessive fury that made her knees suddenly weak. His tongue, supple and wet, invaded her mouth, touching and dancing eagerly, sending chills down her spine.

Winding her arms around his neck, she molded her lips to his. He reached lower, his hands cupping her buttocks, drawing her closer still. Hard-muscled thighs pressed firmly against her, intimately caressing her own bare legs. Her breasts were crushed against the wall of his chest and her heart thudded loudly.

Stop! Stop him now! Don't make this mistake! a voice inside her head screamed, but as one hand reached upward and tangled in the long strands of her hair, she couldn't resist. His weight drew them both downward to a bed of long sun-bleached grass with a canopy of cloudless blue sky.

His beard was rough against her face, his calloused hands hard and demanding as he touched her through her clothes, smoothing the cotton fabric across her breasts and buttocks, creating an ache that streamed through her in wanton invitation. He was half lying atop her, his legs pinning hers as his lips and tongue played havoc with her senses.

Her nipples reacted, puckering to the feel of his hand through the cloth, her breath constricted in her throat and all the while her brain screamed at her that this was wrong—this hot seduction was purely animal lust and had nothing to do with love.

He tore his lips from hers and stared down into her eyes. Slowly he reached for the top button of her cover-up, plucking the button and sliding it all-too-easily through its hole. The second and third buttons gave way.

Chelsea's heart was pounding, her blood pulsing hot through her veins. "You are beautiful," he murmured as he stared at her breasts swelling so boldly. He reached for another button.

"No!" With all the strength she could muster, she grabbed his wrist and stopped him from going farther.

A small smile played upon his lips. "Second thoughts?" he challenged, and she saw his gaze flicker to the rapid rise and fall of her chest.

"And third and fourth and so on," she said back, willing her voice to remain steady, while his finger still touched the bare skin between her breasts and his leg was flung over one of hers, pinning her to the steamy earth.

"What is it with you, Chelsea Reed?" he asked, undaunted as he propped his head with one hand and let his gaze rove lazily up and down her body.

Chelsea swallowed with difficulty. She knew her hair was tangled, her clothes were pushed and pulled, revealing the hollow of her breast and the length of her thigh. She could feel a burn of embarrassment stain her cheeks. Her lips were swollen—still tasting of his mouth and tongue—and her eyelids were still at half mast. She tried to squirm away, to snatch at the gaping cloth over her breasts, but he pressed his weight against her, pinning her at the thighs.

"Don't you want me?"

"I—I don't even know who you are!"

"Well, that's progress," he said, his eyes glimmering seductively. "Maybe you're not so hung up on this Devlin character as much as you believe—or maybe he's just a figment of your imagination."

"What?" she nearly screamed before she noticed the mockery in his eyes. This—this seduction was all just an act! He wasn't interested in her, he was just trying to prove a point! Just a man with a woman—any woman. Just as Devlin had tried to prove a point when she said she was in love with John!

Though Mitch's voice had turned gruff and his eyes still glinted in sensual invitation, it wasn't because she was Chelsea Reed, it was only because she was available and throwing herself at him.

Sick with shame and disgust, she tried to roll away. "Get off me," she commanded and he laughed.

"What's wrong, Chelsea? Tired of your little game? Can't you believe in your fantasies any longer?"

She struggled free and he let her go. Standing, towering over him, her breath coming in short gasps, she tossed her hair away from her face and tilting up her chin said coldly, "You're the most disgusting, self-serving, arrogant son of a bitch I've ever met!"

"Is that a compliment?"

She clenched her jaw tight and asked with quiet fury, "Why is it you get such a thrill out of mortifying me? No, don't answer that—" she scooped up her bag and started for the path "—I don't want to know."

"Just remember who's been chasing whom."

"Chasing?" she repeated in a low whisper. *"Chasing?"* Whirling, she faced him again and almost melted when she noticed the boyish mischief twinkling in his eyes, the way his black hair fell over his forehead so fetchingly. "I've never chased you, Mitch. But I did come down to this island with a purpose and I haven't given up."

His smile faded. He rose slowly and crossed the grassy

strip to stand just in front of her. His eyes narrowed on her lips. "Are you willing to take a chance on that—" he motioned with one thumb to the trampled bed of grass where they'd so nearly made love "—happening again? Because it will, you know. There's something electric between you and me—don't try to deny it. You felt it, too. Call it sexual attraction or raw animal magnetism or just plain sex, but it exists."

"In your mind."

"And your body."

She wanted to slap him, but she couldn't. He was only telling the truth.

"Leave me alone, Chelsea. For your sake and mine. I don't want to get involved with you any more than you want to have a quick meaningless affair with a man you don't even know. Go back to San Francisco. Find another John. Or another Devlin for that matter. But leave me the hell alone!"

For the first time she thought she saw a glimmer of pain in his eyes. "Why did you bring me up here?"

"To point out that you're playing a dangerous game and you'll lose."

"Why is it dangerous?"

"Because you're too involved in this fantasy—this myth—you're deluding yourself, woman. And I don't want to be a part of any dreams that will only end in disappointment."

"And yet you tried to seduce me."

One side of his mouth lifted. "Oh, I beg to differ. You tried to seduce me."

"Me?"

"You're just lucky I'm not that kind of guy."

"What?" she whispered but realized again, when she caught the glimmer of laughter in his eyes, that he was teasing her. There was more to Mitch Russell than he let on, a side to him that she found lighthearted and free. But it was buried deep beneath layers of distrust and anger. "You're absolutely insufferable."

"Probably. Now, Ms. Reed, why don't I take you back to the hotel and you give up with the cameras and the questions and the bulldozing your way into my life."

"Is that what you really want?"

He hesitated, but only for a second. The brackets around his mouth deepened. "It would be best. For both of us."

"Why?"

"Because, even if I wanted to, I couldn't be the man you're hoping I am."

The sincerity in his blue eyes cut her to the bone. For the first time since she'd met Mitch Russell, she thought he might be telling her the truth. Maybe he deserved the same. Drawing a shuddering breath she said, "As you know, I spent a lot of time and effort getting here. And it's hard for me to believe that someone who looks and sounds and feels so much like Devlin isn't he. All I want from you is some time to get to know you, so that I can go back to the States convinced that he's really gone."

He glanced out to sea and his hair ruffled in the wind. "You want time—time with me?"

"Yes."

"How much?"

"Two weeks."

Sighing, he turned to face her again, and this time his face was set in stone. "Three days."

"But that's not enough."

"That's the deal. Take it or leave it."

"A week, then."

"Three days or nothing. And you've got to promise me

that you'll quit spying on me, taking pictures and acting like some kind of bumbling James Bond." He glared up at her. "I mean it, Chelsea. I've got a job to do—a book to write. So, when I'm ready, I'll come looking for you—"

"When *you're* ready?" she repeated.

"Right. I'm not on a vacation."

"But—"

"Take it or leave it!" he snapped.

She didn't have any choice. She could see by the rock-hard set of his jaw that he wouldn't budge and three days was better than nothing, wasn't it?

Besides, where was it written that she had to keep her end of the bargain?

"All right, Mr. Russell," she finally agreed, feeling more than a little trepidation at the white lie. "You've got yourself a deal!"

CHAPTER SEVEN

FEELING AS IF she'd made a pact with the very devil himself, Chelsea slid a furtive glance in Mitch's direction as he drove her back to the hotel. What would he look like without his beard? His build was the same, his eyes so provocative and blue, they had to belong to Devlin.

As if he sensed her staring at him, he shifted down and looked at her in such a way that the back of her throat went dry. "Why don't you tell me about yourself?" he suggested.

"Why?"

"Well, you've been asking a lot of questions. I figured it was my turn."

"There's not much to tell," she said, smiling slightly. "Besides, it's a boring story."

"You? Boring?" He let out a long breath. "You may be a lot of things, lady, but 'boring'? Never!"

Reluctantly, she sketched out her life, told him about her family, her overprotective older sister, her father the cop, her martyred mother, left for a woman less than half her age.

Mitch listened attentively as his Bronco rambled up the slight incline to the Villa. When she stopped talking, he glanced her way. "And what about your fiancé?"

"John," she whispered, feeling a tug on her heart. Sighing, she shook her head sadly. "John was special."

"You loved him very much."

She hesitated for only a second. "Yes."

"But still you look for his friend."

"For answers," she admitted.

"Answers?" Mitch's hands tightened over the wheel as the Bronco broke through the trees and the hotel loomed ahead. Magenta and violet reflected in the windows and the dusty white walls seemed less scarred in the coming twilight.

"I think Devlin might know something about the boating accident that the police don't." She chewed on her bottom lip as he guided the rig into the pitted asphalt lot and cut the engine.

"Then you don't believe it was an accident?"

"No! I mean, it's possible, but it just doesn't make sense, does it? Why would Devlin run if what had happened in the bay were only an accident?"

"Wait a minute—you think McVey might be responsible?" he asked.

"No." She shook her head emphatically. "But I really don't know what to think. That's why I have to find Devlin. There's a reason he took off—a reason John died."

Mitch's hand surrounded her arm and through the open window of the Bronco, fragrant scents of lemon and gardenia wafted in the warm air. "You know, lady, you're setting yourself up for a major fall. In my book, your friend McVey drowned. Period. End of story. No fairy-tale ending. No mystery. No nothing."

The fingers on her inner arm were warm against her sensitive skin and the stare he sent her fairly smoldered. Yet he didn't move to get closer to her. His hand dropped and he turned away. "Good night, Chelsea," he said, waiting for her to leave.

She reached for the handle of the door. "You know,

he even drove a Bronco not so different from this. Not a Jeep, but a Bronco."

"So?"

"Seems like more than a coincidence."

He snorted and shook his head, but when he glanced back at her, she touched him on the arm. "If you are Devlin, Mitch," she said slowly, "I'm going to find a way to prove it and then you're going to have to face whatever it was that happened in that storm." Her eyes held his for a heart-stopping moment. "There will be no more running."

"And what will you do, when you finally accept the fact that you're wrong, hmm? How will you handle the fact that you're attracted to me—and don't try to deny it," he added as if anticipating the protest that leaped to her lips. "Because when you do, you'll be the one who'll be thinking of running."

With that, he rammed the Bronco into gear and as soon as she climbed from the cab and slammed the door he tore out of the lot, thick tires chirping against worn asphalt.

He seemed so sure of himself, so confident. And yet there was an inner man, a kinder man she'd only glimpsed, hidden deep within the arrogant exterior of Mitch Russell.

She watched his taillights disappear around a bend in the drive. Unfortunately for him, he hadn't counted on her tenacity. She'd find a way to prove he was Devlin—even if she had to take dental X-rays to do it.

At the thought, a slow smile crept across her face. No, she wouldn't have to resort to coercing a dentist into helping her, she thought with a smile. There was another way to prove he was Devlin, if only she had the guts to try and find out. Hadn't John, on the night she'd met Devlin, mentioned that he had a birthmark—a distinctive crescent high on his hip?

At the time, she thought John had been teasing, but once, a few months before the boating accident, John had ribbed Devlin about the birthmark. To her surprise, a dark flush had tinted the back of hard-edged Devlin's neck, thereby proving, to Chelsea's way of thinking, that he did, indeed, have the embarrassing mark.

And now, in all the months since the accident, she hadn't really thought about Devlin's birthmark, probably because she'd never seen it. If Russell was, in fact, Devlin McVey, then certainly he'd still have the birthmark, unless along with growing a beard he'd also decided to have some plastic surgery!

Chelsea considered this new idea from all angles as she shoved open the hotel doors and walked through the shabby lobby. Did she have the nerve to suggest to Mitch that he remove his pants in her presence? A tingle of anticipation darted up her spine, and she grimaced.

There had to be another way.

But how?

Short of rifling through his belongings, she had no other way to prove he was lying.

Steeling herself as she climbed the stairs, she decided she'd give herself two and a half days and if, in that time, she wasn't able to know without a doubt that Mitch Russell was just an alias for Devlin McVey—she'd have to find a way to see that damned birthmark.

Sighing, she unlocked the door of her hotel room and dropped her beach bag on the floor. She didn't much care for her plan, but then, she didn't have much choice. Like it or not, she was running out of time.

Of course, she could further the deception and pretend to fall in love with him. Considering how charged the air was whenever they were together, and the explosion of passion that ignited whenever they touched, it wouldn't be too hard to act as if she were caught up in making love to him and then stopping suddenly when he'd bared himself so she could view his naked hip.

That thought turned her stomach. She wasn't used to trickery and there was the distinct chance that her plan could backfire. She had only to think of this very afternoon and how her emotions had nearly gotten the better of her. What if it was she, not he, who was lost in passion?

She'd nearly made love to him on the cliff overlooking the sea. Her face burned as she flopped back on her hotel room bed and stared at the ceiling.

Well, there was a chance she'd see him in a swim suit—something revealing enough that the birthmark would show. She smiled to herself. That was it! She'd ask him to go swimming with her.

"This is for John," she told herself firmly, deciding that if all else failed, she had no recourse but to pretend to fall in love with Mitch to prove that he was Devlin. There was only one way. She had to see his bare hip.

THE NEXT MORNING, after a night of fitful sleep, her conscience still nagged at her.

A headache was pounding behind her eyes when Chelsea met Terri on the beach near the hotel and tried to sunbathe. While soaking up the sun's rays, Chelsea explained everything to Terri, including how Devlin supposedly disappeared and why she'd come to Paradis. She ended by telling Terri how little progress she'd made.

"Sounds like you should have kept that investigator hired on," Terri said, slathering sunscreen on her belly and thighs. She smiled to herself and adjusted her green two-piece suit. "Why would Devlin—if that's who you really think he is—try to hide way down here in the middle of nowhere?"

"I wish I knew," Chelsea replied, squinting against the sun. Sitting upright, she wrapped her arms around her knees and dug her toes into the warm sand.

"Is there a reason he'd want to avoid you?"

"Not that I know of."

"Maybe he feels guilty for—what was his name—Joe's death?"

"John's," Chelsea corrected automatically. Some of the pain of losing John had eased over the past few months and lately, since meeting Mitch, John's image had faded. But Devlin hadn't. In fact, just being around Mitch made memories of Devlin swim dangerously close to the surface of her mind.

"Tell me about your friend," Terri suggested. She fiddled with the beach umbrella to shade her face, but let her long legs stretch into the white sand. "This Devlin. Why're you so interested?"

"I thought I already explained—"

Terri waved impatiently, then dug into her cooler for a can of soda. She offered cherry cola to Chelsea. "I know what you said, and maybe that's what you believe, but, if you ask me, you're not being honest with yourself. Devlin must be much more important than just your fiancé's best friend for you to come traipsing all the way down here, accuse a man with a different name of running away, and never let up." She popped the lid on her can of orange soda. "Tell me the truth, what do you really feel for Devlin?"

"Friendship," she said automatically, then sighed and blew her bangs from her eyes. "Well, it really was kind of a love-hate relationship."

"Love?" Terri asked, her eyebrows lifting over the rims of her sunglasses.

"Not the way you mean."

"Sexual attraction, then?"

What was the point of lying? She'd been kidding herself for nearly a year and a half. "Devlin was the kind of man I always avoided—you know the type."

"Tall, dark and handsome?"

"To begin with. He seemed kind of dangerous and unapproachable. He had a rough edge to him that made me uncomfortable and he was a cop, a detective, like my dad."

"And that was a problem?"

"The problem was that I'd planned to marry John, have a family, a house in the suburbs, a station wagon with wood trim on the side, you know, the whole bit."

"You?" Terri hooted. "Who were you kidding?"

Chelsea bristled a little. "What do you mean?"

Shaking her red hair, Terri wagged a finger at Chelsea. "You're the least likely candidate for P.T.A. president I've ever seen. Oh, sure, you probably want marriage and a family someday, but you've got too much sense of adventure to tie yourself down to an accountant."

"John was an architect."

"Doesn't matter. Unless I miss my guess, you're not cut out for the wife-of-the-executive routine." She shoved her sunglasses onto her crown.

"Why not?"

"Because you're here, that's why. How many women do you know who own their own business and fly off on some whim—some tropical adventure—to meet a mystery man who's supposedly been running away from her and the dark secret of his past?"

"You've seen too many movies," Chelsea retorted, but

sipped her too-sweet cola slowly, wondering why everyone, Felicia, now Terri, even Mitch himself, had accused her of being somehow destined to be with Devlin.

"Don't forget, I was married," Terri reminded her. "I know the difference between caring for someone and grand passion."

Chelsea lifted her brows.

"My husband cared for me—he really did. But I wasn't the—great passion of his life. That was reserved for his secretary."

"Oh. I'm sorry."

"Don't be. I'm not," she said with a trace of bitterness. "I'm still looking for my own grand passion and so are you." Terri drained her drink, then put both empty cans back into her cooler. "And if it does turn out that Devlin McVey is dead, you shouldn't give up on Mitch Russell."

"Meaning?"

"Meaning that he's a man who could set a woman's blood on fire."

Chelsea laughed. "Is there such a thing?"

"Absolutely!" Terri grinned. "And let me tell you, when I find a guy who does that for me, I'm going to sink my hooks into him and never let go!"

Chelsea chuckled as she drew a circle in the sand and thought about Mitch. "You know, I saw him yesterday, with a couple of men and a woman."

"Mmm."

"A beautiful woman," Chelsea corrected.

"Jealous?"

"No! Well, it did bother me."

"Aha! I knew it!"

"I just wondered if you knew her."

"What's her name?"

"I don't know, but she was gorgeous." Chelsea went

on to describe the woman's attributes, remembering her black hair and dark, laughing eyes.

"She could be anyone," Terri said frowning. "But I haven't heard of Mitch being linked romantically with anyone special. I've seen him with a couple of women— like I said, no one special—and I might have even seen him with this one. I really don't remember. But I wouldn't worry too much about the competition."

"It isn't a competition."

"Sure." Terri glanced at her watch and let out a groan. "I'm late! I've got to be at the store in less than half an hour!" Gathering up her things quickly, she added, "I promised to close the boutique this afternoon. I'll see you later!"

"Let me help."

"No reason, I've got everything." Hauling her cooler, umbrella and towel, she headed up the beach toward the Villa. Chelsea insisted on carrying Terri's beach bag and helped her load her equipment into her car.

Once Terri had taken off, Chelsea returned to her room. No messages. Frowning, she stopped at the mirror and checked her reflection. Her turquoise suit brought out the green in her eyes and her auburn hair fell to her shoulders in vibrant waves. Not that it mattered, she told herself. If Mitch found her attractive, fine. If he didn't— she couldn't worry about it. She was only here to prove that he was Devlin.

And what then?

Worried sea-green eyes stared back at her. If Mitch proved to be Devlin, then she would be faced with the fact that Devlin had run from her, from the accident, from his past. And she'd never dealt well with Devlin when he hadn't been hiding his true identity. How would she handle him now?

Would he tell her what she wanted to know? Or would he throw in her face the very fact that she'd been attracted to him from the first instant their gazes had collided?

And now that John was gone—no longer between them—what would happen? She stared at her reflection, and chewed on her lower lip. What did she expect of Devlin? That he would return to San Francisco with her? Clear up the mystery surrounding John's death? Or would he tell her to get lost, mind her own business, remind her that John's death was just an accident he couldn't face?

Her insides knotted and she leaned against the bureau under the mirror. "Oh, Devlin," she murmured, a thick lump knotting her throat as the reality of how much he'd meant to her surfaced. She had cared for him and not only as John's friend; no, despite all her arguments to the contrary, their relationship had run through much deeper, more turbulent emotional waters than pure friendship. Had she met him before John, she might have fallen for him. Now that John was gone…

And now there was Mitch—if, indeed, he truly was just a man who looked and sounded so much like Devlin that her senses were fooled. This man added a new dimension to an already difficult situation. Mitch was attractive—she couldn't deny it.

However, he was callous and cynical and sometimes bordered on being cruel. Yet there was a side to him that she'd seen only in fleeting glimmers, and she felt that his blatant sexuality, his bold innuendos had been meant to send her scurrying away from him, rather than draw her into his arms.

Mitch was dangerous and exciting and she hated herself for falling into his male trap, yet she couldn't stop herself.

Tossing on a cover-up and grabbing her snorkeling

gear, she decided she could wait no longer. She hurried downstairs and checked at the desk, hoping Mitch had called. The thin, bored-looking clerk assured her no one had asked for her.

It figured. She fumed all the way back to the beach.

So what had happened, didn't she still have a "deal" with Mitch? Had he conveniently forgotten that they'd made a pact? Or was his bargain just a ploy to get her out of his hair? Well, it wouldn't work.

Seething, she dropped her equipment near the water's edge. Damn the man, he wasn't going to get rid of her that easily!

Stripping out of her cover-up, she glanced northward, to the stretch of sand that dwindled to the rocks jetting into the sea. Beyond the point was Mitch's cabin. Maybe it was time to visit him again. They had struck a bargain and time was slipping by—much too quickly. She wasn't about to sit around and wait for him to call her—if and when he got around to it.

She grabbed snorkel, mask and fins, then walked across the wet sand to the tide, where the foamy surf tickled her toes. White pelicans squawked and swooped from the rocks nearby, and a double-masted replica of a nineteenth-century clipper ship, filled with tourists, glided across the blue-green water.

She stepped into her fins, adjusted her mask and snorkel, waded deep into the sea, then began to swim just below the surface of the water. Schools of fish in brilliant shades of yellow and orange darted through the coral reefs and hid in the tangles of seaweed rippling with the tide.

Trying to concentrate on the vibrant sea life, Chelsea swam northward, around the point, but she barely noticed the beauty of the shadowy depths. As had been the case since she'd first met him, she continued to think about Mitch.

She was attracted to him, though the man made her blood boil and sometimes tied her stomach in knots. Had her feelings for Devlin been more than she wanted to admit? Well, yes, considering her response to him when they'd been alone at the cabin in the Sierra Nevadas. Did Devlin care for her? Not at all. As for Mitch, he didn't seem very interested, either. Except that she represented just one more female conquest. He'd made it clear he'd only suffered her company because he thought she was coming on to him and he was willing to take her to bed.

The thought did strange things to her. She was offended, but intrigued. Making love to Mitch Russell had crossed her mind more than once, but she feared that the act itself could hardly come under the heading of "love," and just plain sex was out of the question. She was liberated, but not that liberated, and she hoped she never would be. And yet—isn't that exactly what she was planning—a quick seduction for the single purpose of seeing him naked?

But she wasn't planning to go through with it and the only reason she was considering it was for the sake of the truth, the sake of finding out what had happened on the day of John's death.

Sure. John would have approved.

She felt sick inside as she passed the northern point on the beach and swam inland.

Surfacing near the weathered dock, she tossed her hair away from her face and stripped off her face mask. Taking in huge gulps of air, she told herself she would never purposely try to seduce Mitch Russell—well, at least not yet. But, if she couldn't get him in a pair of revealing swim trunks, the time was fast approaching when she might have to pretend to fall in love with him. And then what?

Her heartbeat quickened, and she licked the salt water from her lips. Maybe her plan was too bold.

She climbed onto the dock, then wrung her hair with her hands. Goose bumps appeared on her skin where the sea water still trickled down her neck and arms as she stared at Mitch's cabin.

His Bronco, not so very different from Devlin's, was parked near the house and Chelsea felt her breath catch in her throat. She left her snorkeling gear on the weathered dock, then walked barefoot through the hot sand to the cabin nestled in the trees. The windows of the tiny house were open, the shades stirring in the breeze and as she climbed the steps of the front porch, Mitch's voice caught her attention.

"…you're sure?" he was saying. "Of course we'll be alone—"

Chelsea froze. Coming here had been a mistake. Her heart thudded against her ribs.

"—I'll take care of all the details. But let's meet somewhere else. Someplace private. Away from the island. So that no one surprises us." His voice was so silky, so smooth.

Her skin crawled. She started edging toward the steps. Better to leave now, before Mitch and his raven-haired mistress discovered her eavesdropping. She'd stepped onto the sand when she heard the distinctive sound of a telephone receiver being slammed back into its cradle.

So he'd been on the phone, setting up a tryst with a woman. She had taken two steps when his voice arrested her.

"Was I mistaken or did we have a bargain?" Mitch demanded.

Chelsea turned quickly, nearly stumbling, and when his eyes clashed with hers, she saw him take in a swift, short breath. His gaze raked her body and his lips tightened almost imperceptibly as he apparently noticed the swell of her breasts and nip of her waist beneath the taut, wet fabric of her suit. Was it her imagination or did she notice more than simple male appreciation in his eyes?

Standing in the doorway, his shirt open, his hands stuffed into the pockets of a pair of tan slacks, he glared at her. To her horror, she found him amazingly handsome.

"I got tired of waiting," she responded, angling her chin upward against his height advantage. "And we're running out of time."

"I thought I told you I didn't want to be spied upon."

"And I thought you told me we had three days together."

"We do."

"It's afternoon. The first day is slipping by. I didn't want to waste any time."

One dark brow cocked insolently. "Some of us have to work for a living. Remember?"

"I thought writers had flexible hours."

"I work better under a schedule."

She gathered in her breath. "I thought you could use a break. Maybe we could go swimming. You could show me some of the sights," she said, hoping to sound innocent. "I brought my gear." She waved toward the dock where her equipment lay.

Mitch eyed her for a minute. Rubbing his beard, he lifted a shoulder. "Well, since you're already here, I guess I can take the rest of the day off."

This was an unexpected surprise. Her heart skyrocketed. "Good."

"I'll be just a minute." He stepped back into the house

and Chelsea decided to follow him inside. She saw him duck into a back bedroom and she peeked around the corner. The room was sparse—decorated with a single chair, desk and computer. He punched a few keys, snapped disks from the drive and flipped the machine off. The glowing terminal went blank.

"How's it coming?" she asked.

"What?"

"Your story—whatever it is." She motioned toward the cluttered desk, where reference books, notes, magazines and two empty coffee cups were strewn.

"At least you had the presence of mind not to call it the 'Great American Novel.'"

"Isn't it?"

He grinned and his teeth flashed beneath his beard. "That remains to be seen. Okay—" He shepherded her outside. "Give me a minute to change."

"Take all the time you need," she said, relieved.

He was gone less than five minutes. When he reappeared, he was wearing a pair of khaki-colored shorts that reached his upper thigh, and a windbreaker.

"I thought we were going swimming," she said, disappointed. Now what?

He smiled devilishly. "I've got a better idea."

"Do you?"

"Hmm. But let's get one thing straight," he said. "No more questions, okay?"

"No questions? Then how're we going to get to know each other?"

He cast her a hard glance. "Believe me, Chelsea, when you find out my life history, you'll be bored to tears."

"I doubt it."

"Don't. I'm not mysterious, intriguing, or even interesting."

That's where you're wrong, Mitch Russell, she thought, but held her tongue as she half ran to keep up with him as he strode toward the sea.

"My story's been told a thousand times. I grew up in the midwest, played on the high-school basketball team, got a small scholarship, went to college, got married, and graduated with a degree in journalism. In a few years, I worked at a couple of different papers and then everything went to hell in a handcart."

"Meaning the accident," she said as they walked across the hot sand to the dock where her snorkeling equipment lay unattended.

"Right. The accident." His eyes darkened and he leaned over to untie the lashings that kept the small sailboat, the *Mirage,* moored to the pier. Glancing up at her, he smiled and Chelsea warmed from the inside out. "Come on, let's try out your sea legs. Ever been sailing before?"

She climbed into the small boat. "You know I have."

"How?" He shoved off, then glanced over his shoulder.

Because you were there, damn it! On your boat in the bay! "The pictures I showed you, remember?"

"Oh, right, your fiancé had a boat."

"The sailboat belonged to Devlin."

His lips compressed as he adjusted the boom, then guided the small craft through the clear water. "I'd forgotten. Seems as if McVey had everything. What was it you saw in his friend? Was he rich?"

"John? No. He did well enough, but he wasn't wealthy."

"So it wasn't money, and it wasn't passion—"

"I didn't say that," she cut in.

He slid her a knowing glance. "Then why do I have

the feeling that you were more interested in his friend than your intended?"

"Because you're bullheaded," she said quickly, then regretted it, when he grinned at her. "John was kind and considerate and intelligent and…and he loved me."

"Sounds like you were planning to marry your best friend."

"Something wrong with that?"

"You wouldn't have been satisfied."

"How do you know?" she shot back. "You don't know anything about me." Or did he?

"I've met your kind before."

"Give me a break."

"You like a challenge, Chelsea, and a little adventure." Mitch studied the horizon, the lines near the corners of his eyes deepening as he steered through the very coral reefs she'd swum through less than an hour before. He slipped a pair of mirrored glasses onto his nose and his black hair ruffled in the wind.

The prow of the boat sliced through the water and the mainsail billowed in the wind that kicked in off the tide. White clouds had gathered overhead, blocking some of the sun's heat as they slowly shifted across the sky. The smell of salt and sea mingled together, filling Chelsea's senses.

She didn't want to think that he might be right, that John wouldn't have created in her that same rush of adrenaline that Devlin had induced. But that very rush was exactly what she'd been trying to avoid. She didn't need a man who was explosive and unpredictable—she wanted a safe and sane man—a man who would give her security and laughter, warm smiles and encouragement, not some rake who could set her blood afire, then move along to the next conquest.

Frowning, she wondered at Mitch's words, so like Devlin's. "Let's not play games, Chelsea, you're marrying the wrong man. You and I both know you're marrying the wrong man," Devlin had insisted, and though she'd denied it then and still rejected his accusation even now, there had been a ring of truth to his words, she thought ruefully.

And Mitch felt the same way. Coincidence? Unlikely. Oh, what she wouldn't do to see him without his beard. And without his pants? her mind teased cruelly, causing her to blush.

"Where to?" he asked, as they rounded the point and cut south along the edge of the island. The beach where she'd sunbathed earlier was visible as was the rambling hotel.

"You're the skipper."

"Be careful, I might shanghai you."

She crooked a disbelieving brow. "And take me where?"

Amusement flickered in his sky-blue eyes. "That would ruin the surprise, wouldn't it?" He started to turn the craft into the wind, but Chelsea stopped him.

"Before we go anywhere, I think I should change."

He flicked a glance down her body. "You look fine to me. And you're the one who showed up like that."

"But we're so close to the hotel. Really, it would only take a minute." Since they weren't going swimming, she had to switch gears and now that she'd finally gotten his attention, she didn't want to lose it and by changing into something warmer, she could spend the rest of the afternoon and evening with him, watching him, looking for little idiosyncrasies that would convince her he really was Devlin.

With a shrug, Mitch headed the boat inland and in a

few minutes, docked the *Mirage* against the pilings near the hotel.

Chelsea climbed out of the boat and grabbed her snorkel, fins and mask. "I'll only be a little while," she said as they plowed through the sand to the back side of the Villa.

"You don't want me to come up to your room?"

She caught the glint in his eye. "No more than I did the first night you suggested it," she said, though she knew she was missing out on a chance. If she could get him into the room, pretend to seduce him—all the while waiting to catch a view of his hip… And then what? Lead him into the bathroom for a cold shower?

No, the hotel room was much too obvious. The only reason she would take him upstairs would be to sleep with him—he wouldn't misconstrue her intentions and she needed a place that seemed more spontaneous so that when she backed out at the last minute, he wouldn't suspect he'd been set up.

She didn't much like the turn of her thoughts as she scurried up the stairs. This new, devious side of her nature bothered her, but she shoved her own recriminations aside. If Mitch were actually Devlin, then he deserved every bit of her deception and if he wasn't Devlin, then he needed a lesson in manners. From the first minute she'd spied him, he'd been inconsiderate, rude and irritatingly arrogant.

She stripped off her suit, showered and changed into a denim skirt and white blouse with wide sleeves that she rolled to her elbows. Adding a trace of makeup and a set of silvery bracelets, she slipped into sandals and hurried downstairs.

He was waiting in the bar—the very bar where she'd first made a fool of herself by running up to him and expecting Devlin McVey to wrap his arms around her and tell her how good it was to see her again.

She felt more than one cautious stare sent her way by a few of the regulars, but she didn't meet the interested eyes that followed her. Mitch grinned when he saw her, left some bills on the bar and ignored the rest of his beer.

"You didn't bring an overnight bag," he said.

Her heart began to drum. "Will I need one?"

"That's up to you."

"Are you propositioning me, Mr. Russell?"

"Take it anyway you like." His fingers wrapped around the crook of her elbow and he propelled her through French doors that led to a flagstone patio. A few round tables were positioned near the old wrought-iron railing, but Mitch passed them and headed through a rusty gate.

"Where're we going?"

"Didn't I say you'd be shanghaied?" he asked, his touch heating her skin and sending ripples of that very same heat up her arm and through her body.

"But you were kidding—"

"Was I?" His lips twisted beneath his beard and his eyes glinted appreciatively.

Chelsea had second thoughts. Despite her earlier plan that she would try and seduce him, at least until a point, she felt as if she were suddenly walking on very thin ice. Mitch was taking control of the situation.

"Why don't we just stay at the Villa? I could buy you dinner."

He barked out a laugh at that. "Always the liberated female."

They crossed the sand and Mitch propelled her along the dock, toward the *Mirage*. "I thought we'd go somewhere more private."

Chelsea started to panic. This wasn't how it was sup-posed to happen. "Where?"

"Come on, Chelsea. Where's your sense of adven-ture?" he mocked, teasing and irritating her all at once.

"I'm not the kind of woman who likes to be rough-handled by a man and ordered around."

"No one's rough-handling you. And face it, you *are* the kind who likes a challenge, and a fight, and you enjoy a bit of a mystery—a little intrigue. In fact, unless I miss my guess," he added, untying the lashings, "you love to be surprised."

"I like to be in control."

"So do I," he said, helping her into the boat, his gaze locking with hers for a throbbing instant. Chelsea's mouth turned to cotton and she thought he might kiss her again. Unconsciously, she licked her lips.

Mitch caught the sensual movement and his back teeth ground together. His brow became more furrowed and he forced his attention to the sailboat, guiding the small craft through the shimmering waters toward the open sea.

Though she was loathe to admit it, Chelsea decided Mitch Russell was right about her. She did like a chal-lenge and, despite her fears, enjoyed the adventure of it all. Felicia would call it her personality flaw and right now, alone with Mitch, Chelsea was in no position to argue.

Spray, cast up from the prow slicing through the water, clung to her face and hair, bringing with it the scent of fish and brine.

She dragged her fingers through the water and won-dered where he was taking her. Trepidation skittered up her spine, but didn't account for the breathless feeling that kept her senses alive. True, she didn't know him all that well, and yet she trusted him, at least a little.

The sailboat rounded the southern tip of the island and he dropped anchor, letting the *Mirage* undulate on the sea. Paradis loomed in the distance, dark and green against a lowering sun. Fiery shades of magenta and gold washed over the sky.

"How about dinner?" he asked.

"Here?" She grinned. "What're we going to do— fish?"

He laughed. "And risk the chance of starving? I don't think so. Wait just a minute." He opened a small hold and withdrew a bottle of wine and a couple of white sacks. To her amazement, he spread a blanket between them and placed cartons of pasta salad, marinated shrimp, sliced cheese and crusty bread and two clear, stemmed glasses, on the makeshift table.

"Where'd you get all this?"

"At the hotel—while you were changing," he said with a crooked grin. "I hauled it back to the boat, then returned to the bar."

"It didn't take me *that* long."

Jaw sliding to the side, he found a wine cork and opened the bottle. "It took long enough." He poured them each a glass, offered her one and, clinking the rim of his glass to hers, said, "Salute!"

Chelsea felt her face drain of color. Her glass trembled in her fingers. "You remember," she accused, her throat dry.

He glanced up at her. "Remember what? Is something wrong?"

"The first night we met—the toast—"

"The first night we met you were drinking alone in the bar waiting for—"

"No!" She couldn't be wrong. Her eyes searched the clouded depths of his. "When I met you at John's apartment. He was making dinner and he toasted you—by saying 'Salute!'"

Mitch's mouth turned down. "I thought we weren't going to bring up all this again."

"But you said—"

"It was a coincidence, Chelsea! Nothing more!" His eyes snapped fire and he shoved a hand through his hair in frustration. "I'm sure I say a lot of things—and do a lot of things—that your friend did. But you can't keep looking for farfetched links to your past!"

Quaking inside, Chelsea took a sip of her wine. The cool Riesling slid down her throat, but she barely tasted it.

"Come on," Mitch invited, his voice softer. "Let's eat."

He offered her a paper plate and though her mind was far from food, she managed to serve herself as the boat slowly rocked with the movement of the sea. Don't give up, she told herself, but found she was torn. This new man, Mitch Russell, was free of all the pain of the past. He wouldn't know how Devlin had mortified her, how he'd proved that she was as susceptible to his charms as the next woman. Mitch was taking her at face value— even though he thought she was more than a little obsessed with her past.

She relaxed as the sunset turned to dusk and she even began to taste the food that he'd been thoughtful enough to bring with him. There was more to Mitch Russell than his gruff exterior, she realized, and smiled at the thought. He was handsome and intelligent, if quick to anger.

Stars began to appear as the sky turned from rose to lavender to deepest purple. Chelsea leaned back against a soft cushion while sipping her second glass of wine.

Had circumstances been different, she thought, watching as Mitch moved easily about the small boat, adjusting the sails and raising anchor, she could fall for a man like him.

The thought struck her like a thunderbolt. She didn't know anything about Mitch, except that his temper was all too quick to flare and his attitude toward women, if she could judge by the way he treated her, was the worst! What had she been thinking? Mitch Russell was as diametrically opposed to John Stern as he could be. But not so different from Devlin, her mind nagged.

"Ooh!" Angry with herself, she decided she'd had too much wine and quickly dumped the remainder in her glass into the ocean.

"Something wrong?" Mitch asked as he turned the craft back to the island and the winking lights of Emeraude.

"Nothing," she snapped.

He chuckled to himself, and that was all the more infuriating! Damn the man—how was he able to get under her skin so easily? From the corner of her eye, she could see the pull of his pants against his buttocks and the stretch of his shirt across his shoulders as he worked with the boom, but she kept her gaze fixed on their destination, the poorly lit beach near the Villa.

Once he moored the craft, she hopped out quickly, ignoring the hand he offered.

"Was it something I said?" he asked, his voice mocking as they walked along the path to the hotel.

"What?"

"Something's bothering you. What is it?" he asked, once they were near the hotel again.

"I'm just having a tough time accepting the fact that

you're not Devlin," she admitted, knowing she was skirting the real issue.

"Why?" he asked suddenly, his voice as smooth as velvet.

"Because I miss him." She gazed upward to his night-darkened eyes and caught him staring at her. Her throat grew thick with emotion at her admission. How long had she denied that she'd missed Devlin, even cared for him? She'd pretended that she was down here only on a mission to find out what happened to John, but there was more to it. Oh, God, what she wouldn't do to know for certain that Devlin was alive.

Mitch's arms wrapped around her waist, drawing her quickly to him and his lips crashed down on hers so swiftly she could barely take a breath.

Warm, wondrous feelings shot through her, and though she knew she should struggle and break the embrace, she couldn't. His lips were magical, the splay of his hands thrillingly possessive. His tongue pressed hard against her teeth, demanding entrance. She could do little but part her lips and tremble when his plundering tongue darted in and out of her mouth, tasting and caressing, titillating and creating sensations of warmth and desire that rippled through her body. Her heart thundered and she pressed tightly to him, her breasts flatted against the hard wall of his chest.

"Oh, God," he groaned, shifting so that his thighs molded to hers.

She kissed him back, twining her arms around his neck and twisting his hair between her fingers. His beard was rough against her face, but she barely noticed as desire swept through her. A soft moan escaped from her lips and he answered, pulling her closer still until she could feel that he wanted her as desperately as she wanted him.

"Stop it," he growled. As suddenly as he'd grabbed her, he let her go, stepping away and breathing in short, shallow breaths.

She nearly stumbled backward. Was this another of his damned tests—to prove that he could send her heart racing—to demonstrate how he could dominate her senses and bring her down to the purely primal nature of woman? She gazed into his eyes and saw more than raw sensuality in the stormy blue depths—there was wonder and confusion, anger and despair. "Stop it?" she repeated, hurt.

"I wasn't talking to you!" he muttered.

"But—"

"I was telling myself to let go of you while I still could!" He made a sound of self-deprecation and he shoved the heels of his hands against his eyes—just as Devlin had years ago at the cabin near Lake Tahoe.

Chelsea couldn't speak, could only stare at his bunched shoulders and inside she was sure, sure he had to be Devlin.

"I won't be used, Chelsea," he said, his voice raw with emotion. "You can't pretend I'm someone else!"

"But I didn't—"

"Yes, you did!" Drawing in a long, whistling breath, he turned and faced her, frowning darkly, and gave her one last piece of advice. In a voice that was rough and low, he whispered, "If you want anything more to do with me, lady, you'll have to forget Devlin McVey."

CHAPTER EIGHT

CHELSEA NEARLY STUMBLED up the faded hotel stairs. Good lord, what had she gotten herself into? Was she falling in love with Mitch—or Devlin—or both men? She stopped on the first floor and took in a long, bracing breath.

What about John? She was beginning to wonder if she ever had really loved him. Her heart wrenched at the thought and she hated Mitch for planting the seeds of doubt in her mind. Or had it been Devlin who had started her second-guessing herself? Had Devlin been right all along when he'd accused her of planning to marry the wrong man?

Stomach so tight it hurt, she climbed the second flight of stairs and considered her plan to seduce Mitch. She snorted at her own naïveté. Yes, she'd intended to pretend to fall in love with Mitch, but now she wondered if an act were necessary. In less than a week, she really had begun to fall for him.

She unlocked the door to her room and stepped into her shabby haven away from the emotional turmoil of dealing with Mitch Russell. Sighing in disgust, she flung herself onto the bed and stared at the ceiling. Ever since dating John, she'd known what she wanted in life. She wanted a business of her own, a husband, two children and a nice house. She wanted security and safety and a nice little world that was so predictable it might border on boring.

Until now. Well, no—she had to be honest with herself—Devlin had made her question her values, and yet she'd ignored him. But now, with Mitch, her entire world was spinning out of control—all the things she'd wanted in life—in fact, the very reasons she'd come to Paradis, seemed to mock her.

Furious with herself, she peeled off her skirt and started on her blouse when she noticed the red light flashing on her phone. She wanted to ignore the message, because she wasn't in the mood for one of Felicia's lectures.

Unfortunately, she had to take the call. What if something were wrong? What if their mother were ill? What if there were serious problems at the boutique in San Francisco?

Reluctantly, she dialed the front desk and was told that Ned Jenkins had called her. Her heart started to pump crazily as she scribbled down the private detective's number in San Francisco. What could he possibly want?

She dialed the number, heard the long-distance connection crackle through, then impatiently drummed her fingers as she waited for Ned to pick up. On the fourth ring, his answering machine clicked on and a recorded message asked her to leave her name and number.

"Ned, this is Chelsea Reed. I'm at the Villa on Paradis and the number is—"

"Chelsea!" Ned picked up the phone, his voice battling with the poor connection. He sounded relieved. "God, I'm glad you called. I thought I'd better give you the latest on Devlin McVey."

Chelsea's heart stopped beating and she felt the color wash from her face. Please, God, don't let him tell me that Devlin's body was finally found! "What is it?" she asked quietly, bracing herself for the worst. Oh, Lord, what would she do if Devlin were truly dead? The future seemed suddenly empty and dark....

"I talked with a friend of mine at the police department—the guy worked with Devlin for a while—anyway, I finally managed to get him to open up a little. He wouldn't say much, of course, but the scuttlebutt is that McVey was on the take."

"What?" she cried, disbelieving.

"You heard me. Not everyone in the department goes along with the theory, of course, but he was working on some big drug case at the time of his supposed death. Some of the guys at headquarters think McVey faked his death because someone had figured out that he was working for the other side."

"That's crazy!" Chelsea whispered hoarsely.

"I'm just repeating what my friend said. He claims that McVey was going to be up on charges—or at the very least, investigated by internal affairs. If he's alive, he'll still face criminal proceedings."

"I don't believe it!" Chelsea's fingers held the receiver in a death grip. "Your 'friend' is spreading rumors! Filthy, vile gossip. That's all this is!"

"No way. I had to pry this information out of him. He didn't want to talk. As I said, he worked with McVey and kind of liked him—well, at least respected him, if not his methods. He confided to me that McVey used some very unorthodox procedures while he was working for the department."

Chelsea sank onto the bed. "This is just gossip, Ned, that's all."

"Maybe so. But when McVey disappeared, he did have several debts that hadn't been paid—a bill for nursing care for his mother before she died, another for his car, and a sizeable contract on that houseboat he lived on."

"Just because he owed some money is no reason to think he'd do anything illegal!" she snapped, instantly defending the very man who had once put her on the defensive.

"I know, I know, but I'm just telling you the facts."

"You're insinuating that Devlin killed his best friend on purpose!" she hissed, disgust roiling in her stomach. Devlin might have been ruthless, even slightly unscrupulous where she was concerned, but he'd been a staunch defender of the law and a loyal friend to John. He would never hurt John. Never. What Ned Jenkins was peddling was an outrageous lie!

"No, I don't think McVey planned anything. I think the accident occurred and McVey made the most of it. He wouldn't kill Stern—the police don't even think that— but he might have found a way to get out of his problems, the very problems he was going to talk to your fiancé about on that boat."

Chelsea was trembling. John *had* mentioned that Devlin wanted to discuss something with him—something private. Chelsea had assumed it had something to do with one of his women, though she had worried that he might finally tell John about the night in the cabin and how Chelsea had all too willingly kissed him and nearly fell victim to her unbridled passion. But this…this bizarre tale that Devlin, in desperation, had turned against the law? No way!

"Look," Jenkins was saying. "I just thought you should know what's going on up here."

Chelsea's hands began to sweat. Had she inadvertently brought serious trouble to Devlin by insisting he had to be found? "Did you tell your friend that you'd located Devlin?"

"Nope."

Relief stole through her. "Why not?"

"You're my client. I'm working for you. I figure the police department has enough men on the payroll. If they want to find McVey, they can spend their own time, money and men on the job."

Thank God for Jenkins's perverse code of honor. "Thank you."

"So—you talked to Russell yet?" he inquired.

"Just about every day."

"And he claims that he's not McVey, right? Acts like you're a fruitcake?"

"That's pretty much it."

"Well, be careful. If my sources are right and McVey was a bad cop, he won't appreciate you stirring up any trouble."

"Devlin would never hurt me!"

"If you say so, but desperate men do desperate things. Just take care of yourself, okay?"

"I will," Chelsea promised, staring through the open window of her hotel room as she hung up the phone. Hot injustice swept through her blood. Devlin—a good cop gone bad? Never! Ever since college, he'd been on the right side of the law! Or had he? She'd only heard the story from John and John had definitely been prejudiced where Devlin was concerned. But on the take? Working with drug dealers? Devlin? Not in a million years!

She closed her mind to Jenkins's call. Obviously the police department needed a reason to explain Devlin's disappearance and they'd come up with this ludicrous story about him turning bad. It made her nauseous.

Devlin had been many things—arrogant, cynical, almost cruel when he felt he had to be—but he would never turn criminal, no matter how desperate his money situation had been. In fact, if he'd wanted to talk to John about his problems on the day of the accident, his reasons had probably been to borrow money. After all, John had been well off, and he would have been more than willing to help out his friend.

But Devlin would never have asked for John's help. His pride would have stopped him. So what had been the topic of conversation on that fateful journey into the bay?

If not money, had Devlin intended to tell John that his fiancée had nearly made love to him at Lake Tahoe? Even now, Chelsea felt the heat of a guilty flush climb up her neck.

Tired of the horrid questions that kept circling through her mind, Chelsea stripped off the rest of her clothes and climbed into bed. She picked up a paperback she'd bought in the airport, but her mind kept returning to Devlin and Mitch.

Who was the woman Mitch was planning to meet? And if he had a lover already, why did he kiss Chelsea as if there was a consuming passion between them that couldn't be ignored?

What was going on in San Francisco? Were the police looking for Devlin now? Would they follow her and track him to Paradis?

Sighing angrily, she tossed her book aside. Her emotions were a tangled mess of yesterday and today, the past, the present and the future. Three men kept invading her mind—confusing her and making her doubt everything she'd once considered so very real.

Yes, John had been safe and secure. And though her love for him hadn't been passionate, she'd cared for him very deeply. But not in the same way she was beginning to care for Mitch, the way she'd secretly cared for Devlin.

Both Mitch and Devlin were explosive, passionate

men who bent the rules and did as they pleased. Could there be two men so alike and yet so different?

A headache began to pound behind her eyes. She snapped off the light. Somehow, she had to find out.

THE NEXT DAY, SHE SPENT the morning waiting for Mitch to call. He didn't. She had half a mind to ring him up, but before she dialed the phone, she heard a brisk knock on her door. "Chelsea—are you in there?"

She groaned inwardly when she recognized Emily Vaughn's voice.

"Just a minute!" She hurried to the door and found Emily and Jeff waiting in the hallway.

"We're on our way to St. Jean," Emily said with a bright smile. "Thought you might like to tag along."

Chelsea racked her brain for an excuse to stay here... and do what—wait for the phone to ring?

"We'll only be gone a few hours—back by nightfall," Emily prattled on and Jeff just shrugged. "It'll do you a world of good."

"Do I need one?"

"Everyone does, hon. Now, come along. I hear there are some simply magnificent gardens to explore. Isn't that right, dear?" she added automatically to Jeff.

Gardens were the last thing on her mind, but Chelsea could think of no reason to stay chained to the phone. As for Mitch's deal of three days, he'd obviously had a change of heart. Besides, this was her chance to look around Lagune and some of the smaller villages on St. Jean. This might also be her chance to discover where Mitch went on his regular visits to the larger island. There was even a chance, though a long shot, that she might just spy Mr. Russell in Lagune and find out firsthand what he found so fascinating on St. Jean.

"Okay," she said to Emily, "you can stop twisting my arm. Just let me get my bag."

She grabbed her straw beach bag, a hat and her favorite white jacket, then locked the door behind her as they headed downstairs.

In the lobby, she ran into Chris Landeen. He seemed surprised to see her, but grinned. "Going out?" he asked.

"We're taking the grand tour to St. Jean," Emily replied, her eyebrows rising slightly.

"Are you?" Chris said. "You know, I was thinking of going there myself!"

"You could join us," Emily said. "I'm Emily Vaughn, this is my husband, Jeff, and you obviously already know Chelsea…"

Chelsea wanted to die as Chris introduced himself. The last thing she needed was for Emily to play matchmaker!

"I've got a little business to take care of first," Chris said, "but maybe I'll catch up to you later!"

"We'll be looking for you!" Emily replied with a wave.

Chris winked at Chelsea. "If I don't see you in Lagune, I'll call you later."

"A nice man," Emily said as Chris strode away.

"I suppose."

"But not your Mr. Russell."

"Definitely not." Chelsea shook her head and followed Jeff outside.

A creaky old station-wagon-cum-hotel-bus took them into Emeraude and the driver dropped them off on the docks. They caught the *Anna Marie* to St. Jean and Chelsea couldn't contain the little shiver of excitement that accelerated the beat of her heart. There was a chance that Mitch was already on the larger island and if, by some fluke, she found him, she might have a better understanding of who he really was.

She gripped the rail of the boat and stared ahead, watching as the prow knifed cleanly through the blue-green water. The spray touched her cheeks and curled the hair at her nape and she actually smiled to herself.

Emily, true to nature, was chattering on about the history of the islands, specifically of pirates who had long ago been officers who had lost favor in the French Navy. Chelsea wasn't sure that all the stories were true, but she let the older woman spin her tales.

"And how're things going with you and your friend?" Emily finally asked, when she'd run out of pirate stories and the boat was nearing the harbor of Lagune. "Mr. Russell. Did you ever locate him again?"

"Mmm," she replied. She really didn't want to discuss Mitch.

"And?" Emily asked eagerly, tilting her tiny head upward like a little bird waiting for an expected morsel.

"And nothing." The boat's engines slowed as the captain guided the craft into the harbor. "He doesn't remember me."

Emily's mouth dropped open. *"Humph!"* she snorted indignantly. "Then you'd best find yourself another man!"

Chelsea grinned. "I'll tell him that. Next time I see him."

"Good, because if you don't, I will," Emily vowed and Jeff, long-suffering as usual, rolled his eyes. "Besides," she added, "there are other fish in the sea—that good-looking man we met in the lobby of the hotel, for one."

"Chris?"

"Yes. Nothing wrong with that one."

If only it were that simple, Chelsea thought, gazing toward their destination.

Lagune was a city in comparison with lazy little Emeraude. The streets bustled with traffic and tourists were jammed along the sidewalks. Palm trees offered shade from the sweltering sun and a few cafés with outdoor tables offered refreshment.

As they strolled along the side streets, Chelsea barely kept up with her end of the conversation. Through her sunglasses, she studied the crowd and the city, hoping for some clue as to why Mitch would come here so often. Was he bored with the sleepy pace of Paradis? And if so, why not move to the bigger island? Or was his damned privacy so valuable?

Frowning thoughtfully, Chelsea followed Emily's brisk pace as they hurried to a stop for a tour bus. She felt an odd sensation—as if she were being watched—but one look at the other tourists convinced her they were all strangers. No one was staring at her and no set of eyes was quickly averted.

"You're letting this cloak-and-dagger stuff go to your head," she admonished herself.

"Pardon?" Emily said, craning her neck back toward Chelsea as she boarded the bus.

"Nothing. Just talking to myself."

"Bad habit," Emily reproved with a kind smile. "One I've got myself." She climbed aboard the huge, slightly battered bus. Chelsea followed, feeling out of place as she slid into a seat near the rear. Cracking a window, she was rewarded with a huge whiff of diesel.

Emily and Jeff occupied the seat in front of her and while Emily chatted with the woman across the aisle from her, Chelsea stared out the window and wondered what her next move would be.

In a cloud of black smoke, the bus lumbered away from the curb and headed out of town. Chelsea barely noticed the passing countryside as she thought about Mitch. Where was he today? What was he doing? And how could she possibly pretend to fall in love with him in only a few days? Closing her eyes, she leaned back in her seat.

Emily jabbered incessantly all the way to the old Mediterranean-style villa that had been turned into a museum. Together with the rest of the tourists, Emily, Jeff and Chelsea wandered through cool, high-ceilinged rooms, their sandals scuffing against thick tile floors. The rooms were furnished with antiques and cooled by slow-moving paddle fans.

Outside, they threaded their way through a maze of showy gardens that terraced from the villa to the sea. Flowers in shades of scarlet, lavender and yellow offered splashes of vibrant color and added a sweet fragrance to the salty air.

"Isn't this place glorious!" Emily cried, clasping her hands as she stared at a terrace surrounded by lush greenery and vines that showed off heavy purple and pink blossoms.

The sensation came again—the eerie feeling that she was being observed.

"Absolutely," Chelsea replied, though she glanced over her shoulder, half expecting someone to be watching her. The idea was ludicrous, of course, and yet, she couldn't shake the nerve-racking feeling.

"You know this mansion was built by an infamous French pirate who held his mistresses captive here."

Chelsea giggled. Some of Emily's tales were so outrageous. "Doesn't look much like a prison to me."

Jeff chuckled and offered Chelsea a smile as they joined their tour group and returned to town.

At a bistro near the harbor, they ate an early dinner of

soft-shelled crab and rice in a spicy red sauce. The food and accompanying wine were delicious but filling, and Chelsea finally shoved her plate aside, though she'd consumed less than half her meal. "I can't swallow another bite."

"But we haven't ordered dessert or coffee yet!" Emily countered.

"You go ahead," Chelsea offered, sliding her chair back. "I'll be right back." She was walking through the crowded tables toward the restroom when she felt the weight of someone's gaze on her back. Whirling, she found herself staring at the tables she'd just passed, a crowded cluster of people eating and drinking, barely glancing in her direction.

"You're really losing it," she grumbled to herself, then she froze. Through the window, she spied the woman she'd seen Mitch with earlier. Her long black hair was streaming behind her as she stepped into a speedboat. Before Chelsea reached the door, the boat had pulled away from shore and was heading northeast. To Paradis? To Mitch?

Her heart wrenched at the thought and she wanted to kick herself. So what if Mitch and the woman were together? Chelsea certainly didn't have any claims to Mitch Russell. Nor did she have any claims to Devlin McVey.

Nonetheless the thought that she'd been spied upon made her skin crawl and she shivered. She hurried into the restroom and splashed water on her face. So the woman was watching her.

But why?

Was she on a mission from Mitch?

Angrily she brushed her hair and slapped on fresh lipstick, then returned to the table where Jeff and Emily were lingering over a half-eaten slice of key lime pie.

"About time you got back here. I'm afraid we've nearly killed this pie, though we did remember to get you a spoon," Emily chirped when Chelsea sat down. "Have a bite, the pie's simply divine."

Chelsea shook her head. "I really couldn't," she said. Not only was she stuffed, but her stomach was in tight little knots. Had the black-haired woman been following her today? She slipped her arms through the sleeves of her jacket, though the temperature in the room had to be over seventy.

"Are you all right?" Emily asked, her voice edged with concern.

"I just overate. I'll be fine," Chelsea lied.

A few minutes later, they left the restaurant and boarded the *Anna Marie.* Clouds had rolled in, turning the sky dark.

"Looks like it's going to storm," Emily said, eyeing the horizon, but Chelsea was only half listening. Her eyes were riveted to the far side of the boat where Chris Landeen had settled against the rail. As if feeling her eyes on him, he looked up, smiled and sketched out a wave.

Inexplicably, Chelsea's stomach tightened. Was it just coincidence that Chris and the black-haired woman had been in Lagune? She expected him to head in her direction, but he turned his attention back to a short, balding man and laughed at something he was saying.

Don't make more of it than there is, she told herself as she turned her eyes back to the sea.

The boat pulled out of the harbor and Chelsea sat with Emily and Jeff, anxious to get back to Paradis.

On the ride back to Emeraude, Chris sauntered over and leaned his elbows on the rail. He slid an appreciative glance her way. "How about dinner with me tomorrow night?" he asked.

"I'm not sure I can," she replied.

"Why not? Plans with your friend?"

Her fingers gripped the rail more tightly. "I'll have to check."

Chris frowned and patted the rail. "I can take a hint," he said and walked back to his seat.

"That wasn't smart," Emily told her later as the boat pulled into the harbor. "I wouldn't be too hasty turning that one down. Not unless you're involved with someone else."

Not yet, she thought uneasily, her mind returning, as it had for the past few days, to Mitch.

SHE DIDN'T SEE MITCH that night and he didn't call. By ten o'clock, Chelsea was mentally climbing the walls.

Mr. Russell certainly wasn't living up to his part of the bargain, she thought sourly, as she dialed Sally in San Francisco.

Her partner answered on the fourth ring and just the sound of Sally's voice brought a smile to Chelsea's face.

"Well, have you convinced Devlin to come home and tell all?" Sally asked.

"I'm not even sure he is Devlin," Chelsea confessed as she leaned against the headboard of the bed. She explained about her experiences on the island and Sally sighed dramatically. "There are some things he does—some mannerisms that are just like Devlin's, and he has the same style, he dresses the same, and yet... Oh, I don't know! One minute I think he's Devlin, the next I'm sure he's a different person entirely!"

"Well, don't expect me to feel sorry for you. You're in a tropical haven, sipping rum and coke or whatever it is they drink down there, and sunbathing, while I'm holding down the fort and slaving away."

They talked for nearly an hour. Sally explained that the boutique was low on inventory and high in sales. She stressed again the need to expand. Chelsea, for her part, told Sally about Terri and the Boutique Exotique.

"Don't you dare come back here with some wild animals to brighten this place up," she warned. "I'm not into getting bitten, scratched, clawed or mauled."

"Don't worry," Chelsea said with a laugh.

"The only beast I expect you to bring back is the infamous Mr. McVey."

If only it were that simple, Chelsea thought. They talked a little longer and finally hung up. She drew her knees beneath her chin and wrapped her arms around her calves and sighed loudly. How would she ever get close enough to Mitch to prove that he was Devlin McVey?

She still didn't have an answer when she threw back the covers and crawled between the sheets. Stretching, she frowned when she felt a piece of paper tucked beneath her pillow.

More annoyed than concerned, she withdrew the small piece of white paper and unfolded the creased note. In bold type, the short message read: LEAVE PARADIS.

She gasped and her gaze flew around the room. Who had planted the note? Fear shot through her. Her pulse raced wildly and she broke out in a cold sweat. Despite the fact that she'd locked the door, she walked through the room, looking under the bed, in the closet and shower, and checking the balcony before she felt herself calm a little.

"Don't panic," she told herself, but her fingers shook as she picked up the telephone receiver and punched out the number of the front desk. When the clerk answered, she said, "This is Chelsea Reed, room 243. Has anyone been asking for me?"

"Just a minute," the bored voice replied. "…no."

"There are no messages?"

"I'm sorry."

"And no one has asked to see me?"

"As I said, no one," he replied, his voice sounding more than a little irritated.

Chelsea considered complaining to the hotel security that someone had been in her room, but instead she drew on her courage and said, "Thank you." The clerk clicked off and she slowly replaced the receiver.

Leaving the warning could be Mitch's way of scaring her. She wouldn't put it past him after he'd pulled that stunt of dragging her into the house and snapping off the lights when she'd first shown up on his doorstep.

No, she decided, forcing herself to remain calm, she wouldn't let some little scrap of paper scare her off.

At least not yet.

But that night, she slept with the lights in her room burning brightly.

THE FOLLOWING MORNING DAWNED gloomy and hot. Gray, burgeoning clouds swarmed over the sea, and the air was heavy as it clung to Chelsea's skin. The restless ocean was the color of steel.

Mitch didn't call. Though she spent most of the day in and out of the hotel, he didn't leave a message. "Some three days this has turned out to be," she grumbled, infuriated that she was hanging by the telephone for a man to call. Disgusted with herself, she threw on the white dress she'd purchased from Terri, grabbed her beach bag and headed into town.

Obviously, Mitch had been buying time. He'd never intended to let her get to know him. Or was there something more to it? she wondered as she waited for a cab

near the entrance to the Villa. Ned Jenkins's call bothered her more than she wanted to admit. His insinuations
were ridiculous, of course. Devlin had always been on
the right side of the law. Though he'd bent more than his
share of rules, he wouldn't turn bad. No, something was
rotten at the San Francisco Police Department, but it had
never been Devlin McVey.

As for the note, it was tucked safely into the pocket of
her wallet and she'd forced it from her mind.

A dusty gray wagon pulled in front of the curb and
she climbed in, instructing a round-faced cabby to drive
her into Emeraude. She'd spend the day in town, go back
to the Dauphin Bleu if need be, to find out more about
Mitch Russell and try to discover who had been in her
room.

She remembered overhearing his telephone call and
her mind conjured up the beautiful raven-haired woman
with her bronze skin, full lips and flashing eyes. The
same woman she'd seen yesterday in Lagune. Had she
met with Mitch last night? Was he just stringing Chelsea
along until he could find a way to get rid of her?

"Oh, God," she whispered, resting her head against
the glass of the stifling cab.

"What's that?" the cabdriver asked. A portly black
man with an easy smile, he glanced at her in the rearview mirror.

"Nothing," she said automatically, then decided she
had nothing to lose at this point. "I was supposed to meet
a man today and he didn't show up." That was a bit of
a lie, but stretching the truth earned her a sympathetic
look in the mirror. "I don't suppose you know him? Mitch
Russell."

The driver shook his head. "Sorry."

"Nothing to be sorry for," Chelsea replied as the old wagon wound through the dense rain forest.

In town, she had a late lunch in a small bistro on the waterfront, then browsed through the craft shops and an art gallery before ending up at the Boutique Exotique.

The parrot whistled sharply as Chelsea entered.

Terri, who was balanced precariously on a ladder as she pinned lime green shorts and tangerine-colored tops to the wall over the register, glanced over her shoulder and grinned. "Well, look who's here. I hope you came with credit cards in hand." She shoved a final tack into the wall and with one appraising look at her work, climbed down. "How's this?" she asked, waving at her display.

"Bright."

"Good. It's supposed to be." Terri wiped her hands on her short red skirt. "So what're you doing in town?"

"Looking for company, I guess."

"Uh-oh, don't tell me, the elusive Mr. Russell has vanished again."

"How'd you know?"

Terri eyed her work and frowned. "Because I saw him leave this morning as I was opening up the shop."

"Leave?"

"Umm. I told you he leaves once or twice a week—at least I think it's that often. I don't really keep tabs on the man."

"He left in his boat?"

Terri shook her head. "No, it was a red speedboat, I think. I've seen it around before."

Chelsea's heart sank. She instinctively knew which craft he was on—and with whom. The same beautiful woman who'd stared at her through the restaurant window in St. Jean. "Was the name of the boat the *Lucia?*"

Terri thought for a minute. "I don't know—could've been. I didn't get a good look, and until I met you, I wasn't really paying that much attention to Mr. Russell and his friends."

"His friends?"

"Yeah. The men and woman I've seen him with a few times." She slid Chelsea a sympathetic glance. "If it's any consolation, I don't think they're lovers."

"I couldn't care less—" Chelsea began, but the look in Terri's eyes silenced her.

"Next you're going to tell me what he does with his love life is his business," Terri teased. "Ever since you landed on this island, you've been obsessed with the man, so don't tell me it doesn't matter whom he's seeing."

The parrot squawked loudly as two women entered the store. Terri said, "Just let me help these two and I'll be right back."

While Terri assisted a series of customers, Chelsea spent nearly an hour in the store and ended up buying a necklace, two pairs of shorts and a scarf. "You know I was just teasing when you came in and I told you I expected to see your credit card," Terri said with a grin as she rang up the sale.

"Everything in this bag—" Chelsea patted the plastic sack "—is an absolute must."

"If you say so." Three more women entered the shop and Terri rolled her eyes. "I bet I don't get out of here until midnight," she whispered.

"You love it, and you know it."

"Yeah, but I can think of better ways to spend my evening."

So could Chelsea, but she didn't want to dwell on the night stretching before her. As far as she could tell, she'd wasted another day learning nothing more about Mitch. "I'll see you on Wednesday," Terri promised. "That's my day off. Maybe we'll go over to St. Jean and poke around the beach."

"I'd like that," Chelsea replied, waving as she left the boutique.

Outside, the heat was oppressive, the air dense. Chelsea considered starting with the Dauphin Bleu and asking questions about Mitch. There were some other bars located along the waterfront but the thought of making small talk with strangers in a series of seedy watering holes turned her stomach.

The wind picked up and the sky darkened with the promise of the storm. She wandered along the docks and, as she stopped to swipe at the sweat that had collected on the back of her neck, she spied Mitch's sailboat lashed to the wharf.

"Looking for me?" a voice boomed behind her.

Her heart nearly stopped as she saw him, arms stretched over his head, shirt pulling out of his jeans and exposing a length of lean abdomen, as he worked on the sail. His gaze met hers.

"Now, why would I?" she asked, sauntering closer.

"Well, it could be my devastating personality…"

"Ha!"

"Or my looks."

She raised her brows skeptically.

"Or you could just be after my body."

"That's it," she teased back.

An amused smile touched his lips and she instantly bristled at the thought that he was mocking her as he hopped lithely onto the dock.

"We did have a deal," she reminded him.

"We still do." His eyes gleamed. "Don't tell me you've been waiting for me."

"Not a chance," she lied.

"Then what's the problem?"

Curse the man. "Oh, I don't know. The way I see it, three days constitutes seventy-two hours and in the past sixty-four, I've seen you maybe six or seven tops."

"You didn't specify—"

"Well, I'm specifying now! You promised me seventy-two hours. The way I figure it, you still owe me a minimum of sixty-six."

"So I am in demand," he teased.

"This is business."

"I'm crushed." But he was still taunting her. "Come on," he suggested, motioning her onto the *Mirage,* "since the meter's running, let's not waste any more time."

"Good idea."

"Hop in the boat."

She eyed the small craft and thought of the note left under her pillow. Suddenly she didn't feel quite so safe, but she stepped onto the sailboat anyway. "Where're we going?"

"Back to my place." He climbed aboard and unleashed the ropes securing the boat. "If you're lucky, I'll cook you dinner."

"If I'm lucky?" she repeated. "So you've been planning this all day?"

"Yep. I had some business that I had to take care of first, then I planned to pick you up." He eyed the horizon. "We'd better shove off before the storm breaks."

"A storm?" she said, her voice catching as she thought of John and Devlin and how their boat had splintered apart in the middle of San Francisco Bay.

As if he noticed the sudden morbid turn of her thoughts, he said, "It's nothing to worry about."

"You're sure?"

"Trust me."

Oh, God, could she? She bit her lower lip as they cast off. *Trust me.* Did she know him well enough? Did she know him at all? Or was she attracted to him because he was so much like Devlin? Her mouth turned dry as he moved so effortlessly on the slippery deck, so athletically. His narrow hips, long legs, wide shoulders, just like Devlin. The wind pushed at his white shirt, whipping it and tossing his black hair from his eyes. Oh, God, he seemed so much like Devlin. If only...

She forced her mind back to the present, to the roiling sea and earlier this afternoon when he'd been with the exotic, black-haired woman. With an effort she tried to keep the challenge from her voice as she asked, "What was your business this afternoon?"

He lifted a shoulder. "Just a little research for my book."

"And you had to leave the island?"

"That's right." Shoving a pair of aviator glasses onto his nose, he guided the *Mirage* through the choppy waters of the bay, past an inbound schooner and several fishing boats. "Why the third degree?" he asked, and Chelsea tried not to notice the sensual curve of his lips or the quirk of amusement touching the corners of his mouth.

"I'm just trying to get to know you."

"Or spying again," he guessed. "You found out I was with Bambi and you're jealous. Admit it."

"Bambi? Her name is *Bambi?*" Chelsea repeated, so incredulous that her jaw dropped.

She was rewarded with Mitch's hearty laugh. "No, her name isn't Bambi. But you *were* spying again."

"Someone happened to see you," she sniffed.

"And you were jealous."

"Not in the least!" But she almost smiled. He had baited her on that one, and she'd swallowed the bait along with the hook, line and sinker.

"So you just happened to be asking questions about me," he prodded.

"I thought you'd reneged on your part of the bargain." She considered telling him about the worrisome note, but decided that it was best if she bided her time. Maybe he would slip up and admit that he was trying to scare her off the island. But why? There wasn't a logical reason unless he truly was Devlin and had something to hide.

"If and when I renege, I'll tell you to your face," he replied, sliding her an assessing glance. "You know, I'm beginning to think that the only way to make sure you stay out of trouble is to keep an eye on you."

"Of all the—"

"Not a good feeling, is it?"

Chelsea was more than a little irritated, but she didn't argue. Battling with him wasn't getting her anywhere. No, she'd have to try and get alone with him if she was going to pry any more information from him.

And if you're going to pretend to be in love with him.

A thousand butterflies erupted in her stomach and her throat tightened as she watched him from beneath the sweep of her lashes. His tanned face was set as he guided the sailboat along the small channel between the coral reefs, and his legs were planted wide, for balance.

The air was thick with the scent of a storm and the sea. The tiny boat bobbed as furious gusts of wind billowed the sails and snatched at Chelsea's hair. Sea spray splashed the deck and clung to her face.

"This storm might be worse than predicted," Mitch nearly shouted as the wind tore past in a loud rush. For the first time, Chelsea saw the worry in his eyes.

She stared out to sea and frowned. The aquamarine water had turned dark, reflecting the ominous sky, and sky and sea blended at the horizon. Other boats were heading inland, to the safety of the Emeraude harbor as Mitch rounded the point and steered the *Mirage* toward his own small dock.

"Hope you don't mind dinner in a hurricane," he said with a cynical grin.

"A hurricane?" she repeated, her mouth dry as she scanned the sky. "You took me out in a hurricane?"

"It's not *that* bad. Besides, it's not hurricane season."

"John was killed in a storm like this," she reminded him and the skin of his cheekbones grew taut.

"I'm sorry," he said, eyeing the charcoal gray sky. "I forgot."

"How could you?" she nearly screamed.

"It's not something I remember."

Her hands clenched over the rail. How could he not remember, unless he truly wasn't Devlin? Her stomach twisted. Was he, as he'd been insisting since the first time she'd met him, Mitch Russell? Her heart felt as if it had cracked with a new, fresh pain. Was it possible that she'd been wrong, so horribly wrong?

Mitch guided the small boat toward the dock. "Well, it may not be a hurricane, but it's gonna be rough."

"How long will it last?"

"Who knows?" He lowered the sails when the boat was positioned at the dock, then lashed it securely to the moorings and took Chelsea by the hand. "I'd better get you inside." Rain began to pour from the heavens, dripping on the weathered pier and peppering the sand.

Suddenly, she panicked. The bold chilling reality of what she was about to do hit her with a force that nearly stole the breath from her lungs. How could she, in the privacy of Mitch's house, so far from civilization, pretend to want to make love to him—only to stop once he was stripped and she could view his bare hips? He'd be furious—or worse yet, persuasive and she wasn't sure she could deny him, nor that she'd want to.

How could she get away from him—from her own passionate emotions—in the middle of a storm? After all, this was a man she barely knew.

"Chels—?" he asked and his voice sounded so much like Devlin's that her heart squeezed. He took her hand and she let him help her from the boat. "Come on." He tried to protect her from the rain that began to fall by holding one arm over her head, but her legs felt like rubber and she suddenly wished she was anywhere else on earth but in the middle of a tropical storm with Mitch Russell. She couldn't go through with her act—a false seduction. Be this man Mitch Russell or Devlin McVey, she couldn't lie so brazenly and deceive him with such cool calculation.

"I—maybe I should go home," she said as they stepped onto the wet sand.

"It's too late."

"But—I—well, I can't stay here indefinitely." She stopped in a thicket of palms lining the beach, not far from his cabin. She had to find a way to end this horrid charade, even if it meant running away from him right now.

His fingers tightened over her wrist. "What're you afraid of?"

You! Me! Us! Her throat worked, but no sound escaped.

"The storm will pass."

Staring into the depths of his eyes, lost in his darkening gaze, Chelsea wasn't so sure. The maelstrom of emotions raging in her soul was tearing her apart.

"I won't hurt you," he said so softly she barely heard him.

She swallowed with difficulty. "I—I'm not afraid," she murmured.

"Oh no?" One dark brow cocked insolently.

"You're not *that* devastating, Mr. Russell."

"Well, Chelsea, you are," he whispered, and to her shock he jerked her hard against him and lowered his mouth over hers. Chelsea gasped, her heart knocking wildly in her chest, but she didn't tear herself away.

Instead, against every promise she'd so recently made to herself, her body reacted and she kissed him back. As the wind slashed through the fronds of palms high overhead, whipping the sea into a wild froth, she pressed her mouth to his and thrilled when his tongue claimed hers.

His hands roved anxiously over the back of her dress and her own arms wound tight around his neck.

"Oh, God, Chels," he whispered over the whistle of the wind. Rain began to fall, but Chelsea barely noticed, so captivated was she by the movements of his hands and lips.

He kissed her eyes, her cheeks, her ears. His fingers tangled in her long hair and he pulled gently, exposing her throat to his marauding mouth.

His tongue flicked and danced, tasting of her sweetness, leaving a damp trail that the rain washed away.

Chelsea quivered inside. She felt his hand move upward to surround her breast and knew her nipple had already grown taut. Beneath the damp, white fabric of her dress, she swelled to fill his palm, and a warm wetness oozed deep within her.

"God, help me," he whispered, falling to his knees and dragging her onto the sand. He placed his mouth over her breast and through the rain-dampened fabric, his tongue and teeth sought and flicked, teasing and dancing, drawing a deep, raw moan from her throat.

Desire ran in a wanton dance through her blood and she trembled with the need of him, writhed on the sand with a want so intense it chased away any lingering thoughts of denial.

She held his head close against her as hot, electric pulses shot through her body. Tingling at the touch of him, she tried to force more of herself onto him until, through the white cotton, he was suckling as a babe.

He groaned, and still kissing and nipping at her breast, he found the buttons of her dress and began sliding the small buttons through their holes.

Chelsea, caught in the wonder of his lovemaking, didn't notice. She felt the rain against her face, felt his fingers surround one buttock and pull her anxiously against him, fitting their hips together as he thrust closer and his hard shaft pressed intimately against her abdomen.

Her throat was dry, her mind spinning in delicious circles of desire.

His hands found bare skin and he shoved her dress from her, exposing one lace-encased breast. Anxiously, he yanked on her bra strap, forcing her breast to spill out, bare and full. Groaning, he breathed, warm as a summer wind, against her and his lips found the button of her nipple. He tasted her and anxiously shoved her dress over her other shoulder and past her hips.

His fingers slid easily down her legs and he managed

to cast aside his own clothes as the storm picked up and the sky turned dark as midnight.

She didn't stop him when he unhooked that flimsy, wet scrap of material that was her bra, nor did she protest when he yanked down her underpants.

She could think only of how much she cared for this enigmatic man and the firestorm of passion he aroused in her. He lay with her, his hands sculpting her wet body, her own fingers exploring and touching him intimately.

He was beautiful and hard, his body all sinewy muscle and bone. The dark hair of his chest rubbed against her breasts when he leaned over and kissed her again, his lips molding and searching, his tongue hard and demanding.

He rolled her onto her back, and prodded her legs apart with his knees. Then, poised just over her, he gazed down, his face taut with strain, his eyes scorching. With one hand, he touched her breast almost reverently, watching as the proud dark nipple puckered to attention. Then he leaned forward and kissed that dark little peak.

Desire throbbed deep inside Chelsea, yawning and aching to be filled. With one finger, he stroked her thigh and she writhed beneath him. "Please," she whispered in a voice she didn't recognize as her own.

His throat worked when he tilted his head upward again and stared into her eyes. "I've wanted to do this from the first moment I saw you," he whispered and then, without another word, he lost all restraint of his tense muscles and plunged into her, driving deeply, filling her, sending shock wave after sweet shock wave through her body.

She clung to him, her fingers digging into the corded, rain-slicked muscles of his shoulders as she fused her body to his, arching upward, meeting him in a supreme, blinding ecstasy that tore the breath from her lungs.

She didn't think, only felt the warmth of his body in hers, tasted the male saltiness of his skin as her mouth pressed hard against his lips, throat and chest.

Her eyes closed, though she wanted to see more of him as his tempo increased and she was pushed higher and harder, moving faster, spinning out of control, until a dazzling light splintered behind her eyes and she bucked, convulsing, crying out. But her words were drowned by the roar of the wind and his own primal cry. "Chelsea— oh, God—Chelsea! Oh, sweet, sweet, Chelsea. I knew it would be like this!"

"So did I," she whispered, a warm glow enveloping her, the storm seeming light-years away, the rain a welcome mist as she held him tightly to her and felt his rough beard against her wet breasts.

He licked the raindrops from her skin and she became alive again, her body already anticipating another sweet deluge from him.

Their hearts pounded in time with the fury of the sea. Chelsea clung to him and felt his body instinctively curve around hers, protecting her from the elements.

"Come on," he said softly as her heartbeat returned to normal. "I'd better get you inside. You're going to spend the night with me, in my bed, and I won't listen to a single argument."

Before she could say anything, he stood and picked her up in one lithe movement. All thoughts of denial slipped from her mind. She wrapped her arms around his neck to avoid falling and closed her mind to all the logical arguments that had begun to fill her mind.

Tonight she wouldn't listen to logic.

Tonight she would love him and let tomorrow bring what it may.

She nestled her head against his neck as he did exactly as he'd promised. He carried her, naked as the day she was born, into his house and straight to his bed.

CHAPTER NINE

THE STORM RAGED all night long and Chelsea, kept awake by the pounding of the wind and Mitch's lovemaking, only dozed near dawn. Wrapped in the security of Mitch's arms, she didn't have time for self-doubt or recriminations—at least not until she awoke to find herself in Mitch's bed, with him lying naked beside her.

Oh, Lord, she silently prayed as her gaze traveled over his tanned skin and muscles, now relaxed. Dark lashes swept his cheek and his breathing was slow and even. Black hair fell over his eyes and matched the thick beard covering his chin.

What had gotten into her? she wondered as morning light stole through the room. She'd never, never made love to a man she didn't love before—not even Devlin. Appalled that she'd let her wayward emotions control her body, she realized, regretfully, that there was no turning back.

Also, there was no chance that she could let herself fall in love with him. No, she wouldn't delude herself, she thought, angrily flopping back on the pillows and letting out a heartfelt sigh. What she felt for Mitch was raw, sexual attraction. Love hadn't entered into it. Her heart ached at the thought.

Just because he looked, smelled, felt and tasted like Devlin was no excuse for the way she'd acted.

Glancing over her shoulder at Mitch again, she was

more convinced than ever that he must be Devlin. He had to be. But that didn't mean that making love to him had been right. In fact, making love to Devlin was much more complex than making love to Mitch. She could leave Mitch Russell here in Paradis and never look back—well, she could try. As for Devlin, she doubted he would ever be out of her life, not even if he were dead.

She could attempt to write off Mitch Russell as an island fling—or at least she could try. But her feelings for Devlin were seeded much too deeply.

She bit on her lower lip and slid toward the edge of Mitch's double bed. She had to get away before she let her war-torn emotions control her again. But just as her foot dangled to the floor, she remembered her reason for pretending to fall for Mitch and her cheeks burned all the more brightly. Not once in all their long hours of lying naked together had she looked for the birthmark which would prove without a doubt that the man in bed with her was Devlin McVey.

Didn't she care? How could she have forgotten something so important? Lord, what was wrong with her!

Furious, she tossed back the covers, exposing not only herself but all of Devlin or Mitch or whoever he was in his splendid nakedness. His legs were long, tanned and covered with soft dark hair, his buttocks white, his back long, muscled and sleek. He stirred, growling a little, then looked up at her with eyes so blue they took her breath away.

"Can't get enough of me?" he asked, smiling beneath his beard as he reached for her.

"I don't even know what I'm doing here," she admitted, her mouth cotton dry as she forced her gaze back to his lean hips, searching for that damned birthmark. Where was it?

He shifted and she felt her skin tremble in expectation when his fingers grazed her bare thigh. "This is insane," she muttered, still searching desperately as he rolled over suddenly, exposing all of himself to her.

"Haven't you ever seen a man before?" he mocked and she wanted to die at his lack of modesty.

She didn't answer, just stared in horror at his hip, searching for his birthmark.

It wasn't there! No crescent shaped mark, only an ugly network of scars that mottled his skin.

How could she have been so wrong?

Dying a thousand deaths, she squeezed her eyes shut, then opened them again, willing the damned birthmark to be there.

"Is something wrong?" he asked, concern lining his brow.

Everything! "I—I think we made a horrid mistake," she stammered, her insides raw and hurting. This man *wasn't* Devlin. Oh, God, what had she done?

Mortified beyond words, she tried to scramble from his bed, but he grabbed her quickly. "Mistake?" he repeated.

"Oh, yes, this should never have happened!"

His eyes were clouded with confusion. "I don't get it," he muttered, staring down at her with an intensity that scorched all the way to her soul. "We're consenting adults."

"That doesn't make it right." Oh, God, if she could only get away from him before she broke down!

"What does?"

"Love."

He snorted and she went cold inside. "A dreamer." Levering up on one elbow, he shook his head and stared at her. "You really do live in a fantasy world."

She hated to think that he was right and struggled to free herself, but he pinned her against the bed, his hard body pressed intimately against hers. "Why don't you just relax and enjoy yourself?" he suggested.

Just let me go! "Really, I can't. This is wrong, all wrong!"

"Why?"

"Oh, Devlin, don't you understand?" she flung out before she realized her mistake.

His face washed of all color and his expression turned to stone. "What did you call me?" he ground out.

"Devlin," she whispered, shaking.

"That's what I thought." He swore violently and the passion left his face. He stared at her as if she'd gone mad. "I'm not— Oh, hell, what does it matter? Get out!"

"What?"

"You heard me, get out!" He rolled off the bed and reached for a pair of faded denim jeans. As he did, he half turned and she saw his hip again, white except for a ragged network of scars which ran down to the top of his thigh. She dragged the sheet over her breasts for modesty's sake and for several long seconds, she stared at the scars that convinced her that he wasn't Devlin after all.

Shame and mortification shot through her. Oh, God, why had she been so impetuous, gone so far? Her throat felt raw and her eyes burned with unshed tears. Her entire world tilted.

She forgot that he was angry with her. "What happened?" she whispered, praying for some sign of a birthmark and seeing none.

"I'm just tired of playing your ridiculous games!" He stepped into his jeans.

"No—I mean your scars—what happened?"

"The accident," he clipped. "You remember—the one that took my wife's life?"

"Oh, right," she whispered, filled with self-loathing. How had she made love to this man—this stranger? She glanced up at him, unshed tears filling her eyes, and she felt a painful tug on her heart. Good God, had she convinced herself that she loved him? How pathetic. She shoved her hair out of her eyes and wished she could disappear.

"And don't try and tell me I got hurt in a boating accident with a man I'd never met."

"I—I didn't," she said, shaking her head.

"Good, because if you ask me, the only reason you've convinced yourself that I'm this Devlin character is to smooth over your guilty conscience for making love with a man you barely know!"

"No," she argued, grabbing hold of some of her tattered pride. "That's not true. I've thought you were Devlin from the moment I first saw you!"

He snapped his jeans and pulled up the zipper. "But you wouldn't believe me, would you? And you kept pushing it. Even when it was obvious I wasn't your man."

"He *wasn't* my man."

"Oh, no? Well, from where I sit he should have been. And if what happened between us last night was because you thought I was Devlin, I feel sorry for that poor idiot you were engaged to. God, you must've used him to get at his friend."

"That's not the way it was!" she cried, mortified.

"Well, I wouldn't know, would I? I wasn't there!" he snarled.

Stunned, she couldn't move, couldn't find her voice. She was outraged, but her fury was matched by the dark red patch that swarmed up his neck.

"Now, if you're through digging into my personal life and having sex with a fantasy, just get the hell out of my bed!"

"Only too gladly," she replied tightly. Astounded that he wasn't Devlin and stung that he would make love to her, then order her cruelly away, she rolled out of bed and grabbed a shirt he'd slung over the back of a chair.

He saw her buttoning the shirt and rolled his eyes. Scowling, he shoved his hands into the pockets of his jeans. "I'll get your clothes—"

"Don't bother! I don't want or need any help from you!" she insisted, holding her wobbling chin high as she swept past him and strode out the front door. Tears of embarrassment burned at the back of her eyes, but she set her jaw and trudged along the beach, feeling mortified as she found her sandy bra and underpants and her ruined white dress. Her bag had blown over and she had to scrounge along the beach to find her wallet, keys and sunscreen, gritty from the sand.

She'd really been out of her mind last night—leaving her things unattended, making passionate, wanton love with Devlin—no Mitch— Oh, God, what had she done! Raw inside from his callousness, she wanted to crumple into a heap near the water's edge and break down and cry. But she wouldn't give him the satisfaction of showing how much he'd wounded her. Chin held stiffly erect, she waded until she was knee-deep in the surf and tried to rinse out her soiled clothes.

Choking back sobs, she didn't even hear him approach, didn't know he was in the water beside her until he touched her shoulder. She jumped away.

"Look, I'm sorry," he said, but she stepped farther away, recoiling from his touch.

"You don't have to apologize!" she spat, casting a

"drop dead" look over her shoulder and seeing the first sign of vulnerability crossing his hard-edged features. Turning her back on him again, she swished her clothes in the salt water.

"Chels—"

Oh, God, so much like Devlin—why did he sound so much like Devlin? Tears clogged her throat and filled the corners of her eyes. "Leave me alone!"

"It's just that you're so crazed about me being this other guy," he explained, touching her shoulders and forcing her to turn to face him.

"Stop it!" she whispered. "I—I said we made a mistake. I made a mistake."

"I just want to make something clear. I'm done with being used by you, Chelsea!"

"Used? Used?" she repeated, incredulous. "You think I used you?"

"Yep. So you could play out your fantasies—pretend that you were really making love with Devlin McVey."

That was so close to the truth, it shattered her. Hadn't she convinced herself he *was* Devlin—as if that made making love to him all right?

"I think I'd better leave," she said. "But, just so you don't think I'm totally out of my mind, you should know that I'm not the only one who thinks Devlin may be alive." She turned, starting for the path that led south toward the Villa.

He caught up with her before she'd taken two steps. He grabbed her arm and yanked hard, spinning her around. "What's that supposed to mean?"

"The police in San Francisco haven't completely given up on the idea that Devlin's alive," she said, seeing no reason to hide anything from him. "In fact, they've come up with some theories of their own—the first of which is that Devlin was on the take."

The fingers digging into her arm tightened.

"They think that the drug case he was working on went sour because he tipped off the crooks."

Mitch's eyes darkened dangerously. "And what do you think?"

"Devlin would never have sacrificed his principles. He was a good cop and he would never, never have done anything to hurt John." She swallowed hard. "I know that from my own experience."

"How?"

What did it matter? She forced her gaze to his. "Because you were right about Devlin and me. One night… before I was engaged to John, I was alone with Devlin, not that either of us wanted to be, but, well…" Even now the words stuck in her throat and tears of shame burned the back of her eyes. "One thing led to another and we nearly made love. We didn't, but it could have happened. Devlin was sick with disgust—with himself and with me. I, um, don't think he ever trusted me again. At least he never so much as touched me."

"Maybe he couldn't trust himself around you," he said thoughtfully. "You do have a way of getting under a man's skin."

She shook her head. "Not Devlin's." Taking in a deep breath, she added, "But Devlin, above all else, was a good cop. And now, back in San Francisco, there's even been some talk that he rigged the boating accident and faked his own death."

"Go on," he said, his nostrils flaring slightly.

"I talked to my private investigator the other night. And it seems Devlin's caused quite a stir in the city. Some people even think he might have killed John on purpose!"

The fingers digging into her flesh were almost cruel and the look on his face was desperate and ravaged. "Chelsea, you've *got* to listen to me! For your sake and mine. Whoever this McVey character was, he sounds like trouble and I think it would be wise for you to write him off. Grieve if you have to—cry your tears—but face the fact that he's gone. Forever."

The tears that had been threatening all morning collected in her eyes and her throat closed painfully. She didn't want to break down and cry, but she was so overwrought, so twisted and turned, so pulled one way and the other, she felt as if she might faint. Last night she'd convinced herself that this man was Devlin, this morning she vowed that he was Mitch. How could two men tear her apart so?

At the sight of the tears beginning to track from her eyes, his angular face softened a bit. "I know it's hard—"

"You don't know a damn thing!" she cried, wanting to lash out, to return the pain that had cut her to the bone.

"—but you've got to face the truth."

She knew what he was going to say before the words passed his lips. "Devlin's *not* dead! He's not! He can't be!" she rasped, hearing the desperate, nearly hysterical edge to her voice.

Mitch's arms surrounded her and though she fought him, shoved against his shoulders and when that didn't work, pummeled his chest with her hands, he wouldn't let go. His strong arms held fast as iron bands and even her attempts at kicking him with her bare feet only caused him to flinch.

"I won't believe it, I won't, I won't, I won't!" she screamed as if she were a child.

"You have to."

"No!" Considering a life without even the hope of ever

seeing Devlin again was terrifying. Empty, loveless years stretched long before her. The thought struck her that she had loved him and her knees went weak. Had everyone else seen so clearly that she'd fallen for her fiancé's best friend? Old wounds opened brutally and denial sprang to her lips. "No, no, no!"

Yet the nagging thought wouldn't go away. She'd even considered the possibility herself. In loving Devlin, had she lied to him, lied to herself and lied to John? Letting out a painful cry, she felt as if she were breaking in two. If not for Mitch's strong arms, his tender lips pressed against her crown, the soft, soothing words he whispered against her ear, she would surely have fallen to the sand. "It's all right, Chels. Cry, love, if you have to. Let it all out." His voice, as deep as Devlin's, was filled with emotion. As if he cared!

If only she'd had the courage to admit to Devlin, long ago, that she'd cared, that she'd loved him, that he'd been right and she had wanted to make love to him. If only she'd faced up to the fact and been honest with John.

And now, she had to be honest with this man. If he was a stranger, she had used him, as a replacement for a love she'd never shared. She looked up at him and through the sheen of her tears he still looked so much like Devlin—felt so much like him—that her heart broke into a thousand pieces.

He kissed the tears from her eyes and she wept all the harder at his tenderness. "Don't," she whispered, but he didn't listen and held her close, gently rocking, willing her pain away.

Slowly, as the minutes passed, she regained some of her composure. The tears dried and the anguish tearing through her lessened slightly.

"I'm sorry," he said again, his voice rough, as her sobs subsided.

"So am I."

"It's not easy to lose someone you love."

She remembered his wife and felt a stab of jealousy for a dead woman who could evoke so much reverence in this irreverent man. "No, it's not," she agreed, slowly pushing against him.

His arms relaxed.

"You were right," she said, forcing the horrid words to her throat. "I was using you. I wanted Devlin to be alive so badly that I would have done anything, *anything,* to prove that he was."

"And now?"

"I wish I knew."

"You'll go home?"

"Eventually."

"And in the meantime?"

She glanced past his shoulder to the cozy little cabin nestled between the trees. Sunlight and shadow played upon the roof and debris littered the porch. "I don't know," she admitted, turning away from the house and staring at the sea.

Morning light danced upon the water, causing jewel-like prisms to twinkle on the surface. The *Mirage* rolled restlessly against the dock. "I have a few more days," she replied. "I guess I could stay here."

"Knowing that you'll never finish your quest?"

That was the hard part. Accepting Devlin's death. She ran a shaky hand over her forehead. "I—I'll have to think about it."

Mitch sighed. "And what am I going to do with you?"

Love me, she thought, but avoided his eyes. That was absurd—loving someone he barely knew—a woman he thought was a candidate for the ward of a mental hospital.

One side of his mouth lifted into a crooked grin. "Come on in. I'll make you breakfast and then I'll drive you back to the hotel," he offered.

Chelsea wanted to refuse. She didn't want to be reminded that she'd fallen so effortlessly into his arms, that all the while she'd been making love to him, she'd pretended that he was Devlin. "I should just go back now," she said, wanting to lick her wounds, to find a way to accept that Devlin might be lost to her forever.

"This won't take long. And you can clean these out and dry them," he said, holding up her sandy underwear and bra. Chelsea flushed to the roots of her hair, but she didn't protest when he took her hand in his and walked her back to the house.

It was a cozy, bare cabin, far removed from John's expensive bay-front condo and Devlin's cluttered houseboat. But the simplicity of Mitch's cabin touched her and she thought dreamily of a life here, with him, tucked away from the world.

Inside, Mitch handed her two thick white towels and herded her into the bathroom.

"Call if you need me," he said at the door.

"I'll be fine," she assured him, her heart aching a little at his concern.

While Mitch cooked breakfast, Chelsea showered, letting the warm water run through her hair and down her back. Memories of Devlin assailed her, but those distant thoughts wove intricately with fresher images of Mitch. The two men were so alike yet so different. Was it possible that she'd been in love with them both? And if so, what did that say about her? Was she so fickle that she could love Devlin, while being engaged to John, then fall for Mitch while she was still intent on locating Devlin? Lathering her body and feeling the soap slide down her wet skin, she was reminded of making love to Mitch in the rain. An explosion of emotions tore through her. She leaned against the shower stall and felt ashamed all over again.

"What now?" he'd asked, and she posed the same question to herself. She turned off the water and buffed her body dry with a thick white towel. She had a life back in San Francisco—a thriving business that needed her and a family who cared. Now that she'd accepted that Mitch wasn't Devlin, what possible excuse was there to linger?

She swiped at the foggy mirror and stared at her reflection. Cloudy green eyes glared back at her. The fact that she was beginning to fall in love with Mitch scared her. Just as she'd never admitted that she'd loved Devlin, now she couldn't accept any emotional strings tying her to Mitch.

He was an expatriate, a cynical ex-journalist who was content to plunk a few keys on a computer during the day, and hang out in the local bars at night. Oh, yes, and occasionally he would be seen in the company of one sultry Latin lady.

Not exactly husband material.

And definitely not safe.

She slipped Mitch's robe over her shoulders and rolled up the sleeves. Cinching the belt, she opened the bathroom door and heard him clanging around in the kitchen. Funny, she thought, John had cooked for her, and now Mitch seemed to be filling that void.

The door to the room across the hall was ajar and Chelsea remembered that this tiny room was Mitch's office. Biting her lip, she shoved the door open and stepped inside. The desk was about as messy as the last time she'd seen it, and she, deciding it was now or never, slid into the desk chair.

Quietly, she started the computer, then hunted through the desk drawers, trying to find the work disk. At last, she located it, tucked behind a stack of file folders. Inserting it with shaking fingers, she accessed the file. There it was—the first chapter of a book, written by Mitch Russell, entitled Blue Lightning.

Chelsea scanned the first few lines, then skimmed the entire chapter. From what she could tell, the book was a thriller—the hero a policeman who broke more than his share of rules in his efforts to solve a series of murders. The setting for the novel was San Francisco.

Not South America.

Not Chicago.

Not Paradis.

Her heart stopped beating. The detective in the story could have been Devlin. But Devlin was supposed to be dead and Mitch had never met him.

Unless Mitch had lied. Again.

Trembling, she sagged back in the chair. Raw emotion tore through her and her heartbeat became erratic. She had to bite her lip to keep from breaking down again. What kind of a game was Mitch playing with her mind?

Steeling herself, she removed the work disk and after slowly counting to ten, grabbed what she could of her elusive composure and strode, barefoot, down the short hallway to the kitchen where Mitch was busy over the stove, flipping hotcake after hotcake from the griddle to a plate on the counter.

"You lied to me," she said, stopping near the table, her voice filled with challenge.

"I did?"

"Yes—about this!" She held the damning disk in front of her. As he glanced over his shoulder, he spied the computer disk. His devil-may-care smile slid from his face and once again she was staring at the dangerous man she'd first met on the island. "I read it, you know, all of chapter one."

"What're you doing?" he demanded, a blood vessel bulging in his neck. "You can't go through my things! You actually turned on my computer and—"

She didn't back down. "I want an explanation. You said you were writing a story about some Third World country in South America, but the setting in here—" she shook the floppy disk angrily "—is the good old United States and more specifically, San Francisco."

His muscles tensed and his eyes glittered. "Most of the book is set on the West Coast—Seattle, Portland, L.A. and yes, even San Francisco. But a lot of the back story is set in Colombia and Peru," he said evenly.

"And Paradis?"

"Yes."

"The man in this book could be Devlin McVey," she nearly shouted.

"The hero could be any cop in America."

"Or, more specifically, any cop in San Francisco. Don't do this to me, Mitch. Don't play me for a fool! There are just too many coincidences that don't make a whole lot of sense unless you're Devlin McVey or his twin!"

"Did he have one?"

"Not that I know of," she said, beginning to shake inside. "I'm sick and tired of being pulled and pushed by you. One minute you convince me you're who you say you are, and the next I'm back to square one, believing you're Devlin!"

"Your problem."

"I don't think so!" She shook the disk under his nose. "Mitch, please. Don't lie to me! How do you know about this? Oh, God, if you're Devlin, don't torture me this way!"

His nostrils flared and the pancakes on the griddle began to smoke, but Mitch didn't seem to care. He turned off the grill without so much as a glance at the hotcakes, then grabbed his keys from the counter. "Get dressed," he ordered.

"Why?"

"You're leaving."

"No, I'm not."

"Don't make me show you that I'm stronger than you are," he said with quiet menace. "Go on, get your clothes right now, or I'll dress you myself!" The determined glint in his eye convinced her that he meant business.

She dropped his work disk on the table. "It won't do any good, you know," she warned with steely determination. "You can't get rid of me. Not now."

"Oh, no?" His grin was almost wicked and it caused a shiver of fear to slide down her spine as he tossed her dress and shoes to her. "Just wait and see."

CHAPTER TEN

MITCH'S BRONCO SQUEALED to a stop in the parking lot of the Villa. Seething, he yanked his keys from the ignition, opened the door and strode around to the passenger's side. Tugging open the door with one hand, he reached inside with the other.

"I can get out myself," Chelsea told him coldly, but he grabbed hold of her arm and hauled her onto the asphalt.

She tried to walk by herself, but he was at her side, his hand clamped around her elbow as he propelled her into the hotel, past the front desk and up the stairs. "You don't have to keep this up," she grumbled, hurrying to keep pace with him.

"You haven't left me much choice."

On the second floor, he nearly pulled her down the hall. At her door, she flung his arm off her. "Thanks," she said through clenched teeth. "You've done your duty."

"Not yet."

"I'm here. What more do you want?"

"I want you off Paradis."

"But I have every right to stay here—"

"Open the door."

He was dead serious but she didn't budge. "You can't tell me what—"

With infuriating calm, he leaned one shoulder insolently against the jamb and waited as she dug through her bag for her keys. "If you think I'm going to invite you in—"

"I don't need an invitation," he said flatly.

"You have the most gall of any man—"

"Just open the damned door before I break it down!" he growled and his face was suddenly fierce with impatience.

Chelsea shoved the key into the lock, then shouldered open the door. She took one step inside and her throat closed. "No— Oh, God, no—"

"What the hell happened here?" Mitch whispered. Quietly, he shut the door behind him.

All her clothes were strewn on the floor, her suitcases had been ripped and dumped, the drawers of her bureau were tipped over and carelessly left upside down, and her bed had been stripped of blankets, sheets and even the mattress.

"Looks like you had company," Mitch muttered angrily, his eyes scanning the mess.

"But why…?" she asked, stepping slowly through the piles of clothes and upturned furniture. "Who would do this?" Sick inside, she surveyed the damage. The ugly image of some stranger pawing through her things, touching her clothes, caused her stomach to roil. She felt her face go white and steadied herself against the door.

"Stay put," he whispered. Her heart hammered as he walked quickly into the bathroom, opened the shower, then returned. He looked through the open closet, then opened the doors to the balcony. Satisfied that whoever had ransacked the hotel room was no longer around, he frowned as he stared at the destruction.

"Is anything missing?" he asked, his voice surprisingly kind.

"I—I don't know."

"Take a quick look around," he ordered. "Tell me if you think anything was stolen."

She didn't know where to start. She started picking through her clothes and she thought of the burglar, tossing her clothes, jewelry and papers heedlessly around the room. Her dismay slowly gave way to outrage as she saw her address book, pages ripped out, shredded and torn, littering the floor by the window. The balcony doors were open and a breeze caused the curtains to billow and the torn papers to flutter. Impotent anger burned through her blood. "Don't you think we should call the police?"

"Not yet."

"But—"

"Trust me, Chelsea," he insisted, picking up her scattered dresses, shorts and sweaters, his fingers deftly— almost professionally—going through the pockets of each item of her clothes.

"But I think—"

"Just take a mental inventory, will you? You should be good at that, you own a store or something, don't you?" He tossed a few dresses across the end of the bed, then grabbed her white jacket and began going through the pockets.

She reached for a sundress, but stopped when she heard him draw a quick breath between his teeth. "Well, what do you know?" Mitch said, holding up a tiny vial of white powder and frowning darkly. "This yours?"

She shook her head. "No." She didn't have to ask what it was. With a sinking sensation she knew.

His eyes thinned. "I'd guess someone planted drugs on you. Cocaine probably."

"Are you sure?"

"I don't think it's sugar, do you?"

"But why?" she asked, aghast. To her horror, he pocketed the small bottle.

"Obviously someone doesn't like you poking around."

"But I've only been 'poking around' about you."

"Keep looking," Mitch suggested, and Chelsea, shaken to her roots, started sorting through her clothes. Nothing appeared to be missing. Nor were there any other notes or hidden bottles or packets. But the room was a disaster and her things were strewn around so carelessly she couldn't keep her temper in check. "This just doesn't make any sense," she said, glancing up at Mitch as he shoved the mattress in place, then kneeled to look under the bed. She stopped folding clothes and eyed him. "You acted as if you suspected someone had planted something here."

"I'm suspicious by nature."

"But why would anyone vandalize my room?"

He glanced at her as if she were incredibly naive. "Obviously whoever did this wanted you to be in big trouble with the police."

"Me, in trouble? But I didn't do anything. I don't understand."

"This is probably because of me," he admitted with a scowl.

"You? Why?"

"They must've seen us together."

"They? They who?"

"I'm not sure."

"But you've got a pretty good idea," she said, understanding a little.

"I'll find out."

"How?"

His eyes glittered and she felt a tremor of fear. "Leave this to me."

But she couldn't let it go. All his secrecy hadn't helped at all. "Why would anyone ransack my room and plant drugs here? I just don't get it…" She let her words trail off as she thought that he might somehow be connected with crime, perhaps a drug smuggler hiding under the guise of a would-be author.

She sank onto a pile of clothes. "This has something to do with you, the reason you came down here in the first place—whatever it is you do down here, doesn't it?"

She remembered the first night she'd been bold enough to walk to his house, and the way he'd reacted when he'd thought she'd been followed. Her throat grew tight. The thought that he was tied up in something illegal, something as horrid as drug smuggling, tore at her insides. She forced her voice to remain calm, though her hands were clenched into tight fists. "What's going on, Mitch?"

He let out a snort. "I wish I knew."

"But you know *something.*"

He hesitated, then his eyes met hers again and his gaze was hard and determined. "I know one thing. You've got to get out of here."

"Oh, so we're back to that."

Mitch reacted violently. He sprang across the bed and took hold of her wrist. "*I* didn't do this to your room. You know that. I was with you."

That much was true.

"But you know who did," she insisted.

"Maybe."

She was starting to get scared. "And you won't call the police."

"No." He scanned the room one last time, righted one of her suitcases and began throwing her clothes into it. "You'd better pack."

"No."

His head snapped up and sizzling blue eyes pinned her. "We probably don't have much time, Chelsea, and I'm not going to spend it arguing with you." Kicking an empty suitcase toward her, he said through clenched teeth, "Pack what you want in ten minutes. The rest stays."

Despite the fear that inched up her spine, she didn't budge. "I'm not going anywhere. Not until you explain everything."

With an exasperated oath, he flung her jacket into the open case, then planted his fists on his hips and glared at her. "You don't have much of a choice, do you? Either you leave quietly, my way, or we call the police and they lock you up in one of the worst jails I've ever seen or they transport you to the nearest American city and drop you in the lap of the D.E.A."

"But I'm innocent—"

"Save it for the judge." He went back to his task, flinging her clothes into the case. "Has anyone been following you?"

"I don't know. I'm—I'm not sure," she said, remembering all too vividly how she'd felt eyes watching her from time to time.

He glanced up sharply. "But you think maybe someone was?"

This was no game. He was deadly serious, a trace of fear flickering across his hard features. "It…it was just a feeling I had the other day when I went sightseeing in St. Jean."

"Did you see anyone?"

"Only friends of yours."

"I don't have any friends," he said flatly.

"Well—Bambi or whatever her real name is—was there, along with her two buddies, of course." She watched for a reaction but Mitch didn't move, just stared at her, his face set in granite.

"Anyone else?" he asked.

"No—well, yes, I saw Chris Landeen on the boat."

"Did you happen to be wearing this—" he held up her white cotton jacket "—at that time?"

"Yes, but no one had a chance to put anything in my pocket. Besides, if they had, they wouldn't have had to go through all the trouble of breaking into my room."

"Maybe," he said, rubbing his beard. "Who were you with on St. Jean?"

"A nice elderly couple," she retorted, feeling the urge to protect Emily and Jeff.

"Do they have names?"

"Of course they do, but—"

"Quit fighting me, Chelsea!" he warned, his patience long gone. "Don't you see I'm on your side?"

"No! I don't! I don't know whose side you're on or even if there are sides. I'm still not sure I even know your name."

His jaw clamped tight.

"What I see is that you're trying to scare the hell out of me and you're doing a damned good job of it," she said, her throat catching.

"Oh, God," he whispered, then wrapped her in his arms. His breath fanned across her hair and it felt right to be held by him. Within his arms she felt safe and warm. "Look," he admitted. "I'm scared, too. I don't like this any more than you do, but you've got to help me. Now, come on, Chels, who were you with?"

The way he said her name—so familiarly, as if they'd known each other for years, caused her heart to tear. She had no choice but to trust him now. "I was with Jeff and Emily Vaughn," she said, feeling a traitor. "But they're not involved in any of this!"

"You don't know, Chelsea," he said with such dead calm that her heart began to pound.

"What about you?" she asked, pulling herself free of his comforting embrace. "What're you involved in?"

"Right now, I'm just trying to save your backside." He finished stuffing her clothes into her suitcases and lifted them from the bed. "Can't you take a hint? Someone's giving you a pretty strong warning."

"Do you know who?" she asked boldly, her insides quivering. She didn't want him mixed up in this and yet there seemed no way that he wasn't involved.

"No."

"But you said you could take a guess."

"I could take several, but I won't." He grabbed the plastic sack used to line the trash can, walked into the bathroom and scraped her makeup, shampoo, toothbrush, and anything else he could find off the counter and into the bag.

"And I don't suppose you know who wrote me the note?"

"What note?" he asked, barely listening as he snapped her suitcase closed.

"The note I found under my pillow. The one that suggested rather strongly that I leave Paradis."

He froze, every muscle suddenly taunt. "You received a threat?"

"A warning."

"And you didn't tell me?"

"I thought it might have been from you!" she cried, her fear spreading when she saw the worry in his eyes.

"Someone broke into your room *twice?*"

"Yes—"

"God Almighty! Did you call the front desk, alert security?"

"No."

"Why the hell not?"

"Why the hell aren't you calling the police right now?" she flung back.

"I've got my reasons."

"Yeah, right. Well, I've got mine."

He ignored that and asked, "Do you still have it?"

"I think so." She dug into her purse, pulled out her wallet and opened a small pocket. The scrap of paper was tucked away where she'd left it. As she pulled the folded note from her wallet, Mitch snatched it from her hand.

He paled slightly. "That does it." He picked up the telephone receiver, dialed quickly and after a few seconds spoke in rapid Spanish.

"What're you doing—" But he held up a hand, refusing to listen to her protests.

When he hung up, he said with quiet authority, "You're getting out of here and now!"

"Who did you call?"

"Someone who's going to help us."

"Can't you even tell me who?"

"No. Let's go." He picked up her suitcase, handed it to her, then propelled her to the door where he grabbed the second case. "When did you get the note?"

"The other night."

"When?"

"Tuesday," she said. "I went to bed and found it under my pillow."

"You should've told me," he muttered as they headed for the elevator.

"You haven't made yourself all that available."

"That's because I didn't want to be seen with you," he explained.

Chelsea's heart plummeted and she felt an overpowering sense of disappointment. Crazy as it was, she'd begun to care for Mitch Russell. Despite the fact that he was overbearing, cynical, and a regular pain in the backside, she saw deeper into the man. There was a tender side to him, a gentleness hidden under crusty layers of cynicism and pride. "Am I such an embarrassment?" she asked as they hurried downstairs.

He actually smiled. "Sometimes," he admitted, as he ushered her quickly through the lobby.

"I'll take care of the bill later," he said crisply when she tried to pause at the desk.

"Where am I going?"

He didn't waste any time, held the door open for her and escorted her to the parking lot. "Off the island."

She stopped dead in her tracks. "No way!" She couldn't leave, not yet, not when she was so close to finding out the truth—and so close to Mitch. Their lovemaking last night...

"As I said, you've run out of options." He opened the door to his Bronco and helped her inside. "No funny stuff," he said, his gaze locking with hers as he reached for the door. "This is serious, Chelsea. For once in your life, do as I say and don't ask any questions. I'm thinking about your safety."

"And your hide?" she asked, arching an insolent eyebrow.

His lips curved into a wayward smile. "That's a distinct possibility, isn't it? Think what you want." He slammed the door shut and walked around the Bronco. Once behind the wheel, he plunged the key into the ignition and took off, guiding the Bronco down the winding road that led through the trees to Emeraude.

ON THE WAY INTO TOWN, Chelsea considered all her options. She could throw a fit on the docks, scream bloody murder so that Mitch couldn't send her away, but that would only attract attention.

The warning note, her ransacked room, and the vial of white powder convinced her that she didn't want to cause a commotion. She had to take Mitch at his word that he wasn't behind everything, and she did believe him.

Hazarding a glance from the corner of her eye, she saw the tension radiating from him. His hands were tight and white-knuckled around the steering wheel, his jaw was set and grim and there was a leashed fury in his stiff shoulders.

Not only that, but she'd noticed the glimmer of fear in his eyes. He was worried—worried about her.

Sighing, she shoved her hair from her eyes and wished he'd trust her enough to confide in her. Their lovemaking had only been hours ago, and yet she felt as if it had happened in a distant and faraway world; a world in which he had shown that he cared for her.

He parked on the docks and took hold of her hand. His voice was soft, his eyes piercing. "Please, Chelsea," he said quietly, "Don't try anything stupid. Trust me on this, okay?"

"But—"

His fingers tightened. "This is for real. I don't want you to get hurt."

Her heart squeezed. If he only knew how easily he could wound her. "I—I want to stay with you," she said impulsively. "Whatever this is, we can battle it together."

He hesitated just a second and slowly, as if it was painful, he reached toward her and brushed a wayward strand of hair from her cheek. His fingers were strong and trembled a little when they grazed her skin. "Don't make this any harder than it is, Chelsea. You have no idea what's going on."

"That's because you won't let me!" she cried.

He closed his eyes, then forced them open. "Let's go."

"No, Mitch, please. Let me stay. After last night I know that whatever happens—"

"You were right. Last night was a mistake," he said coldly and she felt as if she'd been slapped. He dropped her hand and leaned back in the seat. "It should never have happened."

"But it did happen!" she cried, disbelieving that he would be so cruel. "You can't deny it!"

"I can and I will!" He reached over and opened the passenger door. "This is where we say goodbye, Chelsea."

"Just like that?"

"Yep." He slanted her a cold glance as she stepped out of the Bronco and he followed suit. Grabbing her bags, he started for the docks, to a pier where a charter boat was anchored. When she stood rooted to the spot, he glanced over his shoulder and asked, "Are you coming with me or will I have to carry you?"

"I'm not going anywhere."

"Have it your way." He dropped the suitcases, fired off some quick Spanish to a deckhand, and started toward her, an unmistakable gleam in his eye. The deckhand hopped onto the pier, grabbed her luggage and hauled it aboard.

"You wouldn't dare!" she said when Mitch reached her.

"Try me," he ground out, taking hold of her elbow and yanking her toward the waiting boat.

"You can't do this—"

"Just watch." His grip was hard and punishing, his stride long and determined. "Remember, this is for your own good."

"Don't patronize me!"

"Wouldn't dream of it." At the end of the dock, she stopped, refusing to take the necessary steps onto the boat. Mitch didn't miss a beat, he spoke again in Spanish, this time to the captain of the *Sea Breeze*. The huge, bearlike man with oversize features, snow-white hair and thick glasses nodded his agreement.

"I'm not a willing passenger!" she cut in.

"Captain Vasquez isn't interested," Mitch replied.

"But you can't just leave me here!"

"I'm not. You're setting sail in fifteen minutes. The captain has money for you and a one-way plane ticket to San Francisco, by way of St. Jean, Miami and Dallas."

"I'm not getting on any plane!" she said staunchly, refusing to leave him now. He needed her. Whether he knew it or not, he needed her and, God help her, she needed him! "You don't have a plane ticket—"

"As I said, I already gave it to the captain."

"When?"

"A few days ago."

Something inside her died. Pain, hot and searing, cut through her soul as she stared into his eyes. "You planned to send me away, and you even bought the ticket, but last night…you made love to me?" she whispered brokenly.

He swallowed hard. "I didn't plan on that."

God, how could he be so cruel?

"It just happened."

"You planned it!" she cried, knowing it to be a lie, but wanting to wound him as he'd hurt her. How could he have loved her so thoroughly last night, how could he have caressed her so sweetly, knowing that he planned to shove her aside? Tears welled behind her eyes.

"I didn't plan on anything," he said.

"Then, please, let me stay with you," she begged, mortified at the sound of her own voice.

"You can't," he whispered, his throat thick. Then suddenly he stiffened and his eyes flashed. "For once, Chelsea, use your head."

"Okay," she said bravely, her heart shredding but deciding it was do or die. "I've thought it through. I want to stay with you."

For a second, something akin to tenderness crossed his features and for the briefest of moments, Chelsea thought he'd change his mind. She flung her arms around his neck and buried her face in his chest. "I love you," she said desperately.

For a heartbeat he didn't move and she thought there was a chance his arms would wrap around her and he'd tell her that he loved her, too.

Instead he ground his teeth together, pushed her to arm's length and, though his blue, blue eyes were shadowed, he said, "I don't want you here, Chelsea."

"I don't believe you!"

"Accept it, Chelsea. It was over before it really began. What we felt—that was all just sex, but now it's dangerous for you here and you can't stay." A muscle worked near his temple but his fingers held tightly onto her, as if he couldn't let go.

She held up her trembling chin and stared at him through the sheen of tears. "I don't care if you're Devlin or Mitch, I love you," she said again.

"Oh, God." He closed his eyes a second, as if in agony, but when his lids rose again, his gaze was cold and distant. "Leave Paradis and forget that you ever knew me," he said, the words biting deep.

"You don't mean it," she said bravely, wounded inside.

"I do, lady. I don't want anything more to do with you." He dropped her wrists. Turning on his heel, he marched stiffly back to his Bronco.

Chelsea stood numbly on the dock, watching him storm away without so much as one backward glance. She felt like crumpling onto the sea-weathered planks and tears streamed from her eyes.

Was it possible that he really didn't care about her? Pain, mocking at her for her naïveté, scraped her soul.

"Come on, missy," the captain said over the rumble of the *Sea Breeze*'s massive engines. "Time to go."

She was vaguely aware that her feet were moving, that she was being guided onto the boat, that the captain was calling off orders in Spanish. Her gaze followed Mitch and she watched in silent desperation as he climbed behind the wheel, gunned the engine and tore out of the parking lot until at last, the old rig rounded a corner and disappeared from sight.

Mitch Russell was out of her life.

CHELSEA DIDN'T REMEMBER THE ride to St. Jean. As the charter boat pulled into the harbor at Lagune, she finally surfaced from the jumble of emotions that had kept her preoccupied since the beginning of the trip. She stared at her hand, still closed around the plane ticket and money the captain, by way of Mitch, had given her.

The boat pulled into the dock and sailors began to leave. Captain Vasquez said, "I will call the cab for you to get you to the airport."

Slowly, she realized that she was still being ramrodded into doing exactly what Mitch wanted. "No—no, thank you," she said, rebelling as she forced a wobbly smile. "I'll do it myself."

"And you will take the plane?"

Not on your life, she thought, though much of the fight had been squeezed out of her. "I don't have any other option," she said slowly, hoping to sound convincingly beaten.

The bearlike captain didn't look like he believed her, but at that moment two deckhands began yelling loudly in Spanish, obviously about ready to tear into each other. Circling on the deck, fists clenched, black eyes glittering ominously, they threatened and snarled.

"Dios!" Captain Vasquez muttered under his breath, momentarily forgetting her. "Juan, no—" He started for the two men and Chelsea grabbed her bags, hurrying down the plank leading to the dock.

She half ran along the crowded waterfront, hoping to disappear before the captain remembered that she was his responsibility. How much money had Mitch paid to get rid of her? she wondered, then gritted her teeth. Well, it wasn't enough! She'd come here with a purpose and, by God, she wasn't leaving until she had finished her mission.

Or before you have one last chance to make Mitch realize that he loves you?

She closed her ears to that nagging little voice in her mind and hailed a passing cab. The driver slammed on the brakes and she yanked open the back door, tossed her bags inside and hopped into the backseat.

"Where to?" the cabby asked, eyeing her in the rearview mirror.

"A hotel."

"Which one?"

Chelsea thought quickly, her mind spinning ahead with a half-formed plan. "I, um, don't have reservations. I just need a room—inexpensive—for a day or two."

"There are many hotels on the island."

"How about one with a view of the docks," she said suddenly as inspiration hit.

"Not inexpensive," he said.

"That's all right. Just as long as it's a small hotel that doesn't attract too many tourists."

"Now you are asking the impossible," he grumbled, pulling into the lazy traffic while trying to avoid pedestrians.

Chelsea settled back in her seat. The beginning of her plan was forming in her mind and with a little luck, she might find out more about Mitch Russell or Devlin.

And what if you do? Suppose you even prove without a doubt that Devlin and Mitch are the same person. Do you really expect him to take you into his arms and say that it was all a horrid mistake, that he loved you all along?

Chelsea frowned, her brows pulled tightly together. No, she thought sadly, the best she could hope for was an answer about John's death. Whether the man she'd fallen in love with was Mitch or Devlin, he didn't feel the same way about her. She'd given him ample opportunity to say he cared and he hadn't.

He's not Devlin, she reminded herself, clenching her hands so tightly they ached.

Her throat closed and she battled tears. She wouldn't cry. She wouldn't. But she had to find out about Mitch Russell. She had no choice. Once she understood him further, found out why her room was ransacked and why he wouldn't let himself love her, she'd leave to start her life over again, without dreams of the past weighing her down.

CHAPTER ELEVEN

THE HOTEL WAS NAMED The Dockside and it was perfect. Slightly run-down and only four stories, it blended into the skyline and waterfront as well as any other and it would serve her purpose.

Chelsea managed to rent a nondescript room on the fourth floor with a view of the bay.

After showering and washing her hair, she ordered lunch and then started working on her plan.

Her first call was to Emeraude and the Boutique Exotique. Terri answered on the third ring.

"Terri, this is Chelsea and I need a big favor," she said.

"Sure, anything," Terri readily agreed. "Just hang on while I help this customer."

Chelsea waited for what seemed like half an hour, though it was probably less than five minutes.

"Okay, what's up?" Terri asked.

Chelsea took in a deep breath. "It's a long story," she confided.

"No problem, things are slow here today. I'm all ears."

Chelsea launched into her tale, filling Terri in. After quickly explaining how she was forced to leave the island, Chelsea ended with, "So, if you can, I'd like you to be my eyes in Emeraude. I can't take the chance of showing up there again—I'm sure Mitch would find me in no time, but if you can tell me anything you see around the docks, I'd appreciate it. The most important thing I need to know is if and when Mitch leaves the island in this direction."

"I'll be glad to help," Terri said, "but I'm kind of stuck here, so I might miss him."

"That's okay, just do the best you can," Chelsea said. "But be careful."

"Now you're really getting me interested," Terri replied, laughing.

Chelsea was worried. She hated dragging Terri into this mess, but didn't see any other option. "Just remember that someone's desperate. They tore my room apart and planted drugs there."

"Don't worry," Terri said. "I can handle it. Look, I've got another customer, I've got to run."

"I'll talk to you later."

She'd barely hung up when room service delivered her lunch. After tipping the waiter, she sat on the balcony and studied her view of the bay while she picked at her avocado salad, sliced cantaloupe and bread. Though she was famished, she barely tasted her food. How long would she wait for Mitch to show up? And what if she missed him?

She thought about returning to Paradis, but knew going back would only make the situation worse. No, if she really wanted to find out what was going on in Mitch's life, she'd have to be patient and wait.

Unfortunately, patience had never been her long suit. She tossed her napkin onto the table and sighed. After reading the chapter in Mitch's book, she'd been certain he was Devlin—and his reaction had been violent. Until then, she'd felt that he'd been falling in love with her, too. Or was he capable of such an emotion?

Mitch. Devlin. The two men blended into one in her mind and she knew that she'd never be able to forget them. Whatever happened in the next few days would probably dictate the course of the rest of her life.

Rather than dwell on the complications of loving Mitch, she took her tray into the room, braced herself, and called her sister.

The recorder flipped on and Chelsea rolled her eyes as she listened to the recorded message. When at last it was her turn to speak, she said, "Hi, Felicia, this is Chels. I've moved to another hotel in Lagune on the island of St. Jean. The number is…" She reeled off her phone and room numbers, then explained that she wouldn't be home for another week. "Tell Mom I'll call her soon," she ended, before hanging up and punching out the number of the shop she owned with Sally.

Sally was in. "Hi," she chirped over the wires. "I wondered when I was going to hear from you again. Don't tell me, you're running off with a rich billionaire who's vacationing down there and fell madly in love with you."

"How'd you know?" Chelsea quipped, feeling better just talking to her friend.

"Because you're living out *my* fantasy!" Sally threw back at her. They chatted for a while and Sally insisted that, though they all missed her desperately, the business was perking along and sales were up. "I'm about to go mad just ordering things," Sally said. "We're already out of some of our fall suits. It's impossible to keep up!"

"Well, when I get back, it'll be your turn," Chelsea said, smiling for the first time in hours. "You can come down here, or visit Tahiti or wherever you want to go."

"Oh, no, when you get back, we'll talk about expanding. I found the perfect spot in Oakland and it's only a half-hour drive and you'll absolutely love it."

"I'll take your word for it," Chelsea said. "I should be

home in a week. I'll let you know the exact date when I buy my ticket."

"Don't worry about it. I'll see you when you get here."

Chelsea hung up, grabbed her purse and dashed downstairs to set her plan in motion. The lobby, as uninspiring as her room, was nearly empty as she shoved open the glass doors.

Outside, the heat was blistering, burning against her scalp and rising in waves from the pavement. She joined the rest of the tourists on the sidewalk that bordered the waterfront. The glare off the water was blinding and only a few trees offered sparse shade.

Chelsea barely noticed as she passed windows of the shops lining the bay. She only slowed as she discovered a camera store that featured binoculars in the front display.

"Perfect," she told herself, and purchased the most powerful pair she could afford. On her way back to the hotel, she stopped at a bakery, a fruit stand and bookstore.

Back in her room, she shoved two chairs and a small table onto her small balcony, hung the binoculars around her neck and settled into one chair while propping her feet on the other.

Then she was ready. She checked the binoculars and grinned as she stared through the thick glasses. Depending upon where Mitch decided to berth the *Mirage,* Chelsea would spot him. All she had to do was wait.

She didn't think in terms of how long. She didn't care. She was going to find out his secret and why he insisted upon pushing her away. Once and for all, she'd find out if he was Devlin, and then, she told herself firmly, when she knew the truth, she'd fly back to San Francisco without him.

Only then would she be able to bury the past.

Her heart squeezed painfully and she ignored it, setting her jaw and resolutely staring through the binoculars.

Her eyes were just beginning to tire when the phone rang so loudly she nearly jumped out of her chair to answer it. "Hello?"

"Chelsea! Thank God you're there!" Felicia said breathlessly. "I just got in and heard your message. You have no idea what's going on! I tried to leave a message at the Villa and the snotty desk clerk insisted you'd already checked out. Mom and I were worried to death!"

"Slow down," Chelsea said. "Why were you worried?"

"Because of Devlin! Oh, Chelsea, all hell's broken loose up here. I've already talked to two policemen—detectives—who used to work with Devlin. It seems they think he must be alive. They asked me all sorts of questions about him—about you."

Chelsea's knees gave out. She sank onto the bed. "And what did you tell them?" she said slowly, her hands beginning to sweat over the receiver.

"Well, the truth, of course!" Felicia replied, slightly miffed. "I'm surprised no one contacted you."

"You told them I was here—looking for Devlin?"

"Yes!"

"Oh, God, Felicia, you didn't!"

"I just told you I did. Why wouldn't I? They were the police, for God's sake!" Felicia was nearly shrieking.

Chelsea tried to stay calm. "When did you talk to them?"

"When? Two—days ago."

"And you didn't call me until now?"

"I said I tried earlier at the hotel—you weren't there!" Felicia snapped.

"But two days!" Panic ripped through her. Chelsea licked her lips nervously, wondering if there were a way to get word to Mitch, to warn him that he would soon be accosted by police who might think he was Devlin. If he hadn't been already.

"What's going on? Chelsea," Felicia asked. "Are you in trouble?"

If you only knew. "No," she said, "but I decided to take a room in Lagune, on St. Jean."

"Why?"

"Paradis is pretty small."

"This has something to do with that Mitch person, doesn't it?"

"He and I had a disagreement," Chelsea admitted.

"You're in trouble!" Felicia pronounced.

"I'm fine," Chelsea lied.

"Well, as long as you're not involved with whoever that man is. Whether he is Devlin or not, and I seriously doubt he is, it's no good trying to resurrect the dead. All those emotions, all those feelings belong in the past. Face it, Chelsea, it's time to move on. And all this business with the police—it's just so awful!"

"Nothing's been proven yet," she said, instantly defensive.

"I know, and they wouldn't tell me much, but I got the impression that Devlin did something illegal. Something worse than faking his death—"

"I don't believe it!" Chelsea snapped, annoyed with herself. She'd probably drawn a map for the police, a map that led right to Mitch Russell's doorstep.

"This is a nightmare! I knew you should never have taken off on this wild-goose chase! You'd better come back to San Francisco. I talked to Sally the other day and she's hot to expand. Maybe you should concentrate on the store. Start in a new location, make some new friends, start dating again. It wouldn't hurt you to have a life."

"I do have a life."

Felicia's voice was hard. "I mean a new life—without any strings to John or Devlin."

"I'll think about it." Chelsea bit her tongue and said goodbye before she said something she'd regret.

Nervous as a cat, she took up her position as lookout again and stared through the lenses. The waterfront was packed with people, tourists and seamen, milling around the piers that stretched out to the sea. Boats of all sizes and shapes were lashed to the moorings, while others headed inland and out to sea.

"This may be impossible," she thought as the sun lowered. She sipped from a bottle of diet cola and considered the fact that she was wasting her time. What if Mitch came after darkness fell? What if he didn't come at all? What if she missed him?

She toyed with the idea of returning to Emeraude and having it out with him once and for all, but he would probably just send her packing again.

But if the police were on his tail, shouldn't she warn him? She could call—tell him she was in the Dallas airport and that she'd talked to someone at home and discovered that the police, too, were looking for Devlin.

He probably wouldn't even take her call. And she had warned him already when she'd told him earlier that the San Francisco Police Department thought Devlin McVey had turned bad.

She chewed on her nails, then left her post to make the call. She couldn't stand the waiting, the not knowing. Face it, Chelsea, you're in love with him. Be he Satan or saint, criminal or upstanding citizen, Mitch Russell or Devlin McVey, you've lost your heart to him.

She shoved her hair from her eyes with shaking fingers and slowly lowered herself onto the bed. She loved him, just as she'd vowed earlier. The impact of loving him hadn't really hit her until now. Until she realized that within days, she'd never see him again.

The thought of learning the truth and leaving for San Francisco, as she had promised herself she would, tore her apart. Even now her insides were churning....

The phone rang and she picked it up quickly, half-expecting to hear Mitch's voice.

"Chelsea? It's Terri. Believe it or not, I think Mitch is heading your way."

"He is?" she whispered, hardly believing that he would risk boating to Lagune only hours after having her shipped here.

"Yep, at least I think that's where he's headed. I was over at the bistro talking to Simone when Tacita—that's the girl we've seen Mitch with—stormed in and demanded to use the phone. She was red-faced and furious and God only knows what she was talking about. My Spanish is pretty rusty, but you can bet she was madder than a wet hen."

Chelsea's breath constricted. "And Mitch was with her?"

"Oh, no! After she took off, I left for the boutique and I saw that red speedboat heading in the direction of St. Jean. I couldn't make anyone out at that distance, but there were three people on board and Mitch's sailboat is still moored down at the docks."

Chelsea's skin broke out in a cold sweat. "When did they leave?"

"Fifteen or twenty minutes ago," Terri said. "Is everything okay?"

"I hope so," Chelsea said fervently. "I'll let you know. Thanks a lot."

"No problem."

Chelsea hung up and walked back to the balcony. The sun had begun to set, the sky was turning dark and the sea had become a deep shade of purple. Lifting the binoculars to her eyes, Chelsea trained her glasses toward Paradis and saw several boats approaching, but the craft that caught her attention was a shiny red speedboat that knifed through the water, leaving a thick white wake behind.

Biting her lower lip, she watched, barely daring to breathe, as the image grew larger. Only when the boat docked did she see the faces of the three men on board, and sure enough, Mitch Russell was in the company of the two swarthy-looking men she'd seen him with before.

She didn't think twice. This was it. Her one chance. She wasn't going to blow it. Grabbing her purse, she nearly flew out of the room and pounded down three flights of steps. Outside, she squinted against the gathering darkness and the crowd on the waterfront until she found Mitch's profile, and her heart turned over. Tall and lean, his shoulders wide, his eyes protected by dark glasses, he was as handsome and mysterious as ever. Her heart jackhammered as she stared after him and his two acquaintants.

Trying to keep a buffer of people between them, she followed slowly, keeping her gaze trained on the three men. They stopped at the door of a seedy bar. Mitch glanced over his shoulder once, but Chelsea was partially hidden by a tall woman with a parasol. Obviously satisfied that they hadn't been observed, Mitch shoved hard on the door and followed his two compatriots inside.

Nervous sweat ran down Chelsea's spine. But she couldn't give up—not now. And she couldn't brazenly follow the men inside, either. So she had to use another entrance. Quickly, she rounded the corner of the block, walked up a side street and ducked into a back alley.

The back door to a row of shops was open. Chelsea found the rear entrance to the bar and slipped inside. The rooms were dark and she followed a short hallway of red linoleum through a small pool room to the main area. She stood at the corner and quickly eyed the place. The bar was filled with smoke, tinny music and harsh laughter.

A few men sat around short tables and Chelsea realized, belatedly, that, as a woman she stuck out like a sore thumb. Mitch and his friends were just seating themselves at a booth in the corner and Chelsea ducked into a table at the opposite side of the bar, behind a chipped stucco post and a row of half-filled bottles of liquor.

Mitch's back was to her and she was grateful for small favors. She ordered a beer and paid for it, ignoring the frosty glass that was set before her on the table and wishing she could find a way to get closer. She already assumed the two men that Mitch was using for "research" were thugs, the kind of surly, angry men that gave her the creeps. From her partially hidden vantage point, she pretended interest in a local paper, but studied them.

The tall man signaled to the bartender and ordered three drinks. He snarled out an order, then frowned when a petite waitress didn't serve them fast enough.

Why would Mitch keep company with such men?

For the first time since she'd arrived in the Caribbean, Chelsea wished she had never come. Seeing Mitch pal around with these two men made her skin crawl, and yet she stuck it out, gritting her teeth in determination. There had to be a reason he was here with them, a good reason! He couldn't be a criminal—she wouldn't believe it!

Her hands were shaking when she reached for her glass and took a sip. At that moment, the taller of the two men spied her. He had been stroking his moustache thoughtfully, but stopped and a look of consternation crossed his features while his black gaze roved over her face.

Chelsea pretended nonchalance, catching his gaze, then ignoring it, as if it were an everyday occurrence for her to step into a seedy bar by herself.

The tall man muttered something to his friend and both he and Mitch turned at the same time.

Mitch froze. Beneath his beard his skin went white. He said something to his friends and shrugged, dismissing her. As if he'd never seen her in his life before.

But a sliver of fear shot through Chelsea. Should she leave or stay? Either way, she thought, seeing the gleam of menace in the tall man's black eyes, might put Mitch's life in danger.

She started to scoot her chair back and the short, thickset man panicked when she reached for her purse. He yelled something in rapid-fire Spanish to his friend, motioning to Chelsea.

"No!" Mitch cut in, sending Chelsea a warning look that turned her blood to ice. "She is nothing to me. She knows nothing! Believe me!" He grabbed the tall man's arm. "Let's go—"

But Mitch was too late. The fat man's lips curled suspiciously. "She has heard too much," he said in a thick Spanish accent. From beneath his light-colored suit jacket, he withdrew a pistol.

Chelsea's blood turned to ice.

"Chelsea!" Mitch screamed, knocking the man's arm, so that his aim went wild. "Jesus! No!"

The gun went off with a *crack!*

Glass shattered behind the bar. People screamed and shrieked, overturning tables and spilling drinks. Men leaped for cover or ran for the exits. Beer and wine sloshed on the cement floor.

Chelsea tried to run, scrambling to the bar as she got to her feet. But the fat man aimed again and Mitch flew over an overturned table, protecting her body with his. The gun went off loudly and Chelsea felt him stiffen as he emitted a loud moan.

Good Lord, he was hit!

"Move it!" Wind whistled through his teeth. "This way," he muttered hauling her to her feet and running with a limp through the bar to a back exit. "Move!"

The tall man sprang forward, hollering loudly in Spanish as he gave chase.

Outside, police sirens wailed. Dogs barked, children screamed and dust caught in Chelsea's throat. Mitch yanked hard on Chelsea's hand, half dragging her down a dark labyrinth of cobblestone alleys that wound in and out of dusty yellow buildings that somehow all looked the same.

"What the hell were you doing in there?" he demanded as they ran. Sweat dampened his brow and his face was twisted in pain. He ran with a limp and blood stained the ground, leaving a scarlet trail behind them.

"I had to know what was going on."

"Hell, you just about got us both killed!" Breathing with difficulty, he yanked her around a corner and through the side street.

Behind them, footsteps pounded the pavement and people yelled or screamed. Two more shots rang through the town and Mitch began to slow, his left leg dragging, blood running from the wound in his thigh, his pants stiff and stained.

"You—you never listen do you?" he gasped, breathing with an effort. Sweat beaded his brow and his face was white. His lips were flat against his teeth as he fought the pain.

"And you never tell me the truth—"

"That's it! Stop right where you are!" a male voice boomed.

Chelsea turned and found a giant of a man bearing down on them. In one hand he had a gun, in the other he flashed a policeman's badge. All she saw were the words San Francisco Police Department and she nearly collapsed. Her worst fears were confirmed. She'd led the police to Devlin—or to Mitch—and because of her, he would probably spend the rest of his life behind bars.

"He's hurt—take him to a hospital," the voice said again and for the first time Chelsea realized there were two other men with the huge police officer, and one of them was a stocky man with red hair and cold blue eyes.

Ned Jenkins.

So he'd told them he thought he'd found Devlin.

"What're you doing here?" she demanded.

"My job," Ned explained.

"But you said—"

"That changed," he replied. "When the D.E.A. got involved."

Chelsea's heart turned to stone. She turned to Mitch. "I—I didn't mean—"

"It's all right, Chels," he said quietly, wincing in pain, his dark hair in sweaty strands against his forehead. "It had to come down to this."

The big man took charge. "Have him stitched up and

then meet us down at headquarters with her," he said, nodding in Chelsea's direction. "Let's just see what they have to say." He turned to Chelsea. "Come on, lady, I can't wait to hear how you got yourself involved in this mess."

CHAPTER TWELVE

"So THAT'S IT?" the policeman asked, watching as Chelsea nervously shredded her foam coffee cup. "You came down here looking for Devlin McVey because you thought he was still alive, and you ended up with Mitch Russell."

"Yes," she said, sitting in an uncomfortable chair in the police station.

Officer Jack Bates, a black man with light brown eyes and a perpetual scowl, shook his head as he finished typing. "I have to hand it to you, you've got guts." He whipped her statement out of his typewriter.

"Thanks," Chelsea said.

"Read this over and if it's right, sign on the bottom," he instructed, handing her a pen.

She read over the typed pages, telling her side of the story, and sighed. Then, with only a second's hesitation, she signed her name quickly.

"Okay, you're free to leave the station. But don't leave the island. We've arranged a room for you at the Duchess Hotel at Roger's Point. We took the liberty of moving your things over. You'll be a guest of the department for a few days."

"I suppose I should be flattered," she said, biting her tongue. She had no right to question the police. As a policeman's daughter, she knew that this man, along with the rest of the force, was only doing his job. "I'm sorry," she said, "It's been kind of a rough day."

He flashed her a sympathetic smile. "Don't worry about it."

Smiling, she picked up her purse and asked, "What about Mr. Russell?"

"On his way here from the hospital," Officer Bates replied.

"Is he okay?"

"So far." His golden eyes showed a little bit of understanding. "I wouldn't be too concerned about him, if I were you. Seems to me Mitch Russell's the type who always lands on his feet."

"I guess you're right," she said sadly.

"You want me to give him a message for you?"

What was there to say? "No, thanks," she said. "Maybe I'll see him later." But she doubted it.

"There's a car waiting for you. Someone will drive you over to the hotel."

"Thanks." Feeling suddenly tired, she walked through the small cinder-block station. Outside, a blue-and-white police car was waiting. The driver, a woman with cropped brown hair and a perpetual frown, gunned the car when Chelsea hopped in. They drove in silence through the winding streets of Lagune to the outskirts of town where the road angled sharply upward, through a forest of lush trees and vegetation.

As she rested her head on the back of her seat, Chelsea thought of Mitch and Devlin and John. San Francisco and John Stern seemed far away, a part of her past that had little to do with her now. Even her image of Devlin was unclear and the feelings she'd once held for him seemed foolish and trite.

But Mitch was a different story. If he were Devlin,

then he'd changed and she couldn't even think of him as she'd once thought of Devlin. No, Mitch was another man entirely, a mystery, an enigma, but a man she knew she could love for a lifetime.

And she'd betrayed him. Innocently, perhaps, but betrayed him nonetheless. Obviously he was at odds with the law and she led them straight to him. Her heart ached. Deep inside, she couldn't, wouldn't believe that Mitch was involved in anything illegal. Hadn't he tried to save her just this afternoon? Didn't that single noble act prove him guiltless?

She closed her eyes for a second and when she opened them again, the driver was pulling into the circular brick drive of the Duchess Hotel. In the center of the grounds a tiered fountain spewed water in thin, perfect streams and well-tended gardens filled with red, blue, orange and yellow flowers offered sweet fragrance. Shiny clinging vines grew in abundance against a tall, whitewashed hotel with a red-tile roof and skirted with wide verandas.

Any other day, this spectacular hotel would have thrilled her.

"You're already registered," the woman officer explained, leaning over the back of her seat and handing Chelsea a key to a room on the third floor. "And all your personal belongings from the Dockside as well as the Villa on Paradis are here."

She could barely believe it. "Thank you," she said as she slid out. She watched as the police car rolled around the gardens and disappeared down the hill.

Squaring her shoulders, she walked stiffly up the few short steps. Inside, the hotel was grander than any she'd seen on either Paradis or St. Jean. The lobby floor was polished tile, the desk a burnished mahogany. Thick walls of clean white stucco surrounded tall, paned windows that offered panoramic views of the gardens or sea. Huge paddle fans circulated the air and thick carpeting in fawn and cream led upstairs.

Chelsea took the elevator to the third floor. Her room turned out to be a suite that filled the entire west wing. Antique furniture, brass lamps and fresh-cut flowers were placed in intimate groupings and each private area was graced with French doors leading to a private balcony.

The police department of St. Jean certainly knew how to live well, Chelsea thought as she picked a mango from a basket of fruit.

She set the mango aside, kicked off her shoes, showered and slipped into her bathrobe. Then, her hair still damp, she wandered out onto the balcony and stared at the palm-lined view of the bay. If only Mitch were here to share this with her, she thought. The breeze, smelling faintly of the sea, caressed her face and lifted her hair from her shoulders. The ocean had darkened with the night. A few stars winked in the sky and a sliver of moon hung low over the sea.

Mitch, Mitch Mitch. Would she ever be able to get him out of her mind?

Leaning against the rail, she stared at the darkening horizon and tried to picture Mitch sailing back to Paradis. Without her.

Click.

She turned, thinking she imagined the noise. Her heart leaped to her throat as the doorknob turned. Her fingers twisted in the belt of her robe. "Who's there?" she called, but her voice was faint. She felt her heart leap as she expected Mitch to stick his head in.

To steady herself, she leaned against the rail behind her and nearly fainted when she spied Devlin—no Mitch—enter the room.

Startlingly clean-cut—without a beard, his hair neatly trimmed—he limped into the room. "Chelsea—" he called before he saw her through the open balcony door.

She could barely believe her eyes. His newly shaven face was tanned only to his beard line and he was wearing faded jeans, a T-shirt and a beat-up leather jacket—Mitch's jacket.

"There you are." His gaze skated down her robe to the V above her breasts and he smiled, that brilliant slash of white that could only belong to Devlin.

Oh, God, he *was* Devlin. And Mitch! Tears sprang to her eyes.

"Thank God you're alive!" she cried, running to him and flinging her arms around his neck and nearly knocking him over. Tears of happiness tracked down her cheeks and she buried her face against him. "You miserable, lying, cheating, son of a bitch," she said, choking on tears and laughter, her heart soaring in the knowledge that Devlin was alive, that he was Mitch, that the two men she loved more than anything in the world were one and the same!

"That's some greeting for a man who just saved your neck!"

"Why did you lie to me?" she cried, still hanging desperately onto him. "Why did you pretend to be Mitch? God, how could you deny it over and over again?"

"It wasn't easy!"

"But you made it look easy. Over and over. You kept denying and telling me that I was crazy, and if I weren't so glad that you're alive, I'd kill you myself!"

He laughed then, tilting her face up to his and kissing her so deeply that she couldn't breathe, could barely think, and suddenly she didn't care about his reasons. "I had to do it, Chels," he said when he finally lifted his lips from hers.

"Why?"

"For John."

"Why?"

His eyes darkened with a private pain. "John wasn't supposed to be killed that day," he said with a sigh. "I was."

"What?" she whispered.

"Come on, sit down." He helped her to the side of the bed and his face grew hard. "I was working on a case, a big drug-smuggling case, trying to break up a ring that moved drugs from South America through Paradis to the U.S. Unfortunately, the men involved were beginning to suspect that I was a cop. What I didn't know is that they planned to kill me, by booby-trapping the boat."

"But why did you want to talk to John that day?" she asked, her throat raw.

"Because I was going to explain that I'd have to disappear for a while. I didn't want anyone to know who my friends were. It was to protect him—and you—and it backfired. While we were sailing, the storm picked up, and we started for shore, but the boat blew up, just out of the blue, probably some sort of timing device on a bomb—it wouldn't take much and not enough of the wreckage was found to prove it. Anyway, I survived. Unfortunately John wasn't so lucky."

"So you were out for revenge."

He nodded. "I swam ashore, got hold of my superiors and demanded a new identity to protect myself."

"Didn't you tell them what you were doing?"

He frowned. "This was personal," he said, his jaw sliding to the side and his eyes gleaming with an inner anger. "So I used all the information I'd gathered during the investigation and moved down here. I assumed the role of an expatriated American and within about three months, I made contact with the drug cartel."

"The same one?"

"Yes, but I was dealing with different people and I'd changed my looks significantly enough that they wouldn't recognize me. Until you showed up."

"Uh-oh."

"Right. I was just about to expose the drug kingpins to the police in a sting operation when you fouled up everything! I couldn't believe it! And I couldn't get rid of you."

"You tried," she charged.

"You bet I did. I was frantic for your safety. I thought that if I was rude and cruel enough, you'd take the hint. But not you, oh, no—I'd forgotten how damned stubborn you can be."

He rolled his eyes and stared at the ceiling. "And then, even when I came on to you like a macho creep, you wouldn't buy it. You kept after me. I tried to stay away from you, I even hired some people to watch you."

"You did what?" she cried.

"Chris Landeen—he'd met you and I asked him and a couple of clerks at the hotel to keep an eye on you. I couldn't risk seeing you myself, for fear that by being with you, showing that I cared about you, I'd look vulnerable to the thugs and, if I ever made them angry, they might turn on you. So I hired Chris and a few others because I had to know that you were okay. And then came the storm." He turned back to her and his eyes blazed with a familiar blue flame. "The damned storm. There you were and I couldn't resist. Hell, I didn't want to."

"And then you threw me out."

"Because Carlos and Ramon were on to you! Who do you suppose put the drugs in your room? Who sent you the note?"

"Them?"

He grinned wickedly. "Well, actually I'd bet Tacita left the note for you—she probably bribed a maid in the hotel."

"Tacita—you mean Bambi?"

"One and the same." His eyes twinkled and she shoved a wet lock of hair from her face. "She's very jealous, you know."

"What was she to you?"

"Nothing," he said softly. "Too wishy-washy. You know me, I go for the mule-headed type."

"Thanks a lot!"

"You nearly ruined everything, you know."

"How?"

"Today, in the bar. That was the final showdown. The local police were in position and, thanks to you, the San Francisco cops were there as well. Everything was set, until you showed up and nearly ruined the arrest and damned near got us both killed!"

She eyed his leg. "You will be okay, won't you?"

"Just a little sore for a while. The bullet grazed my thigh, but didn't hit anything serious." His eyes gleamed seductively. "In fact, I think we should make sure that all my parts are working."

"Maybe you should rest in bed," she suggested.

His eyes gleamed. "Precisely what I had in mind," he said, kissing her again. "And I'm not going to get up for days!" His lips touched her eyes, her throat, her cheeks, "You know, I believed you today when you told me you loved me."

"I do," she said simply, winding her arms around his neck.

He sighed and said hoarsely. "And I love you, Chelsea. God, I've loved you for so long." He lifted his head and gazed into her eyes. "I lied when we were in Lake

Tahoe. I wasn't testing you, I just couldn't keep my hands off you. And I was disgusted with myself because John was my friend. I betrayed him by wanting you."

"It's all right," she said automatically as she smoothed the hair from his face.

"No, it's not. Before she died, my wife cheated on me with a 'friend' of mine. I know how it feels," he ground out, his eyes dark.

"We didn't cheat on John."

"Close enough," he said in disgust, then asked. "Would you really have married him?"

"I don't know. I thought I wanted to at the time, but even then, I had doubts. I guess we'll never know." She felt a tug on her heart at the thought of John and she knew that she'd never forget him. During the course of her relationship with him, she'd known there had been something missing, something vital and passionate and real, something she had with Devlin.

He touched her gently on the cheek. "And what about me? Will you marry me?" he asked so suddenly Chelsea glanced up sharply to see if he were joking. But his expression was serious and the love in his eyes was overwhelming.

"Of course I'll marry you, Devlin," she said, then added impishly. "You know, I'll even marry you if your name turns out to be Mitch."

He laughed and the sound touched a special part of Chelsea's heart. "We could get married tomorrow morning," he said, "and spend our honeymoon down here while the investigation wraps up."

"What then?"

"Back to San Francisco where I'll finish up my book—that is legit by the way." Wrapping his arms around her, he kissed her lightly on the lips. "But one thing worries me," he said.

"Just one?"

"Will you be happy married to a cop? I've been offered my old job back."

"I love you, Devlin, not your job. I don't care if you're a detective with the police department in San Francisco or a writer on Paradis. You know," she said honestly, "I wouldn't even care if we never left the islands."

He grinned widely. "Good, because I think we should keep the cabin on Paradis. It could be our own private tropical paradise for the rest of our lives."

"And our children's lives," she added with a wink.

"Children? You want children?"

"Many—and the first one will be named Mitch or Michelle," she teased.

"No," he said softly, "the first one will be named John." Devlin wrapped his arms around her and Chelsea felt tears build behind her eyes. She loved him—oh, God, how she loved him!

From this day forward she intended to spend the rest of her life proving how much he meant to her.

His weight shifted and they tumbled onto the bed. "Aren't you going to ask to see my scar?" he asked and Chelsea giggled.

"This time I'll remember to look," she said as his mouth captured hers in a kiss that was both fierce and gentle.

Closing her eyes, she yielded, body and soul, lost in the wonder that was and always had been Devlin McVey.

* * * * *

OBSESSION

PROLOGUE

Whispering Hills Hospital

THE PATIENT ROCKED slowly back and forth in his chair. His eyes, deep-set and pale blue, stared at the television screen, and though he didn't speak, his lips moved, as if he were trying to say something to the woman on the small color screen, the cohost of *West Coast Morning.*

Kaylie, her name was. He had a picture of her. The one they hadn't found. The one the orderlies had overlooked. It was old and faded, the slickness nearly worn off, but every night he stared at that picture and pretended she was there, with him, in his hospital bed.

She was so beautiful. Her long blond hair shimmered in soft curls around her face, and her eyes were green-blue—like the ocean. He'd seen her once, touched her, felt her quiver against him.

He sucked in his breath at the familiar thought. He could almost smell her perfume.

"Hey! Lee, ol' buddy. How about some sound?" The orderly, the tall lanky one called Rick, walked to the television and fiddled with the controls. The volume roared, and the singsong jingle for cereal blared in a deafening roar to the patient's ears.

"Noooo!" the patient cried, clapping his hands to the sides of his head, trying to block out the sound. "No, no, no!"

"Okay, okay. Hey, man, don't get upset." Rick held his palms outward before quickly turning down the volume. "Hey, Lee, ya gotta learn to chill out a little. Relax."

"No noise!" the patient said with an effort, and Rick sighed loudly as he stripped the bed of soiled sheets.

"Yeah, I know, no noise. Just like every day at this time. I don't get it, you know. All day long you're fine, until the morning shows come on. Maybe you should watch something else—"

But the patient didn't hear. The program had resumed, and Kaylie—his Kaylie—was staring into the camera again, smiling. For him. He felt suddenly near tears as her green eyes locked with his and her perfect lips moved in silent words of love. It won't be long, he thought, his own lips twitching. Reaching deep into his pocket, he rubbed the worn picture between his thumb and forefinger.

Just wait for me. I'll come to you. Soon.

CHAPTER ONE

"WHO IS THIS?" Zane Flannery demanded, his fingers clutching the phone's receiver in a death grip.

"Ted." The voice was barely audible, rough as a shark's skin. Zane couldn't identify the caller as a man or woman.

"Okay, Ted. So what is it?" Zane's mouth had turned to cotton, and the numbing fear that had gripped him ever since "Ted's" call the day before gnawed at his guts.

"It's Kaylie. She's not safe," the voice grated out.

Kaylie. Oh, God. A knot of painful memories twisted his stomach. "Why not?"

"I told you. Lee Johnston's about to be released."

Zane managed to keep his voice steady. "I went to the hospital. No one there is saying anything about letting him out." In fact, no one had said much of anything. Dr. Anthony Henshaw, Johnston's doctor, had been particularly tight-lipped about his patient. Phrases like "patient confidentiality" and "maintaining patient equilibrium," had kept spouting from the doctor's mouth. He'd even had the gall to tell Zane point-blank that Zane wasn't Kaylie's husband any longer. That Zane had no *right* to be involved. Just because Zane was owner of the largest security firm on the West Coast didn't give him the authority to turn the hospital upside down or "persecute" one of his patients. Zane liked that. "Persecute." After what Johnston had attempted to do to Kaylie.

The man had nearly killed Kaylie, and now Zane was accused of "persecuting" the maniac. Figures.

In the well-modulated voice of one who weighs everything before he speaks, Henshaw had informed Zane that Johnston was still locked away and that Zane had nothing to worry about. As a patient of Whispering Hills hospital, Johnston was being observed constantly and there was nothing to fear. Though Lee was a model patient, Dr. Henshaw didn't *expect* Johnston to be released in the very near future. He *assumed* Johnston would remain a patient for "the time being."

Not good enough for Zane. He didn't work well with words like *expect* or *assume.*

Pacing between his desk and window, stretching the phone cord taut, Zane felt as helpless as he had seven years ago when Lee Johnston had nearly taken Kaylie's life.

"Why should I believe you?" Zane asked the caller, and there was a long silence. Ted was taking his time.

Zane waited him out.

"Because I care," the raspy voice stated. The phone went dead.

"Son of a bitch!" Zane slammed down the receiver and rewound the tape he'd made of the call.

Startled, the dog lying beneath Zane's desk barked, baring his teeth, dark eyes blinking open. Hairs bristled on the back of the brindled shepherd's neck.

"Relax, Franklin," Zane ordered, though his own skin prickled with dread and cold sweat collected on his forehead, underarms and hands. "Son of a damned—"

The door to his office burst open, and Brad Hastings, his second in command, strode in. A newspaper was tucked under his arm. "I called the police," he said, obviously aggravated. His dark eyes were barely slits, his nostrils flared. Not more than five-eight, but all muscle, Brad had once been a welterweight boxer and had been with Flannery Security since day one. Hastings was a force to be reckoned with. "There's nothing new on Johnston. He's locked up all right, just like Henshaw told you. As for the doctor, he seems to be on the level. He's been Johnston's shrink for five years."

And in those five years, Henshaw hadn't told Zane anything about his patient. Zane had checked in every six months or so and been told curtly that Mr. Johnston was still a patient and not much more.

When Dr. Loyola had been at Whispering Hills, things had been different. Loyola had been the admitting doctor. *He* understood the terror his patient inspired and *he'd* kept Zane informed of Johnston's progress or lack thereof. But Loyola was long gone, and no one now employed at the hospital considered Johnston a threat.

Except "Ted." Whoever the hell he was. Zane tried to concentrate. "What about this Ted character?" Zane played back the tape, making a second copy as he did, and as Hastings listened, Zane tried to envision the man who was giving him the warning.

The tape ended. Zane rewound it again and took the copy from the recorder.

Hastings scratched the back of his balding head. "No Ted at Whispering Hills. No Ted listed as a friend or family member of Johnston."

"You checked all the workers at the hospital? Cafeteria employees, nurses, orderlies, janitors, gardeners?"

"No one with the name Theodore or Ted. The last guy to work there named Ted left two and a half years ago. He lives in Mississippi now, doesn't know a thing about what's happening at Whispering Hills these days. I talked to him myself."

Zane felt helpless, like a man struggling to desperately cling to a rope that was fraying bit by bit.

"What about a woman? Teddie, maybe," he said thoughtfully. "Or Theresa, Thea, something like that?"

"You think that—" Hastings motioned skeptically toward the tape "—is a woman?"

"I couldn't tell, but I thought whoever called was disguising his or her voice...." He felt another wave of bone-chilling fear. What if the caller were Johnston himself? What if he'd had access to a phone and Bay Area phone book? What if that madman was calling Kaylie at the station?

Zane grabbed the phone again, punched out the number of the television station where she worked and drummed his fingers impatiently as the receptionist answered, then told him that Kaylie had left for the day.

Cursing under his breath, he hung up and dialed her apartment. A recorder answered. He didn't bother to leave another message, but slammed the receiver down in frustration. *Get a grip, Flannery,* he ordered himself, but couldn't quell the fright.

Why hadn't Kaylie returned his calls? he wondered, panicking. Maybe it was already too late!

"Look, she's all right," Hastings said, as if reading his boss's thoughts. "Otherwise you would've heard. Besides, she was on the show this morning, and you know for a fact that Johnston's still at the hospital."

"For now."

Glancing surreptitiously at Zane, Hastings snorted. "I hate to bring up more bad news, but have you seen this?" He slapped the newspaper onto Zane's desk. The paper opened, and Zane realized that he was staring at page four of *The Insider,* a tabloid known for its gossip-riddled press. A grainy picture of Kaylie and the cohost of *West Coast Morning,* Alan Bently, stared up at him. They were seated at a table, laughing and talking, and Alan's arm was slung over Kaylie's shoulders. The bold headlines read: Wedding Bells For San Francisco's Number One Couple? And in smaller type: Is Kaylie Still His Number One OBSESSION?

"How can they print this stuff?" Zane growled, more irritated by the story than he had any right to be. Half of anything *The Insider* printed was purely sensationalism—nothing more than rumors. Yet Zane was infuriated by the picture of Alan and Kaylie together, and he was sickened at the hint of their marriage. It had to be a rumor just to boost ratings. He was certain Kaylie would never fall for a clown like Bently.

Worst of all was the reference to Kaylie's last movie, *Obsession,* a film that was, in Zane's estimation, the beginning of the end of his short-lived but passionate marriage to Kaylie.

Tossing the paper into the trash, Zane didn't comment, he just strode across the room and opened his closet door. He yanked his beat-up leather jacket from a hanger, and while shoving the copy of the anonymous caller's warning into the pocket of his jacket, he pushed aside any lingering jealousy he felt for Alan Bently. Zane didn't have time for emotion, especially not petty envy. Not until Kaylie was safe. A plan had been forming in his mind ever since the first chilling call from "Ted." It was time to put it into action.

Kaylie wouldn't like it. Hell, she'd fight him every step of the way. But that was just too damned bad. This time she was going to do things his way. He explained his plan to Hastings, instructed his right-hand man to take care of business and put Kaylie Melville's safety at the top of the list. "And give a copy of the tape to the police!"

Satisfied that Hastings could handle the business, he said, "I want every available man on the case. I don't give a damn about the costs. Just find out who this Ted is and what his connection is to Kaylie. And start tracing calls—calls that come in here, or to her house, or to the station where she works. I want to know where this nutcase is!"

"Is that all?" Hastings mocked.

"It's all that matters," Zane muttered, shoving his fists into the pockets of his jacket. He whistled to the dog, and the sleek shepherd lifted one ear, then rose and padded after him.

Kaylie would kill him if she realized what he had planned but he didn't care. He couldn't. Her life was more important than her damned pride.

Outside, the morning air was warm. Only a few clouds were scattered over the San Francisco sky. Zane unlocked the door of his Jeep, and the dog hopped into the back. He had one more phone call to make, he thought, pulling into the clog of traffic.

He made the call from his cellular phone.

Once his plan was set, he went about finding his headstrong ex-wife.

HOURS LATER, ZANE HAD tracked her down. She hadn't been at her apartment, nor had she gone back to the station, so he guessed she'd decided to spend the evening alone, at the house they'd shared in Carmel.

He parked in the familiar driveway and second-guessed himself. His plan was foolproof, but she would be furious. And she might end up hating him for the rest of her life.

But then, she didn't much like him now. She'd made it all too clear that she didn't want him in her life when she'd scribbled her signature across the divorce papers seven years before.

So why couldn't he forget her? Leave her alone? Let her fend for herself as she claimed she wanted to do?

Because she was in his blood. Always had been. Always would be. His personal curse. And he was scared.

He let the dog out of the Jeep, and the shepherd began investigating the small yard, scaring a gray tabby cat and sniffing at the shrubs.

"Stay, Franklin," Zane commanded when the dog attempted to wander too far.

Pressing on the doorbell, he waited, shifting from one foot to the other. The house was silent. No footsteps padded to the door. Leaning on the bell again, he heard the peal of chimes within. Still no response.

Don't panic, he told himself, unnerved that he couldn't find her. Reaching into his pocket, he withdrew a set of keys he hadn't used in years and slid a key into the lock.

The lock clicked. The dead bolt slid easily.

So she hadn't bothered to change the locks. *Not smart, Kaylie.*

With a grimace, Zane pocketed his key and shoved on the familiar front door. It swung open without the slightest resistance, and he stood staring at the interior of the house that had once been his.

Swearing under his breath, he ignored the haunting memories—memories of Kaylie. Always Kaylie. God, how could one woman be imbedded so deeply in a man?

With another reminder to Franklin to stay, he closed the door behind him. Tossing his battle-worn leather jacket over the back of the couch, he surveyed the living room. Nothing much had changed. Except of course that he didn't live here, and he hadn't for a long, long time.

The same mauve carpet stretched through the house.

The windows were spotless, the view of Carmel Bay as calming as he had always found it. And the furniture hadn't been moved or added to. Familiar pieces covered in white and gray were grouped around glass-topped tables. Even the artwork, framed watercolors of dolphins, sailing ships and seagulls, provided the same splashes of blue, magenta and yellow as they had when he and Kaylie had shared this seaside cottage.

But all of the memorabilia from their marriage—the pictures, tokens and mementos of their short life together—were gone. Well, most of them, he thought as he spied a single snapshot still sitting on the mantel.

The picture was of Kaylie and him, arms linked, standing ankle-deep in white, hot sand on their honeymoon in Mazatlán. He picked up the snapshot and scowled at the heady memories of hot sun, cold wine and Kaylie's supple body yielding to his. The scent of the ocean and perfume mingled with the perfume of tropical flowers and a vision of a vast Mexican sky.

Dropping the photograph as if it suddenly seared his fingers, he snorted in disgust. No time to think about the past. It was over and done. Already, just being near Kaylie was making him crazy. Well, he'd better get used to it.

He crossed the room. Freshly cut flowers scented the air and reminded him of Kaylie. Always Kaylie. Despite the divorce and the past seven painful years alone, he'd never truly forgotten her, never been able to go to bed at night without feeling a hot pang of regret that she wasn't beside him, that he wasn't in her life any longer.

Shoving the sleeves of his pullover up his forearms, he walked to the recessed bar near a broad bank of windows. He leaned on one knee, dug through the cabinet and smiled faintly when he found his favorite brand of

Scotch, the bottle dusty from neglect, the seal still unbroken. With a flick of his wrist he opened the bottle, just as, by confronting her, he was reopening all the old hurt and pain, the anger and fury, and the passion.... As damning as it was exciting. Closing his eyes, he reined in his runaway emotions—emotions over which he usually had tight control. Except where Kaylie was concerned.

"Fool." Straightening, he poured himself a stiff shot. "Here's to old times," he muttered, then tossed back most of the drink, the warm, aged liquor hitting the back of his throat in a fiery splash.

Home at last, he thought ironically, topping off his glass again as he sauntered to the French doors.

Through the paned glass, he stared down the cliff to the beach below. Relief, in a wave, washed over him. There she was—safe! With no madman stalking her. She walked from the surf, wringing saltwater from her long, sun-streaked hair as if she hadn't a care in the world. If she only knew.

Wearing only a white one-piece swimming suit that molded to her body, sculpting her breasts and exposing the tanned length of her slim legs, she tossed her thick, curly mane over her shoulders.

His gut tightened as he watched her bend over and scoop up a towel from the white sand. The next couple of weeks were going to be hell.

KAYLIE SHOOK THE SAND from her towel, then looped the terry cloth around her neck. The last few rays of sun dried the water on her back and warmed her shoulders as she slipped into her thongs and cast one last longing glance at the sea. Sailboats skimmed the horizon, dark silhouettes against a blaze of magenta and gold. Gulls wheeled high overhead, filling the air with their lonely cries.

The beach was nearly deserted as she climbed up the weathered staircase to the house. Leaving her thongs on the deck, she pushed open the back door, then tossed her towel into the hamper in the laundry room. Maybe she'd pour herself a glass of wine. Pulling down the strap of her bathing suit, she headed for the bedroom. First a long, hot shower and then—

"How're you, Kaylie?" a familiar voice drawled.

Kaylie gasped, stopping dead in her tracks. The hairs on the back of her neck rose, and she spun around quickly, drops from her hair spraying against the wall. *Zane? Here? Now? Why?*

Draped over the couch, long jeans-clad legs stretched out in front of him, he looked as damnably masculine as he ever had. His ankles were crossed, his expression bland, except for the lifting of one dark brow. However, she knew him too well and expected his pose of studied relaxation was all for show.

His steely gray gaze touched hers, and his lips quirked. For a few seconds she remembered how much she had loved him, how much she had wanted to spend the rest of her life with him. With an effort, she closed her mind to such traitorous thoughts. Her throat worked, and slowly she became conscious that one strap of her swimsuit dangled over her forearm, leaving the swell of her breast exposed.

"W-what the devil are you doing here—trying to scare me to death?" she finally sputtered, adjusting the strap back over her shoulder. But before he could respond, she changed her mind and shook her head. She wasn't up to talking to Zane—not now, probably not ever. "No, wait, don't answer that, I don't think I want to know."

He didn't budge, damn him, just lounged there, on *her* couch, drinking *her* Scotch, stretched out and making himself comfortable. His nerve was unbelievable, and yet there was something about him, something restless and dangerous that still touched a forbidden part of her heart. And she knew he wouldn't have shown up without a reason.

His scuffed running shoes dropped to the floor. "You didn't call me back."

She felt a jab of guilt. She'd gotten his messages, but hadn't worked up the courage to talk to him. "And that's why you're here?"

"I was worried about you."

"Oh, please, don't start with this," she said, reminded of the reasons she'd divorced him—his all-consuming need to protect her. "You don't have to worry about me or even be concerned that—"

"Lee Johnston's going to be released."

The words were like frigid water poured over her, stopping her cold. Zane's feigned casualness disappeared.

"He's *what?*" she whispered. In her mind's eye, she pictured Lee Johnston, a short, burly man with flaming red hair and lifeless blue eyes. And she remembered the knife—oh, God, the long-bladed knife that he'd pressed to her throat.

"Y-you're sure about this?" Oh, Lord, how could she keep her voice from quavering? The look on his face convinced her that he believed she was in grave danger, and yet she didn't want to believe it. Not entirely. There were too many dimensions to Zane to take anything he said at face value. Although she'd never known him to lie.

He hesitated, rubbing the back of his neck thoughtfully. "Someone called me."

"Who?"

"I don't know. Someone who called himself 'Ted.'"

"Ted? Ted who?" she asked.

"I wish I knew. I thought maybe you could help me figure it out," he admitted, launching into his short tale and starting with the first nerve-jangling call from "Ted," and ending with his gut feeling that Dr. Henshaw was holding out on him. "Do you have a recorder—a tape player?"

She nodded mutely, then retrieved the portable player from her bedroom. Zane picked up his jacket and took out a small tape, which he snapped into the machine. A few seconds later, "Ted's" warning echoed through the room.

"Oh, my God," Kaylie whispered, her hand to her mouth. She listened to the tape twice, her insides wrenching as the warning was repeated. Zane, though he attempted to appear calm, was coiled tightly, his features tense, his eyes flicking from her to the corners of the room, as if he half expected someone to jump out and attack her.

Why now? she wondered frantically. *Why ever?*

She bit her lower lip, then, thinking it a sign of weakness, stopped just as the tape clicked off. "Why did this 'Ted' guy call you? Why not me?"

"Beats me," Zane admitted, sipping amber liquor from a short glass, his jaw sliding pensively to the side. "None of this is official. At least not yet." Zane's features were hard, and a quiet fury burned in his eyes. "So far we've only got this guy's—whoever he is—word for it. I talked with Johnston's psychiatrist and I didn't like what he said."

"But he didn't say Johnston would be released." She turned pleading eyes up at him.

"No, but I've got a gut feeling on this one. Henshaw

was being too careful. My bet is that the man's going to walk, Kaylie. Whoever called me had a reason."

"Oh, God." Her whole body shook. Stark moments of terror returned—memories of a deranged man who'd sworn he'd kill for her. "They can't let him go. He's sick! Beyond sick!"

Zane lifted a shoulder. "He's been locked up a long time. Model patient. It wouldn't surprise me if the courts decide he got better."

Her world spun back to that horrible night when Johnston had threatened her, waved a knife in front of her eyes, his other arm hard against her stomach as he'd dragged her from the theater. He'd sworn then that he would kill for her and he wanted her to witness the sacrifice....

In her mind's eye, she could still see his crazed smile, feel him tremble excitedly against her, smell the scent of his stale breath.

She sagged against the wall and felt the rough texture of plaster against her bare back. *Think, Kaylie,* she told herself, refusing to appear weak. Swallowing back her fear, she straightened and squared her shoulders. She couldn't fall apart—she wouldn't! Forcing her gaze to Zane's, she silently prayed she didn't betray any of the panic surging through her veins. "I think I'd better talk to Henshaw myself."

"Be my guest."

On weak legs she walked into the kitchen, looked up the number of the mental hospital, and dialed with shaky fingers. A receptionist answered on the fourth ring. "Whispering Hills."

"Yes, oh, I'd like to talk to Dr. Henshaw, please. This is Kaylie Melville—I, um, I know one of his patients."

"Oh, Miss Melville! Of course. I see you on television

every morning," the voice exclaimed excitedly. "But I'm sorry, Dr. Henshaw isn't in right now."

"Then maybe I could speak to someone else." Kaylie tried to explain her predicament, but she couldn't get past square one with the cheery voice on the other end of the line. No other doctor would talk to her, nor a nurse for that matter. On impulse she asked to talk to Ted and was informed that no one named Ted was employed by the hospital. Before the receptionist could hang up, Kaylie asked, "Please, just tell me, is Mr. Lee Johnston still a patient there?"

"Yes, he is," she said, whispering a little. "But I really can't tell you anything else. I'm sorry, but we have rules about discussing patients, you know. If you'll leave your number, I'll ask Dr. Henshaw to call you."

"Thanks," Kaylie whispered, replacing the receiver. She poured herself a glass of water and tried to quiet the raging fear. *Think, Kaylie, think! Don't fall apart!* She drank the water, then made fists of her hands, willing herself to be calm.

When she walked back into the living room, Zane still sat on the couch, his elbows propped on his knees, his silvery eyes dark with concern. A part of her loved him for the fact that he cared, another part despised him for shoving his way back into her life when she'd just about convinced herself that she was over him.

"Well?"

"I didn't get very far. Henshaw's out. He'll call back."

The furrow in Zane's brow deepened.

Kaylie, trying to take control of the situation, said, "I'll—I'll talk to my lawyer."

"I already did."

"You *what?*" she demanded, surprised that Zane would

call *her* attorney, the very man who had drawn up the papers for their divorce.

"I called Blake. His hands are tied."

She was already ahead of him. "Then I'll talk to Detective Montello. He was the arresting officer. Surely he'd…" Her voice faded as she saw him shake his head, his dark hair rubbing across the back of his collar. "Unless you've already called him, too."

"Montello's not with the force any longer. The guy who took his place says he'll look into it."

"But you don't believe him," she said, guessing, her heart beginning to pound at the thought of Lee Johnston on the loose. Icy sweat collected between her shoulder blades.

"I just don't want to take any chances."

For the first time, she thought about him being in the house—waiting for her when she finished her swim. "Wait a minute, how did you get in here?"

Zane glanced away, avoiding her eyes. "I still have my keys."

"You *what?*" she demanded, astounded at his audacity. He hadn't seemed to age in the past seven years. His hair was still a rich, coffee brown, his features rough hewn and handsome. His eyes, erotic gray, were set deep behind thick black brows and long, spiky lashes. "But you gave them to me," she said.

He offered her that same, off-center smile she'd found so disconcerting and sexy in the past. "I had an extra set."

"And you kept them. So that seven years later you could break and enter? Of all the low, despicable… You have no right, *no right* to barge in here and make yourself at home—"

"I still care about you, Kaylie."

All further protests died on her lips. Emotions, long

buried, enveloped her, blinded her. Love and hate, anger and fear, joy and sorrow all tore at her as she remembered how much he had meant to her. Her breath was suddenly trapped tight in her lungs, and she had to swallow before she could speak. She shook her head. "Don't, okay? Just…don't." She willfully controlled the traitorous part of her that wanted to trust him, to believe him, to love him again. Instead she concentrated on the truth. She couldn't allow herself to feel anything for him. What they'd shared was long over. And their marriage hadn't been a partnership. It had been a prison—a beautiful but painful fortress where their fragile love hadn't had a ghost of a chance.

"Look, Kaylie, I just thought you should know that Johnston's about to become a free man—"

"Oh, Lord." Her knees went weak again, and her insides turned cold.

Zane sighed, offering her a tender look that once would have soothed her. But he didn't cross the room, didn't hold her as he once would have. Instead he rubbed impatiently at the back of his neck and glanced at a picture on the mantel—the small snapshot of their honeymoon. "Johnston was obsessed with you before, and I doubt that's changed."

"I haven't heard from him in a long while."

"No letters?"

She shook her head, trying to convince herself that Lee Johnston had forgotten her. After all, it had been years since that terrifying encounter, and the man had been in a mental hospital, receiving treatment. Maybe he'd changed….

"Don't even think it," Zane warned, as if reading the expressions on her face. "He's a maniac. A psycho. He always will be."

Deep down, Kaylie knew Zane was right. But what could she do? Live her life in terrified paranoia that Lee Johnston might come after her again? No way. She glanced down and noticed that she was wearing only her bathing suit still. "Your information could be wrong," she said, walking to the laundry room, where she snagged her cover-up off a brass hook near the door. Standing half-naked in front of him only made the situation worse. She struggled into the peach-colored oversize top and pulled her hair through the neck hole only to find that Zane had followed her and was standing in the arch between the kitchen and laundry room, one shoulder propped against the wall. His gaze flicked down her body to her thighs, where the hem of her cover-up brushed against her bare skin.

"And the call?"

"A crank call."

"You really think so?" he asked.

"I—I don't know." Kaylie cleared her throat and tried to concentrate on the conversation. "But I think you over-reacted by driving all the way down here—"

"I called, damn it," he snapped, his patience obviously in shreds as his eyes flashed back to hers. "But you didn't bother to call me back."

She felt another guilty pang, but ignored it. She'd considered returning his call and had even reached for the phone once or twice, but each time she'd stopped, unsure that she could deal with him and unwilling to complicate her life again.

"You didn't say anything about Johnston—"

"Of course not! I didn't want to freak you out with a message on your recorder."

"Well, you're doing a damn good job of it now," she snapped, her own composure hanging by a thread. Just seeing Zane again sent all her emotions reeling, and now this…this talk about Johnston. It was just too much. Her nerves were stretched to the breaking point.

Zane's voice was softer. "Look, Kaylie, I think you should take some precautions—go low profile."

"Low profile?" she repeated, trying to get a grip on herself as she walked past him into the kitchen. She couldn't let him see her falling apart; she'd fought hard for her independence and she had to prove to him—and to herself—that she was able to take care of herself. She picked up a small pitcher and began watering the small pots of African violets behind her sink. But as she moved the glass pitcher from one small blossom to the next, the stream of water spilled on the blue tiles. She mopped up the mess with a towel and felt Zane's eyes watching her, taking stock of her nervousness. "And what do you think I should do?" she asked, glancing over her shoulder.

His gaze, so rock steady it was maddening, met hers. "First of all, install new locks—a couple of dead bolts and a security system. State-of-the-art equipment."

"With lasers and sirens and a secret code?" she mocked, trying to break the tension.

"With motion detectors and alarms. But that won't be enough. If Johnston's released, you'll need me, Kaylie. It's as simple as that."

Desperate now, she tried to joke. "You? As what? My bodyguard again?" She watched him flinch. "I don't think so—"

His hand shot out and he caught her wrist, spinning her around. She dropped her dish towel. "I'm serious, Kaylie," he assured her, his voice low, nearly threatening. "This is nothing to joke about!"

Was he out of his mind? The inside of her wrist felt hot, and she fought the urge to lick her lips.

"And I think it would be best if you took some time off—"

"Now, wait a minute, I can't leave the station high and dry!"

"Your career just about did you in before," he reminded her, then glanced down to where his fingers were wrapped around her arm. Slowly he withdrew his hand. "You need a less visible job." Then, as if realizing his request bordered on the ridiculous, he wiped his palms on his jeans and added, "Why don't you just ask for a leave of absence until this mess with Johnston is straightened out?"

"No way. I'm not going to live the rest of my life in high anxiety—especially over some stupid call." Though she was afraid, she couldn't give in to the fear that had numbed her after Johnston's last attack. And the man *was* still locked away.

Tossing her damp curls over her shoulder, she reached down and grabbed the towel from the floor. Her wrist, where Zane had held it so possessively only seconds before, still burned, but she ignored the sensation, refused to rub the sensitive spot where the pads of his fingers had left their impressions.

"Look, Kaylie," he said, his voice edged with exasperation. "I'm just trying to help you."

"And I appreciate it," she replied, though they both knew she was lying, that the question of her independence had been a determining factor in their divorce. "I—I'll take care of myself, Zane. Thanks for the warning," she heard herself say, though a part of her screamed that she was crazy to let him go—that she needed him to keep her safe. She extended her hand, palm up. "Now, I think you have something of mine?" When he didn't move, she prodded him again. "The keys?"

Zane's eyes darkened to the shade of storm clouds.

Her heart began to pound. He wasn't giving up. She could see his determination in the set of his jaw.

"How about a deal?" he suggested, not moving.

"Believe me, I'm not in the mood."

"The keys for a date."

"For a *date?* Get real—"

"I am, Kaylie. You go out with me, just for old times' sake, and I'll turn the keys over to you."

"And in the meantime you won't make an extra set?"

"We'll go tonight. I won't have time to do anything so devious."

Kaylie wasn't so sure. And she was tempted, far more than she wanted to be. Standing so close to Zane, seeing the shading of his eyes, feeling the raw masculinity that was so uniquely his, she was lured into the prospect of spending some time with him again. There had been a time in her life when he'd been everything. From body-guard to lover to husband. Her life with him had seemed so natural, so right…until the horrid night when their safe little world was thrown upside down. All because of Lee Johnston.

Kaylie had fallen in love with Zane, trusted him, relied upon him. Now her throat grew dry, and she shook all the happy memories aside. She couldn't trust herself when she thought of the first magic moments they'd shared—when their love had been new and fresh, before Zane had become so intolerably overprotective and domineering. No. Her dependence on him was long over. Now she was older, and wiser, and on to his tricks. She wouldn't re-peat past mistakes. "I don't think a date would be such a good idea."

"Come on, Kaylie, what've you got to lose?" he asked, his voice low and disturbingly familiar.

Everything, she thought, her palms beginning to sweat.

"You've got other plans tonight?" he asked.

"No—"

"No date with Alan?" he mocked, obviously referring to the ridiculous article in *The Insider.* Her producer had left a copy of the rag on her desk as a joke. She wasn't engaged to Alan and never would be, but no amount of denial to the press had seemed to change the public's view that she and Alan, who had once been costars of *Obsession* and were now cohosts of a popular morning show, were not lovers.

"No date with Alan," she said dryly.

"Then there's no reason not to spend a little time with me. Come on," he insisted, his smile irresistible.

"But—" Why not? It's just a few hours, a voice inside her head teased. Wouldn't it be nice to rely on him just a little and find out what he really knows about Lee Johnston? What could it hurt? She looked up at him and swallowed hard. There was a tiny part of her, a feminine part she tried to deny, that loved Zane's image of power and brooding masculinity, that being around him did make her feel warm inside. But being around Zane was unsafe—her emotions were still much too raw.

"Let's go. I know a great place in the mountains. You can tell me all about your career as a talk-show hostess and maybe you'll be able to convince me that you'll take all the precautions necessary to keep you safe from Johnston."

"Okay," she finally agreed, telling herself she *wasn't* excited about the prospect of spending time with him. "But I'll need time to change."

"I'll wait," he said amiably as he walked back to the bar. She watched him pour a drink, as she'd watched him a hundred times before. His shirt was a dark blue. His sleeves were pushed over his forearms to expose dark-skinned muscles that moved fluidly as he handled the bottle and glass. And his hands... She shouldn't even look at his long, sensual fingers and blunt-cut nails.

She swallowed hard against the memories—erotic memories that she'd hoped she'd forgotten. His gaze found hers in the mirror over the bar, and he smiled a little sexy smile. Her insides quivered.

Turning quickly, before she stared any longer, she headed for the bedroom and told herself that she was a fool, but now that she'd committed herself, somehow she'd get through the evening ahead.

CHAPTER TWO

ZANE TRIED TO IGNORE the disturbing sensations—sensations that were way out of line. Kaylie was his ex-wife for crying out loud, and here he was, pouring himself another drink, feeling like a teenager in the throes of lust. Returning to this house—this cottage by the sea where he and Kaylie had spent hours making love—had probably been a mistake of colossal proportions, but he'd had no choice. Not if he wanted his plan to work. And he did. More than anything.

After the divorce he'd promised himself he'd give her room to grow. When he'd married her she'd been nineteen, and the most beautiful woman he'd ever met. Blonde and tanned, slim and coy. Her laugh had been special, her touch divine.

Though he'd fought his attraction to her, he couldn't resist the wide innocence in her eyes, the genuine smile that curved her lips, her ingenious wit, though it was often used at his expense. His hands tightened around his glass as he remembered the scent of her perfume, the feel of her skin rubbing against his, the wonder of looking down into her eyes as he'd made love to her. And it had all changed the night a maniac had held a knife to her beautiful throat.

Now Kaylie was beautiful but mature, her humor sharper, her sarcasm biting. Yet he still wanted her— more than a man with any sense should want a woman.

And now her life was threatened.

Paralyzing fear gripped him. Living without her had been hell. He'd just have to convince her that they belonged together. Hearing the bedroom door open, he turned, and his throat went desert dry.

She was dressed in a white off-the-shoulder dress, her blond curls swept away from one side of her face, her eyes glinting with a gloriously seductive green light. "Okay, cowboy, this is your ride. Where're we going?"

The line was from one of her movies—she'd said it to him as well, late at night, when they had been alone in bed. Had she remembered? Undoubtedly. Zane's diaphragm pressed hard against his lungs. "It's a surprise."

She tilted her head at an angle. "Well, it had better be a short surprise. I have to get up at five tomorrow to tape the show."

"I'll have you back by ten," he lied, pretending ease as he snagged his scuffed jacket off the back of the couch and walked with her to the front door.

He reached for the knob, but she laid a hand across his. "This is all on the up and up, isn't it? One dinner and then you'll hand over the keys?"

His gut twisted. "That was the bargain."

"Then I'll trust you," she said, the corners of her beautiful mouth relaxing.

He felt a twinge of guilt at deceiving her, but shrugged it off as he opened the door and she swept outside ahead of him. He'd played by her rules long enough. Now it was time she played by his.

KAYLIE WAS NERVOUS as a cat when, as they walked outside, she discovered a large brown-and-black shepherd lying on the porch. "Who are *you?*"

"Man's best friend. Right, Franklin?" Zane said, whistling as he opened the back door of the Jeep and the dog leaped inside.

"You bring him on all your dates?" she teased.

He flicked her an interested glance. "My chaperone," he drawled. "Just to keep you in line."

"Me?" she replied, but grinned as she slid into the passenger side. Maybe this date wouldn't turn out to be the disaster she'd predicted.

Casting a glance in his direction as he climbed behind the wheel, she realized that he would never change. He'd always be strong, arrogant, determined, stubborn and self-righteous. But funny, she reminded herself. He had been blessed with a sense of humor.

Still, she was uneasy. She'd seen his mouth turn down when she'd quoted one of his favorite lines from an old movie. She'd done it on purpose, to check his reaction. He'd tried to hide his surprise, but she'd noticed the ghost of change in his eyes.

So why hadn't she refused to get into the Jeep with him?

Kaylie cast her eyes about, not wanting to confront her actions. A part of her was still intrigued with him. And she'd been lonely in the past seven years. She'd missed him far more than she'd ever admit. Yes, she couldn't handle the way he'd overreacted and tried to treat her like some fragile possession, but she'd missed his smile. She recalled it now with bittersweet poignancy, how that lazy slash of white would gleam against a darkened jaw as she'd awakened in his arms.

Her heart pounded at the memory, and she silently cursed herself for being a nostalgic idiot. So she missed his sexy looks, his playful grin, his presence in her house.

He headed east, leaving the sun to cast a few dying rays over the darkening waters of the Pacific. The sky had turned a dusky shade of lavender, reflected in the restless sea.

Zane drove without saying much, but she could sense him watching her, smell the clean earthy scent of his aftershave. She'd been crazy to agree to this, she decided. She was much too aware of him.

"Why did we leave the city?" she asked, to break the awkward silence stretching between them.

"Because I discovered a place you'll like."

"In Kansas?"

His sensual lips twitched. "Not quite."

"So let me get this straight. You thought, 'Gee, Lee Johnston's about to be released from the hospital—this would be a great time to break into Kaylie's house and take her to dinner in some restaurant in Timbuktu.'"

He grinned. "You're astounding, Kaylie. The way you read me like a book," he said sarcastically. "You know, that's exactly what I thought!"

She rolled her eyes and held her tongue for the rest of the journey.

Two hours later, Kaylie's stomach rumbled as she stepped out of his Jeep and eyed the restaurant he'd chosen. She'd expected him to take her to one of their old haunts along the waterfront in Carmel where they could eat seafood and laugh, drink a little wine and remember the good times—the few carefree times they'd shared as man and wife. When he'd mentioned the mountains, her interest had been piqued.

This place, this ivy-covered, two-storied house that looked as if it had been built before the turn of the century, wasn't like Zane at all. Mystified, she walked up the worn steps to a wide plank porch. A few rockers moved with the wind, and leaves in the surrounding maple and ash trees rustled as they turned with the breeze. *Quaint,* she thought. And so unlike Zane.

She eyed him from beneath her lashes, but his strong features seemed relaxed, his face handsome and rakish, one thatch of dark hair falling over his eyes. He shoved the wayward lock from his forehead, but it fell back again, making him look less than perfect and all the more wonderful.

Get a grip, she reminded herself as they walked into the old house and Zane tied Franklin to a tree near the entrance.

"You sure he won't scare the guests?" Kaylie asked.

"This ol' boy? No way," Zane said, rubbing the dog behind his ears.

Inside, a maître d' escorted them to a small table in what once had been the parlor.

Zane ordered wine for them both, then after a waiter had poured them each a glass of claret, Zane touched his glass to hers. "To old times," he said.

"And independence," she replied.

They dined on fresh oysters, grilled scallops, vegetables and crusty warm bread. Zane's features seemed sharper in the candlelight, his eyes a warmer shade of gray as he poured the last of the bottle into their glasses, then ordered another.

Conversation was difficult. Kaylie talked of work at the station; Zane listened, never contributing. As if in unspoken agreement, they didn't discuss Lee Johnston.

"So where'd you get the dog?" she asked as he topped off her glass. She was beginning to relax as the wine seeped into her blood.

"He used to work for the police."

"What happened—they fire him?"

"He retired."

Kaylie stifled a yawn and tried not to notice the play of candlelight in his hair. "And you ended up with him."

Zane shrugged. "We get along."

"Better than we did?" she asked, leaning back in her chair and sipping from her glass.

"Much."

"He must do just as you say."

Zane's teeth flashed in the soft light. "That's about the size of it."

Kaylie was caught up in the romantic mood of the old house with its wainscoted walls and flickering sconces. A fire glowed in the grate and no one else was seated in the small room, though there were four other tables near the windows.

"How'd you arrange this?" she asked, finishing her second—or was it her third?—glass of wine. Pinpoints of light reflected against the crystal.

"Arrange what?"

She motioned to the empty room. "The privacy."

"Oh, connections," he said offhandedly, and she was reminded again of how powerful he'd become as his security business had taken off and his clientele had expanded to the rich and famous. He'd opened an office that catered to Beverly Hills, another to Hollywood, as well as San Francisco, Portland, Seattle and on and on. In seven years his business had prospered, as if he'd thrown himself body and soul into the company after their divorce.

He refilled her glass. "I thought we should be alone."

"What? No bodyguards? No private investigators?" she teased, then regretted her sarcasm when his eyes darkened.

"I think we should declare a truce."

"Is that possible for divorced people?" she asked, and watched as he twisted his wineglass in his fingers.

"Mature divorced people."

"Oh, well, we're that, aren't we? And I guess you're bodyguard enough, right?" She sipped the wine and felt a languid sleepiness run through her blood. Maybe she should slow down on the claret. It was just that she was so nervous around him. Her muscles relaxed, and she slumped lower in her chair, eyeing him over the rim of her glass. He was so handsome, so erotically male, so... dangerous to be around.

The waiter cleared their plates and brought coffee. He offered dessert, but both Zane and Kaylie declined.

"Well," she said as Zane reached into his wallet for his credit card, "don't forget the keys."

"The what?"

"Your end of the bargain. The keys to my house."

"Oh, right." He dropped his credit card on the tray, then reached into his pocket and withdrew a key ring from which he extracted two keys. He slid them across the table. "There you go. Front door and garage."

She could hardly believe it as she plopped the keys into her wallet. "No strings attached?"

Something flickered in his eyes, but quickly disappeared. "No strings."

Kaylie felt a twinge of remorse for thinking so little of him. Why couldn't she open her heart and trust him—just a little? Because she couldn't trust herself around him, she thought with realistic fatalism.

They walked outside and into a balmy night. The sky had darkened, and jewel-like stars winked high over the mountains. Zane opened the Jeep door for Kaylie, and Franklin hopped onto the passenger seat, growling as Zane ordered him into the back.

"You're in his space," Zane explained. The dog jumped

nimbly into the backseat, but his dark eyes followed Kaylie's every move as she climbed inside.

"I don't know if that's so safe."

"He's fine. He likes you."

"Oh, right."

Once back on the road, Zane switched on the radio, and the soft music, coupled with the drone of the engine and the security of being with Zane again made Kaylie feel a contentment she hadn't experienced in years.

Drowsy from the wine, she leaned her head against the window and glimpsed his profile through the sweep of her curling, dark lashes. His hair brushed his collar, his eyes squinted into the darkness as he drove, staring through the windshield.

The road serpentined through dark forests of pine. Every once in a while the trees receded enough to allow a low-hanging moon to splash a silvery glow over the mountainside.

Kaylie leaned back against the leather seat and closed her eyes. The notes of a familiar song, popular during the short span of their marriage, drifted through the speaker. She punched a button on the radio and classical music filled the interior of the Jeep. That was better. No memories here. She'd just let the music carry her away. Her muscles relaxed, and she sighed heavily, not intending to doze off.

But she did. On a cloud of wine and warmth she drifted out of consciousness.

FURTIVELY, HIS PALMS SWEATING, Zane watched her from the corner of his eye. He noticed that her jaw and arms slackened and her breasts rose and fell in even, deep breaths.

Ten minutes passed. She didn't stir. *It's now or never,* he thought as he approached the intersection. Turning off the main road and heading into the mountains, he guided the car eastward.

There was a chance she'd end up hating him for his deception and high-handedness, but it was a chance he had to take. He frowned into the darkness, his eyes on the two-lane highway that cut through the dark stands of pine and redwood. *Don't wake up,* he thought as the seconds ticked by and the miles passed much too slowly.

It took nearly an hour to reach the old logging road, but he slowed, rounded a sharp corner and shifted down. From here on in, the lane—barely more than two dirt ruts with a spray of gravel—was rough. It angled up the mountain in sharp switchbacks.

He drove slowly, but not slowly enough. Before he'd gone two miles, Kaylie stirred.

The Jeep hit a rock and shimmied and she started. Stretching and swallowing back a yawn, she blinked, her brows knit in concentration. "Where are we?"

"Not in Carmel yet."

"I guess not," she said, rotating the crick out of her shoulders and neck as her eyes adjusted to the darkness. "What is this—a park?"

"Nope."

"Zane?"

He heard her turn toward him. The air was suddenly charged. For a few seconds all he heard was the thrum of the engine and the strains of some familiar concerto on the radio.

Finally she whispered, "We're not going back to Carmel, are we?"

No reason to lie any longer. "No."

"No?"

When he didn't answer, pure anger sparkled in her eyes. "I knew it! I knew it!" she shouted. "I should have never trusted you!" She flopped back in the seat. "Kaylie, you idiot!" she ranted, outraged. "After all he's done to you, you trust him!"

Zane's heart twisted.

She skewered him with a furious glare. "Okay, Zane, just where are you taking me?"

"To my weekend place."

"In the boonies?"

"Right." He nodded crisply.

"But you don't have—"

"You don't know what I have now, do you?" he threw back at her. "In the past seven years I've acquired a few new things."

"A mountain cabin? It's hardly your style."

"Maybe you don't know what my style is anymore."

"Then I guess I'll find out, won't I? I can hardly wait," she muttered, her eyes thinning in fury. She tossed her hair over her shoulder and waited, then quietly, her voice trembling with rage, she asked, "Why?"

"Because you won't listen to reason."

"I don't understand."

"We're talking about your life, damn it. And you were going to go on as if nothing had happened, as if this—" he reached into his pocket and extracted the tape "—doesn't exist! Well, it does, damn it, and until I find out if there's any reason to believe 'Ted,' I'm going to make sure you're safe."

"You're what? How?" she asked, though she was beginning to understand. "I think you'd better stop this rig and turn it around, right now," she ground out.

"No way."

"I'm warning you, if you don't take me home, I'll file charges against you for kidnapping!"

"Go right ahead," he said with maddening calm. He cranked on the wheel to round another corner.

"You can't do this!" she cried. What was he thinking?

"I'm doing it, aren't I?"

"I mean it, Zane," she said, her voice low and threatening. "Take me back to Carmel right now, or I'll make your life miserable!"

"You already have," he said through tightly clenched teeth. "The day you walked out on me."

"I didn't—"

"Like hell!" he roared, and from the backseat Franklin growled. Zane flicked her a menacing glance. "You didn't give me—us—a chance."

"We were married a year!" Even to her own ears it sounded as brief as it had been.

"Not long enough!"

"This is madness!"

"Probably," he responded with deceptive calm, wheeling around a final corner. The Jeep lurched to a stop in the middle of a clearing. "But, damn it, this time I'm not taking any chances with your life!"

Kaylie stared out the window at the massive log cabin. Even in the darkness, she could see that the house was huge, with a sloping roof, dormers and large windows reflecting the twin beams of the headlights. "Where are we?" she demanded.

"Heaven," he replied.

She didn't believe him. Her heart squeezed at the thought of being alone with him. How would she ever control the emotions that tore through her soul?

Oh, no, Kaylie thought, this giant log house wasn't heaven. To her, it looked like pure hell!

CHAPTER THREE

"THIS WILL NEVER WORK," Kaylie predicted as Zane cut the engine.

"It already has." He walked out to the back of the vehicle, opened the hatchback, unrolled a trap and yanked out two suitcases. Franklin scrambled over the backseat and bounded onto the gravel road.

Thunderstruck, Kaylie didn't move. *His suitcases,* for crying out loud! Her heart dropped to her knees. Zane had planned this kidnapping before they left Carmel. And she'd been played for a fool!

"Let's go inside," he said.

"You're not serious. This is a colossal joke, right?" But she knew from the rigid thrust of his chin that he wasn't joking.

To his credit, he did seem concerned. The lines around the edges of his mouth were harsh, and he actually looked disconcerted by her outrage. "Look," he finally said, glaring down at her. "Are you planning to stay out here and freeze?"

"No, I'm going to wait for common sense to strike you so that you'll drive me back home!"

"It's gonna be a long wait."

That did it. She hopped out of the Jeep. Her sandaled feet crunched in gravel as she marched up to him. "This is crazy, Zane, just plain crazy."

"Maybe." He strode up the plank steps, fumbled with a key in the dark and shoved hard on a heavy oak door.

"If you think I'm going in there with you, you've got another think coming!"

He ignored her outburst. A few seconds later, the house lights blazed cozily from paned windows. "Come on, Kaylie," he called from deep in the interior. "You're here now. You may as well make the best of it."

But she wasn't done fighting yet. Crossing her arms over her chest, she waited. She'd be damned if she'd walk into this…this prison for God's sake! She had no intention—

He clicked on the porch lights and stood on the threshold of the log house. Kaylie didn't budge. As if rooted to the gravel drive, she tried to ignore the fact that he nearly filled the doorway, his shoulders almost touching each side of the doorjamb. And she refused to be swayed by the handsome sight of his long, lean frame, thrown in relief by the interior light behind him. She was just too damned mad.

"It's gonna get cold out here."

"I'm not going inside."

"Oh, yes, you are."

"No way, Flannery," she argued, her head pounding from too much wine, her pride deflated. "What's going to happen is that you're going back into the house for your keys, then you're going to climb back into this damned Jeep and take me home. Maybe I'll forget about pressing charges for breaking and entering and kidnapping and you'll be a free man!"

He shook his head and rolled his eyes to the night-darkened heavens. "Don't you know you can't bully me, Kaylie?"

"And here I thought you were the one doing the bullying!" she snapped back. It didn't matter what his reasons for bringing her here were. Whether Lee Johnston was in the hospital or on the loose, Zane had no right, *no right,* to force his will on her. The fact that he'd purposely planned to shanghai her was more than she could take.

Slowly, his face knotted in frustration, he started back down the steps. His eyes were trained on her face. "Come on, Kaylie."

"Out of the question."

"Look, you're getting into that house if I have to carry you in there myself!"

"No way." Her throat went dry as he advanced on her. She had the urge to run as fast as her legs would carry her, but she didn't want to give him the satisfaction of seeing her flee. No, by God, she'd stand up to him. And hold her ground she did, not moving an inch when he strode up so close that his shoes nudged the toes of her sandals.

"We can do this the hard way, or you can make it easy."

"Take me home, Zane," she said more softly. In the shadows she thought she saw him hesitate, and that flicker of doubt gave her hope. Maybe he'd change his mind. She touched his arm and watched his jaw clench. "This is insane. We both know it. Johnston's still under lock and key and I've got to get back. Come on, Zane, this…this…stunt of yours is just no good and I'm—I'm not moving until you assure me we're going back to Carmel!"

"Have it your way," he said softly. His hands circled her waist. "But don't say I didn't warn you."

"No, Zane, don't—" she cried, mortified, as he lifted her easily and her feet left the ground.

"I didn't bring you up here so that you could kill yourself by catching pneumonia." He swung her over his shoulder and hauled her, as a fireman would, toward the house. Her hair fell over her face. All the blood rushed to her pounding head.

"Zane, this is ridiculous!" she cried, clinging to his sweater, feeling his muscles ripple beneath the knit. "Let me down, damn you. Stop! Zane, please!"

Up the porch stairs and into the house. He kicked the door shut behind him and set her, sputtering and furious, on the floor. "You bastard!" she barked, throwing her hair out of her eyes and tugging at her dress.

"Kaylie—"

"This is America, Zane. You can't take the law into your own hands!"

He winced a little at that, and storm clouds gathered in his eyes.

"Just because you're a private detective you don't have the right to go around...around...abducting helpless women!"

"Helpless? You?" he flung back at her, shaking his head as he strode through a pitch-ceilinged living room and beyond. "I'm the one taking my life in my hands by bringing you here!"

"Damn right," she agreed, right on his heels. "All I'll give you is grief."

"Amen." He flipped on the wall switch and walked briskly into the kitchen.

"So you may as well give me the keys—"

"Forget it!" He turned and clamped big, angry hands over her bare shoulders. "Now, listen, Kaylie, this is the way it is. I know what I've done by bringing you here. I don't need a lecture on kidnapping, abduction, the rights of the American people or women's lib! All I'm trying to do is make sure that you're safe."

"Spare me—"

"I have. For seven years." His fingers tightened over her shoulders and his eyes searched her face. She felt his anger, but in his eyes she saw deeper emotions brewing. "Just try to understand," he said quietly. "You've got this job where every morning anyone west of the Rockies can switch on his television and see you and Alan Bently on the tube."

"So?"

"So what's to prevent your personal nutcase, Lee Johnston, from trying to do another number on you?"

"The law! The courts! Henshaw."

Zane snorted, then shoved a hand through his hair in frustration. "I deal with the law and the courts every day. Things don't always turn out like they're supposed to. As for Henshaw and Whispering Hills, I've got my doubts about that setup, too."

"Johnston's been there seven years."

"Then he's probably due for reevaluation," Zane said. "We'll know in a few days."

"A few days?" she echoed. He expected her to stay up here that long?

"That's how long it will take to check out the rumor. Maybe this Ted guy knows what he's talking about. Then again, maybe he doesn't. Believe it or not, I didn't bring you up here just to get you angry. I'm scared, damn it. Scared for you. When I think of what Johnston could have done to you—what he's still capable of…" Zane shuddered. Rubbing his arms, he strode to the window and, leaning his palms on the counter, stared through the glass to the black night beyond.

Kaylie's heart softened a little. Though she was furious with him for abducting her, she couldn't help but feel a kindness toward him, a thawing of that cold part of her heart where she'd kept her memories of their short marriage. She had loved him with all of her young, naive heart, and no other man had ever taken his place. No man could. But she forced all those long-buried thoughts of love aside.

"You have no right to do this," she said quietly.

"I have every right."

"Why?"

"Because I care, damn it." He whirled on her, and his gaze, flinty gray, drilled deep into hers. "I care more about you than anyone else on this planet—even more than your precious Alan Bently. If you haven't figured it out yet, that man's a leech. He only cares about you because he thinks a public romance with you will further his career."

"Oh, save me—"

"It's true."

"How do you know? Have you ever talked to Alan?"

He snorted derisively. "Of course not."

"Well, if you had, you might have found out that I've never been involved with him."

"That's not what the tabloids say."

"*You* read the tabloids?" she repeated, amused.

"No, but where there's smoke, there's fire."

"And you care?"

His lips twisted downward. "I told you—I care about you. As for Bently, the man's the worst kind of opportunist. All those rumors that link you to Alan, I can just imagine what they do to the ratings."

"Wh-what?" she demanded, getting a glimmer of what he was alluding to.

"It's a ratings thing, isn't it? Your morning talk show is pitted against a couple of other shows, isn't it? I'll bet your network thought it would boost viewership if you and Alan got married."

"That's absurd!" she gasped.

"Is it?" He opened a cupboard and found a brand-new bottle of Scotch. With a hard twist of his wrist, he snapped open the cap, breaking the label, and after locating a small glass, poured himself a stiff shot.

He took a slow swallow, and her gaze traveled from his firm chin to the silky way his Adam's apple moved in his neck. God, he could reach her as no other man could. There was an irresistible male force surrounding him, and she was oh, so susceptible. She dragged her gaze away.

"I know you never believed it, Kaylie, but I loved you. More than any man should love a woman. I was the one who was obsessed."

"And now?" she asked, her voice trembling. They were wading in hazardous water. "Did you bring me up here because of Johnston? Or was there another reason?"

His gaze locked with hers for a second. Then he tossed back his drink. "And now I'm protecting you. Period. If you think this is some kind of exotic seduction, guess again. I don't have to go to so much trouble."

"I'd hope not," she said evenly, though emotions were tearing through her, "because if you did, you would've lived a very celibate life in the past seven years!"

"Maybe I have," he said, but he had to have been joking. Dear Lord, when she thought of his passion, his wild lovemaking, his wanton sense of adventure in the bedroom, delicious chills still skittered down her spine. No, Zane Flannery might have gone seven days without a woman, possibly even a month or two, but seven years—never! His sexual appetite was too primal, too instinctive. She studied the rock-hard jut of his chin, the angle of his cheeks, the authority in the curve of his thin lips.

He eyed her just as speculatively. "And what about you, Kaylie?" he asked suddenly, his eyes darkening to the color of a winter storm. "What about your sex life?"

She hadn't blushed in years, but now a red heat stole steadily up her neck and face, stinging her cheeks. "I don't think we should be discussing this!"

"It's just one question. A pretty straightforward question."

She swallowed back the urge to lie and tell him that she'd had a dozen or so lovers. "My work keeps me pretty busy," she hedged. "I haven't had time for too many relationships."

"Neither have I," he replied, his gaze finding hers. The silent seconds stretched between them. Kaylie heard only the rapid cadence of her heartbeat, the air whispering through his lungs. "I wasn't lying when I said I loved you, Kaylie," he added, staring into the amber depths of his glass. "You can deny it all you want, you can even pretend that you didn't love me, but there it is. I handled it badly, I admit. But I just loved you too much." Drawing in a deep breath, he finished his drink, dropped his empty glass into the sink, then started out of the room. "Your bedroom is upstairs to the right. I'm next door. But don't worry about your virtue tonight. I'm just too damned tired from arguing with you to do anything about it."

Her throat closed in on itself as she watched him saunter out of the room, the dog at his heels. The faded fabric of Zane's jeans clung to his hips, and his buttocks moved fluidly, though his shoulders and back were ramrod stiff.

"Good night, Kaylie," he called over his shoulder as

he mounted the stairs. "Turn out the lights when you go to bed."

"And what makes you think I'll stay here?" she replied, following him to the stairs, but remaining at the bottom of the steps.

He paused at the landing, one hand resting on the banister. Turning, he towered over her, and again she noticed the torment in his eyes. "It's dark, and the nearest house is over ten miles away. The main road is even farther. Now, if you want to start making tracks through the wilderness, there's nothing I can do to stop you, but I will catch up to you."

"You have no right to do this! No right!" she screamed.

He suddenly looked tired. "That's a difference of opinion," he said, then mounted the rest of the steps, leaving her, fists clenched in fury, to stare after him. She felt a twinge of regret for the fleeting, giddy love they'd shared, but she shoved those old emotions into a shadowy corner of her heart. Loving Zane had been a mistake; marrying him had nearly stripped her of her own personality, and she wasn't about to fall into that trap again.

She glanced down at her hands and slowly uncoiled her fingers. Though she remembered her love with Zane as being unique, it was based on all the wrong emotions.

And now she was scared—frightened that the ominous warning on the tape was true. If only she could call someone—anyone—and find out the truth about Lee Johnston. Once she knew where she stood, she could face the range of emotions Zane provoked in her.

Shivering, she walked outside and made her way to the Jeep. It was locked; the keys were not in the ignition and, of course, there was no mobile phone. Though she suspected he had a phone somewhere. But where? Miserably, she stared at the darkened dashboard. She didn't know the first thing about hot-wiring a Jeep—or any other car for that matter. Hot-wiring, as well as breaking into a car were among those valuable high school lessons she'd missed while growing up on a Hollywood back lot.

She kicked at the gravel in disgust and felt the breath of a mountain breeze touch her bare shoulders. Rubbing her arms, she stared dismally at the black woods looming all around her. If she left now, she wouldn't get far in sandals and a thin cotton dress. Nope. Zane had made sure escape was impossible. At least for tonight.

Turning on her heel, she started back up the steps. There had to be a way, she thought, refusing to give up. If she couldn't leave tonight, she'd find a way tomorrow.

Back in the house, she searched all the downstairs' rooms for a telephone, but though she found phone jacks, there wasn't one telephone in sight. She clenched her teeth in frustration. Damn the man. He'd made sure to thwart her. In the living room, hidden behind panels, she discovered a television, and she worried about her job. What would happen when she didn't show up tomorrow morning?

She turned on the power to the set but nothing happened. Then she noticed that the connecting cables swung free. Obviously the cable had been switched off.

She tried not to think of her position as cohostess of *West Coast Morning*. There was time enough to worry later. First she had to find a means of escape. And then, once back in the city, she'd check out Ted's warning personally, even drive to Whispering Hills to see Dr. Henshaw in person. With renewed purpose, she continued her quick search. In the pantry she found a flashlight and an old army jacket—not the most elegant or comfortable, but something to protect her from the elements, should she have to walk any distance. But taking off in the woods alone at night was too intimidating, even though it would serve Zane right to discover her gone come morning.

Leaving the jacket and flashlight untouched, she padded upstairs and noted that the lamp in Zane's room was still burning—a sliver of light showed beneath his closed door. She didn't bother knocking, but twisted the knob and found Zane, wearing only the worn Levi's, leaning back on the bed, almost as if he were waiting for her.

His head was supported by two pillows, and his eyes were the color of slate. His chest was covered with a mat of dark, swirling hair that covered a tanned skin and a washboard of rigid abdominal muscles before disappearing enticingly beneath his waistband.

The back of Kaylie's throat went dry. She forced her gaze back to his face. His lazy smile flashed white against a day's growth of beard.

"You room's to the *right,* remember?" His lips curved speculatively. "Unless of course you want to stay with me."

The shepherd, lying on the floor near the foot of the bed, lifted his head and cocked it to one side, as if he were sizing up Kaylie.

Kaylie turned her attention back to Zane. "I just want control of my life again."

Reaching over to the lamp, his shoulder muscles gliding with easy, corded strength, he clicked off the light. "Your choice," he said in the darkness. "Here—" he thumped on the bed "—or down the hall."

"I have a job to get to—"

"Forget it."

"They'll miss me."

He chuckled, as if he knew something she didn't. "Alan will be thrilled to have a chance to show the whole world he doesn't need you."

"You'll regret this, Zane," she muttered as she fumbled in the dark, then finding the door, walked quickly out of the room, slamming the door behind her.

What had she been thinking of? She'd been out of her mind to walk into his room and see him half-naked on the bed. A warmth in the pit of her stomach curled invitingly, and she remembered how lying next to him had been safe, secure, loving. The scent of his body lingering on the bedsheets, the feel of a strong arm wrapped around her waist.

"Stop it," she told herself as she marched to the room designated as hers and closed the door behind her. She surveyed her surroundings with a critical eye. The bedside lamps were lit, and golden light glowed warmly against the pine-paneled walls. The hand-stitched quilt on the double bed had been turned down. "How thoughtful," she grumbled, as if he could hear her as she stared at the plumped pillows. "But you forgot the mints!" She kicked off her sandals and padded barefoot against the smooth floor. The room was inviting, in an elemental sort of way, but she couldn't forget that she had been shanghaied here against her will, even if, as Zane so emphatically insisted, her life were in danger.

She groaned at the thought of what would happen tomorrow morning when she didn't arrive on the set of *West Coast Morning.* There would be chaos; her boss would be furious, and the phones at her apartment in San Francisco as well as at the beach house, would be ringing off the hook. Someone would call her sister, and Margot would worry herself sick.

"Oh, Lord, what a mess!" She grabbed a handful of hair and flung it over her shoulders as she padded to the closet and, out of curiosity, opened the door. An array of clothes—women's clothes—filled every available space.

Skirts, sweaters, jeans and slacks were draped on hangers or folded neatly on the shelves. So she hadn't been the first, she thought cynically. Disappointment welled up in her, and she slammed the door shut. No time for sentimentality.

So Zane had a woman—or women. So what? She didn't really believe that he'd lived the life of a monk, did she? It was only surprising that he would expect her to buy that whacked-out story, what with this closet chock-full of women's things.

Flopping onto the mattress, she tossed one arm over her eyes, trying to relieve the headache that was pounding at her temples. Too much wine, too much fear and way too much Zane Flannery, she thought. But tomorrow she'd find a way to force him to take her back to Carmel or straight to San Francisco, back to her home, her job, her life without him.

She only had to get through one night of sleeping under the same roof with him. One night with him lying, stripped bare to the waist, on a king-size bed only a dozen feet away.

Stop it! she thought, squeezing her eyes shut against the pure, sensual vision of him sprawled lazily across the smooth eiderdown quilt.

She didn't want him! She didn't! And yet there was something so provocatively male and charming about him, that she wondered, just for a fleeting moment, what it would be like to love Zane again.

Tossing the quilt over her shoulders, she started counting slowly, hoping that sleep would envelop her and that by morning Zane would come to his senses!

ZANE CLIMBED OUT OF BED and stared out the window. He wondered if he'd made a big mistake. He'd known she'd be angry, of course, even expected her temper to boil. But he hadn't been prepared for her accusations cutting so close to the bone. Nor had he expected to want her so badly. Already he ached for her, and the thought of a night alone in the bed, with Kaylie only a few steps down the hall, would be torture.

From the foot of the bed, Franklin whined.

"Shh." Zane patted the big dog's head, then resumed his stance at the window, his thoughts drawn, as ever, to the only woman he'd ever loved.

She'd changed in the past seven years, he realized, placing one hand high on the window casing and leaning the side of his head against his arm. She'd grown up.

Gone was any trace of the naive young woman he'd married—the teenager who had made a string of semi-successful movies before *Obsession.*

No, this new woman was strong, forceful and well able to control her own life. He'd have to be on his toes, he thought as he stared moodily into the dense, inky forest, because if he let down his guard for a second, she'd find a way to escape and throw her life in jeopardy. She didn't really believe that Johnston would be set free soon.

But Zane did.

He knew what it was like to have death take those he loved, and he was bound and determined that this time he'd thwart the grim reaper. Even if he had to keep Kaylie locked away for the next six months!

CHAPTER FOUR

THE FIRST FEW STREAKS of dawn crept across the bed. Groaning, Kaylie roused herself.

She was in an isolated cabin. With Zane.

God, what a mess!

Climbing out of bed, she stretched and looked out the window. The sun was rising behind a wall of sharply spired mountains. Golden light shone through the stands of pine, glittering in the dewdrops. What was she doing here?

"Oh, Zane," she murmured, grabbing the quilt and wrapping it around her. What was she going to do? Zane had always been an enigma of sorts, and she'd never learned how to handle him—just, she supposed, as he thought he'd never learned to handle her.

Smiling at the thought, she sat on the window seat and drew her knees under her chin. She remembered the first time she'd seen Zane and the tiny knot of apprehension that had coiled in her stomach, the same warm knot she felt now as she thought about him in the next room. She should be angry with him and she was, but the morning took the edge off her anger.

Had it been ten years ago when she'd first laid eyes on Zane Flannery? She'd only been seventeen at the time, and yet, the first time she'd seen him seemed as though it had occurred only yesterday....

A BODYGUARD! SHE, KAYLIE MELVILLE, with a bodyguard! She almost laughed at the thought. Just because she'd made a couple of pictures and she'd been receiving fan mail—some of it not so nice—didn't mean she needed a bodyguard!

"It's a bodyguard or nothing," her father warned her. "We can't be following you off to God-only-knows where every time you make a movie. So, you tell that producer of yours that you get your own personal bodyguard or you won't be making any more films for him!"

Her father, a short, wiry man with a temper that could skyrocket, wasn't about to take no for an answer.

"That's right," her mother had agreed, as she did with any of Dad's rules. "You listen to your father." Her mother had winked broadly. "No reason to give up your career. Just have the studio hire a guard. I'll talk to them myself."

Kaylie didn't argue. She loved making films. Her first picture had been mildly successful—a teen horror flick that made the studio more money than had been expected. Her second film was meatier, as she played a teenager who fell for the boy from the wrong side of the tracks and had to deal with unsupportive parents and pregnancy. Her third movie, *Carefree,* was a teen comedy that surprised the critics and earned the director, as well as Kaylie, glowing reviews. The film had grossed over a hundred million. Triumph Studios was ecstatic. Barely sixteen, Kaylie had become a household word, a budding star who received fan mail and was asked to do interview upon interview to promote her forthcoming projects. She was compared to other young actresses of the time. People sought her autograph. And the fan mail kept pouring in. Letters of undying love, proposals of marriage, and a few not-so-kind missives from a few tortured fans.

Soon the powers-that-be at Triumph Studios agreed with her father and insisted she retain a bodyguard.

But, at seventeen, she hadn't expected anything like Zane Flannery to walk into the offices of Triumph Pictures and announce that he would be looking after her. Not by a long shot! She had thought she'd be protected by some husky ex-football player with a couple of teeth missing. Or by some man with a huge belly and unshaven jaw who had once been the bouncer at a bar. But, oh no, Flannery was nothing like either man she'd envisioned.

He was younger than she'd expected—in his early twenties, by the looks of him, and much cuter—well, more handsome than any of her costars. His hair was longer than stylish and sable brown, curling over his collar and falling over his forehead in shiny, windblown waves. His face, though rough-hewn, took on a boyish quality whenever he flashed a rakish, devil-may-care smile that turned her inside out.

"Miss Melville," he said, extending a work-roughened palm. They were seated in the cluttered office of Martin York, the producer of her latest film, *Someone to Love.*

Flannery's large palm dwarfed hers as he shook her hand, then released her fingers. Wearing only a leather jacket, jeans and a T-shirt, he looked as if he were one of the stagehands or construction workers on the set, but his eyes gave him away. Gray and penetrating, they seemed to take in all of the office at once as he turned back to the producer.

Martin tossed his Dodgers baseball cap onto a chair behind him. Grinning beneath his beard, he reached over a desk piled high with scripts, reels of film and overflowing ashtrays, and clasped Zane's outstretched hand. "How the hell are you?"

"'Bout the same," Zane drawled, dropping into the chair next to hers and slouching low, his jeans-encased legs stretched out in front of him.

"That bad, eh?"

Both men laughed, and Kaylie repressed the urge to giggle. Their easy camaraderie caused her to feel like an outsider, and when she was nervous, she often giggled. But she didn't want Zane to see her as the least bit girlish. He looked like the kind of person who wouldn't easily suffer fools, and she didn't want to get on his bad side.

"I've known Flannery here for more than a few years," Martin said, looking at her as if suddenly remembering she was in the room. "We knew each other in the navy. So don't let his appearance fool you. He's the best in the business."

Kaylie trained her gaze on the man who was to be her protector. The best in the business? So young?

"Zane's worked on some top-secret stuff for the armed services, then he landed a job at Gemini Security. Now he's starting his own company—right?"

"That's the rumor," Zane replied lazily. He glanced at Kaylie again, and his smile faded. "I'll take care of you, Miss Melville. You can count on it."

"Kaylie," she replied with a shrug. "And I'll call you Zane. Okay?"

"If that's the way you want it."

She looked from Zane to Martin, but Martin, too, lifted a shoulder. "Whatever works."

Kaylie grinned and tried not to be lost in the power of Zane's gaze. But she felt giddy and conspicuous and— What was wrong with her? He was just her bodyguard.

No big deal. Or was it? This man—well, he looked as if one hot look from him could melt a glacier.

"Okay, okay," Martin said, handing Zane an address book. "Now, here's Kaylie's address. She still lives with her folks and her sister, and she'll be working here as well as on location in Mexico and Australia. Her folks won't be going along, so Kaylie will be your responsibility. She's been getting a few crank letters…" He tossed a stack of mail, bound by a rubber band, to Flannery just as he finished copying her address into his own book. "I want you to check them all out—"

"Hey, wait a minute," Kaylie cut in, surprised. "That's my mail, right?"

Martin nodded, his expression growing peevish.

Objecting, Kaylie reached for the small bundle. "Don't I get to read it?"

Martin waved off her request. "Don't worry about it. The secretary will respond."

"No way. I always read—"

"You don't have time," Martin said, obviously irritated. "You've got a plane to catch in three days and—"

"And it's mine," Kaylie said, hoping not to sound too petulant. But she wasn't going to let this new guy think he could boss her around. She'd agreed to the bodyguard but that was all. To Zane, she said, "If there's something else you want to know about me, just ask."

He arched one dark brow, and a smile tugged at the corners of Flannery's lips, though he tried to keep his expression grave as he slapped the stack of envelopes into her hand. "When you're done with them, I'd like to see them again."

Martin was fit to be tied. "We don't have time—"

"It's cool," Kaylie assured him, and Martin rolled his eyes.

"Women," Martin muttered under his breath, but Kaylie, cheeks burning, jaw tight, refused to rise to the bait. She just wanted this bodyguard to understand that she wouldn't be treated like a little kid. As for Martin's bad mood, he'd get over it.

From that point on, Zane was all business. He was with her constantly, but never obtrusively, and she began to relax around him. He helped her with her studies and taught her card games and even ran through her lines with her. Once in a while he'd show her a different side to him—a side that proved he did have a sense of humor. While going over her lines, he'd ad-lib, all very seriously, and she'd foul up her lines and they'd both end up laughing. Once in a while she'd catch him looking at her intensely, his eyes darkening, and she'd feel a tightening in her stomach, a warmth that seeped through her whole body.

When they were together, she felt secure. Even when they went out at night, he was cool and calm, almost relaxed. But at the slightest hint of danger, if any fan got too close and he sensed her unease, every muscle would flex and his eyes would glint with warning.

Being so close to him, closer than she was to any other male, she began to rely on him and fantasize about him. He was as handsome as any of her costars and seemed much more virile and worldly. He didn't party, nor try to impress the stars. He was just there—steady as a rock— with his sexy smile that turned her insides to jelly. They spent month after month together.

In Australia, after grueling hours on the set, he'd swim with her in the ocean, and walk with her as the warm sand squished between her toes. He never touched her, though she'd caught his gaze drifting over her body as the wind teased the hem of her dress or the drops of salt-water dried on her skin.

Once, she caught him staring at the dusky hollow between her breasts. She couldn't breathe for a second. Instinctively she placed her hand over the halter of her swimsuit and his gaze moved, but not before she saw the flame in his eyes. Without a word, he tossed her a beach towel and kept his distance from her for the rest of the day.

It wasn't until the next year, after the success of *Someone to Love,* when they were filming in Victoria, British Columbia, that their relationship changed. Her parents had stayed with her on the set for two weeks, then flown back to California.

Kaylie, feeling restless, paced in her room. From her window, she spied the storm clouds gathering to the west, reflecting her own mood as they shifted in dark patterns on the water. She opened the window, feeling a stiff breeze, smelling the heavy scent of rain. There was electricity in the air, currents as charged as her emotions, and she couldn't think of anything but Zane and what it would be like to kiss him.

She told herself she was crazy, that her mother would tell her she was in the throes of puppy love, that her feelings for Zane were nothing more than a schoolgirl crush.

Nonetheless, she was wild for him.

For the first time in her life she had sexual fantasies, and they always involved Zane. Sometimes she blushed just looking at him.

After filming, she and Zane decided to walk back to the hotel. The wind picked up and the clouds overhead opened. Huge raindrops peppered the ground, forming puddles. "Come on," Zane said, turning up his collar and grabbing her hand as he dashed across a street. "We'll catch a cab."

Laughing, she followed, raindrops catching in her hair and running down her cheeks. They hurried past other pedestrians fumbling with umbrellas, carriages pulled by huge horses and double-decker buses rumbling through the slick streets. But each cab that passed was full.

As a final cab roared past, Zane muttered an oath. Then, tugging at her hand, he said, "I think this is a shortcut." He pulled her through a park. They ran down gravel paths, their shoes crunching, their breath fogging in the air.

Kaylie's legs began to ache. "Hey, slow down," she said, gasping from his quick pace.

He slid her a disbelieving glance. "Out of shape?" he mocked, but tugged on her arm and pulled her beneath the leafy cover of a willow tree. The smell of damp earth and ferns filled the air. Magenta azaleas and pale lavender rhododendrons splashed color through the mist that seemed to rise from the loamy soil.

Zane threw his arm across her shoulders and wiped a drop from the tip of her nose. "I guess even I can't protect you from Mother Nature," he said with a crooked grin. His dark hair fell across his eyes, and raindrops glistened, jewel-like, in the blackened strands.

His gaze touched hers, and in one breathless instant Kaylie knew he was going to kiss her. The arm around her shoulders tightened, his fingers wound in her hair, and, as she tilted her head back, his lips found hers in a kiss that was gentle and fierce.

She responded, opening her mouth to the tender insistence of his tongue. He moved closer to her, his suede jacket smelling of leather and rain, his aftershave tingling her nostrils.

She moaned his name and strained against him—
intimately.

Zane stiffened as if he'd been hit by an electric current.
Quickly he stepped backward until the heel of his boot
scraped against the scarred trunk of the willow. "Damn."
Running a shaking hand over his wet forehead, he stared
past her, over her shoulder, to a point in the distance. "I
can't let this… This just can't happen," he said raggedly,
passion in his eyes as he attempted to fixate on anything
but her.

"But—" She took a step closer.

"No!" Holding up his palm, he shook his head. "My
job is to protect you, not seduce you." His gaze found
hers. "Your parents—"

"Are in L.A.," she blurted out.

"—trust me."

He was right, of course, but she was too young and
stubborn to admit it.

"Come on, let's get out of this downpour…."

Throwing caution to the wind, she flung her arms
around his neck and pressed her anxious lips to his. She
felt him shudder. From his shoulders to his knees a shiver
of desire possessed him.

"No, we can't…. Oh, God." And with that desperate
prayer, he kissed her, long and hard, his arms surrounding her, his mouth exploring. Turning quickly, he pinned
her against the rough bole of the tree, but she barely noticed as she kissed him with all the wild abandonment
she'd dreamed of.

His hands moved upward until the weight of her breast
filled his palm. His hips shoved tight against her, and she
felt the rock-hard force of his desire creating an answering awakening in her. Warm and moist, like the spring
shower, she experienced a want that was dark and dusky

and so demanding she ached for him, wanting him as she had no other.

He kissed her eyes, her nose, her cheeks, her throat, his tongue licking away the raindrops as his hands found the zipper of her jacket. The bleached denim opened, and he lifted her blouse until his damp fingertip plundered beneath her bra, touching and delving, causing her nipples to crest into small, hard buds.

Desire crept up her spine, spilled into her blood, causing her to moan and kiss him feverishly.

Beneath the drooping branches of the willow tree, with the wind sighing and the rain creating a moist curtain, Kaylie wanted to be loved.

"Oh, I should be hanged for this."

"Don't stop—" she cried, feeling him pull away.

"You're barely eighteen," he whispered, once again moving away from her.

"But I love you."

The words seemed to sting. He stepped backward and sucked in a long, slow breath while Kaylie, her breasts still aching, her jacket draped off one shoulder, felt suddenly bereft and empty. Didn't he want her? She had only to look at him to know.

"Those are strong words," he said, his voice so low and rough she barely recognized it.

"But—"

"Shh!" Stepping forward, he placed a finger to her lips, and she kissed his knuckle, touching it with her tongue. He grabbed her roughly. "Stop it, damn you!" he growled. "Don't you know you're playing with fire?"

"I'm—"

"You're eighteen. Eighteen! And I'm being paid to keep you safe!" In frustration, he straightened her jacket.

"Let's get out of here before we do something we'll both regret."

"This is what I want," she pleaded as his fingers clamped around her wrist and he yanked her toward the path again.

"You're too young to know what you want."

"I'm not—"

"And you're too used to getting anything you desire. On a whim," he said with more than a trace of remorse. "I'm not a rich man, Kaylie. And I'm not going to blow this job by getting involved with you." Casting her a dark look over his shoulder, he added, "And I'm not some toy that you'll experiment with, lose interest in, then discard when you're bored."

"What?" she cried, planting her feet and trying to pull free of his grasp.

He stopped and then, as if he were searching for a way to throw away her feelings, he said, "Grow up."

She slapped him. With all the force of offended youth, she hauled back and smacked him across his wet cheek.

"You spoiled brat," he muttered, and she couldn't tell if he were angry or relieved. Maybe he'd baited her on purpose. But this time, when he took hold of her wrist, his grip was punishing, almost brutal as he half dragged her through the park, mindless of the muddy puddles that splashed her boots. The path cut through a rose garden and a thicket of oaks before spilling onto the sidewalk that flanked the hotel. "Thank God."

Furious, she couldn't resist taunting him. "So what're you going to do with me, Zane?" she baited, still reeling from his assessment of her as a "brat." "Turn me over your knee and spank me?"

He stopped dead in his tracks. His face went stark white. His fingers slackened, and he squeezed his eyes shut, pinching the bridge of his nose between thumb and forefinger, as if in so doing he could call up his fleeing patience. "No, Kaylie," he said, slowly opening eyes as hard as glass. "As soon as you're safely back at the hotel, I'm getting the hell out of here."

"Meaning?"

"That you'll just have to find yourself another body-guard."

No! Desperation tore at her. "But I don't want anyone else." She coiled her fingers around the lapels of his jacket and held on tightly, as if afraid he might run. "Don't you understand, Zane. I want you. *You.*"

Staring down at her upturned face, he let out a groan and dragged her closer still, kissing her over and over again. She felt him shudder against her, as if he were trying and failing to rein in impossible emotions.

Oblivious to the pedestrians hurrying, head and umbrellas tucked against the wind and rain, they held each other, she clinging to him as if to life itself, he embracing her as if she were a rare and fragile creature he was afraid to release for fear of never seeing again.

The wind and rain blew past, but they didn't care.

Finally he stepped away, his expression tortured and grim. He took both her chilled, wet hands in his. "This can't happen, you know."

"It already has."

He shook his head, though his eyes betrayed him. "Then it has to stop."

"No!" She knew what she wanted. Zane, Zane, Zane!

"Come on. You're getting drenched," he muttered, twining his fingers through hers as he pulled her up the steps to the glorious old hotel. Built to resemble an English castle, the hotel stretched a full city block. Gold brick, leaded glass, and tall, narrow windows created

seven stories. Lush gardens and brick courtyards surrounded the sprawling building.

Zane, propelling Kaylie by her elbow, hastened her
through the lobby and into an elevator. Once on the sev-
enth floor, he unlocked the door to her room and made
a sweeping search of the suite.

"Take a hot shower and I'll meet you downstairs for
dinner."

She wouldn't let him go. "Stay with me."

"Kaylie—"

"Please!"

He groaned and pulled his hand from hers. "I can't.
You can't. *We can't!*"

"But—"

"Don't you know this is killing me?" he finally admitted as she reached for him again, trying to kiss him,
feeling tears fill her eyes.

"I love—"

"Oh, God, Kaylie, don't!" he whispered, his voice raw
as he left her and closed the connecting door between
their rooms.

Later, at dinner, he refused to talk about their relationship. Instead, he was all business, sitting stiffly across
from her, his gaze moving restlessly over the other guests,
looking, searching for danger that didn't exist.

The meal, in Kaylie's opinion, was a disaster, and
upstairs in their suite again, things didn't improve. He
closed the door between them and refused to kiss her.

"I don't understand," she cried against the door panels, slamming her fist against the wall in frustration, but
she received no answer.

The next few days were torture. Zane acted like a complete stranger. He was distant and proper to the point that
she thought she might scream. She tried to draw him into

conversation, but his replies were quick monosyllabic answers. No more laughing. No more jokes. No more ad-libbing to her lines. Stiff and businesslike, he became the antithesis of the man with whom she'd fallen in love.

On the set three days later, she cracked. She blew her lines for the third time when the director waved everyone off the set and called for an hour break.

Kaylie, cheeks burning, walked straight to the docks. Zane was near her side, though, of course, he didn't say a word. Not one solitary word.

She clamped her hands over the rail and, without looking in his direction, shouted, "What's wrong with you?"

Zane leaned against the fender of a car as she pressed her nails into the painted railing and stared at the rippling blue waters reflecting against a clear, cerulean sky.

Gulls floated on the air currents near the docks, while sailboats and fishing trawlers skimmed across the horizon. Kaylie barely noticed, her concentration centered solely on Zane.

"Well?" she demanded, wanting to shake him.

"Nothing's wrong."

"Like hell! You've changed, Zane!"

"I'm just here to do a job."

"You care about me!"

"You're my client. My responsibility."

She flew at him. Emotionally strung out, she raised her fists as if to pummel his chest, but he captured her wrists and pinned them together over her head before she had a chance to strike. So close she could see her own reflection in his sunglasses, she felt helpless and tired. Tears welled in her eyes and she crumpled against him. "There's more—we both know it. Tell me there's more," she pleaded, her throat closing against the pain of his rejection.

"There can't be." But the corners of his lips turned down, and she knew he was fighting his own ragged emotions.

"I *love* you."

"Kaylie, no!" But his face was pained, and he sighed loudly…sadly. "God, help us," he whispered, releasing her and shoving one hand through his wind-ruffled hair. Looking toward the heavens, he swore. Was he angry? At her? Or himself?

"I do love you, damn it, and I always will." Sobs choked her. "I love you, Zane. Please, just love me back."

"It won't work."

"We'll make it work!" she cried, reaching up and lifting his sunglasses to see the agony in his eyes.

With a moan, he wrapped his arms around her and dropped his mouth on hers in a kiss that nearly strangled her with promised passion.

She closed her eyes to the storm of desire overtaking her. He did care! He did!

When he raised his head, she saw the torment on his face. "This *can't* happen. We can't let it."

But she kissed him again and again. Only when she knew the director would send someone looking for her did she pull back.

That night she expected Zane to come to her. She lay on her bed, wearing a soft pink nightgown, trembling at the thought of what she intended.

She watched the clock as the hours passed. Ten. Eleven. Midnight. Still the light beneath his door shone. At twelve-thirty, she could wait no longer and knocked softly. "Zane?"

The door opened. He stuck his head into her room. "What?"

She swallowed hard. Though she'd played the role before, she'd never seduced a man, never been in bed with a man. "I—I, uh, thought, you might like to come in…." Oh, Lord, why did her voice sound so high-pitched and trembling—like a child's?

"Are you all right?"

"Yes, but—"

"Then let's just leave it, Kaylie," he said, his voice as rough as sandpaper.

"I can't."

"Go to sleep." He shut the door firmly, and she wanted to die of embarrassment.

She couldn't sleep that night, nor the next. She was a failure at rehearsals, and the director, running behind schedule, was in a foul mood.

Zane was adamant. Cool and distant again. And no amount of anger or pleading would change his mind.

Until the phone call.

It came through at eleven o'clock on a rainy Monday night. Kaylie, restless anyway, picked up the receiver only to hear Margot's frail voice on the other end. "Kaylie?" Margot cried, her voice breaking. "Oh, Kaylie…"

"What?" Kaylie's heart leaped to her throat. Fear engulfed her.

"Oh, God, Kaylie. It's Mom and Dad…." Margot wailed. Nearly incoherent and sobbing uncontrollably, Margot cried on and on. Kaylie's insides turned to ice as she understood part of what Margot was saying—something about an accident and Mom and Dad and another car.

Trevor, Margot's boyfriend, took control, and his voice was firm as he explained about the accident. As he spoke, Kaylie understood. The room went out of focus. The floor tilted. Blackness surrounded her as she realized both her parents were dead, killed in a hideous accident on a winding mountain road in northern California.

She wasn't aware that she'd screamed, didn't realize that she'd sunk to the floor, couldn't feel the tears drizzling down her face, but all at once Zane was there, holding her, cuddling her, calming her as he spoke to Trevor.

He hung up and tried to get her to talk, to drink some water, to do anything, but her grief eclipsed all else.

"Shh, baby, shh," he said rocking her, but she was inconsolable.

He must have called the producer, who sent over a doctor, because she was given something to help her sleep. Even in her drugged state, images of her mother and father and a fiery automobile fused in her mind.

When she finally roused twelve hours later, Zane was there, his flinty eyes regarding her carefully, his jaw unshaven, his clothes wrinkled from sitting in the chair near her bed.

"I—I can't believe it," she said. Her head thundered, and her eyes burned with new tears. Her throat was hot and swollen and she felt as if she'd aged twenty years.

He came to her then. Took her into his arms and stretched out on the rumpled bed with her. "Oh, Kaylie, I'm so sorry," he whispered, his voice cracking. "But I'll take care of you," he vowed, kissing her crown. "I promise."

And he had. From that moment on, he'd never left her side. Through the funeral and resulting media circus, Zane was there, protecting her, sheltering her, being her rock in her storm-tossed sea of grief.

When the pain had finally lessened and she was able to put her life back together, Zane had come to her bed as a lover, not a protector. He held her and made love to her and became her reason for living. His caresses were divine, his lovemaking glorious, and she was certain she was in love.

They married in June, and for months Kaylie was in heaven. Living with and loving Zane was perfect. Their happiness knew no bounds, and though Zane sometimes seemed a little more concerned about her welfare than she thought was necessary, she loved him with all her heart.

Then the letters started arriving. Letters about love and lust and weird rituals. An anonymous person wrote her every day, pledging his love, promising that he would "perform an act of supreme sacrifice" for her. These letters were much more frightening than any others she'd received and the fact that the terrifying missives arrived daily put Zane on edge.

Kaylie wasn't concerned, and even thought Zane was overreacting. And he started calling her day and night when he wasn't with her, asking about her friends, checking into their backgrounds.

She began to feel smothered.

Terrified for her safety, he spent every waking hour trying to locate the man who was invading her life. He spent days with the police to no avail, and he transformed their home in Malibu, where they were living at the time, into a veritable fortress, with guard dogs, an electronic security system and remote-controlled gates.

Kaylie, always a free spirit, felt as if she were withering. Her home began to seem like a military compound.

Zane even tried to secure the cottage in Carmel, but Kaylie put her foot down. They needed some normalcy in their lives, she reasoned, and against his better judgment, he'd acquiesced.

But they grew further and further apart. Hell-bent on

protecting her, Zane refused to see that she was dying inside.

At nineteen she wanted an independence she'd never tasted, a freedom to make her own decisions, to live her own life, and all she wanted from him was his love.

They had worked on the marriage. Oh, Lord, she thought now, as she realized that they had both tried and fought to save their dying union. But they just hadn't tried hard enough.

Zane had become autocratic, and she'd become fiercely independent.

The letters had gotten worse, and when Lee Johnston, the anonymous person, finally accosted them at the premiere of *Obsession,* Zane had lost all control.

Now, SEVEN YEARS LATER, Kaylie swallowed the taste of fear that still touched the back of her throat as she remembered Johnston's blank face, his unseeing eyes, his hard body thrust up against hers. And the knife. God, she'd never forget the feel of polished steel against her throat.

If not for Zane, she might have died that night.

But Zane turned paranoid on her. Even though Johnston was locked up and the letters no longer made their way to her mailbox, Zane installed bigger and better security systems and used his best men to constantly patrol their home.

The marriage dissolved in its prison, and Kaylie had no option but to file for divorce.

At first he fought it. And he even tried to change. But he couldn't, and she doubted that he ever would. Even now, after seven years, he was still trying to run her life. Like Don Quixote fighting windmills, Zane was still grappling with the ghost of Lee Johnston.

And so was she.

Now, staring at the sunlight streaming over the mountains, Kaylie tossed off the old quilt. Today she'd talk some sense into him—today when she wasn't tipsy, when she was rational and calm.

She'd find a way to convince him that they couldn't stay up here alone together. Her heart couldn't take it.

CHAPTER FIVE

IT WAS TIME to take the offensive, Kaylie decided when she heard him rattling around downstairs. With renewed determination, she swept down the stairs and into the kitchen to find him seated on a bar stool, one booted foot propped on the bracing of the matching stool as he lazily flipped through the pages of a magazine.

"'Morning," he drawled with maddening calm. "Sleep okay?"

"As a matter of fact I didn't sleep much at all," she said, irritated, struggling to remain calm and rational. "So you've enjoyed your little joke," she said, shivering in her wrinkled sundress. "Now, let's get back to the real world."

Motioning around him, he said, "This, Lady Melville, is the real world."

"I can't stay here, Zane, even if I wanted to," she said, hoping to sound logical. "What do you think is going to happen when I don't show up on the set?"

He shoved the magazine aside. "Not much."

"Not much?" she repeated, hardly believing her ears but his expression didn't change. She glanced pointedly at her watch. "We have exactly forty-five minutes to get to the city."

"We won't make it," he said, climbing off his stool long enough to pour two cups of coffee. "Even if we wanted to."

"We do want to."

"Correction. You want to." He handed her one of the cups and took an experimental sip from his. "Careful. It's hot."

Kaylie's temper soared. "And I have no say in the matter—right? All my citizen's rights have been stripped since you brought me here to this...this prison! Well, I'm warning you, when my producer figures out that I've been kidnapped, there'll be hell to pay!"

He looked maddeningly unconcerned. "Relax. He won't guess."

"But when he calls—"

"He'll get your answering machine."

"Not good enough, Zane," she said, crossing the room and glaring straight into his eyes. For an instant, a flicker of pain crossed those gray irises, and Kaylie thought there was hope. He wasn't as immune to her feelings as he'd like to pretend.

"Crowley won't call."

"Of course he'll ca—" she started to say, but stopped short. Obviously Zane had taken steps to prevent anything from going wrong with this ridiculous plan of his! Of course! Fury caused her heart to surge wildly. "What'd you do, Zane?" she demanded. "I mean besides becoming a major criminal now wanted by the FBI. What *else* did you do?"

"I made sure that you wouldn't be missed." He settled back on his bar stool and propped his elbows on the counter, eyeing her over the rim of his cup.

Now she was worried. "How?"

"By making the appropriate calls."

"What calls?"

"To the station."

"No—"

"And your sister." He took another long swallow from his coffee.

"You called Margot?" she whispered, disbelieving.

"No, but my secretary did."

She believed him, and her heart sank. Finally she realized that this was no joke. He was dead serious. He intended to keep her captive for God-only-knew how long! She slumped onto the nearest bar stool and wrapped her suddenly chilled fingers around the hot cup of coffee. Was he really that worried about Johnston? Licking dry lips, she tried to think and stay rational. "No matter what you think might happen to me," she said, her voice uneven, "you had no right to bring me up here against my will."

"I know."

"But you don't care," she said, seeing him wince. She took a gulp of her coffee. It was hot and burned a path to her stomach. Avoiding his gaze, she glanced around the room and noticed the phone jack. "You took out all the phones," she said. "Afraid I might call for help."

"Afraid you might do something stupid."

"Nothing could top this trick of yours," she said, and to her surprise he laughed.

"I need to make some calls."

He eyed her speculatively, then finished his coffee in one swallow and walked out of the room and headed upstairs. The floorboards creaked overhead. He was down in a few minutes, cellular phone in hand. "Okay. Who do you want to call?"

She couldn't believe her good luck. "First the station, then Margot—"

"How about the hospital again? Or Henshaw's home—I've got the number."

"But—"

"No one else," he said firmly, his gaze hard. "I brought you up here for your safety and we're not blowing it."

Angry, she watched as he dialed a number, then handed the phone to her. Henshaw's answering machine clicked on, and she left a message that she would call back. Zane connected with Whispering Hills Hospital again, but Henshaw wasn't available. Again, Kaylie was stymied in her requests about Johnston.

Then it was Zane's turn. As he drank a second cup of coffee, he called his office and received an update from Brad Hastings.

"Nothing new yet," Zane said, hanging up. "Look, I know you're furious with me for bringing you here, but it's for your own good." When she started to protest, he held up a palm. "And don't give me any grief about treating you like a child. I don't mean to. I—I just don't want to lose you."

The honesty in his eyes cut straight to her soul. Her mouth worked, but no sound came out. *Don't,* she reminded herself, *don't trust him again. It's too easy to get lost in him.* All too vividly she remembered just how much she'd loved him; how she'd waken every day looking forward to his kiss, his laugh, his touch…. She cleared her throat as well as her mind. She wanted to tell him that he'd already lost her, but she held her tongue because there always had been and always would be a frail connection between them.

Phone in hand, he grabbed hold of the back door. "I have to take care of the stock."

"The what?"

"Horses and cattle."

She glanced out the window to the hills. Blue-green pine and spruce were interspersed with thickets of oak and maple. Through a break in the trees she noticed a weathered barn and split-rail fence. "What is this place?"

"It was an old logging camp, then it was turned into a ranch of sorts. I bought it a couple of years ago." He glanced at her, and one side of his mouth lifted. "Kind of a spur-of-the-moment thing. I decided I needed a place to get away from it all. I knew the guy who owned the property, and we struck a deal."

"This guy—your friend—did he abduct women against their will and bring them here, too?" she baited, unable to keep from smiling. There was a modicum of humor in this situation, after all.

His grin was slightly off center. "Not that I know of," he replied, "but you never can tell. Anyway, I sold some of the timber rights, but I decided to keep this house and a few acres for vacations."

"I didn't know you knew the meaning of the word."

"I'm learning," he drawled, "though no one ever accused me of being quick on the uptake."

Kaylie couldn't help but laugh. This was a new side to Zane, a side that was definitely appealing. She'd never thought of him as a person who was willing to kick back. That he, too, needed time to unwind and enjoy life touched her.

She eyed the big kitchen with its hanging copper pots, gleaming brass fittings and butcher-block counters. The room was airy and light, the windows sparkling clean. "So who keeps everything up when you're not here?"

"A retired couple—Max and Leona." Zane opened the door.

"And where are they?" Kaylie asked, hope springing in her heart. If she could just get the woman alone, explain her predicament, maybe Leona would understand and help her....

"Don't even consider it," Zane said, as if reading her mind. "I gave them an extended vacation and said I'd look after everything myself."

Kaylie's hopes crashed to the floor.

His gaze turned tender as he stared at her. What a sight she must be in her wrinkled dress, no makeup and tangled, unruly hair—a far cry from the famous teenager he'd once married, she thought ruefully.

"I'll be back in a minute." He walked through the door, leaving Kaylie alone. She took advantage of her short-lived freedom, hurrying from room to room, looking, with the help of daylight, for any means of escape. He took the phone with him and there was no CB radio! No living soul for miles!

She worked her way from the kitchen, dining room, living room and ended up in the den. A huge river-rock fireplace dominated one wall, and a bank of windows opposite offered a view of the sloping hillside and valley far below. A river, silver-gray against the blue-green pines, glinted through the trees. Autumn had touched the maples and oaks, turning the leaves gold or fiery red. Wildflowers bloomed in vibrant yellow, pink and blue, providing splashes of color in the dark forest.

"Beautiful, isn't it?" Zane asked, lounging in the doorway.

Kaylie whirled to see him staring at her. Goose bumps appeared on her skin. "I suppose it could be, were the situation different."

"It can be different, Kaylie. All you have to do is accept the fact that you're here and enjoy it."

She hesitated. It sounded so perfect. And too good to be true. "I can't."

He shrugged. "Then you're probably going to have a miserable couple of weeks."

A couple of weeks! she thought in horror. She had to get back now, today, as soon as possible. She couldn't be gone for two days, much less two weeks, for God's sake! For the first time she noticed the duffel bag hanging from his fingers. Her bag! "What's in that?" she asked, dreading the answer.

"I thought you might need a change."

"But how—"

"While you were swimming," he said, then his smile twisted. "I didn't have much time, though, so I just threw some things into the bag. It was hidden beneath the tarp in the back of the Jeep."

"You went through my drawers?" she asked, furious as she conjured up the image of him pawing through her clothes, her stockings, her lingerie....

"It wasn't anything I hadn't seen before," he reminded her softly, then cleared his throat. "I didn't think you'd wear anything I bought you."

"You bought me?" she queried.

"There are clothes in the closet upstairs. Surely you saw them—"

"They don't belong to some woman you're involved with?"

He smiled sadly. "They're yours."

"Mine?" Her heart stopped. "Then this was planned, right? For *days?*" So angry she was shaking, she started for the door.

Zane was quick. His hand shot out, and strong fingers wrapped around her wrist. "Kaylie," he said softly, "slow down a minute—don't go jumping to conclusions." His hands were gentle, his gaze fastened on hers. "Yes, this took a little time to arrange," he admitted. "About ten hours, give or take a few minutes. I found out about Johnston yesterday morning. I had my secretary run out and buy clothes—size six, right?—and ship them here via a company van. At the same time I called the Browns—Max and Leona—and offered them a dream vacation that they well deserved and told them to take the telephones with them."

"And what about me, Zane?" she asked, pressing her face closer to his, standing on tiptoe to stare at him. "Did you ever wonder how I'd react? Did you realize that there's a good chance that I'll never forgive you for hauling me up here against my will?"

His jaw slid to the side, and his eyes searched her face. "That would be a shame, Kaylie," he said, his voice husky, and she knew in an instant that he intended to kiss her. She tried to yank away from him, but his fingers tightened around her arm. "Whether you admit it or not, we're good together." In one swift motion, he tugged impatiently on her wrist, lowered his head and captured her lips with his.

Kaylie struggled, but his arms closed possessively around her and his mouth moved sensually against hers. No! No! Her mind screamed, though her body began to tingle and familiar emotions tore at her heart. With all her strength she pushed away from him, away from the seduction of his body against hers. But he held her tighter, kissing her and stealing the breath from her lungs. The harder she struggled, the stronger he became, his will as unbending as steel.

His hands were hot against her bare shoulders, his mouth demanding. His tongue pressed hard against her teeth and gained entrance to her mouth.

A thousand memories—glorious and loving—flitted through her mind.

He groaned softly, and her blood turned to fire. Heedless of the danger signals, she began to kiss him back, passion exploding from anger. He smelled and tasted and felt so right. His hard, anxious body, pressed tightly to hers, caused an ache to burn deep in the most feminine part of her. As if in a dream, she wondered how it would feel to make love to him again.

The thought hit her like a bucket of cold water. Realizing just how easily she could be seduced, she recoiled inside and shoved hard against his shoulders, struggling and breaking free.

"Don't—don't ever—" she gasped, trying to think rationally and failing miserably "—do that again!"

"Why not?" he asked, his eyes gleaming, a satisfied smile plastered across his jaw. "Didn't you enjoy it?"

"No!"

"Kaylie, don't lie!"

She backed up, her cheeks flaming, her feet nearly stumbling over an ottoman. "You took me by surprise, that's all."

He cocked a disbelieving dark brow. "Maybe I should plan some more surprises."

"Maybe you should go out and feed the cows or horses or chickens or whatever it is you've got here and leave me alone!"

One dark brow arched in skepticism. "Leave you alone. That, I'm afraid, will be hard to do."

"Consider it a challenge!" she said, though she knew that being locked in close quarters with him would make it as difficult for her as it was for him.

He didn't leave. Instead he crossed his arms over his chest. To her consternation, he actually grinned—that boyish and adorable grin that wormed its way straight through her cold facade. "We *should* declare a truce. You know, wave the white flag—try to be civil to each other instead of always lunging for the jugular."

"In this situation?"

"It'll make things easier."

"For you!"

"For both of us," he said softly. "Come on, give it a rest. You might just find that you'll enjoy yourself."

She swallowed hard. That was exactly what she was afraid of—enjoying herself. Why couldn't she just hate him? It would be so much easier than fighting these lingering feelings that she couldn't quite forget. "I—I don't know."

"I'll be good," he promised, but a gleam sparked in his eyes.

What would it hurt? She was tired of the constant battle, though she still bristled at the thought of his high-handed technique of kidnapping her. She had rights, rights he had no business ignoring. "You know, Zane, I'd like to trust you—to get along with you, I really would," she admitted honestly, "but it'll be hard."

"Try," he suggested. "I'll be on my best behavior—charming and good-natured and…as fair as possible."

She blew her bangs out of her eyes in frustration. Fair? Impossible. But there was something beguiling about his smile, something she couldn't resist—something she had never been able to fight. "A truce, hmm?" she said, picking up a crystal paperweight and tossing it into the air only to catch it again. "Okay—on one condition."

"Name it."

"That as soon as we find out that Lee Johnston won't be allowed out of the mental hospital, you release me."

His mouth tightened imperceptibly, but he rounded the desk and extended his hand to her. "It's a deal," he said, wrapping strong fingers over hers.

"Deal," she agreed, shaking his hand, then trying to retrieve her palm from his grasp.

But he didn't let go. Instead he tugged slightly and, lowering his head, dropped a gentle kiss across her mouth. Soft as a whisper, his lips lingered against hers. Tenderness flooded her and she felt weak inside.

"I promise you," he reassured, lifting his head and staring into her eyes, "I won't let anything happen to you."

Her throat clogged. "I—I don't need a bodyguard."

One side of his mouth twisted wryly. "I hope you're right." He scooped a felt Stetson from the brass tree near the door and sauntered out of the room.

She touched her lips with her fingertips. Her pulse was thundering, her knees weak. She sagged against the desk and ran trembling fingers through her hair. Oh, Kaylie, girl, you're in a mess this time! You thought he was out of your system for good, but just one kiss and you melted inside.

She closed her eyes, squeezing them shut, forcing her breathing to slow, her heartbeat to quiet. This would never do. She had to think, be on her toes every minute. Or else she would end up falling in love with him again! "Oh, God," she whispered, afraid of the pain and heartache.

She heard the back door slam shut. Taking a deep breath, she moved to the window and saw Zane, his stride lazy and sensual, as he walked to the barns.

After watching him disappear into a weathered building, Kaylie pulled herself together. Hauling her bag with her, she climbed the stairs again. She needed to shower, change and think. But being around Zane made rational thought nearly an impossibility.

In her room, she opened the walk-in closet and studied the clothes neatly folded and stacked on the shelves. Once again, Zane had surprised her. Slacks, blouses, sweaters, shorts, skirts and dresses—all in her size! Now it was blindingly clear that the outfits, purchased from upscale department stores in San Francisco, were intended for her. How could she have thought otherwise?

As Kaylie gazed at the wardrobe, her heart sank. There was certainly more than two weeks of clothes here!

She intended to shower and change, then she'd put escape plan A into action.

"And what's that?" she asked herself as she stripped and stepped under the shower's steamy spray. But she had no answer. She just knew she couldn't let Zane dominate her again. She could handle her life by herself, but the thought of Lee Johnston turned her insides to ice.

Lolling her head back, she forced herself to relax. Warm rivulets of water ran down her shoulders and back. She closed her eyes and thought about Zane again, the power of his kiss flooding her senses.

Unconsciously she licked her lips and shivered deliciously at the memory of his mouth sliding seductively over hers.

Her eyes flew open, and she silently cursed her own weakness. Truce or no truce, she had to get out of here and fast. And it wasn't only because of the way in which he'd shoved himself back in her life. No, she realized fatalistically, she had to get away from him! Because, like it or not, he was right. It wouldn't take long before she might let herself fall in love with him all over again.

CHAPTER SIX

TWO CAN PLAY at this game, Kaylie thought, buffing her body with a towel. If Zane intended to charm her to death, well, she'd just charm him right back, lead him to trust her enough to let down his guard.

And then she'd make good her escape, somehow leaving him high and dry, his plans foiled. A part of her yearned for that satisfaction; she was just plain tired of him trying to run her life, and yet she couldn't fault him completely. He was, or so he claimed, only looking out for her own good.

A breath of wind slipped through the window, and Kaylie shivered. Wrapping the towel around her body, she strode into the bedroom and surveyed it with new eyes. It was a prison, yes, but not a horrible place to stay. Zane could have made the accommodations much worse; as it was, she had a little freedom, which, she supposed, she should savor. He wasn't breathing down her neck twenty-four hours a day, and she wasn't sleeping with him. Opening the closet, she remembered how much she'd loved Zane in the past, how she'd trusted him with her life. In all truth, he'd saved her once before just as he thought he was saving her now.

Her eyes narrowed thoughtfully as she pulled a pair of stonewashed jeans and a peach-colored T-shirt from the shelf.

"Breakfast's ready," Zane whispered from behind her.

She nearly jumped out of her skin. Clutching the bath sheet around her, she turned to find him in the doorway. She'd been so lost in thought she hadn't heard him climb the stairs or push open the door. "Do you mind?" she asked, arching a lofty brow. "I'm trying to get dressed."

"Don't let me stop you," he drawled, an amused smile toying with the corners of his mouth.

"You're pushing it, Flannery," she warned.

He lifted his palms. "We agreed to a truce, remember?"

"Ahh. The truce. Don't you think we should set down some rules to this agreement? And I think the first should be that you quit sneaking up behind me and scaring the living daylights out of me." She tucked her towel more securely over her breasts. "I'll be down in a minute. And next time…knock, okay?"

He rubbed a hand around his neck and cast a devilish glance over his shoulder. "And miss seeing you like this?" He shook his head, and a lock of hair fell over his forehead. "No way. If you want privacy, next time lock your door."

She finished dressing and hurried downstairs where the scents of sausage and coffee wafted through the rooms. The kitchen table had been set for two, and a huge platter of eggs, sausage links and toast was steaming on the counter.

Zane waved her into a chair and poured black coffee into their cups. "I'll be right back."

"Where're you going…?" But he was already out the kitchen door.

A few minutes later he returned carrying a portable television. "Where'd you get that?" she demanded.

One side of his mouth lifted cynically. "There you go again, hoping to get me to divulge my darkest secrets."

"I thought we had a truce," she reminded him.

He plugged the TV into the counter outlet, snapped it on, then fiddled with the antenna. "We do. That's why I'm being so irresistible."

"So *that's* the reason," she remarked dryly.

"Aha!" he said, finally satisfied with the reception.

Kaylie heard the familiar lead-in music to *West Coast Morning.*

"Oh, no," she said, her appetite nearly forgotten as the camera closed in on Alan Bently's handsome face.

"There he is—your fiancé," Zane said good-naturedly, though Kaylie thought she saw a muscle tighten in his jaw. "What a guy! Look at that! Even his makeup is perfect."

"He's not my fiancé." Kaylie shot Zane a warning glance just as Alan made eye contact with the camera.

"Good morning!" Alan said. His brown eyes didn't blink, and his smile seemed a little forced. "You may have noticed that Kaylie Melville isn't with us today," he said half-apologetically. "She won't be with us for the rest of the week as she was called away from the city for personal reasons...."

"I was *what?*" Kaylie cried, astounded.

"Sick aunt," Zane explained, fiddling with the dials at the bottom of the set.

"What?"

"Your aunt. Very ill. Needs care."

"I don't like the sound of this," she said, pinning him with a glare that was meant to bore holes through solid steel. "I don't even have an aunt!" She reached for a piece of toast and thought aloud. "So you must've told Margot something else. She wouldn't buy into the sick-aunt scenario."

"Nope. But your sister thought it was romantic that I was whisking you away to a private hideaway."

"You *told* her?"

"Of course I told her."

"Just wait 'til I see her again," Kaylie muttered, feeling betrayed by her own flesh and blood. Margot might not know it yet, but when Kaylie saw her again, there was going to be trouble. Big trouble! She ripped off a piece of toast and popped it into her mouth.

"Margot will probably defend me," Zane predicted. "In fact, she said she wished some 'knight on a white steed would carry her away to some romantic hideaway.'"

"Oh, give me a break!" But Kaylie could almost hear Margot uttering those exact words. Whereas Kaylie had always been sensible when it came to men—well, men other than Zane—Margot had been the dreamer, the romantic.

"Besides, she's concerned about your safety and she let me know that she doesn't much like Alan."

"She *knows* how I feel about Alan. No two-bit scandal sheet would change her mind."

As Zane buttered toast and scooped eggs onto his plate, Kaylie turned her attention back to the set. Didn't Zane know that Alan wasn't her type? Even years ago, when they'd filmed *Obsession* together and Alan had shown some interest in her, Kaylie had told him in no uncertain terms to keep his distance. She had been married to Zane at the time, and she wasn't interested in a steamy off-camera affair with Alan or anyone else for that matter. In fact, she had been so head over heels in love with Zane that she had actually laughed at Alan's sleazy attempts at seduction. Fortunately, Alan had taken the hint. Long ago.

"Old Alan looks pretty comfortable without you,"

Zane observed, taking a bite. "He kind of glossed over your absence, don't you think?"

"What was he going to say?" she countered. "He's not exactly dealing with all the facts, is he?"

Zane stopped chewing. "When you and Alan did your last picture together, he was the one ranting and raving for top billing, higher salaries, a bigger dressing room."

"A lot has changed since we filmed *Obsession*."

Zane's eyes darkened. "Amen." He shoved his plate aside, half his food uneaten, and touched the tips of her fingers with his. "So if you're not involved with Bently, who is the man in your life?"

Her lungs grew tight, and she quickly pulled her hand away. "Why don't you tell me? You're the one who seems to know everything about my life." She wished he'd just drop the subject; she didn't want to admit that she wasn't romantically involved with anyone, nor had she been since Zane. The dates and publicized relationships over the past few years had never become serious. She hadn't let herself become involved with any one man. However, she wasn't about to tell Zane about her less-than-fulfilling love life. If Zane knew she was entirely unattached, the feelings hovering in the shadows would only intensify the emotions already charging the air between them. No, it was better if Zane thought she was involved with another man.

"There is something more I should tell you," he admitted, his finger slowly rimming his cup in suggestive circles.

Kaylie's throat went dry. "What?"

The honesty honing his features disarmed her, his fingers quit moving on the rim of his cup. "I've missed you, Kaylie. I've missed everything about you."

"Zane, please—"

"You wanted the truth, didn't you? Well, you're going to get it."

She watched as he shoved his chair back and walked to the window. Staring out, his rigid back to her, he said, "I missed coming home to you at night. I missed hearing you sing in the shower. I missed your lingerie draped in the bathroom, I missed your perfume on the pillows, the feel of your hair brushing my face at night, the way you kicked your shoes into the closet…. I missed…" He turned and stared at her, his expression pensive and tormented. "I missed you, Kaylie. All of you."

Her throat tightened, and for a second she thought the tears burning behind her eyes might spill. He sounded so sincere and a part of her longed to believe him.

"So…you've taken advantage of this…situation. Is that what this is all about?" she whispered, her voice shaky, her hands clenched so tightly around her napkin her fingers ached.

The muscles in the back of his neck tensed. "No." Without another word, he walked out the door and it slammed behind him with a bang.

Kaylie tried to eat but the food stuck in her throat. Her appetite was gone. Angrily shoving her plate aside, she attempted to think rationally, to tell herself not to fall under Zane's spell again, but the simple truth was that she still cared about him—maybe loved him.

"You're the worst kind of fool," she muttered, blinking back tears. She ran up to her room, snagged a jacket from the closet and struggled into boots that were a little too tight. Clomping back downstairs, she headed out the front door and nearly ran over Franklin, who, upon spying her, growled.

"I hope your bark is worse than your bite," she said, sidestepping the dog.

The morning air was crisp. Drops of dew glistened on the sun-bleached grass, and sunlight streamed through the trees, warming the ground in dappled patches. Craggy mountains towered over the forests, and a few stray clouds drifted lazily in the blue sky.

This place was a touch of heaven, she thought reluctantly, remembering Zane's description last night as he hauled her up here. And it did seem heavenly compared to her hectic pace in the city and the job she'd left. "The job you were hijacked from," she corrected herself. "Sick aunt, indeed!"

She stopped at the Jeep and checked to see if it was unlocked. But the shiny rig hadn't moved since Zane had parked it and the cellular phone was nowhere in sight. Every door, including the tailgate, was secured. The windows were rolled up and even the hood was latched. "Wonderful," she sighed, dusting her hands.

She headed around the corner of the house and down a gravel lane to several outbuildings. The first small building was locked, so she balanced on her tiptoes on a chunk of wood and brushed aside the dust that had collected on the windowpanes. Shading her eyes, she squinted into the darkened interior. This particular building was a storage shed of sorts. Bags of feed and drums of oil, wheelbarrows and rakes, chain saws and other tools were stacked against the walls. In her peripheral vision she saw movement—a shadow. She braced herself.

"Find what you're looking for?" Zane asked, propping one booted foot against the bottom rail of a fence. Franklin had linked up with him again and flopped down in the shade cast by the barn.

"Here, maybe this will help." He reached into his pocket, withdrew a key ring and tossed it to her.

Kaylie snatched the ring in midair. She couldn't believe he'd give her his keys. Now, if she could make it to the Jeep....

As if reading her thoughts, he extracted a second ring. "These are to the equipment," he said, jangling his keys in the air. Kaylie watched as sunlight glinted against the sharp piece of metal. "But those—" he motioned to the keys gripped tightly in her fingers "—will get you in and out of most of the buildings on the place. Just be sure to lock all the doors behind you."

The man was absolutely infuriating! "Oh, yes, *master*," she mocked. "And when I leave the room, I'll bow at your feet."

"That would be nice," he drawled, with the hint of a smile.

"You're insufferable and overbearing—and a bully to boot!"

Zane's smile disappeared. "Let's get out of here," he said, striding across the gravel that separated them and grabbing hold of her wrist.

"Sounds good to me. This wasn't my idea in the first place!"

"Then you won't object?"

"Me? Object to anything you say? Never!"

"That's more like it!"

Insufferable. That's what he was! But she didn't protest as he tugged on her arm. Though she had to half run to keep up with him, she let him pull her along the short lane to the barn she'd spied earlier from the den. The exterior of the old building was weathered, the metal roof rusted in places, but the fenced paddocks still held a few head of white-faced cattle.

Zane shoved on a huge door of the barn, and it creaked open. They stepped inside. The interior was dark. It smelled of horses and new hay, dust and cobwebs.

"Over there," he said, taking her arm and propelling her across the worn plank floor to the back of the barn where two horses, on the other side of the manger, stood, tails switching, bridled and saddled. "I thought we'd take a ride."

Kaylie cocked a brow. "And what makes you think I won't just take off?"

"On Dallas, here?" he asked, nodding toward a rangy bay gelding. "Not much chance. He knows when it's feeding time and no matter where he is, he hightails it back here."

The horse looked docile enough. Big brown eyes blinked as the gelding studied her without much interest.

"Unless you've taken a few riding lessons in the past seven years, you won't get two miles from this place on Dallas." He grinned deviously in the half light. "Besides, even if you try, this boy, here," he said, hooking a thumb at a muscular chestnut stallion, "will catch you. Meet His Majesty."

She looked pointedly at him and deadpanned, "I thought I already had."

Zane's lips twitched. "He's second in command."

"Oh." Kaylie looked thoughtful. "Let me get this straight. I'm riding a horse named Dallas and you're on His Majesty?"

"You got it." Zane opened the stalls and led both animals out of the barn.

"Figures," Kaylie muttered, blinking against the sudden brightness as Zane shouldered open the door.

They mounted the horses and rode through a series of paddocks holding several other horses and a few head of cattle. The grass was dry, the ground hard, but still the animals grazed, plucking at the few yellow blades, flicking flies with their tails, or standing in the shadows of the nearby forest.

A few spindly legged foals hid behind their mother's rumps and one feisty white-faced calf bellowed as they passed. Zane, surprisingly, seemed relaxed in the saddle and Kaylie, not much of a horsewoman, pretended that it was second nature to sit astride a huge animal with a mind of his own.

"Where're we going?" she asked, shading her eyes and wishing she had thought to bring along a pair of sunglasses.

"To the ridge."

"Why?"

He glanced over his shoulder, and his gray gaze touched hers. "For the view."

Zane was riding a horse up to a ridge in the mountains in order to show her a view? If anyone had told her two days ago this would be happening, she would have laughed in his face. And yet she found Zane's newfound laid-back, get-away-from-the-rat-race attitude appealing.

The ride took nearly two hours as the horses picked their way up an overgrown trail. Kaylie's legs began to ache, and her eyes burned from squinting against the sun. She took off her jacket and tied the sleeves around her waist as Dallas plodded after His Majesty.

As she swayed in the saddle, Kaylie tried to find interest in the wildflowers sprinkled among the trees, or in the flight of a hawk circling high overhead, but her gaze, as if controlled by an unnamed force, continually wandered back to Zane. His dark hair shimmered in the sunlight and curled seductively over his collar. His shoulders stretched wide, pulling at the seams of his shirt. His sleeves were pushed over his forearms, exposing tanned skin, a simple watchband and a dusting of dark hair.

There was something earthy and masculine that surrounded him, an aura she found captivating. She noticed
how his shirt bunched over the waistband of his jeans,
the way his belt dipped in back as he rode.

Right now all she could think about was one man—
the one man who had once been her husband, the man
who had loved her so thoroughly she'd been sure no other
could take his place.

Maybe no one could.

That thought caused her to draw back on the reins.
Dallas sidestepped, snorting and prancing, his ears flicking as Kaylie eased up on the bit. How easy it would be
to fall in love with Zane again. *If you're not in love with
him already.* "No!" she cried, and Dallas reared.

Zane yanked his horse around. His face was grim.
"What?"

"Nothing," she said quickly, feeling her cheeks flame
as she settled her horse. "I—I just lost control for a minute." She couldn't fall in love with him again! Wouldn't
allow herself the painful luxury!

"You're okay?" He didn't seem convinced, and the
concern in his eyes touched a forbidden part of her soul.

"Just fine," she answered with only a trace of sarcasm.

One side of his mouth lifted. "Good. We're almost
there."

The path curved sharply north, and the tall pines gave
way to a rolling meadow of dry grass. A creek cut into
the dry earth as it raced downhill to pool in a lake that
reflected the blue of the mountain sky.

Kaylie, as she slid from the saddle, couldn't help but
be enchanted. "It's gorgeous," she murmured, looking
past this little alpine valley and over the ridge, where
mountains steepled and gray-green forests covered the

lower slopes. Zane tethered the horses, and the two dusty beasts sipped from the stream.

"That's the house," he said, standing behind her and pointing over her shoulder. His sleeve barely touched hers, and yet she was all too aware of him, his earthy scent, the warmth of his skin, the clean, sharp angle of his jaw. He extended one long finger, and Kaylie was mesmerized by the tanned length of arm and hand stretched in front of her.

She followed his gaze and saw, far below, nearly obliterated by fir trees, the roof of the old log cabin.

"You know," she said, "I never saw you as someone who would retreat up here."

He glanced down at her, and his lips pressed tightly together. "I learned a few years ago that some things are more important than business."

Her heart nearly stopped beating. "Did you?"

"You taught me that lesson, Kaylie." The look in his eyes grew distant and guarded. Tension controlled his rugged features. "Seeing you with Johnston on the night of the premiere brought everything into sharp focus. Nothing mattered but your safety. But, of course, it was too late." She watched as his naked pain dissolved to a cynical expression. He swept his hair back with the flat of his hand. "But you've never understood that I only protected you because I loved you and I was afraid of losing you. And I drove you away—did the one thing I was afraid someone else would do."

The air between them hung heavy with silence. Only the lapping of the water, the twitter of birds in the surrounding pines and the painful cadence of her own heartbeat broke the stillness. Kaylie knew the devastating grief of losing people she loved. Hadn't she lost her parents

when she was young? And Zane had been there to pick
up the pieces.

He leaned closer, so close that she saw flecks of blue
in his gray eyes. "Losing you was the hardest thing I've
ever experienced."

Kaylie's eyes burned. When Zane's hand slid upward
and strong fingers wrapped around the back of her neck,
she didn't resist, but tilted her face upward.

His lips brushed intimately over hers, and she parted
her mouth expectantly.

The wind swept through the trees, soughing through
the scented pine boughs. Shadows shifted in the sunlight
as Zane's arms wrapped tightly around her.

Kaylie closed her eyes and tried to think of all the
reasons she should push him away. But the pressure of
his mouth on hers, the intimate caress of his tongue, the
feel of strong fingers splayed possessively along her back
were too seductive to ignore. With the sun warm against
her back, she succumbed, winding her arms around his
neck.

Desire surged through her, and she moved closer to
him, felt his anxious thighs against hers. The sweet pressure of his arms wrapped around her and held her so
close that her breasts were crushed and she could barely
breathe.

Her feet left the ground. He carried her to a thicket
of pines and laid her on a bed of needles near the water.
Then he stretched out beside her and his lips found hers
in a kiss that was hot and wild and filled with emotion.

His hands moved downward, sculpting each of her
ribs, his thumbs brushing the swell of her breasts.

Kaylie moaned softly as her nipples hardened and a
moist heat in the depths of her womanhood swirled. Lost
in battling emotions, she clung to him, laid her head back

and felt the warm moist trail of his tongue as he kissed her throat and tugged on her shirt, exposing more of her skin.

Her breasts ached for his touch, her body quivered in a need that was overpowering.

He rolled atop her, and the weight of his body was welcome, the feel of his skin against hers divine.

She ignored all the voices in her head that still whispered she was making an irrevocable mistake, and she wound her hands in his hair, then let her fingers trail down the strident muscles of his back and shoulders.

"Make love to me, Kaylie," he whispered against her ear, and she could barely think. Blood was pounding at her temples, desire creating an ache so intense, she only wanted release.

He stroked the front of her T-shirt, resting the flat of his hand over her pounding heart.

"You want me."

She stared up at him. His handsome face was strained, perspiration dotted his brow. Above him, branches shifted against the blue, blue sky.

"You want me," he said again.

"Y-yes." She couldn't deny what was so patently obvious. She ached for him, yearned for him, burned deep inside with a longing so intense, she could think of nothing but the feel of his sweat-soaked body claiming hers in lovemaking as savage as it was sweet.

"And I want you," he whispered hoarsely.

He wasn't lying. She could feel his hardness through his jeans, rubbing against her hips, causing a friction that seared to her very core. She moved with him and sighed when he pulled her T-shirt from the waistband of her jeans and reached upward, the tips of his fingers grazing her lace-encased nipples.

"Oh, Zane," she whispered, her mouth finding his as she arched closer, wanting more.

He kissed her again, then his tongue slid down the milk-white skin of her throat, past her breasts, to the sensitive flesh of her abdomen.

"Zane," she whispered, and he buried his face in her.

A strangled sound escaped his lips, his breath fanned against her skin, and when he dragged his head upward and met her gaze, his eyes were glazed and stormy, as if he were fighting an inner battle that tore at his soul.

She reached upward to clasp her arms around his neck and drag his lips to hers, but he grabbed her hands. "Don't," he said, clenching his eyes shut and sucking in a swift breath.

"Zane?"

"Just don't!" The skin across his cheeks was stretched taut, and he dropped her hands, pushing himself upright. He swore violently.

"Is something wrong?" she asked as he rolled away, sitting with his back to her as he drew in long, steadying breaths.

"Everything."

"I don't understand."

"Don't you?" He twisted around, facing her again. "I intended to seduce you, Kaylie. I've planned it ever since I knew we'd be together again."

She could barely keep her eyes raised to his.

"But it's not enough."

"What—?"

"Physical lust isn't enough," he explained, the brackets near the corners of his mouth showing white. "It has to be more!" His fist pounded the dusty ground and he swore at himself between clenched teeth.

"But—I mean, I thought—"

"I know what you thought. And you were right. I planned to have you—right here and now. But I need more than a quick, hot session in the forest, Kaylie!"

She gasped and blushed to the roots of her hair. "I don't understand—"

"Sure you do. I want it all." He pulled her close to him, roughly jerking her against the rock-hard wall of his chest. His face was warm and close, his breath scented with coffee. "Let's go—"

"But—"

He whistled for the dog and climbed onto his mount. Kaylie straightened her clothes, confused and bereft and feeling like a complete fool. Good Lord, she'd nearly made love to him and he'd rejected her!

She gathered up Dallas's reins, and, slapping the leather against the gelding's withers, she wondered how she was ever going to survive the next few days being trapped up here alone with Zane.

CHAPTER SEVEN

"IT'S JUST NOT LIKE Kaylie to leave us in the lurch like this," Jim Crowley, producer of *West Coast Morning,* grumbled. He stepped over the thick camera cables as he made his way off the cozy set, which was designed to look like the living room in one of San Francisco's charming row houses.

He headed down a short hall to his office, with his assistant, Tracy Montclair, following one step behind.

"Even Kaylie Melville has a personal life, you know," she pointed out.

"All of a sudden? In the past six and a half years, Kaylie hasn't missed one show. Not one. This just isn't like her." He shoved open the glass door to his office and stalked to the desk.

The ashtray was overflowing, and he dumped the contents into a wastebasket, then settled into his creaky leather chair.

"Call that sister of hers—Marge, isn't it?"

"Margot."

"Whatever." Jim winced as a nerve in his lower back twinged, the aftermath from a game of racquetball. "Phone Margot and see if there's a number where we can reach Kaylie."

"Oh, come on, Jim. You're not serious, are you? She's with her aunt in a hospital somewhere, for God's sake!"

"Well, even hospitals have phone numbers." Jim tried

to ignore his craving for a cigarette and unwrapped a stick of gum. "I need to talk to her. We've got a helluva schedule next week and I don't think Alan can handle it alone."

"She may be back by then."

"Well, let's not leave it to chance, okay?" He wadded the gum into a small clump and tossed it into his mouth just as there was a quick rap on the door. Through the glass he spied Alan Bently.

"I swear that guy's got radar," Jim muttered under his breath. Alan had the annoying habit of showing up every time his name was mentioned. "What's up?" he asked, as Alan slid into the chair next to Tracy's.

Alan flashed his thousand-watt smile. Though no longer a leading man, he still had an on-camera charisma that attracted the female viewers. "I just thought we'd better discuss the next couple of shows. Unless Kaylie gets back soon, we've got to rethink the format. Starting with Monday."

Jim scowled. "Reformat? How?"

"Well, I assume I'll have to do all the interviews as well as the news." Alan leaned forward, resting his elbows on his knees, looking earnest as he proceeded to explain to Jim that he could host the hour format of *West Coast Morning* all by himself.

FOR KAYLIE, THE NEXT FEW DAYS were torture. Torn between her life in San Francisco and the excitement of this adventure with Zane, she alternately formed plans of escape and talked herself out of them.

She felt as if she were on an emotional battlefield. One minute they were at each other's throats, the next, waving the white flag.

Zane's office hadn't come up with any new information on Lee Johnston. "Ted" hadn't called again. Dr. Henshaw was still out of town, though Brad Hastings promised to visit him at Whispering Hills the minute he returned. He also had an appointment scheduled with the administrator of the hospital.

Zane's nerves were strung tight. He admitted that he felt useless up here, that he should be in San Francisco checking things out for himself, but at the mention of returning to civilization, he blew up. Kaylie was safe here—at least temporarily.

It almost seemed as if they were married again, except of course, they didn't go to bed together. And, as in their marriage, Zane was dominating the relationship.

Half the time Kaylie was furious with him, and yet she could feel her emotions swaying and she was softening bit by bit. Often in the past seventy-two hours she'd caught him watching her when he'd thought she wasn't looking, and she had noticed how he'd avoided even the briefest physical contact. That was the hard part—being so close to him and yet not touching.

During the days, they took horseback rides, mended the fence, worked on the house, took care of the stock, and Kaylie found herself fantasizing about Zane—remembering the good part of their marriage, the love that had been so special. In the evenings they talked, watched television, played cribbage or petted the dog. Franklin still wasn't crazy about her, but he accepted her and even thumped his tail on the floor when she walked into a room. And that was progress.

To her surprise, she discovered Zane had changed, just as he'd said he had—he'd mellowed with the past seven years, and she couldn't help wondering what life would be like now, were she married to him.

But that was an entirely irrational thought.

Now, as he knelt at the fireplace and laid firewood in the grate, she watched the pull of his jeans at his hips, the slice of skin that was exposed as his sweater inched upward. He glanced over his shoulder and motioned to the empty wood basket. "You could help, you know."

"Could I?" She laughed. Seated on the couch and swirling a glass of wine, she added, "And here I thought you were going to treat me to a life of leisure—you know, pamper me to death."

"No way." He dusted his hands. "I thought you were a fiercely independent woman who wouldn't let any man treat you as less than an equal."

"Well, I am, but—"

"Then get some wood," he suggested, nudging the empty basket toward her with the toe of his boot.

"Slave driver," she whispered, taking a last swallow of wine. "You'll pay for this, Flannery." Smiling good-naturedly, she grabbed the basket and marched out the front door.

"I don't doubt it," he called after her.

Outside, a cool breeze swept over the mountainside and a thin stream of moonlight guided her. A few stars winked jewel-like in the black sky and an owl hooted from a nearby stand of pine. The wind picked up, and the air was heavy with the promise of rain.

Kaylie walked past the Jeep and noticed that the interior light was on.

Her heart skipped a beat.

She reached for the door, and it opened.

She hesitated for a second. This was her chance, but did she really want to leave? She chewed on the inside of her lip and glanced at the house. Of course she had to leave—she had no choice! As long as Zane tried to con-

trol her, she had no will of her own. And she was falling
for him again. That was dangerous.

Swallowing hard, she dropped the basket and slid into
the interior, realizing that she didn't have his keys. Crossing her fingers, she silently prayed that he'd left the keys
in the ignition. No such luck. Even though Zane had made
several trips carrying grain from the storage shed to the
barn in the Jeep, he hadn't forgotten his keys. Nor the
phone. It, too, was missing.

"Damn!" she muttered, sneaking a glance at the house.
Light spilled from the windows but she couldn't see Zane.
It didn't matter. He was busy with the fire. He wouldn't
miss her for a good five minutes. But how in the world
did one go about hot-wiring a car?

"Think, Kaylie," she said, deciding that she had to
look behind the ignition and try to find two wires that
when touched, would create an electrical charge. Or at
least that's what she guessed. It seemed logical. And she
didn't have time for any other speculation. It was now or
never. Do or die.

She lay on the driver's seat, her head under the dash,
eyeing the wires that ran every which way. Biting her lip,
she tugged gently on a tangled group that seemed to feed
into the ignition switch. There was a red wire and a black
one—if she pulled them out of the dash, unwrapped the
plastic coating, then touched the wires…?

Hopefully she wouldn't detonate the engine or shoot
herself into orbit, she thought ruefully.

She pulled on one of the black wires.

A low growl erupted from the woods.

Kaylie's heart leaped to her throat.

"Don't tell me. You've decided to take a crash course
in auto mechanics," Zane guessed, his voice so soft she

barely heard him. But Franklin, lurking in the shadows, barked loudly.

She froze, dropping the wires as if they were indeed hot.

Feeling like a fool, she tilted her head so that she could see him, and took the offensive. "I think I've already mentioned your vile habit of sneaking up on people." She pinned the dog with her glare. "The same goes for you."

Franklin wagged his tail, proud of himself, and Zane threw back his head and laughed. "And you, Ms. Melville, have a *vile* habit of trying to run away." He eyed the interior of the Jeep, and his mouth quirked. "So you were trying to start the Jeep without the aid of a key. Well, don't let me stop you." Gesturing grandly to the dash, he swallowed an amused smile. "Go right ahead."

"And have you stop me the minute the engine turns over?"

"A risk you'll have to take."

Her temper started to soar. What she wouldn't do to start this damned Jeep and take off, leaving him in a spray of gravel.

Zane leaned his hip against the fender. "And of course, you could shock yourself while you're at it."

"I realize that!" Sitting upright, she slid out of the car. "If you're done belittling me—"

"And if you're done with this teenaged prank."

She shot him a withering glance. "Prank? After the stunt you pulled by kidnap—"

He held up a palm, and she clamped her mouth shut, determined not to break their fragile truce.

"I thought we'd gotten beyond that," he said, his brows beetling.

"I—we—I thought we had to," she said, knowing he didn't believe her. "But the opportunity to leave just presented itself. You can't blame me for—" She bit her tongue.

He grabbed her by the arm and propelled her toward the house. "Oh, no? Then who should I blame?"

"Yourself! For hauling me up here in the first place. It's been three days, Zane! Three days of being away from the real world!"

"And it's been great, hasn't it?" he said, pressing his face close to hers.

"Just spiffy," she shot back, not letting him know for even a second that he was right, that being here with him was a little touch of heaven.

He picked up her discarded basket and glanced up at the sky. "*I'll* go get the firewood. It's safer. You'd better go inside. It's gonna rain soon." Swinging the damned basket, he strode to the woodpile with Franklin trotting after him.

Later, once the fire was burning in yellow-and-orange flames, Zane left the room for a few minutes. When he returned, he was carrying a small tape player, a bottle of wine and two glasses.

"Okay, it's time to get serious," he said, uncorking the wine and pouring them each a glass.

"About what?"

"This." He punched a button, and the tape of his phone call with Ted started playing.

Kaylie couldn't take a sip.

"Does this sound like anyone you know, anyone you've ever met?"

"I—I don't think so," Kaylie replied, her skin crawling at the sound of the raspy warning.

"Think, Kaylie! This is important." Zane rewound the tape and played it again and again until Kaylie could repeat the conversation word for word.

"I don't know," she admitted, biting her lower lip.

Zane snapped the recorder off and plowed angry fingers through his hair. "Obviously Ted knows you and your connection with me. He also knows all about Whispering Hills and Lee Johnston. And he knows that you and I are together."

"He does?" she cried. "How?"

"You weren't on the show, but that doesn't necessarily mean that you were with me. However, the fact that Ted's quit calling makes me think he's got a line on us."

Kaylie's fingers slipped on her glass. She spilled wine on her pants, but quickly mopped it up. "A line—"

"Well, maybe that's a little drastic. Maybe he would've quit calling anyway. He only called a couple of times. But it's a coincidence and I don't believe in coincidence."

"So, what—what does that mean?" she asked, not feeling safer knowing that some other nutcase might guess where they were.

"It means we stay put until Hastings gets some more information."

"Don't you think this Ted, if he's so smart, might find us?"

Zane frowned into his wine, swirling the glass thoughtfully. "I don't think so. Only a few people know I own this place."

"But he could find out." Fear strangled her. "Do you think Ted is Johnston?" she asked, her thoughts racing ahead wildly. "And that he placed the call to you, knowing that you would drag me up here?"

Zane shook his head, but his expression remained grim. "I doubt it. You were too visible in San Francisco. He could find you more easily. If he's going to be released, he wouldn't want to tip you off." His gaze moved from his glass to search her face. "Don't worry, I'll take care of you."

Surprisingly, that thought was comforting.

"But it would help me a lot, if we could figure out who Ted really is."

He played the tape again, and a headache began to pound at Kaylie's temples. She finished her wine and, before she began feeling too cozy and safe with Zane, set her glass on the coffee table. "I think I'll turn in."

She started to stand, but Zane placed a restraining hand on her shoulder. "Just remember one thing," he said, his voice firm.

"What's that?"

"If you try to escape again, I'll have to make sure that it doesn't happen. And that means I'll stick to you like glue."

Shrugging off his hand, she couldn't help but rise to the bait. "You'll have to catch me first."

"I know." One side of his mouth lifted, and his eyes glowed in the firelight.

She knew then that she loved him with all of her foolish heart. And if she didn't leave him soon, she never would be able to. She would have to give up her freedom and independence for the sake of love.

She hurried upstairs to her room. "Oh, Zane," she whispered, her throat aching. She had no choice but to escape—for both their sakes.

ZANE DRAINED HIS GLASS and wondered how long he could keep up this charade. Soon he would have to go back to the city and he couldn't, even in his wildest fantasies, keep her locked away forever. Tomorrow morning she'd miss another taping of her program and sooner or later the producer would start checking. Margot wouldn't be able to keep Crowley at bay forever.

And he couldn't force Kaylie to love him.

That thought tore open old wounds. He'd lost her once, and the surest way to lose her again was to keep imposing his will on her.

Absently, he flicked on the tape again, and Ted's hoarse voice filled the room. "Who are you?" Zane said aloud. "Just who the hell are you?"

And what about Johnston?

An icy knot curled in his stomach. Maybe this Ted character was wrong. Surely the courts wouldn't set a psychotic like Johnston back on the streets. But it had happened time and time again. He shivered inside. He loved Kaylie; he'd never stopped. But he wasn't going to sacrifice her life for anything—not even for a reconciliation. So, if it meant Kaylie would hate him for the rest of her life, so be it. At least she would be safe.

Or would she?

Even here, Zane wasn't completely at ease.

He walked outside to a shed where he kept his phone and, despite the late hour, dialed Brad Hastings. Something had to happen soon. He couldn't keep Kaylie up here forever.

KAYLIE DIDN'T WASTE ANY TIME. The situation was intolerable. She was getting in much too deep with Zane, and she'd have to leave him soon, or she'd never find the willpower. As for Lee Johnston, she'd take care of herself—hire a bodyguard if necessary.

A bodyguard like Zane?

Her heart turned over and she had to fight the strong pull of emotions.

Upstairs she tossed a pair of jeans, her running shoes,

a sweater and jacket over the end of the bed. She drew the covers to her neck and waited, listening to the sounds of the old house: timbers creaking, wind rattling windowpanes, clock ticking in the hall.

Go to bed, Zane, she silently prayed.

An hour passed before she heard his footsteps on the stairs. He paused at the landing, and she wondered if he'd check on her. How would she explain her clothes? The fact that she was still awake?

Chewing on her lip, her heart pumping crazily, she heard his footsteps retreat and the door to his room open and close.

She let out her breath. Now she could get started. She gave him a half hour to get to sleep, then fifteen minutes more for good measure. At a quarter to one, she slid out of bed and dressed in the moonlight streaming through her window.

Tucking her shoes under her arm, she headed in stockinged feet through her door and into the hallway. Her footsteps didn't make a sound, but her pulse was thundering in her brain.

Slowly she started downstairs, wincing on the third step when it creaked beneath her weight.

She waited, holding her breath, but Zane's door didn't bang open, so she hurried down the rest of the flight, picked her way through the living room to the kitchen, then dug in the pantry where she had discovered the old jacket and flashlight. Carefully she switched on the portable light and was rewarded with a steady, if pale, beam.

Good enough, she thought, unlatching the back door and slipping outside. She closed the door behind her, slid into her Reebok tennis shoes and, using only the faint light from a cloud-covered moon as her guide, made her way to the barn.

Inside, the horses snorted and pawed at the stalls. "Shh," Kaylie whispered, flashing her light until she found His Majesty. "It's all right."

Dallas poked his silken nose over the stall door and Kaylie petted him fondly. "Not tonight," she whispered, feeling a little like a traitor. "Tonight I need speed. I can't take a chance that you-know-who will catch me."

With surprising quickness, she bridled and saddled His Majesty, then led him from the barn. He danced and minced as the wind rushed through the trees, and Kaylie felt the first drop of rain fall from the sky. "Oh, great," she murmured. She tried hard to disregard the fact that she wasn't horsewoman enough for him if he were spooked.

His hoofbeats seemed to echo through the night as she unlatched the main gate and guided him through.

She had no idea where she was going, but intended to follow the long lane until daylight. Hopefully, by then, she'd find a crossroad or two and be able to lose Zane, because, if and when he caught up with her, all hell would break loose.

She didn't pause to consider the consequences of his wrath now. Instead she swung into the saddle and shoved her heels into His Majesty's sides. The horse picked up speed, trotting down the drive as the cold wind rushed against her face.

Kaylie squinted in the darkness, hoping beyond hope that His Majesty had some vague idea where civilization would lie, because she didn't.

The sky was dark—no bright lights over the hillside guiding her. Nope, this time she'd have to let common sense and her mount's instincts lead the way. *And I need a little luck,* she thought with an inward smile as she shone her flashlight toward the sky and caught the reflection of

heavy cable. She'd follow the electricity and telephone
wires. Eventually, she reasoned, the cables would lead
to civilization.

The road was steep, the switchbacks hairpin curves,
but His Majesty picked his way along the gravel without
faltering. Kaylie, tense, forever listening to the sounds of
the night, prayed that Zane would sleep in and not wake
until after nine. By that time she'd be well on her way to
San Francisco. Clucking her tongue, she encouraged the
stallion to pick up his pace as rain beat down in a steady
drizzle.

She'd ridden for nearly an hour before she came to the
first road of any significance. Her shoulders had already
begun to ache, and her fingers and cheeks were slick with
rain. "Okay, boy, what do you think?" she asked, patting
the chestnut's sleek neck and frowning when she noticed
the wires overhead were strung in both directions. One
way would lead to a city, the other could lead to another
isolated, and perhaps abandoned, house in the forest.

"Great," she mumbled to her disinterested horse. "Just
fine and dandy!" No doubt Zane would expect her to
head west, for that was the most likely way to reach civilization. And, blast it, she didn't have much choice as
the mountains to the north and east were forbidding and
there were no roads that led south.

"West it is," she ground out, refusing to think about
the cold water seeping through her collar and running
down her neck. She urged His Majesty forward, her ears
straining for the sound of an engine behind them. But
all she heard was the sigh of the wind, the steady drip of
rain and the rhythmic plop of the stallion's hooves. Occasionally a rustle in the undergrowth would startle the
horse as a hidden animal scurried through the woods

flanking the gravel road. "Squirrels and raccoons and rabbits," she told herself. "Nothing bigger or creepy. No bats or snakes or cougars...."

As the night wore on, Kaylie shone her flashlight whenever there was a crossroads, but otherwise followed the road by using the thick power cables as her guide.

Lightning struck in jagged flashes that illuminated the distant hills for a few sizzling moments. His Majesty shied and reared at the eerie light and the growl of thunder as it echoed over the hills.

"Hold, on, boy." Kaylie's hands tightened over the reins. "Steady."

The night closed in around her, and she felt the silence of the woods, the breath of the wind against her fingers and bare neck, the cold damp touch of the rain. She considered turning back a couple of times, but pressed on. Being with Zane was just too dangerous. Some women were cursed to love the wrong men. She just happened to be one of them.

Eventually, the road grew less steep. Kaylie's heart soared. She closed her eyes and thought she heard the hum of traffic on a faraway interstate. Or was it the rattle of a train on distant tracks? No matter. It meant she was approaching some sort of civilization.

Suddenly His Majesty tossed back his head and snorted violently. Stopping short, he rolled wide, white-rimmed eyes backward. His nostrils distended, and his wet coat quivered under her hands.

"Hey, whoa—" The hairs on the back of Kaylie's neck rose as her mount minced and sidestepped. "What is it?" she whispered, hoping she didn't convey her fear to the horse.

She shone her flashlight ahead, and its tiny beam

landed on Zane, half lying on the hood of his Jeep, soaked to the skin, his back propped by the windshield, his arms crossed over his chest, his expression positively murderous.

"Oh, God." Kaylie's heart plummeted.

Lightning flashed over the hills, and His Majesty reared, but at the sound of Zane's voice, the horse quieted, nickering softly.

"Well, well, Ms. Melville," Zane drawled in a tone so low and angry it rivaled the distant thunder, "I was wondering when you'd finally show up."

CHAPTER EIGHT

"BUT HOW—" Kaylie sputtered, shivering as she stared past Zane to the road beyond. Maybe she could make a run for it—or maybe His Majesty could find a path through the woods, a path the Jeep couldn't follow....

"Don't do anything crazy," Zane warned, shoving himself upright and hopping to the wet ground. "And the way I found you is simple. Most of the side roads around here are old logging trails—roads that crisscross over the mountain but eventually end up here. I knew if I waited long enough, you'd turn up."

"You heard me leave?" she asked, swiping at a drip of rain on the tip of her nose.

"Take my advice—don't apply for a job with the CIA."

"You tricked me!"

"No, you tricked me." He strode over and reached for the bridle, but she pulled hard on the reins and His Majesty's broad head swung away from Zane. Kicking sharply into the stallion's sides, Kaylie tried to spur past Zane, but he was too quick.

With an oath, Zane sprang like a puma and grabbed hold of the reins, ripping the wet leather straps from Kaylie's chilled fingers. "That was a stupid thing to do! Even worse than trying to hot-wire the Jeep!"

A ragged streak of lightning scarred the sky.

The horse reared, and Kaylie, thrown off balance, grabbed wildly at the saddle horn and His Majesty's wet mane.

"Whoa—slow down." Zane soothed the stallion, murmuring softly until the anxious beast slowly relaxed. "That's it, boy." Zane patted the chestnut's shoulder.

Kaylie, her hair tossed around her face, accused, "You pretended to be asleep! You heard me leave and you followed me!"

"Of course I heard you leave. Do you think I'd trust you after I caught you tampering with my ignition?"

"Tampering?" she repeated, furious and cold and hurt. "I was just trying to regain my freedom—you know, one of the basic constitutional rights guaranteed to every citizen!"

"I've heard this all before."

"Well, you're going to hear it again!"

"Get down, Kaylie."

"No way."

"Get down. Now!" he roared.

"You have no right to order me around!" she yelled, tossing her head imperiously.

"Probably not," he admitted, "but it's late and I'm tired and wet. Now let's go home."

"That log monstrosity is *not* my home!" she shot back, frustrated and angry that he'd caught up with her twice. Why, when it was so hard to leave him, didn't he make it easy for her and just let her go?

"Not your permanent home maybe, but for now—"

"Don't you know I'll hate you forever for this?" she hurled down at him, glaring.

Moonlight washed his face, and a sliver of pain slashed through his silvery eyes. "So hate me," he replied, his mouth tightening at the corners. "But while you're hating me, get down." When she didn't budge, he glanced up. "Okay, have it your way. You can ride His Majesty all the way back in this damned rain while I lead him in the Jeep, or you can enjoy the relative comforts of a heater, radio and padded bucket seats. Your choice."

"Get in that Jeep with you?" she challenged, though it did sound inviting, and she wished for just a second that loving Zane were simple. "That's what got me into this mess in the first place!"

"Fine." He tugged on the reins, and His Majesty followed docilely.

"Traitor," Kaylie whispered to the horse, and Zane rolled down the driver's window, climbed into the Jeep and fired the ignition.

His Majesty sidestepped. Kaylie patted the stallion's sleek neck. "It's okay," she said, lying, as Zane rammed the vehicle into gear.

"Last chance," he called, and Kaylie, though she longed to climb down from the saddle and sit in the warm interior of the Jeep, didn't move. Zane shook his head in disgust as the rig crawled slowly forward.

Kaylie grabbed hold of the saddle horn as His Majesty started the long trek back at a fast trot. The brisk pace jarred her, and the cold, wet air seeped through her jacket, but she'd be damned if she'd complain! Gritting her teeth, she tried to keep her mind off her discomfort, though her muscles were already aching, her teeth chattering.

As the incline grew more steep, Zane slowed, letting the horse walk. Kaylie was chilled to the bone, and her arms and thighs burned mercilessly, but she refused to call out and ask Zane to stop. Rain dripped down her nose and neck. Clenching her teeth, she endured the painful journey, head high, jaw thrust forward.

After about twenty minutes, Zane muttered something unintelligible, then stood on the brakes. The Jeep ground to a halt in the gravel and mud. "This is insane,"

he growled, opening his door and splashing through the
puddles to His Majesty's side. "Maybe you don't give
a damn about yourself, but you could give the horse a
break!"

He pulled her from the saddle, and she landed on the
ground so hard, her knees nearly gave way. Zane kept
a strong arm around her. "A little wobbly?" he mocked,
but there was a kindness in his features as he helped her
to the Jeep. And the rain seemed to soften the hard lines
surrounding his mouth. He touched her forehead, shoving a wet strand of curling hair from her eyes. "Come
on, Kaylie," he whispered, his voice so tender it nearly
broke her heart, "give it up for the night."

"I—I can't," she stammered.

"Sure you can."

"But—"

"Please, love," he insisted gently, opening the door.
"It isn't worth it."

"How would you know?"

He rolled his eyes, and a self-effacing smile tugged
at the corners of his mouth. "When it comes to stubborn
pride," he admitted, "I think I wrote the book."

His unexpected kindness pierced her pride. Tears filled
her throat, and she had to grit her teeth to keep from
crying as he gently lifted her into the Jeep. She sagged
against him. The warmth of him, the fact that he so obviously still cared for her, perhaps loved her, caused more
tears to burn in her eyes. She wanted to cling to him and
never let go. Inside the Jeep, she could barely stretch out
her cramped, cold muscles.

Before he slid behind the steering wheel again, Zane
unsaddled the horse and tossed the saddle and blanket
into the back. He found a clean, thick towel, and a worn
sheepskin jacket. "Here, dry off a little," he said, hand-

ing her the jacket and towel and turning up the heat as he shoved the rig into First.

Kaylie glanced his way as the vehicle rolled forward. Blotting her face with the towel, she leaned her head back against the seat and tried to ignore the cramps in her shoulders and legs as she fought back tears and the overwhelming urge to fall against him and be held and comforted; to let him take control.

His narrowed eyes were trained on the winding gravel road. Every so often he would glance in the side-view mirror, checking his stallion. It was romantic, in a way, she thought, how he kept chasing her down, swearing to protect her, saying he loved her. If only she dared believe him…trust him a little…love him a lot.

"Did you really think you could get away with it?" Zane asked, as the silence grew thick around them and the gloom of the forest seeped into the interior.

Shivering, she rubbed her arms, trying to keep her teeth from chattering. "I thought it was worth a shot."

"You cold?" He worked with the knobs of the heater, then, still driving, eased out of his own jacket and laid it across the blanket. "I'll probably end up taking you to the hospital."

"I'll be fine," she replied, still chilled to the bone.

Zane sighed. "And what would you have done if you had, by some miracle, found the freeway? Ride the horse down four lanes?"

"No," she said, her spine stiffening involuntarily, "I intended to stop at the first house and call."

"Whom?" he asked.

"Jim maybe—or Alan. Not Margot since she's in cahoots with you."

"And what would Alan have done?"

"Rescued me!"

"Ha!" He barked out a laugh and twisted hard on the wheel. "So now you want to be rescued?"

"No, I just want my life back," she said, staring out the window and watching the wipers slap away the rain.

"A life without me."

She drew in a steadying breath and tried to lie, but couldn't. The words stuck in her throat. She didn't want him completely out of her life—not anymore. And that was the problem. There was no letting Zane in a little bit. With him it was all or nothing. "All" meant giving up her hard-fought independence. "Nothing" meant never seeing him again. Her heart squeezed painfully at the thought. These past few days had been exhilarating and romantic, and her life back in the city seemed colorless in comparison.

"I thought Alan didn't mean anything to you."

"He's a friend. A coworker and a friend."

He snorted and fiddled with the heater as the windows began to fog. "So what about us?"

"I don't know what to do about us," she admitted, her emotions as raw as the dark night. "Part of me would like to see you burn in hell for what you've put me through."

"And the other part?"

She slid him a glance. "The other part tells me you're the best thing that ever happened to me."

Zane drew a slow breath, then smiled painfully. "I definitely think you should listen to part two."

"How can I," she asked, turning to face him, "when all you've done since you showed up at my house is bully me into doing things your way?"

The honesty in her eyes cut deep into his soul. He knew that he'd gone too far. But now there was no turning back. He'd considered letting her leave, pretending not to hear her sneak out of the house and into the barn.

But what then? Let her show up in San Francisco with his horse and never see her again? The thought was unbearable. "I'll let you go, Kaylie," he promised, forcing the words through his teeth. "Once I'm assured that you'll be safe." He swallowed with difficulty and almost tripped over the lie. "That's all I really want for you."

As the rain stopped, he turned off the wipers and checked the side mirror. His Majesty was tiring. "I think we'd better pull over for a little while," he said, frowning. "Give the old guy a break. He's had a hard night."

"Haven't we all?" she said, but climbed out of the Jeep when it slowed to a halt. Both she and Zane checked the horse, who was sweating and starting to lather. Zane walked him slowly for a while, until the stallion's heavy breathing returned to normal. Zane slanted a glance at Kaylie, and his gut twisted.

She caught his gaze, and her lips moved a little—so seductive and innocently erotic. He wondered how much more of this self-induced torment he could stand.

Time seemed to stand still as they stood, not touching, gazes locked, the earthy, rain-washed forest surrounding them.

"We'd better get going," he said, his voice gruff.

She glanced away, breaking the spell. Nodding, she replied, "I'll lead His Majesty."

Zane didn't argue. Once she was safely inside the Jeep, he handed her the reins, then climbed behind the wheel. The rest of the ride was tense and excruciatingly slow. Several times his fingers, gripping the gearshift, brushed against her knee, and she looked sharply up at him, but there weren't accusations in her gaze. If anything, there was an unspoken invitation.

Zane's fingers tightened over the wheel, and he thought he'd go out of his mind battling the urge to stop,

take her into his arms and make love to her right then
and there!

Finally, after agonizing minutes, he steered the vehicle around the final corner, and the log house loomed in
the darkness ahead.

"I'll take care of the horse," he said as he parked the
rig and looked long and hard at Kaylie. "And you should
take a hot bath, drink something warm and then find
the heaviest nightgown in the closet and wrap yourself
up in about a thousand blankets." She reached for the
door, and he couldn't let her escape. He grabbed her and
pulled. She fell against him. As she did, he covered her
mouth with his, pressing hard, insistent lips to hers and
surrendering to the emotions that had warred with him
ever since he'd seen her walking out of the water on the
beach in Carmel.

His blood thundered, his body burned, and all those
vows he'd sworn to himself—vows to stay away from
her until she was ready—vanished.

She seemed to melt against him, her supple lips re-
sponding, a quiet moan escaping her throat. "Why?" he
rasped when he finally lifted his head from hers. "Why
do you continue to fight me?"

"Because you fight me," she responded, eyes glazed
as she slowly disentangled herself. "And that's what it is
with us—a battlefield—your will against mine. It's always been that way, always will be."

She opened the door and stepped into the darkness,
and Zane, wishing the throbbing in his loins would sub-
side, struggled out of the Jeep. Pocketing his keys, he
said, "I'll only be a few minutes."

She stared at him with wide, vulnerable eyes, then
hurried into the house.

He should have just let her go back to the city, he realized, knowing that he couldn't hold out much longer. Sooner or later, he'd give in to the demands of his body, and then... Oh, God, then who knew what would happen?

There was a good chance that he'd lose her forever.

"If you haven't already," he reminded himself grimly. With a gentle tug, he led the tired stallion to the barn.

KAYLIE KICKED OFF HER SOILED CLOTHES and made a beeline for the shower. She let the hot spray soothe her throbbing muscles and loosen her sore joints, while the warm water restored feeling in her fingers and toes. She felt as if she'd been in the saddle for a millennium.

"As a pioneer woman you're a failure, Melville," she said, chiding herself as she squeezed water from a sponge and lathered her body. "And as a modern woman, you need some lessons on the male of the species." What was wrong with her? she wondered, twisting off the faucets and snatching a bath towel from the rack. Every time Zane touched her or kissed her or looked at her, she turned into jelly.

"Don't let him know that," she warned her reflection as she rubbed away the moisture from the mirror. "You're supposed to be strong, independent and in control!" But the green eyes staring back at her accused her of the lie. When it came to Zane, whether she wanted to admit it or not, she was in love. Always had been.

"And you're a fool," she whispered bitterly, toweling dry her hair.

She flung open the closet door and picked out a white cotton nightgown and a robe.

She'd go downstairs, get something to eat and then try to get to sleep. Right now, she knew that sleep was out of the question.

She started downstairs, only to stop short at the doorway to Zane's room. The door was open a crack, and she could see him, standing in front of the mirror, wearing only low-slung jeans.

His eyes caught hers in the reflection, and the look he sent her stopped her breath somewhere between her throat and lungs. "I thought you were going to rest," he said.

"I'm not tired."

He cocked a disdainful brow. "You should be dead on your feet."

"Nope," she replied, hoping to sound chipper, though she had to stifle a yawn.

Turning to face her, he smiled a small, lazy grin. "So, how're you going to plan your next escape attempt?"

"Next time it won't just be an attempt," she replied, unable to resist teasing him.

"Oh?" One dark eyebrow cocked in interest. He crossed the room and held the door open. "So next time you'll dupe me."

"That's right."

"I can hardly wait," he drawled, baiting her.

"Oh, you won't have to wait long," she promised, though she had no idea how she'd ever pull it off.

"No?" His eyes narrowed speculatively, and Kaylie could feel the air charge between them. "You know, Kaylie, I wonder about all those reasons you concoct to go back to San Francisco." He studied his nails. "The job, the empty apartment, your coworker, that all-fired important life."

"It is important."

"No doubt, but I think there's another reason you can't wait to make tracks out of here." He looked up at her and his gaze was so intense, she could barely breathe.

"And what's that?" she asked, swallowing hard.

"I think you're afraid of me—or at least of being alone with me."

"That's silly."

"Is it?" His gaze accused her of the lie. "I think you're less afraid of dealing with that madman who would like to slit your throat than you are of facing your real feelings for me."

"My feelings?" she asked, licking her lips in unwitting invitation.

"Right. I think you're afraid that if you stay here too long with me, you won't have the willpower to leave."

Though his guess was close to the truth, she laughed nervously. "You always did have an incredible ego."

His smoldering look accused her of the lie. She knew he was going to kiss her. In the intimate room, alone in the wilderness, he was going to take her into his arms and she wouldn't be able to resist. "Please, Zane, if you care about me—"

"I do. I told you that. I also told you that I love you."

"Then, if you love me, take me home."

He hesitated, pain shadowing his eyes. "This is home, Kaylie. You and me together—that's home."

"Not anymore, Zane," she said, forcing the words out. "And never again."

"You're kidding yourself."

"I—I think you're the one doing the kidding."

"Am I?" His expression darkened, and the lines around the corners of his mouth grew tight. He grabbed her wrist and slowly tugged, pulling her toward him. Deliberately he lowered his head, until his lips hovered over hers. "I can't leave you alone," he admitted hoarsely, his face only inches from her, his breath stirring the wet strands of her hair, his gaze moving to the pout of her lips. "Damn it, I want to, but I…just…can't." He tugged on her arm, and his mouth claimed hers in a kiss that burned deep into her heart.

Though a thousand reasons to run flitted through her mind, her love for him still lingered. His lips were warm, his body, hard and long, his arms strong. Tilting her head upward, she wrapped her arms around his neck and kissed him with all the pent-up desire she'd tried so desperately to suppress. Lost in the wonder of his male body pressed urgently against hers, she didn't stop him when one hand tangled in her hair, the other splaying possessively against her back. He kissed her throat and eyes and cheeks, and she tingled everywhere, aching for him.

Slowly he lowered her onto the bed and she didn't protest. His tongue slid between her teeth, flicking against her tongue, causing thrills to chase up her spine.

Her nipples grew hard, and dark peaks pressed against the thin cotton of her gown. Her breasts ached for his touch, and she moved intimately against him, rewarded by the feel of his hands slipping past the cotton, sliding the nightgown over her shoulder, exposing her white skin.

His thumb grazed her nipple, and she moaned. Zane lowered his head, suckling on the tiny dark bud, flicking it with his tongue, igniting her blood. Wanting so much more, Kaylie writhed against him. Impatiently his hands slid the nightgown over her other shoulder, baring both breasts.

With a primal groan he kissed both white mounds and buried his head in the cleft between them, alternately suckling from one, then the other.

"Oh, Kaylie," he rasped, kneading one soft mound as he kissed the other. "Don't ever stop." Slowly his hand lowered to the hem of her nightgown, his fingers grazing her thigh, skimming her skin that already felt on fire.

"Please…" she whispered.

He groaned, ripping the nightgown from her body and dropping to his knees, his hands on her bare buttocks as he touched her heated flesh with his tongue, kissing her breasts and abdomen and lower. Sucking in her breath, she leaned against him, her hands tangling in his hair as he explored and probed until she could think of nothing but the swirling hot void, a vortex of want, an emptiness only he could fill.

"I love you," he vowed, his hands still massaging her buttocks as he stood.

Oh, God, if she could only believe him. The words rang in her ears. But did he know that love and possession weren't the same? Could he learn?

Unable to resist, she boldly touched the waistband of his jeans. He made a primal sound deep in his throat, then tilted her head up to his. "Yes, love," he whispered, eyes glazed with passion.

She slid his jeans over his legs and he kicked himself free of them and wrapped strong arms around her middle. In one swift motion, he whirled her onto the bed and was lying over her, his gaze locked with hers, his tongue rimming her lips. "Just love me," he whispered.

"Oh, Zane, I do."

Closing his eyes for a second, he parted her legs with his and entered her swiftly. She sucked in her breath as he began to move, slowly at first, then with an ever-increasing rhythm that drove all thoughts from her mind.

She was here with Zane, making love, and that was all that mattered. They moved together, fusing, loving, spiraling upward and soaring above the clouds. Heaven and earth seemed to splinter before her eyes and she cried his name as she tumbled on a slow, heated cloud back to earth. "Zane, oh, Zane!"

"I'm here, love," he murmured into her hair. "I always will be."

"I know," she whispered, more content than she'd ever been, snuggling deep in his arms, resting her head against the soft mat of hair on his chest, listening to the loud cadence of his heart. This seemed so right, so perfect.

As afterglow finally faded, his lips found hers again and they made love—more slowly this time—exploring and touching, rekindling old fires that flamed and sizzled, becoming intimate as naturally as if they'd never separated.

Afterward, Kaylie sighed contentedly against him as he drifted into a deep sleep. Closing her eyes, she knew that she loved him. It was that simple. And that complicated.

Moaning, he rolled away from her, then sighed, still sleeping. His face, in slumber, was carefree, his mouth a soft line, his lashes dark against his cheek.

Kaylie touched his hair, and her heart nearly broke. Why was she doomed to love a man who was so smothering? Pressing a soft kiss to his lips, she rolled over, intending to fall asleep and deal with her feelings in the morning with a clear head. Maybe she and Zane could work things out. He was a reasonable man, and she was now a mature woman. If she only explained....

She noticed a reflection of moonlight on the floor—a dazzling flash of silver in the dark pile of his clothes. Her heart stopped when she realized that she was staring at his keys as they poked from the pocket of his jeans.

She closed her eyes for a second, wishing the vision away, but when she lifted her lids, the keys still lay there. Beckoning. Offering escape and freedom.

Her mouth turned to cotton.

Oh, God, she thought, shaking inside. Could she leave him? She glanced at his peaceful, trusting profile, tanned skin in relief against the white pillow, and her heart felt as if it were tearing in two.

She had no choice. She had to control her own life. She couldn't allow him to manipulate her.

Holding her breath and fighting tears, she slipped slowly from the bedcovers and silently picked up his keys. As her fingers closed around the cool metal, she hardly dared breathe. They jangled softly, but Zane just snorted and turned over.

For a few precious seconds Kaylie stood silently in the room, staring longingly down at Zane. If only they could love each other again—if only…but it would never work. Wasn't the fact that he kidnapped her proof enough that he always intended to force her will to his?

She couldn't let him control her! Her heart in her throat, she grabbed her clothes and sneaked out of the room.

She dressed quickly on the landing and fought the overpowering urge to run back to him.

Instead she slipped silently downstairs and outside. The air was fresh from the rain, and the first streaks of dawn illuminated the eastern sky.

Kaylie braced herself, then strode off the porch.

The Jeep waited for her.

CHAPTER NINE

RICK TAYLOR JABBED at a broken piece of pottery with his broom. Rolling his eyes, he cocked his head toward the patient. "He's been this way ever since Friday."

Dr. Anthony Henshaw rubbed his chin as he surveyed the damage in the small room. Books were thrown haphazardly on the floor, the desk chair was overturned, a bulletin board ripped from the wall, papers scattered on the floor and the pieces of clay pottery and dirt smashed against one corner. "What's the matter, Lee?" Henshaw asked the patient with the flaming red hair.

"He won't talk about it," Rick said, tossing the trash into a plastic bag. "But it started the other day during that show he watches, *West Coast Morning.* The woman who usually does the interviews—Kaylie whatever-her-name-is—wasn't on that day. Out for 'personal reasons' the other guy said, and ol' Lee, here—" he cocked his head toward the patient again "—went 'round the bend. I've been cleaning up this room once a day."

Henshaw frowned. This didn't sound good. He'd just returned from a symposium in Chicago and discovered from Dr. Jones that Lee Johnston had relapsed. "You miss Kaylie, Lee?" he asked, but the patient, sitting on the end of the unmade bed, didn't reply, just stared blankly ahead, hands clasped prayerlike on his lap.

Dr. Henshaw scratched his chin. Lee was a difficult

case, always had been. He sat next to the patient. "Does it bother you when Kaylie isn't on the show?"

No reply, just a slight movement of Johnston's thin lips.

"Even people who work on television take vacations. They need time off, too."

"He's not talkin' today," Rick said, shaking his head as he restacked books and magazines in the bookcase. "Won't say a word. Not one. Not to me, nor to Jeff or Pam, either. If you ask me, he's waitin' for the show." Shoving the last book on the bottom shelf, he glanced over his shoulder at the doctor. "Let's just hope she's back. Then maybe Lee here will calm down."

Rick left the room, and Henshaw tried communicating with Lee, but to no avail. Quiet, but obviously still upset, Lee refused to acknowledge the doctor's presence. After ten minutes, Henshaw gave up. He had other patients to see and a staff meeting in half an hour.

Ramming his hands deep into his pockets, he walked down the long hallway, rounded a couple of corners to the administrative offices. His own cubicle was near the back, with one window and a view of the gardens.

Dropping into his chair, he scowled to himself. Johnston obviously still had problems. Henshaw doubted if the man would ever fit into society. Yet there was talk that he might be released soon. Aside from a few incidents like the trashing of the room, Lee had been a model patient.

Henshaw picked up a pen and clicked it several times. Then there was the matter of Johnston's privacy. Several people were interested in his case and wondered about his freedom. Henshaw had been called by Kaylie Melville's ex-husband often enough. The man was obviously still hung up on her. As, apparently, was Lee. And then there was Kaylie's costar, Alan Bently, a man who seemed al-

ways linked with her. There were even rumors of their
engagement. Not that Henshaw cared. What she did with
her life was her business—until it involved his patient.

Henshaw had met Kaylie a couple of times and even
he, happily married for twenty-seven years, a proud father and grandfather twice over, understood a man's fas-
cination with Ms. Melville. Whether she knew it or not,
she had a way of stirring up a man.

The doctor shoved thin strands of hair from his face
and set his glasses on the table. He rubbed his eyes and
wondered how he could get through to Lee. With a long
sigh, he decided convincing Johnston that his obsession
was pure fantasy and in no way reciprocated would take
a miracle. Lee had been obsessed with Kaylie for over
seven years. Making Johnston believe that Kaylie had
no interest in him would be no easier than walking on
water.

RETURNING TO SAN FRANCISCO took hours. During the long
drive through the mountains as the sun climbed higher in
the sky, Kaylie felt more than one twinge of guilt. Gritting her teeth, she shoved the ridiculous feeling aside.
She couldn't start second-guessing herself. Not now. Not
after seven years of living without Zane.

Her throat grew tight at the thought of the love they'd
shared, the passion that had rocked her to her very soul.
She could still remember his whispered words of endearment, smell the scent of him clinging to her skin, see in
her mind's eye his body lying across the bed.

Glancing into the rearview mirror, she noticed shadows in her eyes. "Oh, Kaylie," she said with a sigh, "forget him." Then, her lips twisting at the irony of it all, she
murmured, "He asked to be left up there alone—he *deserves* it for barreling back into your life again!"

But she couldn't forget the fire of their lovemaking, the tenderness with which he kissed her, the passion he used to try and keep her safe.

He was wonderful and horrible, and she didn't want him out of her life. To forget about him, she flipped on the radio and tried to catch up on the news, yet she couldn't shrug off the guilt of leaving him high and dry. "Remember," she told herself, "*he* kidnapped you. You owe him nothing!" But the guilt remained.

She followed the highway signs west toward San Francisco. She'd have to return Zane's keys and Jeep to the headquarters of his security firm. When she squared off with Brad Hastings, Zane's right-hand man, she'd tell him where to look for his boss.

At that thought, she grinned sadly. Zane would be furious! But at least she'd finally gotten the better of him, even if her victory seemed somehow hollow.

Kaylie's fingers tightened around the steering wheel just as the deep green waters of the bay came into view. Sunlight spangled the surface, and the San Francisco skyline stretched to the sky.

Once in the city, traffic slowed and clogged the main arterials. Pedestrians crowded the sidewalk.

The Jeep climbed the city's hills easily, and she parked in the lot of her apartment building. She yanked on the emergency brake, then switched off the ignition. The parking lot was quiet save for the ticking of the engine as it cooled, and Kaylie was left with the empty feeling that she'd left something important—something vital— back at the log house in the forest.

"Don't be a fool," she snapped, locking Zane's Jeep and making her way to the elevator that would take her to her third-floor flat.

Inside, her apartment looked the same as it had when

she'd left it last week, but the atmosphere in the rooms was different—cooler, somehow. Vacant. Though Zane had never lived here.

"You're imagining things," she chided herself, stripping off her clothes and heading for the shower. She needed to clear her mind, make a few calls, and then, when she was refreshed, tackle the issue of Zane again.

Smiling at the irony of it all, she imagined returning the Jeep and explaining to Brad Hastings that Zane was stranded. She stepped under the shower's steamy spray and relaxed. Yes, she decided, Zane, for his high-handedness, deserved everything she'd given him and more.

So why, as she washed, did she still feel regrets that their idyllic time together had come to an abrupt end?

As she dressed and dried her hair, images of Zane flitted through her mind. She listened to her answering machine. Several people had called including Alan, Tracy and Dr. Henshaw. Dialing Whispering Hills, she waited, her stomach knotting, for the receptionist to put her through to Lee Johnston's psychiatrist.

Eventually he picked up. "I'm sorry it took so long to get back to you," he said, explaining that he'd been out of town. Kaylie asked him point-blank about Johnston, and there was a pause on the other end of the line.

"You shouldn't have to worry about him for a long while," Henshaw said slowly.

The relief she should have felt didn't wash over her. In fact, Henshaw's pregnant pause caused her mind to race in a thousand questions. Zane was right—Henshaw seemed to be holding back. "How long?"

"That's for the courts to decide."

"Upon recommendation from you and the other doctors at the hospital."

"Don't worry, Ms. Melville. Lee's not going anywhere. Not for a long, long time, I'm afraid."

"Well, I think you should know someone is saying differently," she said, deciding that confiding in him wouldn't hurt. But he already knew about the two calls from Ted and he dismissed them as a "twisted petty prank."

By the time she replaced the receiver, she was reasonably certain that Johnston would remain at the hospital for a while, and yet she wasn't satisfied.

It's because Zane isn't here, a voice inside her head insisted as she punched out the number for the station.

The receptionist answered and put her through to the producer of *West Coast Morning.* "Kaylie!" Jim shouted, bringing a smile to her face. "About time we heard from you! How's that aunt of yours?"

Kaylie's face fell. How was she going to deal with Zane's intricate web of lies? "She's—uh, improving," Kaylie finally replied, deciding to keep Zane's kidnapping to herself—at least for a while. "Incredible recovery," Kaylie forced herself to say, inwardly cursing Zane. "I'm sorry I didn't call you myself—everything got really crazy...." At least *that* wasn't a lie.

"Not to worry. Margot explained everything."

Not quite everything. In Kaylie's estimation, Margot had a lot of questions to answer.

"We've missed you around here," Jim joked good-naturedly. "The show just hasn't been the same without you. And we've been getting a lot of calls. People wondering how you and your aunt are doing. You might have to bring it up on the show tomorrow. Viewers really get off on all that personal stuff."

The thought of lying on the air curled Kaylie's stomach. But Jim was right. "About those calls," Kaylie asked. "Did I get any from a guy named *Ted?*"

"I don't think so. What is it with that guy? Someone else called about him. Tracy took the call." She heard a muffled noise as Jim placed his hand over the receiver and talked to his assistant. "She says that a guy named Hastings called—a guy who works for your ex. Is something going on?"

"Just a crank call," Kaylie said, quickly explaining to Jim about the threats, though he didn't seem overly concerned when she explained that Lee Johnston was still locked up.

"Another nut. I tell ya, this town is full of 'em," Jim said before the conversation ended.

She hung up the phone, grabbed her jacket and purse and headed out the door.

THE OFFICES OF FLANNERY SECURITY were located on the fifth floor of a building not far from the waterfront. Bracing herself, Kaylie pushed open glass doors and recognized the receptionist. Peggy Wagner was a plump woman, somewhere near fifty, with tight gray curls and wire-rimmed glasses. Peggy had worked for Zane forever.

"Mrs. Flannery!" Peggy cried, a smile gracing her soft features as she glanced up from her word processor. "Are you here to see Mr.—"

"Hastings. The executive vice president," Kaylie replied, hoping that the couple waiting on a low-slung couch in the reception area hadn't overheard. Peggy never had been able to use Kaylie's maiden name. Apparently she still thought of Kaylie as Zane's wife.

"You're in luck. He's in," Peggy said, flipping a switch on an intercom and announcing Kaylie. "I'll walk you back." She ripped off her headgear and motioned to another woman at a nearby desk. "I'll be right back," she said, then guided Kaylie through a labyrinth of corridors.

At the end of one hall, Peggy knocked, then opened a door to a small office. The floor was hardwood, the desk oak and the rest of the furniture was expensive and neat, but far from opulent.

Peggy motioned to a pair of leather couches. "Just have a seat and he'll be with you in a moment. Would you like anything while you wait? Coffee or tea?"

"I'm fine," Kaylie replied, wishing Hastings would suddenly appear so she could explain how he could find Zane, then get out.

Peggy crossed the room again. "It'll just be a little while," she assured Kaylie as she closed the doors behind her.

Kaylie, rather than sit anxiously twiddling her thumbs, walked to the windows and stared through the glass to the city beyond. Skyscrapers knifed upward against a hazy blue sky, and a jet circled over the bay. Below, traffic twisted and pedestrians bustled along sidewalks.

The door clicked softly behind her.

Finally! Grinning to herself, Kaylie reached into her purse for Zane's keys. "I'm so glad you could see me," she said, turning, only to wish she could drop through the floor.

Zane was locking the door behind him.

Her heart slammed against her ribs as she stood face-to-face with him. The keys fell from her hand, and her mouth went suddenly bone-dry.

"Me, too," he replied with more than a trace of sarcasm. His expression was dark and murderous, and every exposed muscle contracted tightly. His eyes were the cold gray of the barrel of a gun, and his lips were razor thin.

He looked dangerous and coiled—like a whip ready to crack.

Kaylie gulped, but stood her ground.

"Surprised?"

"I think the word is *thunderstruck,*" she said, hoping to make light of the tension crackling through the room.

"Well, I've got to hand it to you, Kaylie. You fooled me." His jaw slid to one side, and he shot her a glance from the corner of his eye. "I thought we were making progress, but you decided to take one last gamble. And it worked. Almost." He tossed his leather jacket into his chair and shoved the sleeves of his blue sweater up his forearms. His hair was still wind-tossed and wild, and his pallor had darkened with the quietly repressed fury burning in his gaze. "I guess I should offer you a job. You're the only person who's been able to pull one over on me in a long while."

Slowly he advanced upon her. "You lifted my keys, then stole my car—"

"I warned you, Zane," she said, refusing to back up, though she wanted to retreat desperately.

"Warned me?" He shook his head, and he was so close that the movement fanned her face. "That's a good one." The skin over the bridge of his nose was stretched taut, and his nostrils flared. Little white lines etched the corners of his mouth. He was furious—his eyes flared with savage fire, but she couldn't let him know that he frightened her at all.

"I trusted you," he said quietly.

"So that's why you had to keep me prisoner? Because of your 'trust'?" she tossed back at him.

His lips compressed. "We made love, damn it!"

"I—I know."

"And it meant nothing to you!" he charged, his rage exploding.

"No, Zane, I—"

"You slept with me, toyed with me, then the minute I let down my guard, you took off in the night, like some cheap…" He let the sentenced dangle between them—unspoken accusations cutting deep.

"Like some cheap what?" she threw back at him.

"Oh, the hell with it!" His arms surrounded her suddenly, crushing her against him as he kissed her angrily, passionately, desperately. When he lifted his head, some of the fury had faded from his gaze. "What kind of a game are you playing with me, Kaylie?

"Me? Play a game with you?" she whispered as he searched her face.

"I thought last night meant something."

"It did."

"What?"

"That—that—there's still something between us," she admitted.

"And what's that?"

"I don't know, Zane!" she said in exasperation, her nerves stretched tighter than piano wires as he held her so close that she was all wrapped up in the warm feel and smell of him again.

"You deliberately tricked me!"

"And you deliberately seduced me!"

His lips twisted at that. "If I remember correctly, you seemed to enjoy yourself. And there might be some argument about who seduced whom?"

That much was true, she thought, wrenching herself free so that she could think clearly. Her heart was knocking painfully in her chest, her ears rang with the rush of her own blood. When she reached upward to push a strand of hair from her eyes, her fingers trembled so that she balled her fist and crammed it into her pocket. "How did you get back here?"

His eyes narrowed. "A helicopter. Less than a mile from the cabin," he said, clipping his words. "I was back in the city hours ago!"

"I told you I'd escape—"

"Ahh! But you didn't warn me that you'd sleep with me to lull me into trusting you, did you?"

"You must have expected— Ohh!"

Snagging her wrist in his strong fingers, he pulled her roughly against him. "I didn't expect to be *used,* Kaylie. I didn't think you'd stoop so low as to go to bed with me just to get what you wanted."

"I didn't!" she declared furiously.

"You couldn't prove it by me."

She stared into his eyes and saw a flicker of pain, a shadow of just how deeply she had wounded him. Her heart wrenched painfully, and she wondered if all love were this agonizing.

"I trusted you," he whispered, his breath caressing her face.

"But I gave you ample warning, Zane," she said quietly. "I told you over and over again that I wouldn't be coerced, threatened, kidnapped or held hostage. But you didn't believe me, did you? You know, maybe if you'd just have asked me—invited me to spend a few days with you—things would have been different."

"You would have come with me?" he asked, one dark disbelieving brow arching skeptically. "Do you really expect me to believe that you'd give up your precious job, even for a week or two, to spend time with me?"

"Yes!" she cried. "If I would have thought there was any chance that we could have recaptured the good parts of our marriage. If I'd believed for an instant that we could create something wonderful again, I'd have come with you!"

"But you don't believe we can recreate that happiness, do you?"

She shook her head, her heart twisting. "You showed your true colors by kidnapping me, Zane. You'll never change. You'll always smother and overprotect and try to force me into doing everything you want."

"Like I forced you last night?" he whispered, and her gaze was drawn to his Adam's apple as he swallowed.

Mesmerized, Kaylie was vaguely aware that he smelled of soap and a cologne that brought back far too many memories of lying naked with him. She noticed the rise and fall of his chest. Only a few hours ago, she'd touched that chest, a chest that had been bare and taut, with strong, strident muscles and covered by a mat of dark, swirling hair.

When she glanced up, his features had softened. "Oh, Kaylie…" He sighed. "What am I going to do with you?"

"Nothing, Zane. *You* can't do anything with me. That's the whole point. It's not *your* choice. You don't own me!"

"I've never wanted to own you."

"That's not the way I remember it," she said, though she felt a flicker of doubt. For seven years she'd thought of her short marriage as a prison, but now she wondered if she had only been stronger during the time that she was Zane's wife, if she had stood up for her rights, would those prison walls have crumbled?

"You didn't stick around long enough to know, did you?" he flung back.

Stung, Kaylie said, "I think I'd better leave before we say things we'll regret."

"Leave. And what about Johnston?"

"I talked with Dr. Henshaw. Whoever this Ted character is, he's all wet. Henshaw assured me that Lee Johnston will be locked up for a long, long time."

"And you believe him?"

"The man has no reason to lie."

Zane's expression grew thoughtful. His fist clenched as he attempted to control himself. He didn't trust Henshaw. No, he put more stock in crank phone calls than medical opinion. "I should never have let you escape."

"*Let* me?" she mocked.

"I was crazy to trust you. To let down my guard." A muscle worked in his jaw. "You know," he said slowly, "I had the ridiculous idea that if you and I spent enough time alone together, we could work things out. No matter what it was, we could handle it."

"We didn't before," she reminded him.

"I know. But we're older—wiser, I'd hoped."

"More mature?" she pointed out sardonically. "Think about the past few days! Nothing we've done can qualify under the 'mature' category."

He shrugged. "I guess we haven't acted much like adults, have we?" Shoving his hands into the back pockets of his jeans, he added, "Maybe I was wrong. I thought there might still be a chance that you could love me."

Her throat closed. If only he knew. A tide of emotion swept over her, and she realized she had to get away from him and fast, while she still could. She picked up his keys from the carpet and dropped them onto the desk. "Goodbye, Zane," she said, and the words, as if barbed, stuck in her throat.

"Why are you always running from me?" he asked suddenly. "Do I scare you so much?"

She couldn't lie. "Yes," she said, her voice raw.

He closed the distance between them, and his lips

crashed down on hers so swiftly, she gasped. Her breath was trapped in her lungs, and immediate traitorous heat fired her blood. He pressed her back against the door, and his thighs fit familiarly over hers, his chest crushing her breasts. Memories of the night before enveloped her, and desire swept through her bloodstream in wicked, wanton fury.

Her heart pumped gloriously, her blood rushed through her ears. She pressed her palms against his chest, intending to shove him away, but all her strength fled, and she found herself clinging to him instead.

When at last he lifted his head, his face was flushed, his eyes shining with a passion that seared right to his soul. "Dear God, why can't I get over you?" he rasped.

For the same reasons I can't forget you, she thought, but held her tongue. She tried to move, to slide away from him, but he trapped her.

His hands were pressed against the door, his arms blocking her escape. "Why, Kaylie?" he finally asked. "Why did you leave me?"

Feeling suffocated, she drew in a breath. "For all the old reasons."

His jaw grew tight, and any pain she'd seen earlier was quickly hidden. "Last night you weren't pretending," he said slowly, and one of his fingers traced the line of her jaw. "Last night you felt what I did. And yet you can ignore how good we are together, how we feel about each other and—" he touched her lips with one finger "—don't lie to me. I *know* you feel it, too. So how can you pretend that you don't care?"

"Because I can't care!" she said shakily, her hands scrabbling behind her for the handle of the door. Her fingers found cool metal and she shifted, tugging on the knob.

Zane didn't stop her. Instead he backed away. "Escaping again?" he mocked, bitterness tingeing his words. "Maybe you should seduce me first so that I'll let down my guard."

"You bastard," she bit out, but shrank as if physically wounded.

"You certainly have grown up," he jeered.

"So have you," she replied, tugging on the door until it opened. Then she slid an icy glance in his direction. "Goodbye, Zane," she said stiffly. Marching rigidly through the doorway, she told herself it didn't matter what he thought of her—she had a life of her own to worry about.

A life without Zane Flannery.

CHAPTER TEN

ZANE SLAMMED HIS FIST onto the desk in frustration. The lamp rattled, a coffee cup rolled onto the floor, and his picture of Kaylie, a promotion shot for her second movie, toppled with a crash. The glass cracked, destroying the image of a smiling seventeen-year-old.

Her hair had been longer then, hanging nearly to her waist in luxurious golden waves, and her face had been more rounded, her cheeks fuller with adolescence, her green eyes filled with energy and the innocent sparkle of youth.

He'd fallen for her so hard, he'd felt as if the air had been knocked from his lungs. She'd been so young, so damned young, and he'd been hired by her agent as her bodyguard.

Now, running his finger along the crack in the glass, he remembered all too vividly how he'd come to love her. At first he'd resisted, of course, and she hadn't been aware of his changing feelings. But he, too, had been young, and keeping rein on his emotional downfall and charging lust had been impossible. He'd been with her constantly, to protect her, when, in fact, he'd often felt that he was the predator. He'd wanted her as he'd wanted no other woman, burning for her at night, hungering for her by day.

And though he'd sworn never to touch her, never to let her know that she was forever burning brightly in his mind, he'd succumbed at last, body and soul, foregoing his usually clear thinking and deciding that he wouldn't rest until he made her fall in love with him.

It hadn't been easy. Kaylie had as many reasons for not wanting him as he had for keeping his distance from her. But in time, all the walls disintegrated and they were married. And their marriage had ironically become the beginning of the end.

He frowned darkly to himself. She was right, he realized now, as he twisted a pen in his fingers and stared out the window. Clouds were rolling in from the west, converging over the bay, turning the murky waters as gray as his mood. He had been overprotective, near paranoid in his need to protect her.

He'd lost so many before. Both parents and his older brother had died in a mountain-climbing accident when he was twelve. Only he had survived, with injuries that should have killed or crippled him for life. But his mother's sister, Aunt Hilary, had been patient and caring and, with the reluctant help of her second husband, George, tried her best to raise him. George had referred to him as a teenaged hellion on wheels.

Four years after the mountaineering accident, a hit-and-run driver sideswiped Aunt Hilary's car, killing her instantly. At that point Zane dropped out of school, left home and joined the navy.

So when, years later, he'd fallen so hard for Kaylie, he'd been paranoid that he might lose her. In his efforts to keep her safe, he'd smothered her, and she'd demanded a divorce.

"Idiot," he ground out now, "damned bloody idiot." Shaking off his nostalgia, he reached for the phone, dialed the number of Whispering Hills Hospital and waited impatiently, drumming his fingers, for the receptionist to locate Johnston's psychiatrist.

Henshaw eventually answered, but the call was brief. Even though Zane was one of the biggest names in the security business and Kaylie's ex-husband, the doctor, as usual, was reluctant to give out any information on his patient.

"Damn patient confidentiality!" Zane growled, hanging up. Henshaw had been vague, as if he were holding something back, and the hairs on the back of Zane's neck bristled. Something wasn't right. Though Henshaw had assured Zane there were no plans for Johnston's "immediate" release, he hadn't ruled out that someday Lee Johnston might be stalking the streets again.

"Terrific! Just bloody terrific!" Zane's hands felt clammy, and he wished there were some way to get through to Kaylie. She was and always had been much too cavalier about her safety. Even after the horror of the opening of *Obsession*. Because Johnston was locked up, she had refused to worry, going about her life as if the terror hadn't existed, as if her life hadn't hung by a fragile thread that one man had nearly sliced.

He strode to the recessed bar and poured himself a stiff shot of Scotch. He'd bungled this and badly. Gambling that he could convince Kaylie to stay with him at the cabin, he'd thought he'd be able to protect her, if and when Johnston ever saw the outside of the hospital again. But now things were much worse. Kaylie wouldn't even talk to him.

A cold, tight knot of dread twisted in the pit of his stomach. He wasn't out of this yet. Come hell or high water, he intended to protect Kaylie, even if, in so doing, he might ram a wedge between them that could never be removed.

Her life was more valuable than his love. With that
miserable thought, he drained his glass, pressed the intercom on his desk and told his secretary to arrange a
meeting of his most trusted men.

ON THE DARKENED SET of *West Coast Morning,* Kaylie
guessed that Alan didn't like anything she was telling
him. In fact, he was being bullheaded and stubborn about
an issue that she considered very cut-and-dried.

Maybe, Kaylie thought wearily, Zane had been right
about Alan all along.

"I don't get it," Alan complained, plucking a piece of
lint from his jacket. His mouth pinched together into a
contrite pout. His auburn hair was brushed neatly, and
his suit didn't dare have a single wrinkle. He sat on a bar
stool in the kitchen of the set, his notes spread on the tile
countertop of the island bar, near the gas range where
Chef Glenn cooked up his Friday-morning concoctions.
"What's the big deal about a little publicity?"

"It's not publicity, Alan, and we both know it. Who
started the rumor that we were getting married?"

"Who knows? And who cares?" He lifted his shoulders
in an exaggerated shrug. "If you're in the business and
you're popular enough, eventually you find your name
and face on the front page of *Up Front* or *The Insider* or
some other rag."

"So you think we should be flattered?" she accused.

Alan forced a smile, and seeing his reflection in the
copper pots hanging near the stove, smoothed his hair
with the flat of his hand. "Well, I think the least we can
do is go with the flow. Next week someone else will make
the headlines and we'll be old news."

"That's not the point."

"Hey—just chill out, okay?" he said, irritated as he

noticed a mistake in his notes, clicked open a pen and made a quick slash on the neatly typed pages.

"I'll 'chill out' just as long as both you and I deny this whole engagement thing to the legitimate press."

He lifted his palms. "Suits me." Looking back to his notes for the next day's show, he asked, "So what happened? Does Brenda take some rag that got you all riled?"

"Brenda?" she repeated, not understanding.

"Your aunt. The one who was so sick." Alan glanced up sharply, and a tiny line appeared between his thick brows. "The one you were visiting in the hospital for the past few days?" he prodded, eyeing her suspiciously from behind the wire-rimmed glasses he never wore on camera.

"Oh—no!" So Zane had gone so far as to name her supposedly seriously ill aunt. Kaylie cleared her throat. "No, I just had a lot of time to do some thinking…." Well, at least that wasn't a lie. She'd spent the past four days thinking, thinking, thinking. And she'd gotten nowhere. Her thoughts kept turning back to Zane.

"So?"

"So I thought we should take a professional stand against all this tabloid gossip."

"Tell that to the station. It's my bet that our ratings went up while we were splashed across the headlines."

"Still—"

"So cool it," Alan cut in, chuckling. "No harm done. Right?"

She wasn't so sure. "I just like to keep my private life private, that's all."

Alan's eyes, behind the thick lenses, narrowed as he studied her. He shoved his notes together, straightening the pages on the shiny mauve-colored tiles. When he looked at her again, his expression had turned thought-ful. "Is something else going on with you?"

"Meaning?"

He rubbed his chin pensively. "Before you left to take care of your aunt, Flannery called here a couple of times."

Kaylie didn't flinch. "Right."

"So—does all this talk about privacy have something to do with him?"

"Of course not," she said, rubbing her palms down the sides of her skirt.

"You're sure? Because it seems like a big coincidence, you know, that Flannery calls a couple of times after leaving you alone for years. Then you don't show up for work the next day—and now that you're back, you're all worked up about your privacy."

"You're not making any sense," Kaylie countered.

"If you say so." He touched his pen to his lips. "You know what I think?"

"I'm not sure I want to."

"If you ask me, you never really got over him." Alan set his notes on the table and walked to the front of the cameras to the grouping of couches and chairs that created a cozy living room on the set of *West Coast Morning.* Hands deep in his pockets, he leaned a shoulder against the fake mantel on the brick fireplace.

"Zane has nothing to do with this."

"You always were a poor liar. And, unless I miss my guess, Zane has everything to do with it! Remember—I know you. I've known you as long as he has. I saw the hell you went through during your divorce."

"Let's not dredge all that up again—"

He ignored her. "The way I see it, you never were divorced from him—not emotionally. Oh, I know you went through all the legal hoops and you haven't seen him for a while. But it's glaringly obvious to anyone who knows you that you're still in love with him." He tugged on his tie and flicked open his collar button. She wanted to argue with him, but before she could say another word, Alan went on, "If Zane whistled, you'd go running. You might have wanted out of your marriage a few years ago, but that's changed."

"And how would you know?" she wondered aloud.

"Because I've worked with you, Kaylie—seen you grow. Don't forget, I was at the premiere of *Obsession*. I remember what happened when you were attacked, how Zane reacted. Can't say as I blame him, either. He was scared spitless—and he should have been. Johnston was a maniac."

Kaylie crossed the set and took a seat in one of the rose-colored chairs that she'd sat in for hundreds of tapings. So it was that obvious, was it? Even Alan, self-centered as he was, knew how she felt.

"You know, Flannery was just trying to keep you safe," Alan said, then muttered something under his breath and kicked at one of the ottomans on the set. "I don't know why I'm defending the guy—I don't even like him. But he was right in worrying about Johnston attacking you again."

Kaylie's head snapped up. "What does that mean?" she asked suspiciously, nervous fear burrowing deep in her heart. "Is Lee Johnston going to be released soon?"

Alan, not really interested, lifted a shoulder. "If he is, it's a well-kept secret. But he'll be out someday."

With that chilling prediction, he glanced at his watch and shot to his feet. "Got to run," he explained, reaching for his briefcase and athletic bag he'd tucked near the island. "Got a tennis game with my agent. See ya later." With a wave, he was down the hall and out the door.

KAYLIE SPENT THE NEXT couple of hours at the station, checking her messages, but there was no pink slip asking her to return a call to "Ted." She answered her mail, returned her calls and reviewed the shows she'd missed, talked with Jim and Tracy and got ready for the next morning.

Eventually Kaylie left the station in a car she'd rented for the week—until she could drive to Carmel and pick up her Audi. She had one last errand to run. One very important errand.

She drove over the Golden Gate Bridge, barely noticing that the steel-colored clouds were moving inland and that the sun was once again sprinkling the bay with golden light.

Driving by instinct, she was unaware of the traffic or the change in scenery as the highway was flanked by vineyards. In Sonoma, she guided the rented Mustang up a steep hillside and parked in her sister's driveway. She turned off the engine and listened to the radio as she waited for Margot to get home from work. The interior of the car was warm, so she cranked open the sunroof. At five-thirty, the garage door opened, and Margot's sporty little Toyota wheeled into the garage.

As Kaylie climbed out of her Mustang, Margot shoved open the door of her car and fairly ran down the drive to Kaylie's car. "Kaylie! You're back!" she cried, crossing the asphalt and throwing her arms around her younger sister. Margot's shining coppery-gold hair gleamed in the sunlight, and her sky-blue eyes danced. "So tell me all about your adventure with Zane!"

Kaylie rolled her eyes. "Adventure? Is that what you think it was? He literally kidnapped me and held me hostage for days—"

"Umm—sounds divine."

"That's crazy!"

"Is it?" Margot's eyes twinkled. "I can't wait to hear what happened and I want details, Kaylie. Very explicit details."

"You're an incurable romantic," Kaylie said, laughing nonetheless. Some of Margot's enthusiasm was infectious. "I came over here to do you bodily harm, you know."

"Why?"

Kaylie was speechless for a moment. "You know why! Because you were in on it with him."

"And proud of it," Margot teased. "And don't give me this offended victim routine. It doesn't wash. You're crazy about Zane. Always have been, always will be. I don't know why you just don't admit it and make things easier on everyone. Now, come on, help me carry these groceries into the house and we'll have a glass of wine to celebrate."

"Celebrate what?"

"That you're back in the city. Or back with Zane. Whichever you choose." She glanced over her shoulder, and a dimple creased her cheek.

"I'm *not* involved with Zane."

"Sure you are. You're just too bullheaded to admit it." Opening the hatchback, she eyed her sacks of groceries, chose one and stuffed the ungainly bag into Kaylie's arms. "There you go." Balancing a second sack, she led the way to the house, unlocked the door and was greeted by several yowling cats. "Miss me?" she asked the felines as she deposited the groceries on the kitchen counter.

She was rewarded with a chorus of loud mewing, which didn't stop until she petted three furry heads.

Kaylie set her sack on the counter. Margot's house, which she'd built with her husband, Trevor, clung to the side of a steep canyon overlooking the rolling hills and valley floor of the wine country. Margot loved this house, and though Trevor had lost his life in a boating accident nearly two years before, she'd never moved. The good memories outweigh the bad, she'd always say, when the subject of selling the house would come up.

"You know," Margot said now, pouring dry cat food into three separate bowls, "you're lucky Zane still cares enough to try to win you back."

"You think so?"

"Umm." Margot finished with the cats, washed her hands, then pulled a bottle of zinfandel from the refrigerator. Splashing some of the liquid into two glasses, she said sadly, "I just wish I had the chance to start over with Trevor." A tiny crease marred her forehead.

Kaylie felt a jab of remorse. "But Trevor was different from Zane."

"Not so much," Margot said, shaking her head. "He was stubborn, arrogant, prideful and—" her voice cracked "—loving and wonderful."

Wishing she could help Margot quit grieving for a man who'd never return, Kaylie said, "I miss Trevor, too. He was a great guy."

"The best." Margot's voice turned husky, and she blinked rapidly against gathering tears. She took a sip of wine and sniffed. "I guess that's why it's just so hard for me to understand why you're willing to throw away something so precious as Zane's love when he so obviously still wants to work things out."

"I just need to be independent."

"Oh, that's a cop-out and you know it. Let's take these drinks and go outside onto the deck." Margot opened the sliding door with her back. "Grab that bag of chips," she said, motioning to a sack of tortilla chips. "And there's homemade salsa, Chef Glenn's best recipe, in the fridge."

Kaylie poured the chips into a bowl and found the salsa. On the deck, she dropped the snack onto the round table and took a seat under the shade of the green-and-white umbrella. Margot was propped on the chaise longue, rolling her wineglass between her palms.

Kaylie dunked a chip in the salsa and took a bite.

"Believe me, I've had it with independence." Margot gazed dreamily over the rail to the sunset blazing in the west. "If I could have just one more day with Trevor…" She frowned and shoved her hair from her eyes. "You know, the night he left, we fought." Her teeth sank into her lower lip. "I never had a chance to take back all the horrid things we said to each other. But you—" she glanced over at her sister and arched a fine, dark brow "—you have the chance to make things right with Zane."

"It's not that easy," Kaylie admitted. "He kidnapped me, remember? Took me away against my will. Thrust his will on me without the least little concern for me."

"Well, this might sound strange, but I'd give anything for Trevor to come back and try to protect me…." she whispered wistfully. Then, as if realizing she'd said too much, she cleared her throat and took a quick sip of wine. "Well, I guess that's not going to happen, is it?"

"I don't think so." Trevor's body had never been found. For months Margot had believed he was alive and would eventually show up, healthy and robust, but time and reality had finally convinced her that he had been killed.

They sat in silence for a while, listening to insects hum in the trees and watching the sun sink lower in the sky.

"Maybe you're too hard on him," Margot finally said, reaching into the bowl of chips and thinking aloud.

"No way. He lied to me, Margot. And that cock-and-bull story about Lee Johnston—"

"That wasn't a lie." Margot shook her head, and a tiny furrow creased her brow. "You and I both know they won't keep Johnston locked up forever. Zane's just being careful."

"Oh, save me."

"I mean it, Kaylie. So Johnston's not on the loose right now. He may be soon. According to Zane, there's been talk. Now, come on...." The sparkle returned to Margot's blue eyes. "Let's hear it, Kaylie. What was it like being whisked to some romantic hideaway with Zane?"

Kaylie's lips twitched. "I don't know," she said sincerely. "I can't decide. I felt like I was caught somewhere between heaven and hell."

Margot dunked another chip. "Uh-oh, that's passion talking."

"Maybe," Kaylie admitted, wrinkling her nose. "And I haven't forgiven you for your part in this, you know. You sold me out."

"I only tried to help."

"I don't think I need it, thank you very much."

"Oh, get off it, Kay." Margot grinned and leaned closer. "Let's hear all about it, and don't you dare leave out one tiny detail!"

It was after eight when Kaylie finally parked in her own garage. She and Margot had gone out for Chinese food, and after Kaylie had told Margot everything about her stay with Zane—well, almost everything—she'd returned to the city. Margot would never understand leaving a man after making love to him, and Kaylie wasn't sure she did herself.

She noticed Zane immediately. Leaning against his

Jeep, his arms crossed over his chest, he was waiting for her, and from the looks of him, had been for some time.

"What're you doing here?" she demanded, ignoring the tug on her heart at the sight of him.

"Waiting for you."

"Why?"

"I just wanted to know how things went today at the station."

"Sure." She didn't believe him for a minute. He didn't give a damn about her job. "What is it you really want, Zane?"

"You did go to see Margot, didn't you?"

"How'd you know that?" Kaylie cried, and then a fresh sense of betrayal washed over her. "No, don't tell me, my sister called you!"

"The minute you left her house."

"Why?" Kaylie whispered, wanting to throttle her meddling sister.

"She's a romantic," Zane said, cutting her off. "She seems to think we're destined to be together." He started forward, advancing on her, and Kaylie didn't know whether to throw her arms around him or run for cover. Instead she unlocked the door. "Why did she call you?"

"She seems to think there's still a chance for us."

Oh, Margot, how could you? "She didn't hear our argument this afternoon."

"Look, Kaylie, I'm sorry," he said suddenly. "I went off the deep end today at the office. I said some things I didn't mean, and I...I don't want to leave it like that."

"I don't think there's any other way."

"Sure there is," he cajoled, cocking his head toward his Jeep. "How about a drive?"

She laughed. "We tried that once before," she said,

shaking her head. "I'm not going to make the same mistake twice."

With a flip of the wrist, he tossed her the keys. "You drive. I'll let you take me anywhere you want to go."

Her fingers surrounded the cold bits of steel.

"Come on, Kaylie. It'll be fun."

"No tricks?" she asked.

He lifted one hand. "On my honor."

"Now we are in trouble," she said, but couldn't resist. "I must be out of my mind. We'll take my car. That way there's no mix-up with the keys. You seem to have a problem with that." He laughed and caught the keys she tossed back to him.

She climbed behind the wheel of her rented Mustang, and Zane folded himself into the passenger seat. "Anywhere I want to go?" she repeated, ramming the car into gear.

"Anywhere."

From the minute the car's wheels hit the pavement, she knew where she'd take him—a remote stretch of beach that she'd discovered on the other side of the peninsula.

Zane didn't say a word as she parked the car near the sea. He'd driven to her apartment on impulse, unable to let her go. Now, as she tucked her keys in her pocket, he knew he'd made the right decision.

The night-darkened ocean stretched for miles, disappearing into an inky horizon. Kaylie climbed out of the car. Rushing off the ocean, a breeze danced through the beach grass and trees, swirling and rustling leaves overhead. A pale moon, guarded by flimsy clouds, offered soft illumination and cast Kaylie's blond hair in silver light.

The scent of the sea mingled with Kaylie's perfume as they walked toward the frothy waves. They passed a few people, an elderly couple walking their dog and a group of teenagers bopping to the music cast from their radios.

As they neared the surf, Kaylie kicked off her sandals, cast an impish glance in his direction and taunted, "Bet you can't catch me."

Then she took off. Bare feet pounding on the sand, she laughed and headed for the pounding surf.

Zane grinned at the chance of a challenge. He struggled out of his shoes and socks, and though she had a huge head start, tore off after her, determined to catch her as he watched the wind stream through her hair and heard the soft tinkle of her laughter over the roar of the surf.

"You'd better run, Melville," he yelled, exhilarated as the distance between them shortened.

Kaylie felt the wet sand beneath her feet, smelled the briny scent of the sea and heard the slap of Zane's feet against wet sand as he shortened the distance between them. His breathing was loud, his footsteps pounding a quick, even rhythm.

Don't let him catch you, she thought, wondering why she'd started this stupid game. She should have known that Zane would rise to the challenge!

Hazarding one glance over her shoulder, she saw him bearing down on her. In the moonlight his features appeared more harsh, and the gleam in his eye made her already thudding heart slam against her ribs. She pushed herself farther, the air burning in her lungs, her legs beginning to protest. Several large rocks loomed ahead. If she could just make it past them....

With a laugh, he caught up to her, grabbed her around the waist and spun her around, toppling them both in one quick movement.

He landed on the wet sand with one shoulder and dragged her on top of him, twining his fingers through her hair. He kissed her lightly on the lips. "Did you really think you could outrun me?"

"I hoped."

"Foolish girl."

"Woman," she corrected, and he laughed again, his teeth flashing white in the black night. Screened by the boulders from the rest of the beach, they were aware only of each other and the night surrounding them.

"Woman," he replied just before his lips claimed hers in a kiss as wild as the violent sea. Kaylie could do nothing but kiss him back as he shifted, rolling over so that he was above her.

Any thoughts of denial receded with the tide, and she wound her arms around his neck and curved her body to his. Why was it always like this with him? she wondered as his mouth moved from hers. Softly he kissed her eyes and cheeks before his lips returned to the corner of her mouth again and his tongue delved and tasted, rimming her parted lips and touching her teeth.

Vaguely she was aware of the foam that touched her bare legs and toes, the cool sea against her skin. They were alone on this part of the beach, hidden by the rocks and the blackness of the night, as if they were the only two people on earth.

She shivered, but not from the water, as he slowly discovered the hem of her cotton sweater and his fingertips brushed the bare skin of her abdomen. His weight pinned her to the sand while his lips and tongue explored her mouth and neck, playing havoc with her senses.

Moaning softly, she kissed him back, her fingers coiling in the thick hair at his nape, her body arching to his. She didn't stop him when he lifted her sweater and dampened the lacy edge of her bra with his lips. Nor did she protest when his tongue dipped beneath the delicate fabric, gently prodding and wetting the edge of her nipple until her breast swelled and ached.

"Tell me you want me," he persuaded. His breath whispered across the wet lace, tantalizing her with its warmth.

"I—I want you."

"Forever?" he questioned, and in the moonlight she saw one of his dark brows cock.

He's playing with me, she realized, but couldn't control her body as he bent over her breast again and began, through the now-wet fabric, to suckle, gently tugging at her nipple with his teeth and lips. "Hmm, Kaylie?" he said huskily. "Forever?"

"Y-yes," she whispered, a familiar ache beginning to burn deep and hot.

He groaned and rubbed against her, suckling and petting, his breath hot and wet, his body lean and hard. She felt the grit of sand against her bare back, but she didn't care.

He shoved her strap over her shoulder, and her breast spilled out of her bra, translucent and veined in the moon glow, her nipple dark and standing proudly erect.

"You are beautiful," he murmured, reverently touching the hard bud before laving it again with his wet, hot mouth.

Kaylie closed her eyes and cradled his head against her, wanting more, feeling the hot ache of a void only he could fill. Anxiously she moved against him, and her fingers fumbled with the buttons of his shirt. With a growl, he ripped the offensive garment off, then returned his attention to her pants. Groaning, he yanked her skirt away and kicked off his trousers.

"Love me, Kaylie," he whispered, his hands on her

shoulders, his gaze delving deep into hers and burning with a primal fire.

But before she could say anything, he moved over her, his perfect, sleek body poised above her, his knees parting her legs. "I can't help myself," he cried as he entered her and she arched upward to meet him.

Her fingers clung to the hard, strident muscles of his back as he moved, thrusting inside her with a passion so fierce she could barely breathe.

She met each of his impassioned lunges with her own. Time and space ceased to exist, and her mind spun out of control. The sound of the sea receded, and all she could hear was her own throbbing heartbeat and Zane's ragged breathing.

Staring up at him, watching the play of emotions across his strong features, she let her body control her until there was nothing in the universe save Zane and her. Hot and wild, she felt him stiffen, and a wondrous release caused her to cry out. "Zane— Oh, Zane!" Her world tilted out of control as spasm after glorious spasm enveloped her.

"I'm here, love," he answered, before falling in exhaustion into her waiting arms.

CHAPTER ELEVEN

SHE LET HIM STAY. Telling herself she was every kind of fool, Kaylie let Zane spend the night. She was allowing herself one more night of pleasure without thinking of the consequences, and they spent the early hours of the morning making love.

At five, she reluctantly rolled out of bed. Zane turned over and groaned but didn't wake up. She showered quickly. As she dressed, she glanced at him still sprawled across her peach-colored quilt and blankets.

Her stomach twisted painfully when she thought that this might be the last time they would ever be together. She couldn't afford to become emotionally tangled up with him again, but a part of her longed for the marriage they had once shared, the happiness they'd held for so brief a moment.

She loved him still. As much, if not more, than on the day they married. Now, as she gazed at his sleeping form, all tangled in her sheets, she felt a rush of hot tears in her throat. If only things had worked out differently....

"Stop it," she muttered, clasping a gold necklace around her neck and swiping at her eyes. She wouldn't cry now. Nostalgia would serve no purpose.

"What?" Zane growled, opening a sleepy eye. "Stop what?" His jaw darkened with the stubble of a beard, his eyelids drooping seductively, his bare muscles moving fluidly as he adjusted the covers. He looked so virile and male, she had to glance back to her reflection before she did or said anything stupid. "Were you talking to me?" he asked with a yawn.

She brushed her hair until it crackled. "No, I was talking to myself, but since you're awake, remember to lock the door when you leave." She adjusted her turquoise-colored skirt and slid her arms through a matching jacket. "And leave the extra set of keys on the table."

"You're throwing me out?" he asked, disbelieving. He stretched lazily, his skin dark against the sheets. His sable-brown hair fell rakishly over his eyes, and his lips twisted into a thin, sensual smile.

"I think it would be safer that way."

"For whom?"

"You," she quipped, seeing her eyes twinkle in the reflection as she added earrings and a dab of perfume. "You just never know when I might decide to have my way with you."

"So have it!" He tossed back the covers to display all too vividly his well-muscled body, his mat of dark curling chest hair, his firm legs and much, much more.

Kaylie's breath caught in her throat, and she had to swallow in order to speak. "It's, uh, tempting—very tempting, but really, I've got to go—"

"Call in sick," he suggested.

"Not on your life!" She slipped into bone-colored heels. "After already being gone while 'Aunt Brenda' was taken so ill, I don't think calling in sick would go over so well."

Zane grinned devilishly. "I could arrange it so that your aunt had a relapse."

"You're impossible!" Kaylie threw her brush at him, then strutted down the hall.

Zane scrambled off the bed, the glint in his eye unmistakable. Kaylie giggled as she half ran to the kitchen. Stark naked, he tore after her through the house and caught up with her at the back door.

"Zane, don't," she protested, fighting more laughter as his arms surrounded her and he kissed her passionately, holding her hostage against the back door. She squirmed and wriggled, but his kiss was warm and wet and reminded her of the way he'd felt the night before.

"Don't what?" he whispered, his tongue flicking sensually between her teeth.

She couldn't speak until he lifted his head.

"Don't muss my hair or clothes or…" The words faded away as he kissed her again, his tongue darting between her teeth, claiming her mouth, his hands moving downward to cup her buttocks and bring her hips hard against his.

"Or what?" he prodded, not abandoning his assault on her senses.

Kaylie's knees turned to jelly, and though she knew she should shove him away, she couldn't find the strength. "Or I might just—"

"Have your way with me?" he mocked, his eyes dancing with gray light as he lifted his head and stared at her.

"Or worse!" she tossed back.

"Worse?" A wicked grin slashed across his jaw. "Believe me, I'm ready."

"I can tell," she teased. Glancing over his shoulder, she noticed the time on the wall clock and groaned. She was already late! "You wouldn't want me to lose my job, would you?"

He growled and kissed her again. "Yeah, that would be a real pity!"

"I'd never forgive you!"

"No?" He lifted a disbelieving brow, and his eyes were alight with challenge.

"I mean it!" She reached behind him until she found the door knob, then sidestepped him and hurried onto the covered porch leading to the parking lot. "I don't expect you to be here when I get home."

"Not even if I make your favorite dinner?" he asked in a high, falsetto voice.

"Oh, you're impossible!"

She climbed into the Mustang. But as she adjusted her side-view mirror, she caught a glimpse of Zane, naked as the day he was born, standing in the open doorway, arms crossed over his chest, one shoulder propped against the frame, not in the least concerned that the neighbors might see him.

"It would serve you right if you get arrested!" she yelled through the window, missing his response as she slammed the car into Reverse.

Zane laughed, and the rich sound lingered in her thoughts as she drove toward the heart of the city.

"LEE?" DR. HENSHAW TOOK a seat in the chair next to his patient. But Johnston didn't look up. As if he were rooted to the cushions of the old couch facing the television in the recreation room, Lee Johnston sat, waiting, the blank screen reflected in his icy eyes.

"Lee, can you hear me?"

Johnston scratched at a scab on the back of his right hand. But still he stared at the TV.

"No use trying to talk to him," Rick said, walking in and switching on the set. Music blared. Rick adjusted the volume with the remote control. A children's cartoon show was in progress. Johnston didn't move. "Until *West Coast Morning* comes on, he won't say a word."

Henshaw exchanged glances with the orderly, and he thought about the messages he'd received and had to return. Flannery had called again, as had Kaylie Melville herself. He'd have to talk to them both, which didn't present any particular problems.

It was the other call that bothered him, a call he didn't want to return. But, of course, he had no choice.

Rick, still cleaning off a table in the corner that had recently been used for arts and crafts, shook his head at the doctor. "Let's just hope you-know-who is on the show today," he said, placing the palates, brushes, paints and other tools onto a cart. He wheeled the cart next to Lee's chair just as a heavyset orderly named Pam rushed into the room. "Dr. Henshaw? There's a problem in 301," she said breathlessly, her pudgy face red. "Norman is upset—I mean really upset. He threw his breakfast all over the room and…and…" Seeing Lee for the first time, she gained control of herself. "Maybe you'd better come, too," she said to Rick.

Rick mumbled something inaudible under his breath, but gave the cart a shove. The corner caught on the edge of the couch, and several paint mixing tools and palates clattered to the floor.

"Son of a—" Rick caught himself and reached down, grabbing the paint-spattered knives and brushes. The floor was smudged with yellow ocher, Christmas green and scarlet. "Great—just great!"

Henshaw was already following Pam out of the room. Rick, in a foul mood, snarled at Lee, "Maybe you'd just better go back to your room until I clean this up. I don't want you messin' this up any more than it already is! Come on, get going! You'll be back for your stupid program!"

Rick prodded Lee on the shoulder. Johnston jerked

away, his nostrils flared slightly. He didn't like to be touched. Not by Dr. Henshaw and especially not by Rick, the know-it-all with the smug smirk. Rick really thought he was crazy and he looked down on Lee, but Lee intended to show Rick and Henshaw and all the others just what he was made of. Reluctantly, he got to his feet.

"Hurry up, I don't got all day," Rick growled, looking around for a towel or mop.

Lee, spying a knife that had slid just under the couch, hazarded a sly look at Rick, whose back was turned as he unlocked a closet. Quick as a cat, Lee grabbed the dull knife, stuck it into the side of his shoe and pretended to be tying his laces.

"You still here?" Rick asked, facing him again. "Well, come on, come on." He touched Lee again, and Lee recoiled, his stomach turning over.

Only one person had the right to touch his body. And that person was Kaylie…sweet, sweet Kaylie. He licked his lips and scratched absently at the itch on his hand as he stepped into the hallway. He'd missed Kaylie the last few days, but her absence from the program had brought one thing into perfect focus. He had to see her again, touch her, smell her, taste her. Soon.

His bloodless lips curved into the faintest of smiles as he felt the knife, wedged tightly between sock and leather, rubbing against the side of his foot.

KAYLIE'S FIRST FULL DAY BACK at work started the minute she shoved open the glass doors of the building. She waved to the receptionist and made her way through the series of hallways toward her office. On the way, Tracy flagged her down with a sheaf of papers.

"Today's guests?" Kaylie asked.

Tracy nodded and slapped the papers into Kaylie's outstretched hand. "Yep. Just a little more information that came in late. Isn't that always the way?" She lifted her slim shoulders and turned her palms toward the ceiling.

"Always." Kaylie laughed, glad to be back in her normal routine. She didn't even think about Zane standing naked in her driveway—well, she didn't *dwell* on the vivid image she'd seen in her side-view mirror.

She stopped by the tiny cafeteria and saw a couple of technicians and cameramen.

"Great to have you back, Kay," Hal said as he grabbed a doughnut from the box of pastries lying open on the glossy Formica table. Hal, thin and balding, was in charge of the sound booth.

"We missed you around here," his partner, Marvin, agreed.

"It didn't look like it," Kaylie replied, picking up a cinnamon twist and a napkin. "I saw the program."

Hal snorted. "Old Alan was in his element, no doubt about it. He was snapping orders around here like he owned the place."

Marvin, his slight paunch jiggling, chuckled. "The funny part was, no one paid him much mind."

"I bet that went over like the proverbial lead balloon."

"More like a lead zeppelin," Marvin said. "Hey, how's that aunt of yours anyway? What was wrong with her? Heart problems?" He dusted the sugar from his fingers.

Hal, wiping the last crumb of a jelly doughnut from his mouth, said, "I heard she was in an accident of some sort—ended up in a coma."

"She's fine. Her heart did act up after the accident, and she was in and out of consciousness, but she's fine now, out of ICU," Kaylie replied, improvising, mentally cursing Zane for his lies. She breezed out of the cafeteria, balancing a coffee cup, her pastry and napkin in one hand, her briefcase swinging from the other and the notes Tracy had handed her tucked under her arm.

"Welcome back to the rat race," she told herself as she dropped into the chair behind her desk. Sipping her coffee, she retrieved her notes from her briefcase. As she added in the information Tracy had handed her, she jotted down a few new questions and underlined background information she considered important.

She finished with the notes and her pastry just as the door of her office flew open and Audra, the hairdresser and makeup artist, scurried breathlessly inside. "Lord, what a day! Sorry I'm late. Alan's toupee, you know. He's never satisfied with that damned rug, and there's only so much I can do with it. If he hates it so much he should break down and buy a new one. Or go without. Hell, I think a man is much sexier in nothing than something, and that goes for hairpieces as well as clothes." She laughed at her own joke and unzipped her oversize makeup bag. "Well, anyway, I didn't mean to rush you."

"No problem," Kaylie said around a smile. Audra, with her fast tongue, stiletto heels and bloodred lipstick, was always a breath of fresh air in this conservative old building.

Audra eyed her critically. "Nope. You look none the worse for wear," she agreed, rifling in her bag with her red-tipped nails. "In fact you look pretty damned good for hanging around a hospital for four or five days." She frowned thoughtfully as she pulled out a comb and swirled it in some cleanser. "How's that aunt of yours? Heard she had a gallstone operation."

"Uh, it was her heart—no operation," Kaylie replied. Thanks a lot, Zane, she thought as Audra smoothed a few errant strands of her hair into place.

"Well, at least you got away for a few days," Audra

said, pointing an aerosol can in her direction and spraying a cloud of mist over her locks. "And don't be worrying about this—ozone friendly. See, right here on the can." She pointed to a symbol Kaylie couldn't read through the mist. "I'm an environmentalist now."

"Good," Kaylie said, coughing as she reached for her coffee.

Audra snatched the cup away, sloshing a few drops of brown liquid onto Kaylie's notes. "Oh, no, you don't. No, sirree! Your lipstick's perfect. Let's not be messing it up by leaving it on this here cup."

"Aye-aye, Captain," Kaylie teased, saluting Audra as the makeup artist picked up her gear, zipped her case closed and exited.

There was a rap on her door and the familiar sound of Tracy's voice. "Ten minutes, Kaylie!"

She scanned her notes one last time, then dashed to the set. Alan was already waiting. As Kaylie's microphone was pinned onto her jacket, she caught his glance and smile. He seemed genuinely glad to see her.

"Don't worry about a thing," he said, as she settled into her chair. He patted her hand affectionately. "I've got everything covered today. All you have to do is sit there and smile and be your gorgeous self."

"You're kidding," she replied. "Besides, I'm all set."

On the floor in front of camera three, Tracy was motioning for all quiet on the set.

At a silent signal to the sound box, the lead-in music filled the small auditorium. Kaylie took a deep breath, smiled and wondered if Zane was watching. Giving herself a mental slap, she forced thoughts of him aside.

The show went well. She interviewed a rock star named Death, a woman who grew an entirely organic garden, as well as the snake handler from the zoo, along with his favorite python and boa constrictor. She held the snakes and let them crawl across her shoulders as she spoke to their handler.

Alan handled the national news and talked with Hugh Grimwold, a pitcher for one of the bay area teams.

After the local news, and another sports update, both Alan and Kaylie spoke with two high school seniors who had started their own recycling business.

In the final segment, Alan announced the guests for the next show and reminded the viewers that on Friday, Chef Glenn was going to create his famous Cajun breakfast. The credits began to roll as music once again drifted from the speakers positioned around the set.

"Good job, Kaylie," Jim said, clapping her on the back and smiling broadly. "You know, the show just didn't feel right without you." He waved and sauntered toward the reception area while Kaylie headed toward her office.

From the corner of her eye she noticed the dark look that Alan passed her way, but she ignored Alan's foul mood and bathed in Jim's compliments. Jim Crowley didn't hand out praise often.

At her desk, she pulled the cap off her underlining pen with her teeth and started reading the bio information on the guests for the next day.

The door to her office opened and slammed against the wall.

Alan, face scarlet, eyes blazing, stormed into the room. "You don't even have an Aunt Brenda!" he charged, crossing his arms indignantly over his chest.

"What?" she asked, nearly dropping her pen.

"Don't lie to me, Kaylie. I checked."

"You did *what?*"

"I called around, checked with some of your friends. Eventually I even talked to Margot. *She* told me the truth.

She didn't want to—at least not at first—but she came clean. Jeez, Kaylie, I think she gained some perverse pleasure in telling me that you'd lied." His red face turned almost purple.

"Oh."

"'Oh' is right! You let me and everyone else here think you were on some mission of mercy when all the time you were shacking up with Flannery!"

"Now, wait a minute—" Kaylie's voice rose indignantly. Slowly getting to her feet, she wished she could throttle her meddling sister as well as Alan.

Alan made an impatient motion with one hand. "Oh, Margot didn't exactly fill me in, but she made enough broad hints that I figured it out. You were with Flannery last week, weren't you?"

This couldn't happen! Kaylie planted her palms on the top of her desk and tried her best to remain calm. "What I did or didn't do isn't really any of your business."

"You left us in the lurch, Kaylie!"

"You seemed to handle everything well enough without me. And if I remember correctly, I covered for you a couple of years ago—when you bruised your backside and your ego while snowboarding."

Alan's face went white. "But I couldn't tell Jim or the rest of the crew that I'd…" His voice dropped off, and he swallowed hard.

"That you ended up with a broken tailbone trying some silly teenaged stunt with a ski bunny who'd been busted for drugs?"

"Oh, God." The wind disappeared from his sails. "You know about all that?" He ran a shaking hand across his hair, and his toupee slid a little. Kaylie almost felt sorry for him. Almost.

"So what happened?" he asked, his face puddling into

a pout as he slid into a chair near her desk. "I thought it was over between you and Flannery."

"It was."

"But…?"

She was through lying. In fact, as soon as she was finished talking to Alan, she'd go and explain everything to Jim. If the powers-that-be in the station decided to fire her, so be it. At least she wouldn't have to walk this tightrope of lies any longer. "Zane stopped by the other night and we went to dinner. He persuaded me to go to the mountains with him for a few days."

"Just like that?" Alan snapped his fingers.

"Oh, no, it took a lot of convincing," she said, swallowing a smile as she remembered how Zane had fireman-carried her into the lodge. "A *lot* of convincing."

"For God's sake, why did you agree to have dinner with him in the first place?"

"It was part of the deal."

"The deal?" he repeated, shaking his head. He rolled his eyes and tossed his hands up. "So now she's making deals with her ex-husband! Kaylie, do you know that the press has us practically married?"

"We discussed this. It's a dead issue."

"I know, I know. But…well, I thought we could let it ride awhile. What could it hurt? But you running off with Flannery, well, that about kills it."

"Good!"

Alan left a few minutes later, and Kaylie marched into Jim Crowley's office to tell him the abbreviated truth. Jim took the news in stride. He wasn't happy, of course, and he warned her to "call next time—about ten days *before* you plan to leave." But she left his office with her pride and her job intact.

HOURS LATER, SHE RETURNED to her apartment. Zane was long gone, but the scent of him still lingered in the air. The bed was made, but she couldn't resist taking a pillow and breathing deeply. The feathers still smelled of his aftershave. "Oh, Melville, you've got it bad," she chided, still clutching the pillow as she fell back on her bed and stared up at the ceiling. "Real bad!"

Realizing that she sounded like an adolescent in the throes of puppy love, she tossed the pillow aside and walked into the kitchen.

The red light on the answering machine was blinking, and she played back the messages only to hear Zane's voice, as if he were there.

"I guess I'm hung up here at the office awhile," he said with a sigh. "So I won't be over."

"Too bad," she murmured, though she did feel a jab of disappointment.

"But I'll call you later and I'll see you soon."

He hung up, and she listened to a couple more messages—one from Margot begging her to call and another from an insurance salesman.

After popping a dinner into the microwave, she dialed Margot's number.

"Hello?"

"I should tar and feather you," Kaylie announced.

"I guess you talked to Alan."

"Screamed would be the appropriate word."

"I know I shouldn't have said a word to him, but he had the nerve to call here asking about you, and I just had to set him in his place. If you ask me, that guy's got a screw loose."

"Alan?" Kaylie laughed.

"I'm not kidding. I bet he's the one that gave all

those papers the idea you two were engaged. Anyway, I couldn't resist hinting around about Zane. He deserved it."

Kaylie couldn't stay angry with Margot for long. "It's okay, I guess. I was tired of talking about this fictitious Aunt Brenda and I told Jim the whole story—well, most of it. Fortunately I still have my job."

The microwave beeped, and as they talked, Kaylie pulled out her dinner—a pathetic-looking concoction of chicken, peas and potatoes—while Margot asked about Zane.

"He's not here," Kaylie said, nearly burning her fingers as she opened the plastic cover.

"No?" Margot sounded worried.

"He does have his own life."

"I know but—"

"Look, Margot, I know you think that Zane and I should reconcile and live this storybook existence, but it's not going to happen."

"Why not?"

Exasperated, Kaylie replied, "For one reason, he's not Prince Charming and I'm not Snow White or Cinderella or whoever it was Prince Charming was linked up with."

"Oh, Kaylie," Margot said cryptically, "if you only knew."

AT ELEVEN-THIRTY, ZANE was finally caught up. His work, while he'd been off in the mountains with Kaylie, had piled up. He'd had to deal with a complaint about one of his men in the Beverly Hills office, double-check two new security systems in offices downtown, hire three more men as well as go over the books quickly to keep his accountant appeased.

And through it all, he'd thought of Kaylie, worried about her, wished to God that she was with him.

He reached for the phone, but decided not to call her. It was too late. She'd be exhausted. And he'd promised himself to let her live her own life.

Lifting his arms over his head, he felt his spine pop from hours of restless sitting. He stood, walked to the window, and stretching the muscles of his back and shoulders, caught a glimpse of the city at night. Cars rushed by, their headlights cutting into the semidarkness, their taillights small red beacons. A few pedestrians scurried along the sidewalks, black forms visible in the lamplight.

He'd called Whispering Hills earlier in the day and been assured by Dr. Henshaw that Johnston was going to stay locked up for a while. But, though the good doctor had been forthcoming, Zane had a feeling Henshaw wasn't telling him everything.

It wasn't anything Henshaw had said; it was the hesitation in his voice that had caused the hairs on the back of Zane's neck to rise—it was as if the doctor were trying to hide information.

"But why?" Zane wondered aloud, rubbing the day's growth of beard on his chin. Maybe Kaylie was right. Maybe, where her safety was concerned, he was paranoid.

Even the tape from Ted could be a hoax. But why? *Why?*

He'd had gut feelings before and he never second-guessed his instincts. Right or wrong, he had to be careful. This was Kaylie's life—her *life,* damn it. He wasn't about to fool around.

He rotated his neck, closing his eyes. She would be furious if she even guessed that he'd sent someone to watch her apartment, to follow her, to protect her when he wasn't with her.

"You're getting in deep, Flannery," he told himself as he grabbed his keys and snapped off the lights. No, that was wrong. Where Kaylie was concerned, he'd always been in deep, so deep that he felt that sometimes he was drowning.

He wanted nothing more than to drive to her apartment and stay the night, make love to her and awake with her wrapped around him. But he couldn't.

"Breathing room," he muttered as he locked the door of the building behind him. "She wants breathing room."

ALAN BENTLY SWIRLED his onion in his glass and stared broodingly at his drink. Seated at a private table in an expensive restaurant, he was alone with his own bleak thoughts. He was past forty—pushing forty-five—and his hair was little more than a memory. Though he worked out every day, his physique was suffering and his career looked as if it was on hold. Or worse.

For a while, with all the hype and speculation about Kaylie and him being romantically involved, things had started to look up. His agent had talked about a possible part in a movie, and there was even a rumor that a big-name producer was interested in putting Kaylie and Alan back on the silver screen together—to do a sequel to *Obsession*. True it had been over seven years since the original movie had been released, but that didn't matter. Sequels were the thing now.

But Zane Flannery seemed hell-bent on ruining everything. It didn't matter that he and Kaylie had disappeared for a while, though Alan would have liked to milk that disappearance for a little publicity, and he'd enjoyed being the star of the show. Now she was back and definitely not interested in anything but Flannery. Again.

So all his dreams seemed to be slipping away. Like a ghost from his past, fame eluded him. Alan Bently wanted the big time and he'd tasted a little of it once. Not that his job with the station was anything to sneeze at. *West Coast Morning* was big—at least on the West Coast. But it wasn't as glamorous as a successful movie. He wanted his name in the credits. He was still young enough to be a leading man, but he couldn't wait much longer.

Alan tossed back his drink. He knew that his career was teetering on the brink. One wrong move and the fickle public would forget him. But, with the right amount of publicity and interest, he could reach the big time again.

Smiling as the liquor slid through his system, sending a cozy warmth through his bloodstream, he motioned to the maître d' for a telephone and made the call that would ensure his fame again.

CHAPTER TWELVE

THE NEXT MORNING Kaylie felt a pang of loneliness. Zane wasn't lying in the sheets, nor was he winking at her, nor making jokes with her, nor, as she headed for the door, tossing off the blankets and, without a stitch on, chasing her down the hall.

"This is what you wanted," she told herself as she grabbed a piece of toast, slapped some butter on it and munched as she locked the door behind her.

She felt restless and anxious. For seven years she'd lived without Zane, and now, she told herself as she drove toward the station, she couldn't stand one night away from him.

Her thoughts still clouded by Zane, she flipped on the radio, hoping to hear the news, and tried to concentrate on what was happening in the world—to no avail.

At the station's lot, she parked her rental, snatched her briefcase and climbed out of the car. In her peripheral vision, as she locked the car door, she noticed a silver Ford Taurus parked on the other side of the short hedge that separated the station's lot from the street. The driver didn't get out of his car, but pulled a newspaper from the seat beside him and began scanning it as if he were waiting for someone.

A car pool?

Had she seen the car before—yesterday morning? She couldn't remember, and deciding the man had every right to read his paper in the car, walked briskly to the station doors.

Inside, she poured herself a cup of coffee, and after talking with a few coworkers, none of whom asked about Aunt Brenda, fortunately, she made her way to her office where she sequestered herself with the intention to go over her notes on today's guests: a heart surgeon from Moscow, a woman who wrote a diet book for people who love chocolate, and a new young actor promoting his latest movie.

She'd no more than sat down when there was a tap on the door, and Alan, already in makeup, poked his head inside. "I'd like to talk to you after the show," he said as Audra rushed by him with her huge case and a quick "'Scuse me."

"Sure. What about?"

He glanced at Audra then shook his head. "It'll wait."

"Good, because I can't!" Audra said, unzipping her case and eyeing Kaylie. "Now, you don't look as good as you did yesterday."

"Thanks a lot," Kaylie teased, but she knew the hairdresser was right. Two nights ago she'd slept soundly in Zane's arms, only to be awakened to make love to him. Last night she'd tossed and turned, angry with him one minute, missing him the next. She hadn't gotten much sleep.

"A few eyedrops—a little blush, and you'll be good as new," Audra announced, but Kaylie wasn't convinced.

However, Audra worked her magic and Kaylie felt better. The show went well, and aside from Alan sending her silent messages she didn't understand, the segments passed without a hitch.

Afterward she had lunch in the deli across the street, then spent the rest of the afternoon in her office, review-

ing the tape of the day's show and making preparations
for the next program.

There was a quick knock on the door, and Alan once
again poked his head inside. "Got a minute?"

"Sure. What's up?" She tossed her pencil onto the desk
as Alan closed the door behind him.

"There's talk about a sequel to *Obsession*."

"I've heard."

"The producer's talking with the writer of the original script as well as to Cameron." Cameron James had
been the director of *Obsession*.

Alan's face was split with a huge grin. "This could
revive both our careers," Alan went on, pacing on the
other side of Kaylie's desk.

"No one's approached me yet," she said.

"And if they do?"

"I—I don't know." A shiver of fear slid down her spine
as she remembered the premiere.

"'Don't know'?" he repeated, aghast. "Kaylie, just
think of it. You never had a chance to prove yourself as
anything but a child star, but now you could show how
you've grown up, how your character has matured!" He
was excited. His eyes practically glowed, and his hands
became expressive. "This is an opportunity we can't pass
up."

"No one's shown me a script yet."

"It'll happen," Alan predicted, buoyed. "I spoke with
my agent last night and again this morning. Sequels are
all the rage. Look at *Back to the Future,* the *Rocky* films.
Not every one is a blockbuster, but some are. And they
don't have to be action films. There's *Texasville*."

Kaylie considered the idea. She'd been approached to
do small parts in several movies over the years, but had

always declined. "I'm happy here—doing what we do, Alan."

"Well," he said, rubbing his hands nervously, "it hasn't happened yet, but when it does, just promise me you'll keep an open mind. I know that the *Obsession* premiere was a real bummer, but it was a once-in-a-lifetime thing, and look at it this way, the publicity didn't hurt the ticket sales."

"Alan!"

He grinned as he reached for the door handle. "Just a little joke. You know, you're too serious, Kaylie. Much too serious. You need to lighten up."

"I'll keep that in mind."

He left, and Kaylie, a headache beginning to pound behind her eyes, decided to call it a day. She was tired of Alan and his schemes. How could he talk about the premiere of *Obsession* as if the entire horrifying experience were nothing more than a publicity stunt?

If only it had been....

But the memory was too vivid, the images too terrifying and real. Frowning darkly, trying not to dwell on the brutal image of that night, she shivered and told herself to shake off the lingering fears.

She didn't see him, so much as feel his presence.

"Kaylie?" Zane's voice drifted to her as if in a dream. Standing in the doorway, filling it with his broad shoulders and narrow hips, Zane was watching her. His hair was mussed, and Kaylie guessed he'd sprinted across the parking lot.

"Is something wrong?" His features were taut with concern.

"Oh—no, nothing." She decided there was no reason to worry him just because Alan had mentioned the premiere of *Obsession*.

"Nothing?" He closed the door behind him and crossed the room. "Something's bothering you," he challenged, hooking one leg over the corner of her desk. "What happened?" Concern etched the lines of his face, and she thought guiltily that she should be thankful that he cared.

She couldn't lie. "Well, for starters, Alan seems to think I should jump-start my movie career by agreeing to costar in *Obsession II* or whatever it may be called."

Zane didn't move.

"Never mind that there's no script or director, yet."

"You couldn't—"

"And that was on top of a pretty bad week to begin with."

"Bad?" he said, a small smile tugging at the corners of his lips.

"Well, you see, I have this ex-husband, who has been ramrodding his way back into my life." She crossed her arms over her chest. "You probably know the type— pushy, arrogant, opinionated."

"But handsome, sexy and intelligent."

"That's the one," she said, her bad mood beginning to evaporate.

"And you don't like him pushing you around, right?"

She avoided his eyes for a second and fingered the strand of pearls at her throat. "Well, the problem is, I do like him—a lot. More than I think I should. But I don't appreciate him trying to dominate me. But he knows that—"

Zane reached across the desk and took her hand in his. "Kaylie, I love you." The words hung in the air suspended by unseen emotional threads.

Her mouth went dry, and she had trouble finding her voice. As she stared into his eyes, she whispered, "Love isn't based on possession, Zane, and you've tried to possess me for as long as I can remember."

"Hey, Kaylie, about tomorrow's show—" Alan said, opening the door without knocking. With one glance at Zane, he froze.

To Kaylie's surprise, Zane actually smiled, releasing Kaylie's hand and facing Alan. "Bently," he drawled, as if seeing a long-lost friend. "I was just asking Kaylie if she's seen the front page of *The Insider*."

"You what…?" Kaylie asked, feeling a cold lump form in her stomach. Alan licked his lips.

Zane reached into the inner pocket of his jacket and withdrew a folded piece of newsprint. He smoothed it on her desk, and she read the bold, two-inch-high headline: Lover's Spat Forces Kaylie Off Morning Show.

"What is this?" she demanded, skimming the article that insinuated that she and Alan, still planning marriage, had been involved in an argument that sent her running away, seeking solace for her wounded heart. "This is absurd. I did no such thing!" she said, glaring first at Alan, then at Zane. "You're the reason I left. You kidnapped me!"

"Kidnapped?" Alan repeated, his mouth falling open, his gaze moving from Kaylie to Zane and back again. "Wait a minute. Let me get this straight. He *kidnapped* you?"

Zane shot her a look that cut to the bone.

Alan lounged one shoulder against the wall. "Is that what you call *persuading* you to go to the mountains?"

Zane pushed himself to his feet and said quietly, "Kaylie and I need to talk. Alone." He grabbed her jacket from a hook near the door. "Let's go."

Alan was amused and couldn't help the grin that toyed

with his lips. "Well, Kaylie, what happened to all that independence you were so hell-bent to earn, hmm?"

"Oh, give it a rest, Alan," she snapped as she and Zane
walked out of the building. Still stung by Alan's remark,
she said, "I'll drive."

To her surprise, Zane didn't argue, just slid his
long body into the small interior of the Mustang. As
she cocked her wrist to twist the key in the ignition, he
slanted a sexy, knowing smile in her direction. "I suppose it would be too much to expect you to kidnap me
to a private lodge in the mountains."

"Way too much," she said as the engine started. But
she laughed. "Okay," she said, and eased out of the parking lot and into the late-afternoon traffic. "Talk."

Sighing, he stared out the window. Evening shadows
stretched across the town as traffic moved sluggishly
along the hilly streets. "Well, I've spent the last—" he
checked his watch "—thirty-six hours staying away from
you, giving you some space, and it's been hell. I just
wanted to be alone with you again."

Kaylie's heart turned over.

"I'm trying to give you space—breathing room—all
those things you figure are so important, but, if you want
to know the truth, I don't like it much."

"Neither do I," she admitted, trying to concentrate on
traffic as she switched lanes and stopped for a red light.
As the light changed, she tromped on the accelerator and
the car sped forward again.

"Then let's change things," he said quietly.

"How?"

"Pull over—"

"What?"

"Over there." He pointed to a side street near a park.
Kaylie found a parking spot and turned off the car. Zane

climbed out of the Mustang, and she followed, not sure what he was going to say.

The sun, partially obscured by a few flimsy clouds, was low in the sky and shadows lengthened over the ground. Leaves danced across the grass, pushed by a cool breeze. In the distance, children played football while dogs bounded in the thickets of trees nearby. Women pushed strollers, and squirrels chattered in the high branches of the oaks and maple trees.

Kaylie's heels scraped against the path. Zane took her hand, his warm fingers linking through hers. "I think we should try again," he said quietly, his voice rough with emotion as he looked down at her.

"Try?" she repeated, but she knew what he meant, and happiness and fear surged through her.

He brushed a strand of hair from her forehead, his fingers warm and gentle. "Marriage. I want you to be my wife again. Marry me, Kaylie."

She wanted to say yes, to throw her arms around his neck and kiss him and tell him that they could live together happily ever after. Tears sprang to her eyes, and she bit her lip. "I—I don't know," she whispered, blinking rapidly.

"Why not?"

"We tried marriage once before—"

"And we were young and immature. Both of us. This time it would be different. Come on, Kaylie." He drew her into the protective circle of his arms, and his lips brushed gently over her forehead.

God, how she loved him! Her arms wrapped around his back, and she laid her head against his chest, hearing the steady beat of his heart. She closed her eyes for a second. Living with Zane would either be ecstasy or torture—heaven or hell.

When her eyes opened, she focused on the street, where the cars whipped by, wheels spinning, horns blaring.

"Well?" he asked, holding her at arm's length.

Say yes! Don't be a fool! This is your one chance at happiness! "I just don't know," she admitted, and the pain that surfaced in his eyes cut through her heart. "I love you, Zane," she confessed. "I always have." His arms tightened around her.

"So what's the problem?"

"I just don't want to fail again."

"We won't," he promised, kissing her crown.

"Then...I...I need a few days to think it over."

Zane sighed, his breath ruffling her hair. "Why? So you can analyze our chances?"

"Last time we rushed things—ran on pure emotion. This time—if there is a this time—I want to make the right decision."

For a second she thought he'd be angry. His face clouded, and he dropped his hands. "Okay," he finally said, shoving a hand through his hair in frustration. "You have time to think it over, but don't take too long, okay?" He strode back to the car and climbed inside. She followed and slid behind the wheel.

"Why don't you take me to dinner?" he remarked as she checked her side-view mirror and tried to pull into traffic.

"I have a better idea—you take me."

"Only if I can persuade you to marry me."

She grinned inwardly. At least he wasn't furious with her. Signaling, she eased the car into the right-hand lane and noticed that a silver car about a block behind her followed suit. She frowned as she realized the car was a Taurus, but so what? The city was crawling with them.

Zane placed a hand on her knee. "How about some-place elegant—French dining overlooking the bay."

"How about pizza?" she countered, and he laughed.

"You're the driver, Kaylie. You can take me anywhere you want."

"YOU DID WHAT?" MARGOT NEARLY dropped her glass of Chablis as Kaylie finished her story about her relationship with Zane.

Margot had driven Kaylie to the house in Carmel so that she could turn in the rental and pick up her car. "I told Zane that I'd consider it. Then we went out for pizza and I took him back to his car."

"Oh, boy, are you crazy." Margot took a long sip of wine and shook her head. Seated at a round umbrella table on the back deck of Kaylie's house in Carmel, she eyed her sister as if she had truly lost her mind. "Some women spend their entire lifetimes looking for a man like Zane Flannery. And you know what?"

"What?" Kaylie asked, not really interested in Margot's big-sister wisdom, but knowing she was going to hear it one way or another.

"They never find him, that's what! Men like Zane Flannery don't exactly grow on trees, you know!"

"Thanks for the advice."

Margot smiled. She was on a roll. "And you got lucky and found him twice! If I were you, I'd march right into the house and call him right now."

"And say what?" Kaylie teased.

"That you've already found the preacher, for crying out loud!"

Kaylie twisted the stem of her wineglass. She'd thought the very same thing and had even made it as far as the telephone a couple of times, but in the end she'd backed down. "I don't want to make the same mistake we did before."

"You won't. You're older now. And, most importantly, the man loves you, with a capital *L*. So why are you fighting it?"

Kaylie let her gaze wander out to sea. Margot had a point, she admitted to herself.

"And you miss him, don't you?"

Kaylie sighed and shrugged. "Yeah," she admitted, trying to sound indifferent when deep inside she missed him every minute of every day. She hadn't stopped thinking about him, couldn't sleep, plotted ways of bumping into him.

"Look, if it's a matter of pride—"

"It's more than that," Kaylie admitted, remembering the way Zane kidnapped her—just hauled her into the woods without even asking her first. "I can't accept a man who insists on dominating and pampering me."

"You did once."

"That was before."

"Right," Margot said, as if she'd just made her point. "Before that damned premiere of *Obsession!* Until then, you and Zane were comfortably ensconced in marital bliss. To tell you the truth, I was envious."

"You?" Kaylie's eyes rounded on her sister. "But you and Trevor—"

Margot waved impatiently, and sadness stole over her features. "I know, I know. But the truth of the matter was, my marriage wasn't perfect."

This was news to Kaylie. For as long as she could remember, Margot had been in love with Trevor Holloway.

"Oh, don't get me wrong. I loved Trevor more than I should have and I know that he loved me. But—" she

lifted a shoulder "—we had our problems, just like anyone else."

"What kinds of problems?" Kaylie asked.

"It doesn't matter—they seem stupid now and petty.
I'd gladly take all our problems back if Trevor were still
alive." Margot sighed and squinted out to sea, watching
the sun lower in a blaze of brilliant gold that scorched the
sky and reflected on the water. She seemed to focus on
a solitary sailboat that skimmed across the horizon—a
sailboat not unlike the one on which Trevor had lost his
life.

Kaylie thought she was finished, but Margot settled
deeper into her deck chair and continued, "No marriage
is perfect, but some are better than others and some are
the best. I have a feeling that you and Zane had one of
the best—at least until that creep Lee Johnston decided
to mess things up." Margot shuddered.

"Even before the premiere, Zane was...autocratic."

"He was scared. You'd been getting those letters and
he was terrified that something might happen to you—
which it did." Margot leaned across the table, her gaze
touching her sister's. "Give the guy a break, Kaylie. All
he's ever done is love you too much. Is that such a crime?"

"I guess not."

"I know not!" Margot finished her glass of wine. "The
point is that Zane's crazy about you. Also, he's handsome,
successful, caring, dependable, honest, intelligent and
has a great sense of humor. What more do you want?"

"Someone who'll let me make my own decisions,"
Kaylie replied before smiling and adding, "but of course
he'll have to be handsome, successful, caring, dependable—and all the rest of those qualities you reeled off."

"Then if I were you, I wouldn't look any farther than
your ex-husband," Margot said as she climbed out of

her chair and stretched. "Mark my words, Kaylie, you'll never find a man who loves you more than Zane does. And, if you'll stop long enough to be honest with yourself, you'll realize that you'll never love a man the way you love him." She reached for her purse and concluded, "You just have to ask yourself what you really want in life—to be lonely and independent or to take a chance on love—real love. I'll see you later. Think about what I said."

Kaylie figured she didn't have much choice. She watched Margot leave and knew her older sister was right. She'd never love a man as she loved Zane.

ZANE PACED AROUND HIS OFFICE. He'd spent the better part of the afternoon listening to his accountant argue that another office, located in Denver or Phoenix, was just what the company needed. Zane wasn't interested. Expanding the business suddenly seemed trivial.

For the past week he'd tried to stay away from Kaylie. He hadn't called her, he hadn't visited her, he hadn't even shown up on the set of *West Coast Morning,* though he had tuned in every day and had sworn under his breath whenever Kaylie and Alan shared a smile or a joke.

"It's just her job," he told himself, but he couldn't stem the stream of jealousy that swept through his blood. More than once, he had snapped off the TV in disgust, only to click it on again.

But he was giving her time to come to a decision—the most important decision of his life!

He slumped back into his chair, picked up the accountant's proposal, then tossed it into his wastebasket. He didn't need another office to stretch the corporate tentacles of Flannery Security. He didn't really care if he never made another dollar. He just wanted Kaylie.

"You're obsessed," he told himself, not for the first time, as he strode to the bar, found a bottle of Scotch and poured three fingers into his glass. Then he checked his watch. Barely one-thirty in the afternoon. Disgusted with himself, he tossed the drink into the sink, strode back to his desk and fished the figures for the new office from his wastebasket.

"Concentrate, Flannery," he ordered himself as he picked up a pencil to jot notes. But the letters and numbers on the pages jumbled before his eyes, and Kaylie's face, fresh and smiling, framed in a cloud of golden hair, swam in his mind.

His pencil snapped.

Muttering an oath aimed at himself, he grabbed his jacket and marched out of the office. "Cancel all my appointments this afternoon," he told Peggy as he headed toward the elevator.

"And where can I reach you?"

"I wish I knew," he replied. The elevator doors whispered open, and he climbed inside. He thought of a dozen schemes to contact Kaylie again, but dismissed them all. He'd just have to wait.

THE FOLLOWING FEW DAYS Kaylie was nervous as a cat. Margot's advice kept running through her mind. She half expected Zane to fall back into his old pattern—and she suspected that he might have her under surveillance.

But he never showed up at her apartment or the beach house again. Nor did he call or leave a message on her machine.

It was as if she'd finally gotten through to him and he was going to leave her alone.

"That's what you wanted, wasn't it?" she asked herself one evening. It was Friday and had been raining all day. Alan had been in a bad mood on the set, and the taping hadn't gone well. By the time Kaylie reached the beach house, she'd acquired a thundering headache and her shoes were soaked from her walk across the television station parking lot. All she could think about was a hot shower, a cup of tea and a good book.

And Zane of course. She let herself in with her key and smiled sadly. She never had bothered to change the locks; she hadn't had the heart to lock Zane out. And yet he'd never so much as tried any of her doors since the night he'd spirited her away.

And now he wanted to marry her. She was warmed by the thought. Her only hesitation was the thought of failing again, of the pain of divorce. She would never put herself, nor Zane for that matter, through all that pain again. Stripping off her clothes, she continued toward the bathroom.

The phone rang and she grabbed the bedroom extension, half expecting the caller to be Zane. "Hello?" she answered, smiling.

No answer.

"Hello?" she asked again, and there was still silence on the line. "Zane—is that you?" She waited, but heard nothing, and her nerves stretched taut. "Is anyone there? Look, I can't hear you. Why don't you try again?" She hung up slowly and waited, staring at the rain sheeting against her bedroom window and the dark, threatening clouds rolling in from the sea.

The only sounds were the distant rumble of thunder, the rain peppering the roof and the sound of her own heartbeat. The minutes ticked slowly by. "It was probably just a wrong number," she thought aloud, then continued toward the bathroom. She'd hoped the caller had been Zane, and her heart tripped at the thought that he'd tried to reach her.

Maybe Margot had been right, she finally decided, maybe it was her turn to reach out to Zane. Maybe there was a chance that they might start over again. If given the chance, surely Zane would treat her as an intelligent, mature woman.

He had to.

Because she loved him. With all her heart, she loved him and always would. There was no other man for her—no white knight lurking in the wings ready to dash up and carry her away. Zane was the only man in her life—always had been, always would be and she'd been a fool not to realize it before.

Wrenching off the faucets, she heard the phone ring again. She barely took the time to wrap a bath sheet around her before she dashed into the bedroom, leaving a trail of water behind her.

"Hello?" she called into the phone, her voice breathless, just as the caller hung up. "No! I'm here!" she yelled, feeling in her bones that the caller had been Zane. "Well, there's only one way to find out," she decided, throwing open her dresser drawers and yanking on her underwear. Tonight she was going to drive all the way back to the city, back to Zane's apartment and tell him she loved him. They'd have a chance to start over again.

RICK TAYLOR GROANED. HIS hand went to his head and he felt something sticky and wet on the floor where he lay. Blinking hard, he forced his eyelids open only to close them again at the glare from the single shaft of light near the floor. He slipped back out of consciousness before jerking awake. His skull pounded, the pain creating orbs of light behind his closed lids.

"Wha-what the hell?" he muttered, licking his lips. He remembered walking into that loony patient Johnston's room. But Johnston had not been in his bed. Turning to sound an alarm, Rick had felt the hot flash of pain in his abdomen and, doubling over, the crash of something against the back of his head.

Now he propped himself on one elbow, feeling the wound in his side tearing open. "Help," he tried to cry, but the sound was barely a rattling whisper. How long had he been here? Seconds? Minutes? Hours?

But surely he'd be missed. Trying to push himself upright, he fell back and attempted to call for help again. The narrow sliver of light, coming from the hall outside the door, wavered in front of his eyes.

"Help me! Please!"

Using all his strength, he pulled himself toward the door and the hallway. Pain ripped through his body, pounding at his temple. The room, barely ten foot square, seemed to stretch on forever as he inched his way to the door.

With each agonizing tug, his muscles shuddered and sweat poured over his bleeding head. "Somebody help me!" he said again and again until he reached the door. His bloody fingers surrounded the knob and he tugged. But the door didn't budge. He tried again, then realized that the door was locked from the outside.

Swearing, Rick fumbled on his belt for his keys only to discover that his entire key ring—the keys to the hospital, his apartment and his car—was missing.

"Oh, God," he cried, using his last ounce of strength to pound on the door before slipping into unconsciousness again.

"Answer, Kaylie, answer!" Zane whispered, before giving up. "Damn it all to hell!" He swore violently as he slammed the receiver into the phone cradle. His heart was thudding, his palms sweating as he stared at the phone message stating that Lee Johnston had escaped from Whispering Hills Psychiatric Hospital.

Zane's hands were shaking as he walked into the reception area where Peggy was bent over her word processor. "Dial 911. Ask for the police. Tell them that a patient who escaped from Whispering Hills threatened Kaylie once before and give them Kaylie's address—her apartment in the city as well as the house in Carmel." Uncapping his pen with his teeth, he scribbled out the information for her. "But first order the company helicopter to stand by," he commanded. "Tell Dave I want him to take me to Carmel and drop me off at the Buxton building."

"He's already waiting," Peggy said. "He was going to fly Hastings to—"

"Cancel that and have him wait for me."

"Will do." Peggy turned to the telephone and Zane raced out of the office. Heart thumping with fear, he took the stairs two at a time.

On the roof the helicopter was waiting, its gigantic blades churning in the night. Rain and wind lashed at Zane's face as he dashed across the wet concrete to the pad where Brad Hastings was climbing out of the passenger seat.

Covering his head with his briefcase Hastings yelled over the whir of the helicopter blades, "You just about missed us!"

"Emergency," Zane yelled back as he climbed into the copter and Brad dashed for cover. Glancing at the pilot, he said, "Carmel, on the double. Radio ahead for a company car—a fast one. And get me a backup."

"You got it," Dave replied, talking into his headset as

Zane strapped himself in. The helicopter lifted off and Zane sent up a silent prayer. Fear tore at his guts as his worst nightmare played through his mind. He only hoped they weren't too late.

KAYLIE GRABBED HER PURSE and squared her shoulders. She wasn't very good at eating humble pie, but Zane was worth it. This time, she decided, her pride wouldn't get in her way. Snatching a raincoat and umbrella from the hall closet, she headed through the kitchen and slung the strap of her purse over her shoulder.

She punched the answer button on her answering machine and locked the door behind her. In the garage, she heard the phone ring, but ignored the call. Even if the caller were Zane, she found the idea of surprising him in person appealing. If only she had a set of keys to his apartment, she'd turn the tables on him and wait for him in the dark…maybe in his bed with champagne?

She smiled to herself and reached for the button to open the garage door when she heard the sound—a small sound—like the scrape of leather on concrete.

Kaylie froze. Her skin crawled. Telling herself the noise was only her imagination, she strained to listen. Maybe she heard the scurry of a mouse or the neighbor's tabby cat. He was always hanging around when she stayed here. He could have been locked in the garage.

She punched the button but the door didn't open. Nothing happened. When she flicked on the light switch next to the opener, the garage remained dark.

Fear cut a swath into her heart, and she fumbled in her purse for her keys. She glanced nervously around the garage, to the shadowed corners. "Who's there?" she called, but heard nothing. "It's just your nerves," she told herself. Something moved in her peripheral vision.

Kaylie didn't wait. She shoved open the door to the house, letting the interior lights illuminate the darkened garage. Two steps inside a cold hand grabbed hold of her arm. Kaylie screamed.

Lee Johnston, his icy blue eyes blank, stared straight through her.

"Kaylie." His voice was rough and gritty. His flame-red hair was plastered to his head and the drip of rain ran down his neck and beneath the wet collar of his blue shirt.

Her knees went weak, but she pulled hard, intending to escape.

"Leave me alone," she screamed, but the words were only in her mind. Her throat was frozen. Light from the kitchen refracted off the knife in his hand.

Dizziness overwhelmed her. The premiere of *Obsession*. Her life flashed to a series of stills. Zane, oh, Zane, I'm so sorry, she thought.

"Kay-lee," her assailant mumbled and she tried vainly to wrench herself free. But he was strong and compact and determined. Thoughts ran through her mind. She needed a weapon. Tools in the garage. Knives in the kitchen. Anything!

"Kay-lee," he said again, his voice as chilling as the howl of a wolf. She backed up, stumbling over the edge of rakes and shovels. Lee kept up with her, his fingers biting into her arm, the knife's blade somewhere in the dark beside her.

"Let—let me go," she demanded, trying to stay calm, to hold at bay the panic that surged through her brain. Maybe she could talk him out of this! He'd never hurt anyone before—not really. But then, as he passed by the window, she saw the dark smudges on his shirt and knew the stains were blood. Not his, certainly. But whose?

Zane's? Her thoughts rambled crazily, and she thought for a blinding moment that Johnston might have sought his revenge on the man who had captured him years before. The only man she'd ever loved. *Oh, Zane. No, please, God, let him be alive.* Why hadn't she listened to him? Why?

Her knees threatened to buckle. If Zane were dead or lying hurt and wounded…

"No!" she wailed, throwing her body hard against Johnston. He tripped on a rake or shovel, and his fingers slackened. She leaped forward, and he lost his balance. The kitchen! If she could just get into the kitchen and run outside.

"Help!" she screamed, and scrambled past her car.

She rounded the trunk, moving slowly backward, listening to Johnston's movements in the dim light. Was he following her or trying to cut her off by rounding the front of the car? If only the garage door weren't locked! *Think, Kaylie, think!* There was an ax— Oh, God, where was it? Or a crowbar. Anything to protect herself. And the garage door opener—by the back door.

Heart pounding, she inched toward the door.

She heard voices—or was it her imagination? No, there were voices. Johnston heard them, too. He quit moving, though his breathing sounded close—between her and the kitchen. But where?

She stopped, listening, trying to focus. Moments passed. Tense, terrible moments.

Footsteps outside. "Kaylie! Kaylie!" Zane's voice rang through the house. "Oh, God, where are you?" He was alive! Kaylie's heart soared.

From a shadowy corner, Johnston lunged at her.

She screamed. "Zane! Don't come in here!" she cried. "He's got a knife—" But Zane came flying through the door, and in one quick motion, he threw himself into the darkness.

"Oh, please, no!" Kaylie cried as Zane propelled himself through the air and landed on Johnston and his raised knife. The blade flashed up, then swiftly down, landing with a thud in Zane's back before being torn out with a hideous sucking sound.

The two men struggled, and Johnston freed himself, struggling to his feet. Zane pulled himself upright, but swayed.

Kaylie thought she'd be sick. "No!" she screamed as Johnston raised his bloody knife again. She fell back against a shovel. Without thinking, she picked up the rusted tool and using all her strength, swung it, catching Johnston's knees. He dropped like a stone.

Zane sprang, quick as a cat. Blood oozed from the sleeve of his shirt. He rolled on top of the flailing man.

"Freeze!" A strong male voice yelled from the doorway, and Kaylie looked up to see a man in jeans and a sweater training a gun on Zane and Johnston.

"No!"

"Kay-lee, Kay-lee!" Johnston cried.

Kaylie shuddered.

"Back off!" the man in the doorway ordered, his face contorted in rage, his revolver aimed at Johnston's chest. "You okay?" he asked Zane.

"I thought you'd never get here."

"I radioed the police. Now, come on, let's get this low-life out of here."

Sirens screamed outside. As Zane struggled to restrain Johnston, two policemen ran through the house and, pistols drawn, charged into the garage.

"Police! Everybody hold it!" the taller man said, his gun trained on Johnston and Zane.

"Call for an ambulance!" Kaylie cried, watching in horror as a scarlet stain spread across the back of Zane's shirt.

"Already done. Okay, someone called in about an escapee from Whispering Hills. What's going on here?"

Zane, his face white and drained, tried to explain, but Kaylie, frantic for his life, told the police that she'd answer all their questions once Zane was in the hospital. She wouldn't listen to the officers when they demanded answers. Instead she climbed into the back of the ambulance and held Zane's hand all the way to the hospital. He tried to smile, but failed, and his eyes closed wearily.

"You're okay," she said, her voice trembling as she assured herself more than him.

But he didn't respond, and she knew that he'd lost consciousness.

"Don't die, Zane," she whispered, clinging to his fingers as if she could will the life to remain in his body. She heard the whine of ambulance tires spinning against the rain-washed streets. She only wished she'd told him how much she loved him—how much he meant to her.

Lord, she'd been stupid; she knew now. Because of her stubbornness, Zane had nearly been killed. If only she'd listened to him, trusted him, relied upon him, *leaned* on him! If only she'd loved him enough to work with him to save their marriage. Oh, Lord, she'd been such a fool, she thought, tears tracking down her cheeks.

Now it was too late. Too late. Maybe much too late....

CHAPTER THIRTEEN

KAYLIE DIDN'T LEAVE Zane's bedside. The doctors assured her that Zane was fine, that the wound was shallow. The blade of Johnston's knife had only penetrated Zane's shoulder muscle. Though he would be sore for a while, the team of experts at Bayside Hospital were convinced that Zane would be "good as new" in no time. Nonetheless, she camped out at the hospital that night.

"He's sedated. He won't wake up for hours," Dr. Ripley predicted. "You can't do anything for him now. Tomorrow, unless he takes a turn for the worse, I'll release him."

"I want to be here when he wakes up."

"I'll have the nurse call you." Ripley was a thin man in his early fifties with freckles splashed all over his face, neck and arms. His once-red hair was turning to gray, but he seemed as fit as most thirty-year-olds.

"I'd rather wait. It's important," Kaylie insisted.

The doctor slanted a brow. Motioning toward Zane, he said, "He might not be in the greatest mood when he wakes up."

"I don't care."

"Well, okay. Have it your way," the doctor finally agreed, instructing the nurse that Kaylie was to spend the night.

She spent the night in a chair, alternately dozing and waking with a start, her muscles cramping. The small room was never dark. Light from the parking lot street-lamps filtered through the blinds, and illumination from the hall made the shapes in the room visible.

In her fitful hours of sleep, she relived, over and over again, the horrible moments in the garage. The knife. The blade plunging into Zane's shoulder. Blood pooling on the floor. Johnston, dead-blue eyes staring at her, laughing maniacally as she threw herself on Zane's unmoving body. Tears choked her throat. She couldn't lose him… she couldn't….

"Zane! No! Please, no!" She woke to find herself in the hospital room, Zane sleeping on the bed, the worst over.

Relief brought tears to her eyes.

ZANE BLINKED TWICE, shifted and felt a brutal pain rip through his shoulder. He sucked in a swift breath. Shadowy images flitted through the mists in his mind—terrifying visions of the madman and his knife. Kaylie—where was she? His eyes blinked against an intense light.

"Zane?"

Kaylie's voice was like a balm to the pain. Thank God she was alive! Relief flooded through him. Those last frightening minutes in the inky garage, the maniac with his weapon…

Through the fog of his memory, Zane recalled leaping into the dark garage, flying at Johnston and struggling for the knife.

Now he focused with difficulty and discovered Kaylie standing on the other side of the bars of his bed, her hands white as she gripped the rails, her eyes clouded with worry. Her hair was tangled and mussed, her makeup long washed away, her clothes, the same as she'd been wearing the night before, wrinkled and smudged with blood—his blood. Her eyes were red-rimmed and cloudy green and her eyebrows pulled together with worry.

And she was gorgeous. He managed a smile. "You look like I feel."

Letting out her breath, she blinked against a sudden bout of tears. "So you're going to rejoin the living after all?"

"The jury's still out on that one," he grumbled, realizing he was in a hospital bed, bandaged and swathed, an IV dripping fluid into his wrist. Wincing, he attempted to sit up, but Kaylie's hands, cool and soft, restrained him.

"Slow down, cowboy," she said, and he noticed the tremor in her voice and saw the tracks of recent tears on her cheeks. "We've got all the time in the world."

"Do we?" he asked, his gaze locking with hers.

She sniffed loudly. "The rest of our lives."

"Why, Ms. Melville," he drawled, suddenly feeling no pain, "is this a proposal?"

She laughed, though her eyes were wet. Sniffing loudly, she brushed her tears aside with the back of her hand. "You bet it is. And I don't expect to end up a widow before I'm a bride, so you just take care of yourself."

"So now you're giving orders."

"And you're taking them," she announced firmly, though she swallowed hard. "After all, someone's got to protect you."

He laughed at that. "So what're you? My personal bodyguard?"

"No, Zane. Just your wife."

He reached up, and pain seared through his shoulder. Emotions clogged his throat. "You don't know how long I've waited to hear you say those words," he admitted, then with his free hand, playfully grabbed her. "I wish I had a tape recorder, because, no matter what, I'm holding you to it."

Her fingers linked through his. "I wouldn't have it any other way."

"Breakfast time." A nurse, pushing a rattling tray, shoved open the door. "But first I need to take your temperature and pulse and…"

Zane groaned, and the nurse winked at Kaylie. "Looks like he's out of the woods. Why don't you run down to the cafeteria and get yourself something to eat and a cup of coffee."

"Sounds like heaven," Kaylie admitted.

While the nurse tended to Zane, Kaylie made her way to the ladies' room where she washed her face as best she could, repaired her makeup and ran a comb through her wild hair. Glancing in the mirror, she snorted. "Not exactly the glamorous talk-show hostess today, Melville."

For the first time, she thought about her job, and tucking her comb and brush into her purse, she walked toward the lobby. Spying a pay phone near the admitting area, she dredged up a quarter and dialed the station. The receptionist answered on the second ring.

"Hi, Becky, it's Kaylie."

"Oh! Kaylie, let me put you through. Jim's been trying to get hold of you."

"I'll bet," Kaylie remarked as the phone clicked several times and Jim Crowley finally answered.

"You made the front page," Jim announced. "And not of *The Insider* for once. You're in the *Times*."

"I'm not surprised," she drawled.

"You okay?"

Kaylie wondered. She was still shaken by the incident, no doubt about it. Her skin prickled at the horrific memory, and yet she felt better than she had in years.

She loved Zane, and planned to be with him for the rest of her life. "I'm fine," she assured Jim.

A pause. "You sure?"

"Absolutely."

"It's pretty late. I don't suppose you'll be in." He sounded hopeful.

She laughed without much mirth. "Not today."

"That's okay. Alan already said he'd fill in, though he'd like to interview you about last night."

"No way."

"I told him that's what you'd say. Anyway, since it's Friday, I'm asking Chef Glenn to add a couple of appetizers to go with whatever today's concoction is."

"Hot and Spicy Chicken Linguine," Tracy said in the background.

Jim snorted. "Yeah, some Italian thing. I'll see you Monday."

She rang off and took the stairs to the cafeteria. There she ate alone, devouring a bagel and cream cheese and fresh fruit along with two cups of coffee. She felt more than one curious look cast in her direction and heard a few whispered comments.

"Kaylie Melville...yes, channel fifteen...a crazed mental patient went after her.... Yeah, maybe it was the same guy...the guy she was with is up on the second floor... no, not Bently...some other guy...you know those Hollywood types.... Her husband? *Ex*-husband, you mean... are you sure...? Well, what's she doing with him?"

Ignoring the wagging tongues, Kaylie cleared her tray and picked up a newspaper near the lobby. Page one was splashed with the story. Pictures of her house in Carmel, photos of the retreating ambulance, and older shots of Zane and Johnston and her at the premiere of *Obsession* years before graced section two under Local News. "Terrific," she muttered under her breath. "Just great."

Perusing the paper quickly, she decided Zane wasn't up to reading all about the "drama in Carmel" and stuffed the paper into the trash on her way back to his room.

The nurse had left. His breakfast, uneaten, had been pushed aside. Zane was propped up in bed, staring at the television, where a newscaster was reporting Johnston's escape and the attempt on Kaylie's life.

"Well, your name's on the tip of everyone's tongue today," he drawled.

"So's yours."

Zane rolled his eyes. "This is no good," he said. "The problem with all these reports is that it sensationalizes the crime. Who knows what nut is watching and thinking he'd like to get his name and picture on the television by imitating that maniac?" Scowling darkly, he scratched at the back of his hand. A bandage covered the spot where the IV needle had recently been attached to his skin.

"I think I'm safe," Kaylie replied. "Johnston's locked up."

"But how many more like him are out there?"

"It's the price of fame," she said, then nearly bit her tongue. Here it was. The same old argument. And she'd just inadvertently offered him a perfect opportunity to exploit his position. Still frowning, he clicked the remote control, and the lead-in music for *West Coast Morning* filled the room.

"Let's see what *your guys* say about it," Zane said, and Kaylie held her tongue, not wanting to let him know that Jim had already mentioned an interview to her.

Alan's face, gravely serious, was centered on the screen. "I'll be hosting the show alone today," he told the viewers, "because last night Kaylie Melville was viciously attacked by a knife-wielding assailant. The suspect is in custody, his alleged crime nearly identical to his assault on Kaylie seven years ago."

To Kaylie's horror, she watched old footage of the premiere of *Obsession*. Of course the cameramen had been there for quick peeks of the rich and famous. Those cameramen, who had been interested in showing who was dating whom and what dress Kaylie wore to the first showing, hadn't expected to capture a madman lunging at her on film. Nor had they intended for the terrifying drama to unfold in front of their lenses. But it had happened, and every heart-numbing second had been captured on film—from Kaylie's bloodless face, to Zane's heroic act that saved her life.

"Yes, history repeated itself last night at Kaylie Melville's beachside home in Carmel. Fortunately, once again her ex-husband, Zane Flannery, was on the scene to save her from a man who has been obsessed with her for years...."

Alan went on and on, recalling the details of last night's attack as well as bringing up the premier of *Obsession* again. He even publicly admitted that he and Kaylie were just friends, but very special friends, and he looked earnestly into the camera to wish her well.

"I think I'm gonna be sick." Zane clicked off the set.

"It's just his way," Kaylie said lamely, but she could hardly defend Alan. For, though he appeared concerned for her well-being, the entire segment reeked of publicity-seeking and she couldn't help but think that all his references to *Obsession* were to drum up public interest in the old film in the hopes that the viewers and fans, as well as the studio heads, would demand a sequel.

"Well, for all his supposed friendship, he sure doesn't give a damn about exploiting you."

She couldn't argue with him and didn't. The less she thought about last night's attack, the better. She and Zane were together. Johnston was locked away. They were safe and in love. Nothing else mattered.

Zane was released just after noon, with strict orders to take care of himself and not strain the wound. "You've lost a lot of blood and you're carrying around fifteen stitches, so don't do anything foolish," Dr. Ripley told Zane as he signed the release forms.

To Zane's ultimate humiliation, Kaylie pushed him out of the hospital in a wheelchair and helped him into the passenger seat of his Jeep. Then she settled behind the steering wheel. The look she cast him should have tipped him off. Her green eyes danced with mischief as she headed east.

"Where're we going?"

"Can't you guess?"

He eyed her thoughtfully. "Don't tell me, you're kidnapping me to a certain mountain retreat...."

She laughed gaily. "I thought about it, but no, I've got something else in mind."

"What?"

"Lake Tahoe," she replied with an impish grin. "I know this great little place there. It's called the 'Chapel of No Return.'"

"No!"

"Scout's honor." She lifted one hand as if to pledge.

"So where's Franklin?"

"Your neighbor—Mrs. Howatch—called while you were sleeping and offered to watch him for the weekend." She grinned. "I hope she knows what she's getting into."

"Franklin likes her," Zane replied.

"Oh, it's just me he has problems with?" she teased.

"He'll get used to you. I did. Now, lead on, Ms. Melville," he suggested, settling back in his seat and staring at her as if he thought she might vanish and this entire fantasy would give way to cruel reality.

Kaylie beamed. She felt as if she'd finally grown up enough to accept Zane as her husband. Yes, he'd been dominating and overzealous in his protection of her, but now she understood him better. She knew how frightened he must have been for her safety.

The few hours he'd been unconscious had been hell. She finally understood just what losing him would cost her. She didn't doubt that she loved him, always had loved him and always would. She didn't see that love as a curse any longer, but as a blessing. She wanted to spend the rest of her life with him, as his wife, as the mother of his children, as the lifelong partner with whom he would grow old.

And now, at twenty-seven, she felt secure and mature enough to handle him. No more temper tantrums—well, not too many. From here on in, they were partners.

She drove straight to Lakeside Chapel, and when Zane climbed out of the Jeep, stretched and grumbled that he wouldn't be married in anything less than the "Chapel of No Return," she offered to take him straight back to the city.

"I guess we'll just have to forget this whole marriage thing," she told him blithely.

At that he grabbed her roughly, spun her to him and growled in her ear, "Not on your life. I've waited too long for this."

She lifted her shoulders and rounded her eyes innocently. "Whatever you say, honey."

For that she was rewarded with a swat on the bottom. "Come on. No reason to keep the minister waiting."

Within thirty minutes they were married. The ceremony was simple. The preacher was a lively man who was pushing eighty, and his wife, a sparrow of a woman, served as pianist and witness. Another woman, heavyset and beaming, was the second witness, and at the end of the short ceremony, Kaylie and Zane were presented with a marriage certificate, a bouquet of roses, a brochure for Love Nest Cabins and a bottle of champagne.

"Not quite as elaborate as the first ceremony," Zane drawled, once they were back in the Jeep.

"But more lasting," Kaylie predicted.

"You think so?" His dark brow cocked insolently, but his gray eyes were flecked with humor.

"I'm sure!"

"So where to now?"

"Well, we could either go gambling…or…"

"Or what?"

"Or I could take you to the hotel and—" she lowered her voice suggestively and touched his thigh "—we could start the honeymoon."

He placed his warm palm over the top of her hand. "I'm definitely in favor of option two."

"Me, too." Her spirits soaring, she wheeled the Jeep into the parking lot of the hotel. Blue-green pines softened the lines of a rambling, three-storied lodge. With peaked dormers poking out of a sharply gabled roof and a covered porch that skirted the main floor, the rambling building rested on the shores of the vibrant blue lake.

"This is as close to 'heaven'—isn't that what you called your place in the mountains?—that I could find."

"I guess it'll just have to do," Zane drawled, as if he gave a damn about the hotel. All he wanted was Kaylie.

It took twenty minutes to register and have their bags carried to their third-floor suite. Impatiently Zane slapped a tip into the bellman's palm, then, when the young man left, locked the door behind him.

"Now, Mrs. Flannery, what was that you were saying about starting the honeymoon early?"

She laughed, the sound melodious as he wrapped his arms around her and lowered hungry lips to hers. Though his shoulder ached, he ignored the painful throb and got lost in the wonder of his wife.

Kissing her, holding her close, undressing her and feeling her clothes drop from her supple body, Zane felt a desperation that ripped through his soul.

Only hours before her life had been threatened by a knife-wielding madman intent on killing her.

The image was vivid and excruciating. What if he had lost her? What if Johnston's blade had found its mark? His heart nearly stopped at the thought, and he pulled her roughly against him, intent on washing away the horrid images in the smell and feel of her.

The nightmare was over. They could celebrate their lives and love.

Her body was warm and soft, yielding as he caressed her bare shoulder with the rough pad of his finger. She quivered at his touch, and her mouth opened easily at the gentle prod of his tongue. Her fingers were everywhere, as if she, too, felt the urgency of their union.

Life was so fleeting, so very precious, there was no time to waste. Her fingers pushed his shirt over his shoulders, and he flinched as she tugged on his sleeves and the wound in his upper back stung.

"Love me, Zane," she whispered, kissing the hairs on his chest, fanning the fire deep in his loins as her tongue touched his skin, rimming his nipples, lapping at his breastbone, tasting of him and causing wave after tormented wave of pure lust to wash through him.

With a groan he shifted his weight, shoving her slowly back against the down coverlet on the bed. He touched the outline of her bra with his fingers and mouth, kissing the soft curves of her breasts, kneading the white mounds until dark, petulant nipples peaked beneath the white lace. He teased those rosy buds with mouth and fingers as Kaylie writhed beneath him, arching anxiously, bucking her hips against his, silently begging for release.

Slow down, a voice in his mind protested. *Take your time.* But his body, and his desperation to love her, to prove that they had survived the terror of a madman's knife, wouldn't listen. His hands moved anxiously over her, tearing off her bra, stripping her of her underwear.

And she was just as desperate. Her hands worked at the waistband of his slacks, sliding them off his legs and kicking them aside as he mounted her.

With the first thrust, pain shot down his arm, ripping through him with a blinding agony that was matched only by the exquisite torture of her body moving in tandem with his. But he couldn't stop, and soon, as their tempo increased and their sweat-soaked bodies fused, he felt nothing but the sheer ecstasy of her body sliding against his.

"Kaylie, love," he cried, his voice as raw as a December night. He tried to hold back, resist, but the feel of her fingers digging into the muscles of his good shoulder and the deep-throated sound of her moans of pleasure brought him to quick and immediate release. He plunged into her with a primal cry that echoed through the room, and she shuddered against him, clawing and clinging, her face upturned in rapture, her low moan rippling through her body.

Collapsing against her, he held her tight, afraid that if he let go, he'd lose her. Rationally he knew that she was here, with him, and had pledged her life to him, but for so many years she'd been lost to him so that he clung to her as if to life itself. "I love you," he murmured into the sweat-darkened strands of her hair.

Propping up on one elbow, she gazed down on him with eyes that shifted from green to blue. "I thought the doctor said to take things easy," she teased.

"With you, nothing's easy."

Tilting her head back, she laughed, and the sound drifted to the rafters, high overhead. "I promise not to try to be impossible."

He slid her a knowing glance. "Don't make any rash statements."

"You're asking for it, Flannery."

His eyes sparked. "You bet I am." And with that, he grabbed her again, ignoring his doctor's instructions completely.

On Sunday morning Kaylie dragged herself out of bed, showered and dressed in clean jeans and a rose-colored sweater.

"What're you doing?" Zane asked, opening one sleepy eye and groaning as he watched her gather her hair into a ponytail and run a tube of lipstick over her lips.

"Duty calls," she replied, tilting her head to loop a gold earring through her earlobe. "I'm still a working woman, you know. I've got a million and one things to do before the show tomorrow."

He grunted, and Kaylie sensed the first argument of their short marriage. "You can call in and explain to Jim—"

"No."

"But wouldn't you love to prolong the honeymoon?"

"Absolutely. But I can't. I've already missed more than

my share of work lately." She caught his reflection in the oval mirror above an antique dresser. Draped across the sheets, wearing only his bandage and a day's growth of beard, he grinned that sexy grin that caused her heart to trip.

Still, she couldn't let him push her around and try to dominate her life. They had to start off on the right foot.

"You don't have to work, you know. I can take care of us."

"It's my job, Zane. A job I happen to love. I'm not going to give it up."

"Not ever?"

Turning, she said, "Ever's a long time. But certainly not in the foreseeable future."

"So how long do you *plan* to be hostess of *West Coast Morning?*"

"How about for as long as I want to? Or as long as the station wants me? You know, this job won't be indefinite. Whether the producer admits it or not, there is some age prejudice involved." She expected him to object, to give her reason upon reason why she shouldn't continue with her career, but he only lifted a shoulder.

"Whatever you want," he muttered.

She could have been knocked over with a feather. "Wait a minute," she said. "Whatever *I* want?"

"Umm. Long as you take care of yourself."

"And you trust me?"

"I'm trying," he said, his smile fading. "It's not easy."

Surprised at his turnabout, she snagged a pair of his jeans from the floor of the cabin and tossed them at him. "Come on, get dressed."

"I could use a little help," he suggested, one brow lifting craftily.

"Could you?" She couldn't help but play along with his game.

"Well, I *am* an invalid."

She laughed out loud. "That'll be the day. You didn't seem like much of an invalid last night!"

To her surprise, he leaped off the bed and, catching her with his good arm, jerked her up against him. His lips came crashing down on hers with a savagery that stole her breath. "I lied about the invalid bit," he admitted, dragging her back to the bed and burying his face in the lush thickness of her hair.

"I know."

"I thought maybe I needed an excuse to get you back into bed."

"Never," she whispered against his lips. They tumbled onto the rumpled sheets together.

"YOU'RE MARRIED?" ALAN'S chin nearly dropped to his knees. "To Flannery?" Disbelief nearly choked him. "But you can't be.... He—he—"

"He's my husband," she replied. Polishing an apple with a paper towel in the station's cafeteria, she ignored the opened box of pastries and settled for a cup of coffee instead.

Alan tried desperately to recover. "Well, I read all about Johnston's escape," he said, "and I know that you must have been terrified. I mean, talk about nightmare déjà vu! But marriage? My God, Kaylie, what were you thinking?"

"That I loved him," she said, offering him a bright smile as she poured a thin stream of decaf coffee into her cup.

"You thought that once before."

"And I was right," she said, refusing to argue with him.

She set the glass carafe onto the warming tray. "We—uh, just took a wrong turn." She took a sip from her cup and stared at him over the rim. "We won't make that mistake again."

Alan looked about to argue further, but snapped his mouth shut instead. Throwing his hands into the air, he shook his head. "Well, I guess there's nothing left but to congratulate you." To Kaylie's amazement, he hugged her. "Good luck, Kaylie. You know I've only wanted what was best for you. I hope this time you're happy." She almost sloshed coffee all over him.

"I am," she assured him. "And thanks."

MARGOT WAS ECSTATIC. KAYLIE and Zane arrived on her doorstep with a bottle of champagne and celebrated. "I'm so happy for you!" she said, tears streaming from her eyes. "I'm just sorry it took that awful Johnston to get you two together."

"At least that's behind us now," Kaylie said. "He won't be released for years—maybe ever."

"You hope," Zane replied, his expression guarded.

Kaylie wanted to ask him more, but Margot changed the subject and she forgot about the maniac for a while. After all, Lee Johnston was out of their lives forever!

THE NEXT TWO WEEKS SPED past in a blur. Kaylie moved into Zane's apartment in the evenings after work, and Zane, still recuperating, divided his time between the office and home. They talked, laughed and made plans for the future, and slowly Franklin accepted her. At first the dog lay next to Zane, never leaving his side, but as the days passed and Kaylie became a permanent fixture in the apartment, Franklin relaxed, even following Kaylie after mealtimes.

Occasionally Zane and Kaylie argued, but Kaylie tried to keep her temper in check and Zane did a decent job of letting her maintain a certain level of independence.

All in all, the marriage seemed to work, though sometimes, if Kaylie's name or picture appeared in the tabloids, Zane would explode about "invasion of privacy, libel and yellow journalism," and threaten to "sue the living hell out of those bastards." But once he was assured that Lee Johnston was locked up for a long time, Zane took everything in stride.

A model husband, she thought as she pulled into her parking space at the station one morning. Fog had blanketed the city, lingering in a chill mist that seeped into Kaylie's bones.

Unconsciously, she glanced over her shoulder, to see if the car that often stopped at the curb when she arrived at the station was in tow. But no silver Taurus emerged from the fog and she told herself to stop worrying; Johnston had been apprehended—no one else would follow her. Besides, she'd only spotted a car a couple of times. Once in a while a blue station wagon would occupy the same spot. Obviously the drivers were just another couple of early-morning commuters. Maybe they even carpooled together.

She locked her car and walked briskly into the studio where Tracy met her in the reception area. "Here are the updates for today's show and you're supposed to join an emergency meeting with Jim and Alan in Jim's office."

"Emergency?" Kaylie repeated. "What happened?"

"There's a problem with scheduling, I think. One of Friday's guests is backing out."

"And that calls for an 'emergency meeting'?"

"Go figure," Tracy said, rolling her eyes. "Alan is into high drama these days."

Well, that much was true, Kaylie thought as she tapped on the glass door of Jim's office and entered when he waved her in. Alan, already seated near Jim's desk, flashed her a smile.

"Problems?" Kaylie asked as Jim motioned her into the vacant chair next to Alan.

"Two cancellations on Friday's show," Jim explained, reaching into his drawer for a pack of cigarettes. "First the author who wrote the self-analysis book calls and explains that he can't make it for, quote, 'personal reasons' and would we be so kind as to reschedule him? Then we get a call from Jennifer Abbott's agent and Jennifer won't do the show."

"Why not?" Kaylie asked. Jennifer was one of the most controversial actresses on daytime television. Though always in the running for an Emmy, she was notorious for her contract disputes.

"Seems as if Jennifer is keeping mum until after the final round of her contract negotiations, whenever that may be. So for now we're out of luck."

"I thought Tracy had a list of local people who were willing to pinch-hit."

"We've been through it," Alan interjected. "And we've got a couple of 'maybes'…" He cast a quick glance in Jim Crowley's direction, and Kaylie had the distinct impression that they were holding back on her.

"So?" she prodded, uneasy.

Alan leaned forward, as if to confide in her. "So, I called Dr. Henshaw—you know, Johnston's psychiatrist—"

"I know who he is," she said tightly.

"And I asked him to appear."

"You did *what?*" She couldn't believe her ears. No way. *No damned way!*

"Well, face it, Kaylie. The public would like to know more about the man who attacked you. And since you're the cohostess, what better medium than our program to give the viewers a little insight into the complexity of the man?"

"And the police will allow this?" she asked, turning stricken eyes on Jim. "Won't it interfere with Johnston's trial? And what about patient confidentiality?"

Jim reached for a cigarette, then tossed the pack in the drawer and wadded up a stick of gum. "You don't understand. You wouldn't be asking him questions about Johnston…at least not directly. Actually, he'd be on the hot seat. We'd ask him to talk about an ordinary day at Whispering Hills, the makeup of the patients, that sort of thing, and then question him on Johnston's escape."

"I don't believe this," she replied, shocked. "I don't know why he'd agree."

Again the two men exchanged glances. Jim said, "Well, Henshaw does have something to gain from it all."

"What?"

"A little glory for himself," Alan explained. "He's been writing a book for years."

"What kind of a book?" Kaylie asked, dreading the answer.

Jim stepped in. "Apparently he's been working on psychological profiles of star stalkers for a few years. Must've started it before he got the job at Whispering Hills."

"Don't tell me," she said. "Lee Johnston is one of the cases in the book."

Alan grinned. "You got it. Anyway, the book is about done, and suddenly a few publishers are interested. His agent is pushing for big bucks."

"And the publishers are interested because of Johnston's escape and all the press recently," Kaylie suggested.

"Bingo." Alan practically beamed. "Of course, after Johnston's trial, Henshaw can add a final chapter."

"Of course," Kaylie said dryly.

"How'd you find out about it?" she asked.

"I called." Alan's face turned crafty. "I figured there was a lot of public interest right now. I would have liked to have that orderly who was hurt in the escape, but the hospital won't allow it—nor will the police."

"But it's all right for Henshaw."

"As long as we zero in on the book and the escape. But we can't talk about the attack on you."

Kaylie, who had tried to keep as calm as possible during the whole discussion, shook her head. "I can't do this," she said, her stomach churning at the thought of reliving the horrible ordeal again. She looked over at Jim. "You can understand, can't you, why I can't do this? I was attacked—by a madman. And Zane could've been killed."

"Oh, Kaylie—" Alan interjected. "This isn't personal. It's just business."

She took a deep breath. Facing Johnston's psychiatrist, talking about the attack of seven years ago, reliving all the hellish details again. For what? To satisfy America's curiosity? To gain viewers? To sell Henshaw's book? To further Alan's career? To further hers?

It all seemed so petty. A headache erupted behind her eyes. She closed her lids and rubbed her temples. In her mind's eye she saw Johnston's knife thrust into Zane's back. She opened her eyes and shook her head. "I—I don't think I can separate personal from professional on this one."

"You got a better idea?" Jim asked, popping the gum into his mouth.

"A dozen of them," she said, her mind spinning to any other possibility. "There's the leader of the senior citizens' rights group, Molly McGintry. She's in town. Or Consuela Martinez, the woman who came into the country illegally, had her baby so that he could be an American citizen, then went public with the fact to fight our immigration laws. Or how about Charles Brickworth, the guy who's tearing down one of the most historic buildings in the bay area?" she asked, but she could have been talking to walls for all the good it did her.

By the time the meeting was over, Dr. Anthony Henshaw had agreed to be Friday's guest, and Kaylie, along with Alan, would get the grand privilege of interviewing him.

The thought turned her insides to jelly.

And she couldn't complain to Zane. What could he say except, "I told you so"?

No, all she could do was find a way to get through the interview.

"Don't worry about it," Alan said, clapping her on the back as she reached for her purse. "If we work things right, we could generate enough interest not only for a sequel to *Obsession,* but there might be enough of a story in Henshaw's book for a made-for-television movie or documentary."

"Oh, Alan, forget it," she snapped, angry at the situation.

"Loosen up, Kaylie," he replied. "You may not know it yet, but this is the best publicity we've ever had. And, face it, sure you were scared—hell, you went through a lot of pain and agony—but no one was really hurt, were they?"

"No one but Zane and an orderly at the hospital," she replied dryly, "but maybe they can cut movie deals of their own."

"There's no talking to you!" Alan muttered, grabbing his briefcase and athletic bag and storming out of the building.

Kaylie hiked the strap of her purse over her shoulder. How was she going to break the news to Zane?

CHAPTER FOURTEEN

ZANE KICKED AT HIS wastebasket, sending it rolling to the other side of his office. He'd wrestled with his conscience for weeks.

He strode down the hall. Wincing as his wound stretched, he rapped sharply on the door of Brad Hastings's office.

Brad was behind his desk. Tie askew, thin hair standing straight up from being repeatedly run through with his fingers, Hastings stared into the glowing screen of a computer terminal. He glimpsed Zane from the corner of his eye, typed a few quick commands and swiveled in his chair. "What can I do for you?"

"I think it's time to take Rafferty off the case."

"You sure?" Hastings had never before questioned Zane's judgment. But this was a difficult situation. "I thought you were still concerned for Kaylie's welfare."

"I am. But if she found out I was having her tailed, she'd hit the roof."

Hastings chanced a grin. "So who wears the pants in your family, eh?" He ribbed his boss, hazarding Zane's considerable wrath for a chance to needle him.

"Kaylie's big on independence."

"Whatever you say." Hastings shrugged and bit on his lower lip. "I could use Rafferty over on the McKay building."

"Trouble?"

"Looks that way. There's a glitch in the security system, probably a short or something and McKay wants to post a few extra guards. He's got some big client coming in with a truckload of jewels." Hastings consulted his screen again, and Zane looked over his shoulder, trying to show some interest in Frank McKay's import/export business. But all the while he talked with Hastings, he had the gnawing feeling that he was making a mistake—that Kaylie wasn't safe, that she needed his protection.

Paranoid, that's what he was, he decided.

Later, as he walked back to his office, he still wasn't convinced he'd made the right decision. But he had no choice. This was the way she wanted it, and he'd be damned if he was going to blow this marriage.

"Here are your messages, Mr. Flannery," Peggy said, waving the pink slips of paper as he started for his office.

"Oh, thanks."

"And your wife called."

His wife. It sounded so lasting. Grinning, Zane leaned across Peggy's desk. "I don't think I ever thanked you for getting through to the police so quickly. They were at the house in Carmel practically as soon as I was." Reading the messages, he started back to his office.

Peggy adjusted her headset. "I don't think you should thank me. By the time I got through, they'd already been called."

Zane stopped dead in his tracks, then turned on his heel. "They'd already been called?" he repeated slowly, his mind spinning ahead. "By whom? Someone at Whispering Falls?"

"I—I don't know," Peggy stammered. "I didn't think to ask. It took quite a while to connect with the right number in Carmel because I called the San Francisco Police

Department first—you know, to check out her apartment here in the city. When I finally got through to the police in Carmel, I'm sure the dispatcher said something about already sending a unit over to her house. I—I guess I should have told you sooner, but everything turned out okay, and as soon as you were out of the hospital you took off to get married in Lake Tahoe…and…" She lifted her palms and blushed to the roots of her hair. Peggy prided herself on her work. "I didn't think it was that big of a deal."

From Peggy's reaction, Zane assumed the look on his face must be murderous. A hundred questions raced through his mind, but not one single answer filled the worrisome gaps. Who had called? How would that person know that Kaylie was in Carmel?

"Mr. Flannery…?" Peggy asked, apparently still shivering in her boots.

"Don't worry about it," he said, trying to keep his expression calm while inside he was tormented. He'd thought that having Lee Johnston readmitted to the hospital would solve the problem, but there were still some loose ends. It took all of his willpower not to march back to Hastings's office and order not only Rafferty, but six extra men to watch Kaylie every waking hour that Zane wasn't with her. "Call the police, get all the information you can.… Never mind, I think I'd better do it myself."

Back in his office, he shoved aside the desire to pour himself a stiff shot. He knew several detectives on the force, men he'd worked with at Gemini Security ages ago, before he'd started his own company. Now, because of his position as owner of a private detective/security firm, he shouldn't have to wade through a lot of red tape to get the information he wanted. He picked up the phone and rested his hips against the desk. "Come on, come on," he muttered as the call was finally routed to Detective Mike Saragossa.

"Hey, ol' buddy!" Mike drawled lazily from somewhere deep in the bowels of the SFPD. "'Bout time I heard from you. What can I do for ya?"

KAYLIE'S DAY HAD GONE from bad to worse. After the meeting with Jim and Alan, she'd muffed the introduction of a newspaper reporter who was investigating crime within the city government, and Alan had rescued her. Then during an interview with a woman running for mayor, there was trouble with her microphone and, once again, Alan had to take over until the station break. The defective microphone was whisked away and a new one clipped quickly onto her lapel. Meanwhile, the candidate, Kathleen McKenney, was more than a little miffed at the inconvenience, and pointedly ignored Kaylie from that point on.

The last half of the show ran more smoothly, but by the end of the program, Kaylie couldn't wait to climb off her chair, wipe off her smile and relax. She headed straight to the cafeteria, drowned herself in a diet soda, then, after going over the problems with Jim, grabbed her notes for the next day and left the station. All she wanted to do was go straight home and curl up with a good book and spend the rest of the evening with her new husband.

But first, she thought as she climbed into her car and flicked on the ignition, she'd surprise Zane. Rather than wait for him at home, she'd catch him at work. She guided her car out of the lot and merged into traffic. Adjusting her rearview mirror, she spotted a car, not a silver Taurus, but a blue wagon, roll into traffic behind her. No big deal, she decided, but she'd spied that wagon before—on days when the Taurus hadn't been around the parking lot.

So what? Lots of people go to the same place every day. The driver was probably someone who works around here. She drove a couple of blocks, turned right twice, doubling back, and couldn't help but check the rearview mirror. Sure enough, about four cars behind, the wagon tailed her.

Fear jarred her. *Oh, Lord, not again!* She nearly rear-ended the car in front of her. *Stay cool, Kaylie. Get a grip on yourself!* But her heart slammed against her rib cage, and a cold sweat broke out over her skin. Her fingers clamped the wheel in a death grip.

At the next stoplight she slowed, checking the mirror every five seconds.

The light turned green, and she tromped on the gas, her concentration split between the road ahead and the mirror. The blue wagon followed three cars behind. Kaylie shifted down. Timing the next light, she sailed through a yellow and the wagon got hung up on a red.

Her hands were sweating, the steering wheel felt slick as she drove ten blocks out of her way before turning again and heading for Zane's office. She felt numb inside. No one would be following her. Johnston was locked up.

But Zane's words, spoken in an angry blurt at the last mention of Johnston in *The Insider,* came back to haunt her. "The more the press makes of this, the more likely some other wacko is going to try to duplicate the same sick crime. If not with you then with someone else—no one who's famous is safe!" He'd slapped the paper onto the table in front of her to make his point, and she'd pointedly picked it up with two fingers, rotated in her chair and dropped the entire paper into the trash.

"I didn't know you subscribed," she'd mocked, though part of his anger had been conveyed to her.

He'd scowled at her and motioned impatiently toward

the trash. "Articles like that only cause trouble. Believe me, I know." And he did. One part of his business, especially in his office near Hollywood, had grown by leaps and bounds, patronized by stars who needed protection from overly zealous or crazed fans. Any one of those "fans" could potentially endanger the star's life or the lives of members of his or her family.

Kaylie shivered. Her heart knocking crazily, she drove into the parking lot, slid into an open space, then turned off the engine and, with a shuddering sigh, leaned her head against the steering wheel. "You're okay," she told herself, and slowly her pulse decelerated. Should she tell Zane about the cars—the Taurus and the wagon? Would he think she was imagining things, or worse yet, would it send him into the same paranoid need to protect her that had destroyed their marriage once before?

She wanted to be honest with him. Good marriages were based on honesty and yet, just this once, she might let the truth slip.

And what if you're followed again?

Oh, Lord, what a mess! She grabbed a handful of hair and tossed it over her shoulder. Climbing out of her Audi, she stood on slightly unsteady legs just as another car eased into the garage. Glancing over her shoulder, she gasped. Fear petrified her. The car cruising into the lot of Flannery Security was the same wagon that had followed her. The tail she'd thought she'd lost. Oh, God! How could he have known?

The blond man behind the wheel stared straight at her and she saw his face—young and hard, flat nose, cold eyes and straight hair—stare back at her. He opened the car door, and Kaylie didn't wait. Closer to the elevator, she sprinted across the cement and pounded on the button. The doors opened as the taste of fear settled in the back of her throat.

Zane! she thought desperately. She had to get to Zane! Inside the elevator she slapped the door panel. The doors swept shut, blocking out the blond man, and Kaylie sagged against the metal rail as the car moved upward with a lurch. Now, if only the man didn't run up the stairs faster than the elevator.... Again, fear tore at her.

"Zane, oh, God, Zane," she whispered, trying not to fall apart. When the doors opened, she half expected the man to be waiting, aiming a gun at her chest, but she found herself in the reception area of Flannery Security. She flew down the hall, past Peggy's desk and bolted into Zane's office.

"Kaylie?" He was standing at the windows, a dark expression on his face. She threw herself at him and clung to him, refusing to sob. "What the devil's going on?"

Trembling, she knew she was scaring him and wished she could calm down. "Call the police," she cried, "or send out your best man."

"Wh—"

"There's a man following me!" she cried, and Zane drew her closer to him, his muscles strong and hard.

"You're okay," he said, reaching behind him and pushing the button of the intercom, "Peggy, call Brad. Have him seal the building and send out a search team—an armed search team. There's a suspect somewhere in the building."

"The parking lot—" Kaylie clarified, glad for the feel of Zane's arms around her. Still holding her, Zane reached into the top drawer of his desk and pulled out his revolver.

"What's up?" Brad Hastings's voice boomed through the speaker.

"Someone followed Kaylie here. Check the exterior lot and the basement lot, all the staircases."

"You got it!" Hastings replied.

Zane checked his gun for ammunition.

Within seconds, the door to his office opened. "Is everything all right?" Peggy asked.

"Y-yes, fine," Kaylie stammered.

"Could I get you a cup of coffee?"

Kaylie shook her head, and Peggy, with a quick glance at Zane, stepped into the hallway and closed the door behind her.

"Oh, God, I didn't mean—I'm sorry."

Zane held her close and kissed her forehead. "Sorry for what?"

She had to tell him. She'd be foolish to keep information like this inside. Trying to calm down, she let him lead her to the couch.

Peggy knocked quietly, then left a tray of coffee for two on Zane's desk. When Kaylie tried to protest, the secretary held up a hand. "I know you said you didn't want anything, but frankly, you look like you could use a cup of coffee and a shot of bourbon." With those words of advice, she left the room again and locked the door behind her.

"Okay, so what happened?" Zane demanded, his lips a thin, dangerous line as he handed her one of the steaming cups.

Kaylie found strength in the warmth of the cup cradled between her palms. She hadn't known she felt cold, but now that the fear had subsided, she felt chilled to the bone. Haltingly, between sips, she found the words. "This isn't the first time," she admitted.

"What?" he nearly screamed. "What the hell do you mean 'isn't the first time'?"

"Just don't get mad…okay? I had this…feeling…for a few weeks now, but I told myself I was just overreacting to Johnston's attack. You know, seeing ghosts in every corner."

Zane became very still, every muscle in his body rigid and hard. "You should've told me."

"I know, but I didn't want to scare you."

"You just did."

"Maybe it was all in my mind," she said, then shook her head. "There are lots of Taurus cars on the road, and blue wagons are a dime a dozen."

Zane sucked a breath between his teeth. "You were followed here by a Taurus?" he asked, laying his gun on the table.

"No—it was the blue wagon." She explained about losing the car that had been chasing her only to run into it again in the parking garage.

She thought Zane would call additional men to seal off the garage, but instead he walked to the desk and punched the intercom. "Peggy, send Tim Rafferty in, if he's here."

A few seconds later a blond man of about twenty— the very man who had been behind the wheel of the blue station wagon—walked into Zane's office. Kaylie nearly screamed.

Zane dragged a hand through his hair. "Is this the guy?"

"Yes, but—" Cold realization started in the pit of her stomach and crawled up her spine.

"Tim works for me," Zane admitted, his face ashen. "Tim, this is my wife, Kaylie Melville. Kaylie…Tim."

"But—"

"I told him to follow you," Zane clarified.

"But why— Oh, God, no, don't tell me," she said, her

heart dropping to her knees in disappointment. "You've already started it again, haven't you?" she whispered, her voice ragged.

"I had some of my men assigned to follow you for a few weeks—ever since I got the phone calls from Ted." He motioned for Tim to leave the room, and the blond slipped out, shutting the door behind him.

Kaylie was furious. Her heart pounded in her ears as she realized they were replaying the same mistakes all over again. Her voice so low she could barely hear her own words, she said, "How could you?"

"Because I love you, damn it. And I wasn't going to lose you again."

Her throat worked, but no words came. Strangled with disappointment, she stared at her hands.

"I told Brad just this morning to take all the men off the case."

"All the men? You mean there were more than one?"

"Six men rotated."

"Six? Tim must've missed the message."

"Don't make this any harder than it is, Kaylie," he said, returning the revolver to his desk drawer.

"Oh, Lord, Zane, you don't trust me at all, do you?"

He snorted. "I just don't trust the public."

Closing her eyes against the tears that threatened, she shook her head slowly from side to side. "I should have known you wouldn't change," she said, dying a little when she noticed the band of gold and diamonds on her left ring finger.

"I have changed."

"Not enough." Why had she been so foolish? A tear slid from the corner of her eye, and she dashed it away. "I—I wanted this to work."

"It will, Kaylie. We'll make it work."

"Will we?" She sniffed loudly, then squared her shoulders. She'd been played for a fool, a childish, simpleminded fool for the last time. "And how will you handle the fact that one of the next guests on *West Coast Morning* might be Dr. Anthony Henshaw?"

Zane's eyes narrowed. "Johnston's doctor? Is this some kind of morbid joke?"

"I wish," she said with a sigh. She rubbed her arms as if suddenly chilled and explained her conversation with Jim and Alan.

"And you agreed to this?" Zane charged.

"I didn't have any choice. The decision had already been made."

"But that's crazy," Zane said, pacing between the desk and the window. "It just promotes—" He clamped his mouth shut and, though still tense, leaned his hips against the windowsill. His eyes, when he stared at her, still burned, but his expression was soft. "You look like you've had a rough day. How about I take you home and cook you dinner?"

She rolled her eyes and struggled out of her chair. "You don't have to—"

"I want to," he said, trying to break the tension, though apprehension grappled with his forced calmness. What the hell was going on at *West Coast Morning?* Didn't they know that they were potentially setting up Kaylie as a target for the next publicity-hungry nut?

And what about "Ted"? Who was he?

Alan's name kept popping into his mind, but the voice on the tape didn't sound like Alan at all. And he didn't suspect Jim Crowley. So who? *Who?* Someone at the television station? One of Kaylie's friends? Or someone at the hospital who had invented a fictitious name?

They drove separately back to the apartment, and

Franklin, the traitorous beast, padded after Kaylie when they walked inside.

Zane, true to his promise, poured them each a glass of wine, then began fixing dinner. But as he broiled steaks on the grill and steamed potatoes in the microwave, he thought about the upcoming show.

All his instincts told him the program was a big mistake. But his hands were tied. Kaylie had about come unglued when she'd found out he'd had men watching her, and, he supposed, glancing over his shoulder to the counter where she was chopping vegetables for a salad, he didn't blame her. He hadn't played fair.

And now he had to.

"Hey—watch out!" Kaylie cried. "Medium-rare, remember? I'm not into 'burned beyond recognition.'" She grabbed a long-handled fork from the drawer in the cooking island and flipped the steaks on the interior grill. Without asking, she dashed a shot of lemon pepper over the two T-bones.

"You're fouling up my recipe," he said with a good-natured gleam in his eye.

"Recipe?"

"I watch Chef Glenn on Friday mornings."

"Oh, give me a break," she said. "This is all well and good, Zane, but you don't know a curry sauce from a fruit compote—"

He whirled, grabbed her and swept her off her feet. One of her shoes dropped to the floor. "Watch it, lady," he growled in her ear, "or I might have to take my spatula to you."

"Promises, promises." She giggled as he carried her into the bedroom. "Hey, wait. Zane," she cried, laughing. "You can't—" He tossed her onto the bed and, while standing over her, ripped off his shirt in one swift motion.

"But the steaks," she protested, forcing her eyes away from the wide expanse of his chest.

"I've decided 'burned beyond recognition' is the best way to serve T-bones."

"But—"

He dropped onto the bed and covered her mouth with his. She was still laughing, but as his kiss deepened, her giggles gave way to moans. "Zane, please," she whispered, still thinking of the steaks sizzling into charred bones.

The smoke detector started beeping loudly.

"Saved by the bell," she said with a giggle. For that remark, she was rewarded with a pillow in the face. Zane, muttering under his breath, jumped off the bed and hurried into the kitchen. In a state of dishabille, she followed, laughing when she saw the T-bones—small, black replicas of steak.

Zane turned off the grill and opened the windows to air out the kitchen. "How about take-out Chinese, Mrs. Flannery?" he asked, a slightly off-center smile curving his lips as he tossed the burned meat into the sink. The smoke slowly dissipated, and the smoke alarm quit bleating.

"Anything's fine with me."

"But first we have some unfinished business," he said, thinking aloud, a menacing glint in his eye. He grabbed her again, and this time they weren't interrupted.

ON FRIDAY MORNING, KAYLIE WAS nervous as a cat. She and Zane hadn't discussed the show again, and she'd finally forgiven him for having her followed. *It's going to take time,* she reminded herself. Zane was used to being in command, and slowly, with visible effort, he was allowing her to make her own decisions. Though, she suspected with a smile, it was killing him.

For the past few days there had been no silver Taurus, no blue wagon, no car or man following her. She couldn't help looking over her shoulder occasionally and checking her rearview mirror more often than usual, but she was convinced that Zane had kept to his word.

And she'd kept hers. She was more careful than she'd ever been and more in love.

She had great faith that this time, no matter what fate threw their way, she and Zane would make it. Together.

ZANE COULDN'T GET HIS MIND off of today's program. He itched to go to the station, to watch Kaylie, to make sure that she was all right. Rationally, he knew that nothing would happen to her. Johnston's psychiatrist wasn't a madman; Henshaw couldn't hurt Kaylie.

But some other fruitcake could. He drove to work and dropped by Hastings's office. Brad, as usual, had been working for hours, though it was barely eight o'clock. He glanced up from his computer terminal when Zane walked in.

"Got a minute?" Zane asked.

"Sure. What's up?"

"This." Reaching into his jacket pocket, Zane withdrew the tape of his last conversation with Ted. "Did you find anyone who could have made this call?"

"Nope." Brad shook his head slowly. "But several of the guys here are convinced the voice is that of a woman."

"A woman." That didn't make things any easier. Zane stuffed the tape back into his pocket.

"You want us to keep working on it?"

"As long as you've got leads."

"Well, we're about dried-up. As for the tracer, most

of the calls that we can't identify came in from booths—different booths located usually in the financial district."

"Well, that's something," Zane said, thinking aloud. "I don't suppose anyone we suspect lives or works there."

Hastings shook his head. "No one we've scared up so far."

"What about Alan Bently?"

"He'd be my guess as suspect number one," Hastings agreed. "He seems to have the most to gain by all this publicity. Want a printout on the guy?"

"Sure."

Hastings turned back to his computer, and his nimble fingers flew over the keys. A printer whirred to life, and soon a four-paged single-spaced report was lying in the tray. Brad handed the pages to Zane. "Here you go. Everything you always wanted to know about Alan Bently but were afraid to ask."

Zane's mouth stretched into a grin. "That's what I keep you around here for, Brad, that lousy sense of humor of yours."

"Nope, boss. You keep me 'cause I'm the best."

Zane laughed. "Well, that might be part of it," he agreed, sauntering down the hall. He grabbed a cup of coffee, settled into his desk chair and began perusing the report, line by revealing line. Most of the information, he'd read before. The names, the places, the people who were associated with Alan Bently.

"Maybe you're barking up the wrong tree," he told himself as he leaned back and propped his feet on the desk. He dialed the police department in Carmel, hoping someone there could tell him who the anonymous caller was. Someone had called the police, and if he guessed right, that someone had called long distance.

When the police couldn't help him, he dialed the phone

company. He had a friend in administration who owed him a favor. Maybe he could finally get some answers—answers his own phone surveillance hadn't uncovered.

While waiting to be connected to his friend, he pushed a button on the remote control for the television and waited for Kaylie's show to begin.

DR. HENSHAW WAS THE guest scheduled for the first segment of the show. Kaylie, more nervous than she'd been while interviewing the president's wife, flipped through her notes one last time.

"Fifteen minutes," Tracy called through the door, and Kaylie let out her breath. She straightened her skirt and made her way to the set, where she and Alan were introduced to Dr. Henshaw by the assistant producer.

A small man with a beard that rimmed his chin and no mustache, he seemed as anxious about the interview as she was.

"Ms. Melville," he said, clasping her hand and forcing a thin smile.

"Mrs. Flannery now," she replied, "but, please, just call me Kaylie."

Tracy cut in. "Okay, now look Kaylie or Alan in the eye when they talk to you. Forget about the cameras. When I give you this signal…"

Kaylie had heard the spiel a hundred times before.

"Places, everyone!" Jim said loudly, and people scurried. Tracy led Dr. Henshaw to his spot on the end of the couch, Alan perched in his usual chair and Kaylie sat in her usual chair.

"Quiet, please, and five…four…three…"

The lead-in music filtered through the speakers, and Kaylie forced herself to smile calmly, as if every day she interviewed the man who was her attacker's doctor.

"Good morning," Alan said, grinning confidently into the cameras, and the show was off.

Kaylie worked on automatic. They talked about the doctor's forthcoming book, which he'd sold just the day before to a major publisher, and they discussed psychosis in broad terms. Alan brought up Johnston's name, but only in regard to the premiere of *Obsession.* Not only were clips from the film shown, but also footage of the original attack. It took all of Kaylie's professional acting skills to appear calm and detached when inside, her heart was thumping and sweat was beading along her spine.

Just let me get through this, she prayed inwardly as she turned to Dr. Henshaw and asked him about security at the hospital. The doctor became slightly defensive, but soon the interview and the ordeal were over.

Later, after the final segment where Chef Glenn whipped up his favorite apple torte, Kaylie left the set on unsteady legs. This has to be the worst, she thought, content to stay in her office for the rest of the day. She flipped on the radio, answered her mail and gathered some ideas for future shows. She wasn't going to be caught in a lurch again!

At three o'clock, Alan knocked on the door and stepped into her office. "Well," he said, smiling broadly. "Did you hear? The phones haven't stopped ringing. Today's show was a bona fide success! From the response, Jim thinks it may be in the top ten for the year."

Great. "It must've been the apple torte," Kaylie said, and Alan rolled his eyes.

"You should've seen the switchboard! Becky was going crazy out there. And that's not the best news."

"No?" Kaylie tried to sound interested, but her heart wasn't in it. Alan didn't seem to notice. "I've had a million calls but only two that really count. One from my agent, the other from Cameron James. He's agreed to direct again, and he's got a screenwriter lined up to work out a sequel to *Obsession!* Triumph Pictures is interested in producing, and one of the major studios—probably Zeus—is backing the film. It's only a matter of time!"

Kaylie didn't know what to say. Alan was flying so high, he was so exhilarated that she didn't want to burst his bubble by saying she wasn't interested. "What about *West Coast Morning?*" she asked quietly.

"Oh, who knows! It would only be for a few months... Jim would understand."

"I don't know," Kaylie began.

"You don't know? *You don't know?* What's to know? This is the opportunity of a lifetime and *you don't know?* What is this? Are you already trying to squeeze a little more money—"

"Of course not."

"Then you're afraid, right? Afraid of failure? Or afraid of some loony taking after you again? Or is it something else?" he said, thinking aloud as he closed the distance to her desk. "Don't tell me, it's Flannery, isn't it? You're afraid of him—of what he'll say, aren't you?"

Kaylie's temper got the better of her tongue. "I don't think it's even worth discussing. I haven't heard anything concrete yet. No one's offered me a part and so, as far as I can see, it's a moot point."

Alan threw his hands into the air. "God, Kaylie! We are talking major motion picture here! And you're not even willing to pursue it? What's gotten into you?"

"Maybe she's just using her head." Zane was standing in the doorway, and his face was a mask of slow-burning fury. Something was wrong. Kaylie could read it in the set of his jaw. Slowly, he reached into his jacket pocket, withdrew a tape and flipped the tape onto Kaylie's desk. "How about explaining this?" he suggested to Alan.

"What—a tape? Music? Rap? What?" Alan shrugged and lifted his palms. "What's going on, Flannery?"

But Kaylie knew. On the tape was the voice of "Ted." The warning. But Alan? No way. Her gaze flew to Zane's, but he was concentrating on Alan.

"Nope. Just a conversation with a friend of mine. His name's Ted," Zane said, crossing his arms over his chest.

"Ted who?" Alan asked, sending Kaylie a glance that insinuated Zane was walking around with more than one screw loose.

"I don't know his last name. Maybe you can fill that part in."

"Me?"

Zane slipped the tape into the radio/cassette player on Kaylie's credenza.

"Zane, I don't think…" Kaylie began, but the tape started to play and the conversation between Zane and Ted filled the room.

Alan stared at the tape player as if he couldn't believe what he was hearing. Zane swung one leg over the corner of Kaylie's desk and leaned closer to the other man. "The voice on this tape is that of a woman—I don't know her real name—but I think you do."

"A woman? But—"

"It's disguised of course, but it's probably someone you know—maybe someone you date. And no, I'm not talking about Kaylie, because you've never dated her, but have led all the tabloids to believe it."

"Are you out of your mind?"

"I don't think so." Zane let the words sink in, then once he was certain he had Alan's undivided attention, continued, "I talked to the phone company, and it seems there are several long-distance phone calls on your bill. Calls to the Carmel Police Department on the night that Kaylie was attacked by Johnston and calls to reporters for *The Insider* and a couple of other tabloids. Unfortunately there aren't any calls from your phone to my agency when 'Ted' rang me up. But we have the general vicinity in which the calls were made. My guess is that one of your girlfriends made the call. My men are checking into that right now."

"That's ridiculous," Alan said, but the lines around the corners of his mouth were tightening, and the glare he sent Zane was pure hatred.

Kaylie couldn't believe her ears. Not Alan. He couldn't, *wouldn't* put her life in danger!

"It only makes sense, Bently," Zane continued, rewinding the tape and playing it again, letting Ted's warning bounce off the corners of the room. Sweat dotted Alan's upper lip.

Zane motioned toward the recorder. "You've been pushing for more publicity for the past year and a half. You've moved behind the scenes to make people aware of you—and my wife."

"You're wrong, Flannery."

"Am I?" Zane clucked his tongue, and his foot swung slowly as he turned to Kaylie. "You know why Henshaw agreed to come onto this program, don't you?"

"Because of his book," Kaylie said.

Zane nodded. "And the movie rights tied into that book—rights dealing with Lee Johnston, rights to your story, our story and Alan's story."

Alan's face drained of color. "You're jumping to conclusions."

"Am I?" Zane demanded, his eyes narrowing on the shorter man. "I don't think so. In fact, I've already had a conversation with the good doctor. He seems to remember placing a call on the night of Johnston's escape attempt, and not just a call to the police. He called you, Alan. So that you could milk this for all it was worth."

"That's ridiculous!"

"At first I thought Henshaw might have been in on Johnston's escape—helped him along a little. But he convinced me and—" he stared pointedly at his watch "—right now he's convincing the police that you and he only took advantage of a situation that had already occurred. So, when Johnston escaped, he called you and you eventually called the Carmel police. Why?"

"I didn't—"

"There are telephone records, Bently."

Kaylie's stomach lurched. Surely Alan wouldn't have done anything to hurt her—to put her life in danger.

Alan turned to Kaylie, and all of his bravado escaped in a defeated rush. He fell into a chair and buried his face in his hands. "I didn't mean to hurt anyone," he whispered, his voice muffled.

"Oh, Alan, no!" Kaylie cried, tears of anger building behind her eyes. "You couldn't have!"

"You got it backward," Alan admitted, his voice barely a whisper as he looked up, his eyes filled with regret. "That night—the night he escaped. Johnston called here, asking for Kaylie. I didn't know who he was…but by the tone of his voice I guessed. And later, Henshaw called with the news."

"Oh, God," Kaylie whispered.

"So you gave him her address in Carmel," Zane said, not letting up for a second.

"But I called the police—almost immediately! I—I…" The look he sent Kaylie was pathetic. "I just didn't know that he was already over halfway there, that he'd been hitchhiking and so…I called Henshaw back and told him I'd already taken care of everything and that Kaylie was all right and that I thought he and I should do some business together. I'd talked to him before—about a movie on Johnston's life and now, together, I thought we could put something together. Viewer interest would already be high," he said, as if the American public's wishes erased all of his mistakes.

"And that's why he agreed to appear on your show?" Zane persisted.

"Yes—to promote his book and to get people interested in Lee Johnston's story."

"You'd better call an attorney, Bently," Zane suggested, his voice filled with loathing. "A good one. You're up to your neck in this, and the police are bound to show up any minute. I gave them a full report." He reached across the desk and grabbed Kaylie's hand. "Let's get out of here."

She picked up her purse from habit, but her entire world seemed to be turned upside down. Alan? A man she'd worked with forever had used her, betrayed her, felt so little concern for her life? Lord, how had she been so blind?

"Kaylie," Alan said, his features set and grim. His voice broke. "I—I'm sorry. I never—"

"So am I," she managed to say as she let Zane guide her out of the television station. The police were already in the reception area, two squad cars parked outside, four officers charging through the connecting room.

News cameras, some from the station itself, others from rivals, whirred, and reporters were already gathering information for their nightly reports. Microphones were thrust at Kaylie, and cameras chased them as Zane and Kaylie, arms linked, dashed across the parking lot.

"Ms. Melville—can you give us some insight on the reports that Alan Bently was involved in Lee Johnston's escape?"

Kaylie refused to answer that one.

"How do you feel—"

Zane spun around. "No comment," he growled, glaring at the reporters.

"Mr. Flannery—you're Ms. Melville's husband and—"

"Right now I'm her bodyguard," he clarified, his face thrust within bare inches of the slim man who was wielding his microphone like some jousting lance. "And, if you don't want me to get physical, you'd better back off!"

With that, he turned, helped Kaylie into the Jeep and climbed behind the wheel. He roared off, leaving the cameras still whirring.

"My bodyguard?" Kaylie repeated, sagging against the seat and lolling her head back as she looked at her husband. "Oh, boy, I can hardly wait. 'Talk-show hostess demotes husband to bodyguard. Film at eleven.'"

"That little jerk deserved it," Zane insisted, cranking on the wheel hard to round a corner.

"I work with that 'little jerk.'"

"You have my sympathy."

"My *bodyguard?*" she asked again, chuckling at the ludicrous title.

"That's right. Your bodyguard, your husband, your lover, your spouse, your fantasy and hopefully the father of your unborn children!"

He touched her hand, and tears blurred her vision. Yes, Zane was all of the above, and much, much more. He was her life. "I should wring your neck," she whispered without much conviction.

"I think you can be more imaginative than that," he

said, slanting her a sexy grin. "My body parts are willingly at your disposal…."

"You know what I mean," she replied, unable to smother a smile. "You're supposed to be letting me live my life."

"I just don't like to leave any loose ends dangling." Downshifting, he wheeled into the parking lot of their apartment building. "'Ted' was a loose end. The call to the police was a loose end. Those *Insider* lies about your relationship with Alan were loose ends!"

They rode up the elevator together, and Franklin, whining, greeted them. While Zane took the shepherd for a short walk, Kaylie dug through the pantry and found a bottle of champagne they'd never opened—the bottle from the chapel where they were married.

She should be furious with him, she supposed, but she wasn't. In fact, she liked the fact that he'd wrapped up all the loose ends. He hadn't stopped her from working, hadn't even objected when she'd mentioned that she might consider another movie. He was trying…and so was she.

She popped open the champagne and poured two glasses. Then, on a whim, she poured a little bit into a bowl. When Zane and Franklin returned, she set the bowl on the floor for the dog and handed Zane a glass.

"What's this?" he asked, but his gray eyes glinted.

"A celebration."

"Of what?"

"Kaylie Flannery's new independence." Without any more ado, Franklin began lapping from his bowl.

"This is sounding dangerous," he said, but he wrapped one arm around her waist, and she giggled as they both sipped from their glasses.

"Well, I've become so independent, you see, that my husband's meddling in my life doesn't even bother me."

"I never meddle," Zane argued.

Franklin sneezed.

Kaylie laughed and, while balancing her glass, wrapped her arms around Zane's neck. "Don't ever stop caring, Zane Flannery," she said, her eyes crinkling at the corners.

"I never did," he vowed, and pressed champagne-laced kisses upon her waiting lips. "And I never will."

* * * * *

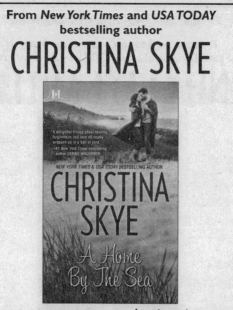

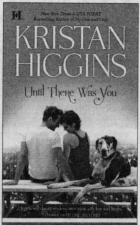

REQUEST YOUR FREE BOOKS!

2 FREE NOVELS
FROM THE ROMANCE COLLECTION
PLUS 2 FREE GIFTS!

YES! Please send me 2 FREE novels from the Romance Collection and my 2 FREE gifts (gifts are worth about $10). After receiving them, if I don't wish to receive any more books, I can return the shipping statement marked "cancel." If I don't cancel, I will receive 4 brand-new novels every month and be billed just $5.99 per book in the U.S. or $6.49 per book in Canada. That's a saving of at least 25% off the cover price. It's quite a bargain! Shipping and handling is just 50¢ per book in the U.S. and 75¢ per book in Canada.* I understand that accepting the 2 free books and gifts places me under no obligation to buy anything. I can always return a shipment and cancel at any time. Even if I never buy another book, the two free books and gifts are mine to keep forever.

194/394 MDN FELQ

Name	(PLEASE PRINT)	
Address		Apt. #
City	State/Prov.	Zip/Postal Code

Signature (if under 18, a parent or guardian must sign)

Mail to the **Reader Service:**
IN U.S.A.: P.O. Box 1867, Buffalo, NY 14240-1867
IN CANADA: P.O. Box 609, Fort Erie, Ontario L2A 5X3

Not valid for current subscribers to the Romance Collection
or the Romance/Suspense Collection.

Want to try two free books from another line?
Call 1-800-873-8635 or visit www.ReaderService.com.

* Terms and prices subject to change without notice. Prices do not include applicable taxes. Sales tax applicable in N.Y. Canadian residents will be charged applicable taxes. Offer not valid in Quebec. This offer is limited to one order per household. All orders subject to credit approval. Credit or debit balances in a customer's account(s) may be offset by any other outstanding balance owed by or to the customer. Please allow 4 to 6 weeks for delivery. Offer available while quantities last.

Your Privacy—The Reader Service is committed to protecting your privacy. Our Privacy Policy is available online at www.ReaderService.com or upon request from the Reader Service.

We make a portion of our mailing list available to reputable third parties that offer products we believe may interest you. If you prefer that we not exchange your name with third parties, or if you wish to clarify or modify your communication preferences, please visit us at www.ReaderService.com/consumerschoice or write to us at Reader Service Preference Service, P.O. Box 9062, Buffalo, NY 14269. Include your complete name and address.

ROM11

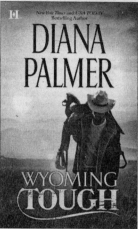

LISA JACKSON

77578 STORMY NIGHTS   ___ $7.99 U.S. ___ $9.99 CAN.

(limited quantities available)

TOTAL AMOUNT $ _____
POSTAGE & HANDLING $ _____
($1.00 FOR 1 BOOK, 50¢ for each additional)
APPLICABLE TAXES* $ _____
TOTAL PAYABLE $ _____

(check or money order—please do not send cash)

To order, complete this form and send it, along with a check or money
order for the total above, payable to HQN Books, to: **In the U.S.:**
3010 Walden Avenue, P.O. Box 9077, Buffalo, NY 14269-9077;
In Canada: P.O. Box 636, Fort Erie, Ontario, L2A 5X3.

Name: _____
Address: _____ City: _____
State/Prov.: _____ Zip/Postal Code: _____
Account Number (if applicable): _____

075 CSAS

*New York residents remit applicable sales taxes.
*Canadian residents remit applicable GST and provincial taxes.

HARLEQUIN®
HQN™   www.Harlequin.com

PHLJ1111BL